MURDER IN THE PARISH

A gripping crime mystery full of twists

FAITH MARTIN

Detective Hillary Greene Book 20

Joffe Books, London
www.joffebooks.com

First published in Great Britain in 2023

Cover art by Nick Castle

ISBN: 978-1-80405-802-2

CHAPTER ONE

An overnight thunderstorm had left massive puddles in the road, and Puff the Tragic Wagon was most displeased. Once or twice, ex-DI Hillary Greene's ancient Volkswagen Golf spluttered and foundered and made alarming choking noises whenever traffic forced her to keep to the side of the road and plough through the mini lakes.

She only hoped her feet stayed dry until she made it into Thames Valley Police HQ in the heart of Kidlington. She didn't fancy doing a day's work accompanied by the squelching soundtrack of sodden footwear.

Although Puff didn't let her down — or break down — once she parked, she bent down to do a quick check of his undercarriage. She wouldn't put it past him to have rust down there just on the verge of falling off and leaving her feet dangling in mid-air.

To her untutored eye, however, all seemed to be well. As she rose to a standing position she felt a familiar scratching in her chest and began to cough spasmodically. This lasted for far longer than she would have liked, and for a moment or two, she had to lean against her car for support and wait for the latest session to pass. A quick glance around assured her that nobody was near enough to witness the show.

Eventually the tickling sensation — along with the compulsive urge to cough — passed, and she reached into her bag to open a packet of tic tacs and popped one into her mouth. She'd found, over the past month or so, that keeping her mouth moist helped.

With a sigh, she slung her capacious bag over her shoulder and headed towards the main building.

A tallish woman in her late fifties, her chestnut-coloured hair, cut into a bell shape, was showing more and more signs of silvering, and she was still debating that age-old problem (or old-age problem?) of whether to dye, or not to dye. Did you bite the bullet and age gracefully? Or say, sod that, and give the silver the finger?

Since she had more things to worry about right then, however, she decided to leave the decision for another day.

She was dressed in moss-green trousers, paired with a mint-green blouse and a dark cream jacket with moss-green piping. The trousers, she could feel, were just a little loose on her now. Years ago, she'd had trouble with keeping the weight off, but the loss of her partner a while ago had changed all that. And the persistent cough that had plagued her since the summer had reduced her appetite even more.

She nodded at the desk sergeant as she swept across the entrance foyer and headed down the stairs to the basement area, where the Crime Review Team and other not-particularly-high-priority teams were forced to hang their hats.

On automatic pilot, she made her way to the former stationery cupboard — literally, it had once housed typing paper and other office equipment — that had been her office since returning to Thames Valley on a consultancy basis working cold cases. Once there, she squeezed behind her tiny desk.

There she turned on her computer and checked her emails. The first one she opened was from her GP, Dr Beatrice Waxman, confirming her appointment for 4 p.m. that afternoon at Deddington Health Centre. The results of the X-ray she'd arranged for Hillary to have taken at the

Horton Hospital at Banbury the previous Saturday had come in, and as she'd said over the telephone yesterday, they needed to have a discussion.

Since today was only Tuesday, they obviously weren't hanging about.

Hillary read the short message through twice, then shrugged it off, refusing to speculate uselessly about it beforehand, and began checking out her other, work-related messages instead. That done, she checked her watch, saw that it was now gone nine, and got up.

She walked the short distance down the permanently artificially lit corridor to the door marked 'Superintendent Sale' and knocked briefly, before pushing open the door and walking in.

After Hillary had retired as a DI more than five years ago, it hadn't taken long for Commander Marcus Donleavy to lure her back as a civilian consultant, with a remit to reinvestigate cold cases under the supervision of a senior, serving officer.

That officer had been Steven Crayle. At first, their relationship had been a bit rocky. Hillary, decorated for bravery and with a crime solve rate second to none, had always been a bit of a station legend. And Steven had felt that having her back, minus any official status but still working murder cases under him, needed some delicate handling on his part.

Soon, however, this professional 'delicate handling' had taken, to their mutual surprise, a far more intimate turn, resulting in her finally moving into his place some months later.

His subsequent death of a heart attack whilst working on a particularly stress-ridden case had left her once again alone, and back to living on her narrowboat, the *Mollern*, which was moored on the Oxford canal in the nearby village of Thrupp.

Superintendent Sale was Steven's replacement — and whereas once she might have waited for him to bid her enter before sailing into his office uninvited, they had quickly developed an easy working relationship. An older man, just slightly running to seed, this posting was, they both knew, his last one before retirement, and he had quickly come to understand that he could leave the actual investigation of cases to her, leaving him free to cope with all the other aggravating guff that seemed to cling to higher-ranking officers like barnacles.

He looked up now as she walked in, and an amiable smile lit up his somewhat fleshy face. 'Morning. Up for a new case?' were his opening words, and music to her ears.

She'd had to admit a rare defeat on their latest 'second look' at a killing that had taken place seven years ago and which looked set to remain stubbornly unsolved. There was simply no new evidence or leads to warrant keeping the file active.

It still clearly rankled her, however, and Roland 'Rollo' Sale had no doubt that she'd keep niggling away at it in her spare time for some months to come.

She was looking paler and thinner these days, and he thought it high time that she was given something new to get her teeth into. He therefore reached for a file and nudged it towards her, a bit like a retriever nudging a ball hopefully towards its owner.

Hillary needed no second bidding and reached for it eagerly as she took the seat in front of his desk, and instantly began rifling through it.

As she did so, the superintendent leaned back in his creaking chair, the bald patches of his receding hairline gleaming under the light of the fluorescent tubes above. Pretending not to notice, Hillary listened attentively as he proceeded to run through the bullet points for her.

'The victim was a parson, or rector or vicar, I never can tell the difference — if there is one. Reverend Keith Coltrane, who was thirty-five at the time, was hit over the head just inside the door of his church in Lower Barton and left to die there. Forensics comparisons prove the most likely murder weapon to be a spade of some kind, and it was in fact proved that a groundsman had left a spade in the porch that day, which was subsequently never found or accounted for. This was just before Christmas. He was eventually found by some poor sod of a tourist, would you believe, who liked to spend his days off seeking out unusual grave notations.'

'Serves him right then,' Hillary grunted unsympathetically, still reading avidly. 'He should have stuck to getting sunburnt at Margate and fighting off the seagulls as he ate his fish and chips like everyone else. Although at that time of year, he'd have been more likely to get frostbite,' she conceded.

The superintendent grinned. 'I daresay the shock of it cured him of his nasty habits anyway.'

'I see the original SIO was Ben Keating,' Hillary said, turning over a page and checking out the signature at the bottom.

'Yes, you know him?' Rollo had joined the team from out of county and didn't have that much knowledge of local officers.

'Yes, when I was younger. A good officer,' Hillary said. 'What you'd call solid. Maybe not one to think out of the box — whatever the hell *that's* supposed to mean — but at least he'll not have stinted on anything. He must have retired a good ten or fifteen years before I did, but unlike me, had the good sense to stay gone. I think I can find out where he hung his hat. I just hope he's still with us. But he'd be . . . what . . . in his late seventies, early eighties by now.'

She shook her head, unwilling to believe that time could just vanish as it seemed to.

Rollo nodded. It was always helpful to be able to pick the brains of the original investigators, but it was not always a luxury they had when investigating cold cases.

Hillary checked the original date of the crime and grunted. 'This is thirty years old,' she said. She was not complaining, merely stating. To her it didn't matter if a victim had been dead a day, or three decades. 'Ah, at least it was 23 December when he died. Being so close to Christmas Day, that might help fix the time in people's minds.'

'Ah yes, Christmas, the time of peace and goodwill to all mankind,' Rollo said sardonically.

'A time of family rows, disappointment over presents, indigestion from too much turkey and hangovers from too much Baileys,' Hillary laughed. 'Mind you, on the day before Christmas Eve, I doubt anybody had started celebrating much yet. Too busy Christmas shopping and attending office parties.'

'Well, I'll leave you to get on with the battered reverend,' Rollo said magnanimously. 'I've already asked Records to send you all they've got. Some of it might even be on the database,' he added. 'And now I'll get on with trying to get us another recruit for the team.'

'Good luck with that,' Hillary said cynically, gathering up the folder and retreating to the door.

Her small team consisted of herself, Claire Woolley, who was, like herself, a retired police officer lured back by a civilian contract, and a former soldier, Gareth Proctor, who'd been wounded and left handicapped by the war in Afghanistan.

And what with budget restrictions and staff shortages everywhere, if the superintendent could persuade the powers-that-be to shell out for another pair of hands to boost their productivity, Hillary might begin to believe in Father Christmas all over again.

* * *

When she was confident that she'd acquainted herself with the basics of her new case, she left her office and headed down to the communal office, where Claire and Gareth shared a large desk. The arrival of at least a dozen dusty-smelling cardboard boxes showed that the Record elves had been and gone in record time. No pun intended.

'I take it we've got another case then, guv,' Claire Woolley said laconically, nodding at the odoriferous stacks. At five feet ten, and heftily built, she had short black hair that tended to curl, and dark brown eyes.

Hillary wondered if *she* dyed her hair.

'Gareth wanted to dive in, but I told him best to wait,' she added.

Over at his desk, Gareth was sitting at attention. It wasn't something that Hillary had known was even possible until the former soldier had joined her team.

She nodded at him, dragged out a chair, sat down and instantly began to cough. Inwardly cursing, she dragged out a handkerchief and held it over her mouth, apologising around the whoops and splutters.

'That chest infection doesn't seem to be going anywhere in a hurry, guv,' Claire said, careful to keep her tone neutral.

'No, the bloody antibiotics I'm on seem to be useless,' Hillary agreed, finally getting her breath back. 'I've got to see the quack at four this afternoon and get a different batch,' she lied, glancing at her watch. 'So, let's get on with this.'

She nodded at the boxes and outlined their latest cold case. She concluded by doling out assignments. 'So, the usual routine. We need to read every scrap of paper, take our own notes, acquaint ourselves with the victim, any suspects originally flagged by DI Keating's initial investigation, and the forensics. Gareth, you can concentrate on the forensics if you like — this murder happened in 1992, and since then, leaps and bounds have been made in crime-scene processes. Liaise with the boffins down the hall and see if any of the original material evidence can be given the once-over with their new magic wands.'

'Yes, ma'am.'

Gareth, she knew, as the youngest member of the team, was best suited to this task.

'Claire, witness statements especially need to be gone through meticulously. We'll take a box each and then pass it on, so each of us has a good overall view of what we're dealing with. Our biggest problem is going to be tracking down the current whereabouts of the people involved. Inevitably, after this much time, a few of them will have died. Or retired to Eastbourne.'

'Not sure which is worse, guv,' Claire couldn't resist it.

Hillary grinned and grabbed a box at random and took it back to her office.

For the rest of the day, they would have nothing more exciting to do than read dusty reports and try to remember what they were doing, and what the world was like, back in 1992. For her and Claire, it would mean a trip back to their early days in uniform.

It was rather depressing to realise that for Gareth, he hadn't even arrived in the world yet!

* * *

Even as she studied, however, Hillary was aware of the time ticking away inexorably towards her doctor's appointment, and with it came that low-level feeling of inconvenient dread that had slowly become worse ever since her persistent cough had begun.

Her first thought, naturally, had been that she'd caught something, but when no common cold or flu symptoms appeared, but the cough persisted, she'd managed to secure an appointment with her doctor — no mean feat in these days of chronically overworked and under-supported medical staff.

She'd been, for some reason, rather surprised and genuinely alarmed when, after listening to her chest and back through her stethoscope, Dr Waxman had told her that she would like Hillary to have an X-ray.

It was only then that Hillary realised that she'd been expecting the doctor to tell her that it was nothing — a mild chest infection, say, that could easily be treated by a course of antibiotics.

Although nobody who knew her could ever have called her an optimist, she'd always thought of herself as a *realist*, and she knew that, when it came to medical problems, most people tended to think the worst, only to discover that their worries were unfounded. Which meant that she had been genuinely disconcerted by this worrying development.

So it was that she had attended her X-ray appointment with a more thoughtful and far more cautious attitude.

Now her mouth felt just a little dry as she packed up her things and left her desk at just gone three thirty. It felt strange to be leaving work at that time, and she didn't bother to poke her head in the door of the communal office, hoping that her team wouldn't even notice that she was gone.

The drive to Deddington was a straight run along the Oxford-to-Banbury road, with the village of Deddington lying much closer to the market town than to the city.

The doctor was running very late, but this didn't surprise her, and when she was finally ushered into Beatrice Waxman's office, the younger woman looked tired. In her early forties, with short no-nonsense brown hair and a make-up free face, she gave a small smile as Hillary sat down. Instantly she set about pulling up Hillary's file on her computer.

'Hello, Mrs Greene,' she said, barely turning her face away from the screen.

'Hillary, please.'

'Yes, sorry, Hillary.' Apparently satisfied that she was au fait with her latest patient's case, she finally swivelled around and looked Hillary in the eye. 'As I mentioned when we spoke on the telephone previously, the results of your X-rays have now come through. And it appears that the radiographer has noted an anomaly.'

Hillary felt her breath catch slightly in her throat, which made her want to begin to cough. Determinedly fighting off the urge to start whooping and spluttering, she managed to control her breathing and slipped another tic tac into her mouth instead.

Then she nodded. 'I see,' she said flatly. 'Could they tell yet what kind of anomaly we're dealing with?'

'Not with any degree of certainty, no, which is why we need to progress quickly onto the next step,' the doctor said candidly, tapping away once more on her keypad. 'I see you have private health insurance?'

Hillary nodded. 'I took it out when I retired as a DI from the police force. I was travelling around on my narrowboat, and it seemed easier to take out private insurance than to keep registering with different NHS clinics wherever I happened to be,' she explained.

The doctor nodded but seemed to be listening with only half an ear as she surveyed the computer screen. 'Splendid, that will mean that we can now advance more quickly. I've arranged for you to have a scan at the John Radcliffe . . . let's see . . . the day after tomorrow.'

'Thursday?' Hillary clarified, glad that her voice sounded calm and matter-of-fact.

'Yes. Does 9.15 a.m. suit you?'

'That'll be fine. Do I need to do anything specific — not eat, or drink caffeine or anything like that?'

'No. During the procedure, you'll be given an injection that will dye your blood, which helps produce a clearer image, but that shouldn't affect you in any major way. Just drink plenty of water afterwards.'

'So I can go straight on to work?'

'If you want to, certainly.'

Hillary nodded. 'I see.' She waited in silence as the doctor wrote something on a form and handed it over. 'You need to give this to the clinic. You'll also need to provide them with proof of your insurance. Once the results are through, they'll send them to me and I'll contact you right away. You may have to come back here so that we can then discuss them going forward.'

'Not a problem.'

The doctor finally looked away from her admin duties and regarded her patient with a tired but compassionate gaze. 'Please try not to worry too much, Mrs Greene. I know that's not always easy, but stress is always something you should try to avoid. And until we have a clearer idea of what we're dealing with, speculation is pointless anyway. At this stage, all we can say is that there's a shadow on your left lung that needs further investigation. And I know that, at times like this, you immediately start to think about cancer and all sorts of other scary things, but at this stage that's very premature, I assure you. And please, if you'll take my advice, you won't research this sort of thing on the internet. There's so much unreliable and sometimes downright misleading and irresponsible things out there that people can frighten themselves silly for no good reason.'

Hillary nodded. 'Understood.'

'Any questions?'

'I don't believe so,' Hillary said, and stood up. She thanked the doctor, wished her a good day and left.

Outside, she walked to Puff, opened the door and sat down. She was aware that her knees felt a bit jelly-like, and her heart rate was higher than normal.

Annoyingly, she began to cough. She wound down the window and let in some air and September sunshine. A flowering bush nearby droned with the sound of bees and dozy wasps. A song thrush sang from an apple tree in someone's garden.

Hillary listened to the thrush with pleasure and waited for her chest to sort itself out. But when the coughing spell passed, she continued to sit in her car, just thinking.

Her mother's strategy had always been 'hope for the best, plan for the worst'. Her father had preferred to cross his bridges when he came to them.

But as Hillary sat there contemplating a future that suddenly seemed far more uncertain and unclear than it had during the summer, the thought that eventually rose most significantly to her mind was that Lower Barton, the village where the Reverend Keith Coltrane had lived and died thirty years ago, was barely two miles from where she was now sitting.

So she could either go and check out the place where her new cold case had occurred, or she could sit in a car park fretting about who-knew-what, and what, if anything, she could or should do about it.

With a grunt, she turned on the ignition and headed back onto the main road. Less than three minutes later, she indicated right to take the Duns Tew turn-off, then about 300 yards later noticed a turn-off to Lower Barton.

* * *

It was a typically attractive Oxfordshire village, with the almost obligatory creamy Cotswold-stone cottages — most of them rose-bedecked, naturally — a rambling, old village pub, and a church with a Norman tower that was probably close to being a thousand years old, give or take a century or two.

She parked by the lychgate and climbed out into a mellow September afternoon. The sun was warm but not intrusive, and she could smell autumnal flowers wafting from the gardens surrounding the ecclesiastical building. A green woodpecker flew up in noisy alarm from a grass patch between two graves, giving its usual 'yaffle' laughter-like call as it fled. Hillary pushed open the gate. From the way the ironwork screeched on its unoiled hinges, Hillary was surprised that the residents of the two graves didn't join in. It had certainly been loud enough to wake them.

The church was, of course, firmly locked. When she was a child, such a thing would have been unheard of, and she felt a pang of nostalgia for things that were lost. Then she reminded herself that 'the good old days' were hardly ever as good as you thought they had been, and turned away from the vast wooden door to inspect instead the noticeboard set up inside the damp stone porch.

Yoga. Mindfulness. A mother-and-daughter group. A pop-up café. The church seemed to offer everything except religious services.

She smiled at the thought of signing up for a mindfulness session. She'd probably start a riot. Lips twitching, she turned and headed off across the grass — perpetually in need of mowing — towards the newer section of the churchyard, idly noting the names on the stones as she passed.

As in most small villages, one family name appeared more often than others, and here it was Busby. The last of them, however, seemed to have died out in the 1970s.

Suddenly, she stopped at a traditionally arched, plain and simple stone, and read the notation carefully.

Reverend Keith Marcus Coltrane
1956 — 1992
Vicar of this Parish
'Well done, good and faithful servant.'

So, he was buried here, Hillary mused, and wondered why she should feel slightly surprised by that. Perhaps because this was where he had been murdered. She'd assumed he would be buried in the village in which he had been born and raised — and if her memory served her right, the files had put that up near Preston somewhere.

Or perhaps she'd subconsciously formed the idea that her latest murder victim was one of those 'trendy' vicars, who believed in cremation over burial. If so, she'd have to watch herself. As of yet she had no idea what kind of man the dead vicar had been, and it didn't do to go into a case with preconceived ideas.

She heard a movement behind her, and quickly shot around, her hackles rising instinctively. Before she'd thought about it, she'd taken one aggressive step forward, and her both her hands were coming up, as if getting ready to fend off an attack.

Whether it was because she was in a churchyard and thus subliminally aware of every horror film she'd ever watched, or whether she was still feeling unsettled and out of sorts after her visit to the doctor, she didn't know. But she could tell that her nerves were more highly attuned than usual, and hovering way too close to the surface of her skin for comfort.

She saw a small woman shy back in alarm at her sudden movements, and abruptly felt guilty. Her companion had to be well into her seventies at least and was one of those OAPs who seemed so thin and frail that an autumn gale might send them off into orbit at the first gust.

'Sorry about that, I was so deep in thought that you gave me a bit of a fright,' Hillary said, smiling an apology.

At this, the old lady gave a wry smile of her own. She had very suspect peach-coloured hair and wrinkles galore, with a pair of deep-set dark brown eyes that still managed to twinkle somehow. 'Been a long time since I scared anyone, my duck. You a friend of the Reverend then?' she added, nodding at the gravestone.

Hillary had a split-second decision to make. Sooner or later, it would get around that the police were reviewing the murder which had occurred here. But did she want to pre-empt the rumour mill? Would this woman, who was almost certainly a parishioner, be more or less likely to talk to her if she knew her business there?

She decided to err on the side of caution and not introduce herself officially.

'No, I never knew him personally. It just struck me how young he was. Thirty-six or five?' she said instead, her warm tone inviting confidences.

'Yes, he *was* young,' the old woman agreed. She had a bunch of flowers in her hand, a mishmash of blooms probably just picked from her garden, and with a sigh, she bent down at the grave three along from that of the Reverend and began removing browning blooms from an urn. The urn was set in the middle of a green mound that bore no stone.

'There you go, my duck,' she muttered to the unseen resident, as she replaced the old stems with the colourful new ones. When she stood up she winced a little, but Hillary couldn't tell if it was her back or her knees that were giving her the trouble.

She also wondered, idly, if the old girl was a widow visiting her spouse, or if the grave belonged to one of her children, or a sibling.

'He was murdered, you know — our vicar. Right here,' she suddenly said, pointing at the church with the discarded slimy green stems. Spotting them, she grimaced slightly, giving the impression that she had forgotten she still held them in her hand. 'I must get rid of these.' She turned to head towards a low dry-stone wall, where the council had obligingly put out a garden waste refuse bin.

Hillary casually followed her. There was a weathering wooden bench by the bin, and she sat down at the far end, leaving plenty of inviting room beside her. Behind her, ivy had colonised the stone, and bees and Red Admiral butterflies drowsily trawled the tiny flowers for pollen and nectar.

As she'd hoped she would, the old lady sat down on the other end of the bench and sighed, absently rubbing her green-stained hands clean on a handkerchief that had been slipped up her sleeve. 'Lovely day,' she said politely.

Hillary nodded. 'Yes, it is. The village must have been very shocked — by the murder, I mean.'

'Oh yes, none of us could believe it. The vicar were a lovely man. Lovely to look at too,' she added slyly, making Hillary give her what must have appeared to be a very comical double take. Had she misheard, or had this peach-haired, wispy little old lady just intimated that the murdered man had been a bit of a looker?

Hillary's lips twitched.

'He had all the village ladies in a dither, I can tell you,' the old woman swept on blithely. She wasn't looking at Hillary, but rather was watching the erratic progress of a little white butterfly that was blundering from stone to stone in search of non-artificial flowers.

'You've lived here long?' Hillary asked.

'All my life, my duck. Which is more than most can say now. They come, they buy a house, do it up, sell it on for a fortune, and are off again. Used to be I knew everyone. When the Busbys were in the manor, like. Now I don't hardly know a soul.'

'Did the Reverend get on with the incomers?' Hillary asked curiously.

'Oh, vicars always get on with everybody, don't they, my duck? It's in the job description I suppose.'

'You were in the village when he died then?'

'Course I was. Nowhere else to go, really. And it was Christmas too. You don't like to be away from hearth and home when it's Christmastime, do you?'

'No, I suppose not,' Hillary said. 'But what an awful time to have such a tragedy. You said it happened in the church?'

'Yup. Some stranger found him and let out a yell, so they say, and Simon Greaves, who was working in the grounds nearby, came running. Well, not running . . . Simon was seventy if he was a day. He used to keep the place tidy like — bit of an odd-job man and gardener. Helped tend the graves and so on. Just inside the door, he was, on the floor. Dead as a doornail, poor duck.'

Hillary blinked. The old woman sounded almost cheerful. Then she reminded herself that this had all happened thirty years ago. Time enough for it to have fallen into the realms of myth and legend. Certainly, any grief felt for their fallen vicar must long since have faded.

'Poor chap. Was he a nice man? Not all vicars are, are they?' Hillary said, feeling confident now that she could say almost anything she liked to the woman beside her, and not shock her.

'Oh ah, he were nice enough, in his own way. Some people said he had funny ideas, mind, but I just thought that was because he was a bit out of his depth, here in the countryside. Probably bored silly! He might have fared better in a town or city, I reckon. Mind you, he was happy enough with his church. And the saint especially.'

Hillary frowned slightly. 'Not sure I'm following you there. The saint?'

The old woman snorted a laugh. 'The church — St Anthony.' She nodded at the large stone building looming in front of them. 'Vicar was impressed by *him* all right. Used to mention him in his services often enough. Can't quite remember now why he was so taken with the chap. Might'a been he was a martyr or something. Truth to tell, I never did listen to the services much. I preferred singing the hymns.'

Hillary nodded and opened her mouth to ask another question, but before she could pump her newest informant for any more titbits about the life and times of the dead vicar, the old lady got abruptly to her feet.

She winced. 'Well, I'd better be off. I'm gasping for a cup of tea, and I've got a nice coffee and walnut cake waiting. Always buy 'em in the shops now, cheaper than making them yourself nowadays. Nice meeting you, my duck.' And without looking back, she set off for the gate.

Hillary watched her go, a shade bemused. Then she shrugged. In the coming days or weeks, she'd probably run into her again sometime. Hopefully, though, she wouldn't be the only resident of the small village willing to share their memories of the dead man.

Otherwise, they were in real trouble!

CHAPTER TWO

The next morning Hillary retrieved two more boxes from the stack of records in the communal office, took them back to her stationery cupboard and began to read.

Intrigued by the old lady in the churchyard yesterday, and the comment she'd made about the murdered man's good looks, she made a point of studying the photographs of the late reverend. Not the pathology shots, naturally, but the family photos of an alive and presumably happy young man.

And she could see at once why he might have set the hearts of his female parishioners fluttering. From the bare vital statistics, he had stood at six feet one inch, weighed eleven stone two pounds at the time of his death — none of it flab — and had had a lush head of black or near-black hair. His eyes had been blue, and he had been, without doubt, handsome in a rather conventional way. The sort who, if he'd been an actor, would have been put in a scarlet uniform and been cast as the smooth-talking villain in a Jane Austen novel.

In the family snapshots, however, he was dressed in mundane jeans and jerseys, but put him in a vicar's black garb and dog collar and Hillary could well see how Keith Coltrane could have presented a challenge to many a female heart.

Had he been celibate? Hillary thought it rather a big ask, but then, never having known the man, she had no idea what kind of man of God he'd been. Or not been.

The fact that he'd been murdered certainly raised interesting possibilities, however. She paused, wondering if she'd become hopelessly cynical. Then shrugged.

She turned back to the rest of the reports, concentrating on DI Ben Keating's account of the investigation's progress, and quickly learned that the SIO had initially looked long and hard at a woman in the village called Anthea Greyling. But finding no corroborating joy there, began to fix his sights more firmly on the dead man's only sibling, his younger sister, Moira.

At this point, Hillary returned to the family snapshots and picked out the woman in question. Like her brother she was black-haired and blue-eyed, but she looked almost skeletally thin. Not surprising, since from DI's Keating reports, she had been, from her mid-teens, a drug addict.

However, scan the documents though she might, she couldn't find any reasons that offered up an explanation for this fact.

The Coltrane family had been middle class, with both parents having well-paid professional jobs. They'd lived in a pleasant mock-Tudor house, in a 1960s-built cul-de-sac, in a picturesque market town not far from Preston. Both children had attended the local grammar school, but whereas Keith had gone on to take a degree in theology and enter a Church of England seminary, Moira had left school at sixteen with no qualifications to speak of.

A series of short-lived jobs had then followed, interrupted by two pregnancies by different fathers and in quick succession. Neither father, it appeared, had remained on the scene for long.

Hillary leaned back in her chair and took a deep breath, which started a coughing fit. She swore silently, and sat up straight again, willing the episode to pass.

When it did, she stared at an old calendar hanging on the wall of her office that was only a few years out of date, her mind drifting back thirty years, and trying to put itself alongside a disaffected and troubled teenager.

Had Moira Coltrane fallen in with a bad crowd at school, who had subsequently introduced her to soft drugs? Had she then forsaken education for work, in order to pay for harder drugs? It was possible, she supposed, and happened far more often than parents liked to think.

Or had the problem been more subliminal? A pretty young girl with an older brother who wanted to be a vicar would probably be ripe for teasing and peer pressure, which could well have resulted in a show of rebellious spirit. Especially if their parents had been proud of their son's career choice. What better way to stamp her own individuality by veering off the other way, and becoming a bad girl?

Mind you, Hillary warned herself, that was assuming quite a lot. What if the Coltranes *hadn't* been happy with their only son's choice of career? Even back in 1992, the Church had hardly been a powerhouse any longer. Professionals themselves, with lucrative careers, they might have thought his choice lacked enterprise and been bitterly disappointed in him.

She made a mental note to ask Gareth if he could track them down, but she suspected that, given the thirty-year time frame since the murder, one or both of them might since have died.

She took up the SIO's reports again, and over the course of the next hour, picked up various titbits on the Coltrane family dynamic. She was not surprised to find that both of Moira's children were taken into care at various points along the way. Taken to a nearby children's home, they were then sporadically allowed 'chaperoned' visitations with their mother.

When she was sober. At some point in her life, it seemed that drugs gave way to alcohol — probably because it was cheaper.

The Reverend, although thirty-five years old at the time of his murder, had not been, or ever been, married. Hillary found that vaguely interesting. Weren't vicars — not those of the Roman Catholic faith, naturally — encouraged to marry and have a stable home environment? Didn't the Church hierarchy believe that happily married men were more experienced in human relationships, and would therefore have more in common with the vast majority of their flock? And, underneath all that, didn't they worry about the possible temptations for a single, attractive male?

Hillary tried yet again to cast her mind back thirty years. Perhaps by 1992 things were getting more progressive? Or perhaps the Reverend had simply not yet met Mrs Right? And, of course, after the events of 23 December 1992, would never be given the possibility of finding her.

Hillary nodded. Yes. That was at the heart of it all. Murder was such a personal, drastic, irrevocable act. It took away a person's future, a chance to atone or achieve, and opportunities to find love and develop or grow. To take that away from someone required either a stunning indifference to the sanctity of life, or, conversely, could only be an act fuelled by some sort of massive and powerful emotion.

Fear? Hate? Love? Revenge? Self-preservation? What could a country vicar have done to engender any of those in his killer?

Well, it was Hillary's job to find out.

With a grunt, she continued to read, paying close attention to the various reasons why the original DI had funnelled the bulk of his investigation towards the dead man's sibling.

To begin with, the neighbours up at the Lancastrian family home had often overheard arguments in the Coltrane household over the years. Several interviews with neighbours confirmed the fact that Keith and his sister didn't get along. Although they'd seemed to be close when they were little.

The consensus was that Neil and Pamela Coltrane couldn't cope with the growing addictions of their daughter, and the inevitable problems it brought. By the age of eighteen, she'd been caught and convicted of theft — an embarrassing enough social stigma for them. But to make matters worse, and unhappily for the Coltranes, Moira had gone on to specialise in burglarising their immediate neighbours, since she knew their routines, and in some cases, had been friendly with their own children and so knew where the spare keys were hidden or which windows had dodgy latches.

A spell in prison, however, hadn't made her see the light, and over the next five years, she was regularly pulled in for soliciting.

This shame finally forced the family to move from the market town to Oxford. Whether they wanted to be nearer their son, who had now been given a living in the county, or whether the new job opportunities they'd been forced to consider had happened to lead them to the university city, wasn't noted.

Naturally, Moira followed them. Any drug addict and alcoholic wouldn't let their main source of income out of their sight, and whenever Moira was desperate for money, she knew her parents couldn't say no. Tossing her out on the street was as good as a death sentence, and they knew it.

According to DI Keating, the family rows continued and grew more and more virulent, again most prominently whenever the Reverend was visiting. He, it quickly transpired, was the most vociferous in his efforts to get his sister into rehab and off the drugs.

Moira, however, and not surprisingly, hated rehab and the withdrawal symptoms that went with it. As Hillary — and anyone in the drugs squad knew full well — an addict had to desperately want to get clean and possess a fierce willpower in order to do so. And to succeed, they needed to have an overwhelming motivating force to help them focus on kicking the habit — the birth of a child, the loss of a loved one, or a really bad health scare for instance. And even then, success rates weren't good.

But Moira, it seemed, had no real desire to kick her bad habits, and bitterly resented her brother's attempts to force her parents to cut her off unless she went into clinic after clinic.

Hillary nodded. Yes, she could well see why DI Ben Keating had liked the little sister for it. A junkie would regard any threat to their next fix with a savage hatred and would fight tooth and nail to get rid of the cause of it. And any love or affection that might have existed between a brother and sister would stand no chance against the lure of drugged oblivion.

Unfortunately, as she discovered as she read on, in spite of his sister now living within ten miles of his parish, and there being an acknowledged and bitter estrangement between them, DI Keating had been unable to find anyone who had seen Moira Coltrane in the area at the time of her brother's murder.

Moreover, forensics hadn't been able to find any trace of her at the crime scene.

Hillary paused to glance at her watch. No doubt a thorough perusal of the forensics file would take her through the rest of the morning, and she was already feeling hemmed in by her tiny office. Time to get out and breathe some fresh air.

Grabbing her bag and jacket she headed down to the communal office. There she asked Gareth to get on with tracking down the whereabouts of Mr and Mrs Coltrane senior, then eyed Claire.

'I'm going to see if I can catch up with DI Keating's prime suspect. Want to come?' Moira, according to the latest update in the files, had been living at the same address for decades.

'This is the little sis with a drink and drugs problem?' Claire asked. She'd obviously already worked her way through the personnel files of the suspects and was currently trawling the witness statements from the villagers. 'You don't have to ask twice.'

Hillary grinned, and then nodded at Gareth. 'You can help me out on the next field trip. Claire's a bit of an expert when it comes to youngsters who've had a hard life, and I want her input on the older — if probably not any wiser — Moira Coltrane.'

She didn't have to explain herself or her choices to the others, of course, but she felt better for doing so. And it was true, Claire had worked with victims for all her career, mostly in the domestic violence unit. And there would be very little Moira Coltrane could do or say that might shock her.

'Ma'am,' Gareth said with a nod.

Hillary nodded at him, coughed once, then backed out of the office, a hand up to her throat as she struggled not to start whooping again.

She didn't see the concerned look that flashed between the somewhat motherly Claire and the straight-backed former soldier.

If she had done, she wouldn't have liked it.

* * *

Moira Coltrane lived in a part of Oxford that would never find itself marked on any tourist map. For a start, there was not a dreaming spire to be seen, even in the distance, on the 1960s-built, decaying council estate. Even with the September sun still shining, the area managed to generate greyness somehow. The blocks of low-rise flats had a defeated air, as if the original architect's vision of a bright new future had gone the same way as flower power and the hippies.

A solitary black-and-white cat sat on a low wall and watched nervously as they passed, its ears lying back on its head in feline suspicion. And somehow, Hillary just knew that the round-eyed moggy was going to be the friendliest thing that she would meet here today.

'Lovely spot,' Claire said facetiously.

Hillary grunted. 'We're looking for Mandela House, flat 41. See any signs?'

'Most have been nicked for their scrap metal value, guv,' Claire predicted. 'Oh, hold on. Someone on the council has got wise — they've taken to painting the names on the walls. Over there, guv.'

She pointed to a block of low-rise flats that was identical to the others, and Hillary nodded, telling herself that she really would have to bite the bullet and get glasses soon. There was only so much squinting — and bluffing — a person could do.

Claire followed her up the cracked concrete path to the unlocked front lobby, her nose wrinkling at the stale, unhealthy smell that leaked out with the opening of the vestibule door.

'Take the lift?' she asked uncertainly, looking at the pair of steel grey doors that stood off to one side.

Normally Hillary wouldn't risk it, preferring to go up the stairs, but she wasn't certain if she could do so without setting off another coughing fit, so sighed, and pressed the button.

The lift, surprisingly, arrived. It was, even more surprisingly, relatively free of detritus when it did so. She pressed the button for the top floor, figuring that since the building was four stories high, flats beginning with the number four would be on that floor. It was for such clever mental cogitation as this, she supposed wryly, that she had once risen to the dizzying heights of detective inspector.

The public areas were uniformly grey and chilly, the rows of corridors long and stingy. A door cautiously opened and then was instantly slammed shut, somewhere off to their left. Hillary wondered which one of them — herself or Claire — had 'cop' written all over them. Then acknowledged it was probably her.

'You go left, I'll go right. Whistle if you find number forty-one before I do,' Hillary said.

Claire gave a grunt and turned away. Hillary watched her back for a while — just to make sure that whoever it was who had opened and shut that door hadn't had time to decide that it might be fun to make trouble — and then began to explore in the opposite direction.

As she walked, she could feel a familiar tickle in her throat, and reached for the tic-tac box to slip one into her mouth.

She knew that Claire wasn't stupid and wondered for how much longer either she — or Rollo Sale for that matter — would continue to swallow her story that she had a lingering chest infection. At some point she was going to have to level with the superintendent, at least. Come what may, she would need to take medical leave. But she'd cross that bridge when she came to it.

'Guv, here,' she heard Claire's voice calling, and turned about and backtracked past the rows of identical doors, glad to have her wandering mind wrenched back to the job in hand.

Claire rang the bell as Hillary approached, grimaced, stuck her head to the door and rang the bell again. Then she sighed, and hammered her fist on it instead.

Hillary wondered why she'd bothered trying the bell at all. She doubted that maintenance in places like these were a top priority with the council, given the current economic environment.

Behind her, Hillary heard the front door of the opposite flat open. But as she turned her head to see which nosy neighbour was so interested, the door was already shutting. It didn't, however, close right to. Somebody, obviously, had an active curiosity.

Moira Coltrane's door finally opened, and Hillary very vaguely recognised her as the woman from the Coltrane family photographs that she'd been studying only a few hours ago. The black hair was now long gone, and straggling grey had taken its place. The eyes were still blue, but faded and unfocused. Only the scrawny figure of someone who ate too little and habitually abused their system remained.

Dressed in a dirty blue tracksuit and falling-apart sneakers, Moira Coltrane looked back at them from a thirty-year distance.

'Yeah? You the council, you can piss off. You'll get the rent when my benefits come in. If you're lucky.'

Hillary held out her Thames Valley ID card, and Claire did likewise. Had Moira taken the trouble to look, she'd have seen that both of the women on her doorstep were consultants, not fully paid-up members of the constabulary. But Moira didn't bother.

She simply gave a twisted grin, showing teeth that would make a dentist shudder, and stood back. 'C'min then. You're lettin' in a draught.'

Claire and Hillary stepped into a tiny hallway with a handkerchief-sized square of carpet that felt tacky underfoot and three doors leading off it. One of them was standing open, revealing a small living room. Moira shuffled in front of them into this room and collapsed onto a small two-seater settee. The television was on — some property show about first-time buyers looking over a doer-upper, whilst the narrator cheerfully informed everyone how DIY could save you a fortune.

Hillary glanced around the flat. It seemed it hadn't been decorated since the seventies. The carpet in here was so worn that the original floor showed through in several places. The furniture probably came from a last-chance-saloon charity shop. There was the smell of booze in the air. No prizes, then, for guessing how her money was spent.

'Whaddya want then?' Moira asked, eyes fixed firmly on the television set. She looked and sounded as if she was utterly disinterested in their answer.

'We're taking another look into the murder of your brother, Miss Coltrane,' Hillary said crisply, succeeding in drawing the other woman's now startled gaze from the television set.

She gave a huge, ugly laugh. 'D'ya wha'? Wha' the 'ell for? The bugger's been dead and gone for yonks. And good riddance to him too, the bloody hypocrite. Nobody's been missing 'im since Mum an' Dad died, that's for sure. Well, nobody but his randy village harem, dozy cows.'

She turned her attention back to the television screen. Then added, 'So you can piss off. I didn't have nothing to say to that tosser who tried to pin it on me when it 'appened, and I ain't got nothing to say to you lot now.'

Hillary sighed and walked to the filthy window to look out. A large house spider lurked in one corner, the remains of a daddy longlegs ensnared in its web silently telling the tale of a meal in progress.

The view outside — what she could see of it — was of another block of flats. A horse chestnut tree, showing signs of the common disease that was currently plaguing the species, was already beginning to drop its black-spotted leaves on the pavement immediately below her. On the street, the black-and-white cat was playing chicken in the road with a delivery van.

It was all so far removed from the bucolic, idyllic surroundings of Lower Barton that Hillary didn't wonder at the heartlessness of Moira's sentiments. But it was going to be a bit of a pain. She knew this type of witness only too well, and getting any useful information out of her was going to take some doing.

'Do you blame him for *everything,* Moira?' she asked quietly, and heard the rustle of the other woman's clothes as she craned her neck around to glare at her. But Hillary was still staring out of the window.

'Piss off,' Moira said succinctly.

'You don't care who killed him?'

'Piss off.'

'Was it you?'

'Piss off.'

'The original investigating officer thought that it *was* you.'

'And he can piss off an' all.'

Hillary suddenly grinned. She couldn't help it, and the other woman caught the reflection of it in the dirty pane of glass and stiffened warily. In Moira Coltrane's experience, grins like that, on faces like hers, only meant one thing. Trouble.

'I'll be sure to pass on your sentiments to him when I see him,' Hillary said mildly, turning away from the window. Trying to get anything out of her witness now would be pointless. She caught Claire's eye and gave an infinitesimal jerk of her head, and wordlessly the two women walked towards the front door.

'Don't bother to stir yourself, Miss Coltrane, we'll see ourselves out,' Hillary called pleasantly over her shoulder. Then looked at Claire, and both women silently mouthed to each other the response which inevitably came, right on cue.

'Piss off!' Moira shrieked.

Outside the door, Claire began to laugh. But it didn't last long. The same gloom that had settled over Hillary seemed to have taken her under its unwanted wing as well. 'Well that was a waste of time,' she said.

But Hillary wasn't so sure. Whilst Moira had been determined to be as obstructive and unhelpful as possible — probably her standard response to any interview with authority — she had, unknowingly, said something that Hillary had found interesting.

It would probably turn out to be nothing, of course. But then again . . .

Hillary glanced at the door opposite and saw that it was still open half an inch. Whoever had been eavesdropping had been intrigued enough to wait for her neighbour's visitors to leave. A friend — or foe — of Moira? But even as Hillary debated whether it would be worth her while to find out what the unseen voyeur was up to, the door closed with a gentle 'snick'.

Hillary shrugged. They would be back here before long anyway. One way or another, she would have to get the dead man's sister to be more forthcoming — when she'd had time to gather a little more ammunition with which to penetrate her clam-like shell. And if she was still curious about the nosy neighbour, she could do something about it then.

With a sigh, she called HQ, and told Gareth that Keith's parents were probably dead, but to check the register and make sure. If Moira told her that the sun was hot, she'd want to check in with a scientist, just to be certain.

* * *

29

As soon as the sound of their steps had stopped echoing along the corridor, the door opposite Moira's flat reopened, and a woman stepped out.

Sara Reese had lived in the block of flats almost as long as Moira, but prided herself on being a good cut or two above her neighbour. Though only a few years younger, her hair was dyed a becoming shade of red, and she was dressed in proper slacks and held down three part-time jobs. And had never in her life been arrested.

With a sense of pleasant anticipation — her friend's visitors had been of a higher calibre than Moira's usual lowlife acquaintances — she tapped on the door and waited, rearing back a bit as the door was flung open, Moira looking ready to snarl something filthy at her. Oh my, she had been hitting the booze even earlier than usual, Sara thought with mild disgust, but then Moira's face softened.

'Oh, s'only you. Sorry, Sara, thought it was the bloody coppers back again.'

At this, Sara perked up even more. As a woman who'd always had to look out for herself, she forever had her eyes peeled for ways to make a bit of extra money, and right away she scented the whiff of a possible opportunity.

'You not been up to your old tricks again 'ave you, Mo? At your age too,' she added, giving Moira a nudge with her elbow and a dirty snigger that wouldn't have shamed a *Carry On* film actor. 'You gonna invite us in then or what?'

'You got a bottle?' Moira asked craftily. She knew how much Sara liked to know everything that was going on — especially when it was none of her business — and she didn't see why she should provide the entertainment for free.

Sara nodded and nipped back to her own place for two cans of cider, moving faster than she had done in some years. Moira regarded the offering with disgust, then shrugged. 'Better than nothin' I s'pose,' she muttered gracelessly, nodding at her to come in.

Once seated in front of the telly once more, she popped open the can and drank half of it straight down.

'So, what's up then?' Sara asked, without even the pretence of casual conversation. 'Nothing bad, I hope?' she added, with shameless insincerity.

'Nah. You'll never guess though,' Moira said, and began to gurgle with laughter.

'What? It's not Clara-Jane is it? She hasn't got herself into any bother?'

Moira drank some more of the cider and regarded her neighbour with a jaundiced eye. 'Naw, she ain't then. Don't know why you and she are so thick as thieves, neither,' she muttered. 'The ungrateful sod couldn't care two hoots for either one of us.'

Sara shrugged, feeling annoyed by the put-down — perhaps because, deep down, she suspected that Moira was right for once — but knowing better than to take the bait anyhow.

It would only set Moira off into one of her tantrums.

She'd known Moira's daughter, Clara-Jane, since she was a nipper. And during the periods when she hadn't been taken off by the social and put in some home or other, Sara had often babysat her, whenever her mother failed to come home at night. And fed her, when her mother failed to come home at mealtimes.

Sara had never wanted kids of her own, and her magnanimity was half-hearted at best, but she had to admit to a sneaking fondness for the daughter of her neighbour. Perhaps because Clara-Jane reminded her of herself. Snarky, irrepressible, and never willing to give a sucker an even break.

'So what's the plod want then?' she pressed.

Moira, cat-like, made Sara wait until she'd finished the can of cider, then looked pointedly at the can in her neighbour's hand.

Sara sighed, took a gulp from it, then — reluctantly — handed it over. 'Come on then, give! And it better be worth it,' she said, nodding at the can that Moira now tilted greedily towards her face.

Moira snorted.

'The silly buggers have only gone and opened my brother's case again,' she said, eyes dancing. And didn't *that* give the nosy cow something to chew over!

'Your Keith? Never! That must be twenty years ago,' Sara said.

'More like thirty,' Moira said bitterly. 'Bastard.' And went on to list her usual grievances about her family.

But Sara, who'd heard it all before, was already zoning her out, as her mind began buzzing. The reopening of an old murder case might not be top-notch news, but she was sure she could sell it to the local rags or true-crime bloggers. Desperate for news, they were, what with podcasts and whatever. And the murder of a randy vicar — all vicars, to the news media, were randy, right? — would have to be worth a few bob in the right places.

With a bit of luck, she could eat steak — well, stewing steak —tonight.

Leaving Moira staring at the television screen without even so much as a token goodbye, Sara hurried back to her flat. There she paced, and getting her phone out, started hunting down possible sources of income.

And whilst she was at it, she thought, she might as well give Clara-Jane a call — if she was still using the same number. It must be a couple of years now since they'd spoken, and it'd be nice to catch up with her and see how she was doing.

And she'd be bound to be interested that her dear dead uncle's murder case was being looked into again.

Sara hummed happily to herself as she set to work. She always had liked being the bearer of interesting news!

CHAPTER THREE

Hillary and Claire returned to HQ, chatting mostly about Claire's children and grandchildren and their latest triumphs and disasters. Once or twice, Hillary noticed Claire open and then close her mouth, as if about to say something, then thinking better of it.

And she thought she had a good idea of what it was on her colleague's mind and was grateful that she kept her counsel. She had no wish to discuss her health — or, at this point in time, even think about it much. Time enough for that when she knew what she was dealing with.

Back in the communal office, Gareth looked up as they entered, his eyes speculative.

'Claire, can you write up the interview, such as it was, and put it in the murder book?' Hillary asked a shade wearily. Whilst uncooperative witnesses were a daily hazard, that didn't make them any more palatable.

At the beginning of each case, she always set up an open, on-going file she dubbed 'the murder book' that was to be kept constantly updated by every member of the team. That way, any one of them could use it for reference, and meant they didn't repeat themselves chasing the same data.

'Guv,' Claire said, and added wryly, 'shouldn't take me long.'

'I take it she wasn't very forthcoming then?' Gareth ventured with a brief smile. He was beginning to feel a part of the team now, Hillary noted with satisfaction, and with a couple of murder cases under his belt was becoming more confident, getting to grips with what was expected of him.

'You could say that,' she responded with a grimace. Then, 'Do you have a current address for DI Ben Keating?' One of the tasks she'd set him earlier was to find out if the original investigating officer was still in the land of the living, and if so, where.

'Yes, guv. He didn't go far — just over the border into Northamptonshire, in fact.'

'Cheaper houses and cheaper prices,' Claire said. 'It may not be far in geographical miles, but it's amazing how much further your pension goes when you're not in the OX postcode. My better half keeps threatening that we should do the same and keeps leaving me real estate brochures on the coffee table.' She rolled her eyes to show what she thought of the idea.

Gareth nodded absently, only half-listening. The former soldier might be getting more accustomed to life in civvy street, Hillary mused, but he still retained his pinpoint focus on the job in hand whilst at work. 'He's eighty-one now, ma'am, but I don't think he's gone into care. The address suggests a private residence, anyway.'

Hillary glanced at her watch. There was plenty of time to fit in another interview. 'All right. I promised you the next shout. Fancy a road trip to the outer wilds then?'

Gareth's lips twisted slightly — which was his equivalent of a grin. 'Ma'am.' He rose, reaching for the walking cane that was his constant companion.

'I'll meet you in the car park,' Hillary said. 'I just need to go and update the super. You can drive.' Nowadays, she tried to spare Puff the longer journeys.

'Ma'am,' Gareth said, hoping that he'd successfully hidden his relief. He was happy with his adapted car and preferred to be in the driving seat. Moreover, he was never totally convinced that his superior officer's car would actually arrive at their intended destination on any given occasion.

Claire watched him limp out, and with a sigh got down to her typing.

* * *

Ben Keating lived on a small housing estate not too many miles from the Silverstone racing tracks. Hillary wondered if he was a petrol head and had moved here to take advantage of it, or whether it was coincidental. Most ex-coppers she knew took up golf. Why, she had no idea.

She only hoped his memory was still good. For all she knew, this might be one of his children's residences and they acted as a carer for him, in which case, their journey would have been wasted.

The house was a bland, neat semi, probably a council house in its former life. The front garden was small, with a neat square of lawn with a single flowering rose bush that had been planted dead centre in the middle of it. The path was weed free, and the privet hedge surrounding the property recently trimmed.

Hillary noticed Gareth giving it all an ex-soldier's approving nod and quickly hid her smile.

She rang the bell, and was slightly surprised, but very pleased, to see a sprightly, white-haired man open the door. Although lean, he stood without aid, and his slightly sunken brown eyes were taking her in with a sharpening interest. His eyes shot to Gareth, and then instantly back to her.

Yes, the former DI still had all his marbles all right, Hillary noted with relief. Even now, she could almost hear him mentally placing her as being in 'the job'.

'Hello there,' Ben Keating said.

Hillary smiled at him and fished out her identification. As he read it, his eyes widened slightly. Even though he'd been retired for many years, he'd heard of Hillary Greene.

Then he noted her civilian status, as declared on the laminated card, and raised an eyebrow.

As Gareth showed his own ID, the old man's eyes took in the former soldier's badly injured left hand, and the way he stood, left side leaning on his stick, and looked slightly puzzled.

'Mr Keating? Former DI Keating?' Hillary said, protectively drawing his attention back to herself.

'That's me.'

Hillary smiled. 'Hello, sir,' she said, determined to get him on side at once. And showing deference was a sure way of doing that. 'We're hoping you can help us. We're civilian consultants with your old firm, taking a second look at cold cases. Like you, I retired at the rank of DI. My colleague here was recently in the army. We're hoping you can help us with our current investigation.'

'Ah, I heard about all that. Budget cuts, I 'spect?' In his day, the force had been well-staffed, and specialist outside consultants hadn't been heard of. But he'd heard about the CRT unit, and a division being created to keep old files active.

Hillary sighed and nodded. 'You know how it is, sir,' she said, again reinforcing the 'us and them' scenario, with herself and the old man definitely grouped together in the 'us' division. 'We do answer to Superintendent Sale though,' she clarified, knowing that the mention of a high rank wouldn't go unnoticed.

She had the feeling that in Ben Keating she was dealing with an old-fashioned copper, who liked things done the old-fashioned way, and that by bringing in a 'proper' copper's name she'd help soothe away any misgivings he might still have.

The old man slowly nodded. 'Fair enough. Come on in then,' he stood back, revealing a small but uncluttered hall. He led them straight through to the kitchen. Full of natural daylight, it had a view of a tiny back garden with a lone apple tree and was decorated mostly in shades of green and cream.

It had room for a small table and chairs, and it was to these that he indicated.

'Tea or coffee? Milk, sugar, lemon?'

They put in their orders as they took a seat each, and watched the old man set about with the kettle. 'So, which case of mine are you interested in?'

'The murder of a vicar, Keith Coltrane, back in 1992, sir,' Hillary said, getting out her notebook and biro. She noticed that Gareth had his phone at the ready and had detached what looked to her like a small rubber-tipped pen that he used to tap on the tiny keypad. She saw Ben Keating give the tech a disdainful glance and tried not to do the same. Although she had to accept modern gizmos, she did so grudgingly.

'Oh yeah, I remember *that* one, right enough,' Ben said, which boded well. Then he rather spoiled it by adding succinctly, 'Odd.'

He filled the mugs and brought them back to the table one at a time. Hillary noticed that his hands had a slight tremble and wondered if he had the onset of Parkinson's. Her own father had suffered with it, and in the former DI's rather shuffling and careful gait, she thought she recognised another of the symptoms.

'Odd how, sir?' she asked politely.

Ben brought his own mug of tea and set it on the table, then pulled out a chair and sat down with a sigh.

'It's hard to say, really,' he began, then immediately smiled wryly. 'Sorry, I daresay that's the last sort of thing you want to hear from the former SIO. I'll try and get more specific.'

He took a sip of tea and paused. He had big bushy white caterpillar-like eyebrows, and they had the disconcerting habit of moving up and down seemingly independent of any other part of his face. She saw Gareth watching them as if mesmerised before hastily looking away.

'There are some cases when you just never seem to be able to get a hold of the real meat and gravy of it,' Ben

Keating began. 'Do you know what I mean?' He looked at her closely.

Hillary felt her heart sink, because she *did* know what he meant — only too well. 'Yes. I know just what you mean. I've had a few cases like that, and they're always a bugger.'

Ben gave a grunt of laughter, then sighed. 'True. So, in the case of the Reverend, well, for a start, there was the victim himself. You don't often come across murdered clergymen do you? I mean, statistically, they're not in a high-risk category. Well, not back then, they weren't. Nowadays, well . . .'

He paused and shrugged philosophically. Then he took another sip of his tea.

Hillary wasn't about to chivvy him. She knew when patience was required.

'But it wasn't just his job, so much as the fact that I could never get a real sense of the *man*,' Ben Keating continued. 'According to which witness you talked to he was clever, or charming, or down-to-earth, or funny, or up himself, or genuine or . . . You get the picture?'

Hillary nodded glumly. She got it, all right. 'He was all things to all men?'

Ben grunted. 'I suppose, in a vicar, that was a good quality to have. And I daresay he just got in the habit of doing or saying whatever it was that any particular member of his parish expected of him at the time. I mean, it was his job to be pleasant, and soothe ruffled feathers and what have you.'

Hillary leaned back in her chair with a sigh of her own. 'Good for the Church of England, but a bit of a sod for us,' she acknowledged. 'And I daresay the villagers weren't all that forthcoming. "Don't speak ill of the dead" and all that. Which would have gone double for a murdered vicar?'

'You can say that again!' Ben Keating snorted, his white bushy eyebrows doing a veritable fandango on his forehead. 'Trying to get any useful insight into the man from the people who knew him was a bloody nightmare. Usually, you can get a feel for who might kill someone by learning who the victim was. But in this case . . .' Ben sighed.

'Yes, I can see that you would have been up against it,' Hillary said, with genuine sympathy. 'At least, that's where we have the advantage over the original team. After thirty years, people are bound to be more willing to talk. Our problem is going to be finding people still alive who remember him!'

'Rather you than me.' The old man looked at her and raised his mug in salute. 'The best of British luck to you,' he added with a cheeky grin.

Hillary grinned back. 'From the case files, you seemed to finally hone in on the younger sister as your prime suspect?'

Ben shrugged. 'Only because she seemed to have the most compelling and understandable motive.' He visibly hesitated, then shook his head in frustration. 'But there again, it was all so *unsatisfactory*. Those siblings had been fighting for years. What prompted Moira to take a spade to her brother's head at that particular point in time? And I couldn't track down any evidence of a recent or almighty row between them that might have precipitated it.'

'But there were other suspects too?' she prompted gently. 'You seemed to question . . .' For a moment Hillary's mind wouldn't come up with the name of the woman she wanted, and — worse — felt the now familiar urge to want to cough. Then the name popped into her head, and she took a sip of coffee in an attempt to stave off the tickling in her chest. 'Er . . . Anthea Greyling, wasn't it? You went back to her a time or two?'

But it was no good; she reached into her handbag to bring out a tissue, and began to cough into it. 'Sorry, don't worry, it's not catching,' she said between gasps. 'I've had a chest infection for ages and can't seem to get rid of the damn thing,' she explained, patting her sternum.

'Oh, I've had them too,' the old man said in solidarity. 'And you're right, they're sods to get rid of. And to answer your question, yeah, Anthea Greyling did stand out from the crowd. I mean, a lot of the women in the village flocked around him, but she was by far the vicar's biggest fan,' Ben Keating said, politely ignoring his visitor's coughing fit.

Gareth shot Hillary a quick glance, only relaxing when the coughing fit ended.

'Yes, I've seen his photos,' Hillary said, taking a careful sip of her coffee again. 'And there's no doubt he was a handsome man. But given the dog collar, I don't suppose we could label him a ladies' man exactly, but just as someone who seemed to acquire his fair share of attention, like it or not?'

'I'll say. And all of them were willing to dish the dirt on the other.'

'Did you get the feeling that he *liked* the attention though?' Hillary asked.

'Can't say that I did, really,' Ben said, absently rubbing a shaking finger against the side of his face. 'I mean, all those that I talked to who were neutral, as it were, seemed to think that the vicar did his best to ignore or downplay his fan club.'

Hillary nodded. 'But Mrs Greyling stood out from the crowd?' she prompted.

'Yes. She was a pretty redhead, I seem to remember, somewhere in her mid-thirties at the time. She'd married well, I seem to recall. Her husband . . . can't remember his name . . . was pretty well off. But she fell hard for the Reverend, no doubt about it. Started attending church regularly once he came to the village, whereas before she'd never seemed to bother. Joined groups that used the church, volunteered to do the flowers and run a stall at the village fete. You know, all the things that would bring her into his orbit. But she became so obviously besotted that she became a bit of a joke. Not nice, that, when that sort of thing happens in a small community.'

'No,' Hillary agreed. Was it possible that Anthea Greyling had had a shameful moment of clarity, and saw herself as others saw her? And in that moment of intense humiliation, had taken it out on the object of her desire? 'How did the husband take it?'

'He'd just served divorce papers on her by the time the vicar's body was found,' Ben said.

'Yes, I remember reading that in the case files.' Hillary clicked her fingers. 'He'd actually been to see the Reverend on the morning of his death, hadn't he? Bit of a big red flag that, even though the victim was seen alive and well by several people afterwards.'

'That's right,' Ben said. 'And I never completely ruled him out, but to my way of thinking, he'd got most of his anger out of his system already. Given the wife the boot, and no doubt enjoyed giving the vicar a good tongue-lashing as well. Vented his spleen and all that.'

Hillary nodded, following his reasoning with ease. 'And bashing someone over the head with a spade does sound like a spontaneous outburst of sudden rage. And all of *his* rage would probably have been spent by that point. Yes, I can see why you put him at the bottom of the list.' But she made a mental note to revisit just how strong the husband's alibi had actually been for the afternoon of the vicar's death.

'And Max Walker?' Hillary turned to her next topic, ticking it off on her to-do list in her notebook.

'Ah, now there's another prime example of how slippery that case was to get a proper hold of,' Ben complained. 'Max owned the land next to the churchyard. He was one of those who came from the city, wanting to live the good life — you know?'

Hillary smiled. She'd caught up on this particular file in the car on the journey over. 'A former accountant wasn't he?'

'Something like that. I can see the man now. He looked the part, I'll give him that — big, but muscular, florid-faced, and all that. He looked like a proper son of the soil. But I don't know that the bucolic dream was working out all that well for him. You couldn't really make much of a living from a smallholding, even back then. So he was already looking for ways to diversify.'

'Going back to his big-city ways,' Hillary put in with a grin.

Ben gurgled into his tea. 'Yeah. Trouble with him was, I think all his work colleagues had joshed him so much about his quitting a good job and were just waiting for him to come crawling back with his tail between his legs, that he was desperate to prove them wrong.'

'Couldn't face the humiliation of admitting to failure, huh?' Hillary mused.

'Not him! So he had come up with this plan about buying the field next to the church and setting up a campsite of some kind. I seem to recall that the field in question abutted his own property on the east, so it would have been ideal. Trouble was, the vicar had his eye on it for a cemetery. The churchyard was filling up, and although the village isn't huge, it would inevitably need to extend its burial site.'

'Ah,' Hillary said. 'So they were battling it out with the land owner? Or the parish council?'

'Both, probably, if I know anything about villages,' Ben predicted grumpily.

'Any idea who eventually won?'

'Nah,' Ben said with a shrug. 'Things like that can rumble on for years. By then, I'd long been pulled off the case and reassigned. And I've never been back to the village, so who knows? There's probably been a bloody great housing estate been built on it by now or something.'

Hillary, who'd been to the church just yesterday, could testify that *that* at least hadn't happened. Well, not yet anyway.

'That sort of argy-bargy isn't the sort of thing that usually ends in murder though, is it?'

'No. Not usually,' Ben said, but something in his tone caught her attention. As did one of his bushy eyebrows, which slid downwards to overshadow one of his eyes.

Hillary paused in the act of raising her mug. 'You think this might have been one of those *un*usual times?' she asked quietly.

Ben Keating sighed and hesitated, clearly trying to think of the best way of articulating his feelings. Eventually, he said, 'I think Max Walker was desperate to succeed. And I think his temper wasn't the best. And since someone grabbed a spade that happened to be near at hand and whacked our victim on the back of the head with it — yeah, I could definitely see Max Walker doing that, if rage and frustration got the better of him.'

'Did Keith Coltrane strike you as the bolshie kind? Would he have fought persistently for what he wanted?' Hillary asked.

'I dunno,' Ben admitted. 'Now we're back to where we started. I never really could get a proper handle on the man. But I can tell you that when he took over the church, the congregation was pitiful. And he'd built it up — mainly with women, I'll grant you, but he was also attracting a fair number of younger members, which I imagine was no mean feat. So I can see him being reasonable and calm on the surface, but for all that, being determined to get his own way.'

'Yes, he must have had something about him,' Hillary agreed. 'A backbone. Some cunning. Perseverance. And charisma.'

Ben nodded. 'And somewhere amongst all that, he rubbed somebody up the wrong way so badly that they lashed out.'

'The spade was left in the church porch by the old groundsman. You ever like him for it?' Hillary asked.

'Nah,' Ben said dismissively. 'Far as I could tell, he got on all right with the Reverend. And he just did the occasional odd jobs and was paid for it. So, where's the motive? No, I think he just left his garden equipment lying about, and somebody saw the spade, and when he or she had the final showdown with the vicar just inside the door, they reached out and grabbed it.'

Or that might just be what they want us to think, Hillary mused silently. According to Ben's investigations, the groundsman had been digging out ivy early that morning, and had left off sometime before ten, intending to come back and finish the job before it got too dark. That left the spade in the porch, in plain sight, for most of the day. And so close to Christmas, there was no saying how many people might have been around the church and seen it there. The women who

43

were decorating the halls with boughs of holly. Parishioners putting Christmas wreaths on loved one's graves.

Suppose one of them had seen and noted the spade, and it had given that same someone an idea? What if they'd then subsequently *planned* the murder in advance? What if it wasn't luck or coincidence that they had happened on the vicar at a time when he was alone in the church?

Perhaps, right from the start, Ben had been misled into thinking this was a spur-of-the-moment thing, when it wasn't. *That* might account for his feeling of never being able to get at the meat and gravy of it.

Hillary sighed. Or then again, maybe not.

'We believe both his parents are now dead, so I can't talk to them. What was their take on things at the time?' she asked curiously.

Ben finished his mug of tea and pushed it aside.

'Well, they were shook up, as you can imagine. I got the feeling that when I turned up on their doorstep with that look on my face — you know the one I mean?'

Hillary did. In the past, she'd had to turn up on doorsteps herself with that same look on her face. She nodded solemnly.

'Yeah. Well, I got the feeling they were bracing themselves to hear bad news about their girl. Not surprising, given the circumstances. She was a junkie and had been working the streets. So when I had to tell them that it was in fact their son . . .'

Hillary coughed, then reached into her bag for a tic tac. 'I suppose they thought he was safe, being a vicar. In a country parish and all?'

'Yeah, I suppose they did,' Ben said heavily. 'Well, when I went back to them after a few days and the worst of the initial shock and disbelief had passed, they just seemed bewildered. Neither of them could offer up anything of use. According to them, Keith hadn't been behaving any differently before his death. He had no money worries. He wasn't courting — their words, not mine. He was looking forward to the Christmas services — his favourite, apparently. He had no quarrel with anyone, not that they knew.'

'Well, we know that's not right,' Hillary put in. 'He had Max Walker and Anthea Greyling's husband to contend with, for a start. So he obviously didn't confide much in his parents.'

'Well, I suppose he wouldn't. Being a vicar and all, I suppose he thought he had to keep his parishioners' business private,' Ben reasonably pointed out. 'And that, at least, *was* one thing that was consistent about him. Everyone I spoke to had to admit — either grudgingly or gushingly — that he was good at his job. He seemed very happy with his church. And his bosses were happy with him too. His bishop made a note of telling me that Keith had one of the best attendance rates of any of his rural churches.'

'So, in summation,' Hillary said, 'he was a good vicar, who was everything to all men, with a rotten sister, a land-grabbing neighbour, and a besotted, attractive married woman and her unhappy husband to contend with.'

'Yup, that about sums it up all right,' Ben Keating said with a sigh. 'So you can take your pick, and like I said before — the best of British luck to you.'

* * *

'So, what do you make of all that?' Hillary asked, as they returned to Gareth's car.

Gareth frowned thoughtfully. Then said, 'I think this one is going to give us gyp, ma'am.'

Hillary burst out laughing. She couldn't help it. And then she started coughing. And that made her swear.

Gareth, his face showing no expression at all, drove them back towards Kidlington.

* * *

Later, Hillary turned into the car park of the Boat, the pub on the Oxford canal where she moored her narrowboat, and parked Puff in her favourite spot near an elder hedge. It was a lovely, late golden afternoon, with the nip of autumn in the breeze, and a hedge sparrow singing lustily from somewhere across the canal.

As she set off along the towpath on the short walk to the *Mollern* she was accompanied by a mallard drake, who kept pace with her, quacking insistently. So much so, that once she'd climbed aboard the boat, she instantly went to the small galley and chucked some pieces of brown bread out of the porthole to keep the feathered little sod quiet.

That done, she hunted in the small cupboard under the sink for a tin of something, coming up with some meatballs in tomato sauce. She checked the use-by date suspiciously and then dumped it into a pan. Whilst it heated, she kicked off her shoes and collapsed into one of the two armchairs her tiny home boasted.

Slowly, she leaned her head back on the chair rest and stared at the ceiling, which, on a narrowboat, was never very high above her.

Tomorrow she would have to go for her scan. She mentally kicked herself as she realised that she'd forgotten to inform Rollo Sale that she'd be late in to work. Again. Quickly she sent him an email, promising to make up for the missed hours by working late, and giving no details about why she needed to rearrange her hours.

That done, she returned to the galley to rescue her supper from sticking to the bottom of the pan and dumped the lot into an old soup bowl that was handy. She then drew out a small stool, rifled in her cutlery drawer for a soup spoon, and sat absently eating, watching the mallard drake defend his own supper of brown bread from another of his kind.

As the outraged quacking rose to a crescendo outside her window, she told herself that everything would be fine.

All she had to do was make herself believe it.

CHAPTER FOUR

Thursday began overcast and spitting lightly with rain. Hillary heard its gentle patter on the roof of her narrowboat as she lay, still tossing and turning in her narrow bed, with the dawn beginning to lighten the sky outside the porthole window.

So much for trying to get a good night's sleep, she thought dryly. She'd spent most of it chasing around half-formed ideas and thoughts on a murdered vicar, and the rest of it dragging her mind back from the abyss whenever it insisted on straying onto today's hospital procedure, and its possible ramifications.

Not surprisingly then, she felt woolly-headed and grumpy, which meant that at half past six she was already up, showered and dressed for the day. She couldn't face breakfast — not even a slice of toast — and so after drinking way too much coffee, left the narrowboat wearing a navy-blue skirt and blazer under her best waterproof mac.

By now the rain, being intermittent, was taking a short break, and she decided on the spur of the moment that rather than walking towards her car, she'd take a short walk along the canal in the opposite direction instead.

After all, there'd be no point calling in at work early just for the sake of getting forty-five minutes or so of paperwork done. That was besides the fact that she didn't want to give any of her co-workers the opportunity to ask any unwanted questions about her imminent absence.

On the other hand, she didn't want to be too early at the hospital either. Hanging around an antiseptic environment and waiting for an unknown procedure to begin would probably send her blood pressure skyrocketing.

No, she'd rather be out here, where she could appreciate the sights, sounds and smells of nature. She took a couple of slow, careful breaths and looked around her appreciatively. Here the willow tree's leaves were just starting to turn a soft lemon colour, the first of them being shed onto the still, khaki-coloured water of the canal. Lining the waterway, the big butterbur leaves were browning and curling at the edges, and the big stems of reed mace, often wrongly thought to be bullrushes, were beginning to form their velvet-like dark brown overcoats. There was not a swallow in sight now, having all set off back for Africa, and Hillary missed their swooping dips along the canal tops as they hunted for midges.

A robin was singing happily in a hawthorn bush though, and as she breathed in the soft, damp air, for once, and paradoxically, she felt no urge to cough. Typical, she thought. She was about to get a scan on her lungs, and here they were, behaving themselves impeccably for once. Did they somehow know — like pets, when a visit to the vet was on the cards? And like naughty children caught out in a misdemeanour, were they pretending that her current problems were nothing to do with them?

The whimsical thought made her chuckle softly to herself and shake her head. No two ways about it, she needed to get a grip! She walked leisurely for ten minutes or so, then turned back and retraced her steps, going past the *Mollern* and beginning to pick up her pace a little as the rain returned.

By the time she trotted up to Puff, she was damp about the shoulders and beginning to shiver. Great. It would be just her luck to catch a cold and get a *real* chest infection now.

She turned the ignition and hopefully turned on the heater to high. Puff, naturally, thought she was having a laugh.

Still shivering, she turned and headed out of Thrupp, getting caught up in the usual rush hour of traffic heading into Oxford. It felt strange not to turn off into the HQ parking lot, but to continue straight on to the roundabout, and from there set out for the Oxford suburb of Headington.

The John Radcliffe hospital sat like a big white elephant on top of a hill and was visible for miles around. Parking, as might be expected, was a game of patience, skill, luck and sheer bull-headed ruthlessness. It only took her twenty-five minutes to secure a place, which she thought was probably a record.

As a native, however, she'd set out with over an hour and a half to spare, so she didn't have to rush towards the CT unit, which was just as well, because it took her another quarter of an hour to find the bloody thing!

As she finally entered the waiting room, she was aware that her heart was beating a little too fast, and there was a low-level feeling of dread hovering somewhere in the pit of her stomach.

Like a lot of people, she was not fond of hospitals. Or needles. Or the unknown.

The waiting room was typical of its kind. Generic carpet tiles, generic furniture, and a low table with a smattering of months-old periodical magazines scattered atop it. The walls were adorned with the usual mixed bunch of 'warning' posters that were designed to scare you silly, and breezily informed you that if you were experiencing such-and-such symptoms you might have galloping gut rot and your insides were in danger of falling out. Or something.

A single receptionist sat behind a screen in one corner of the room and smiled at her brightly. Hillary nodded at her with a not-quite-so-bright smile and checked in, handing over the letter explaining the reasons she was there, and at what time she'd be needed.

There followed the usual tapping on the computer keypad, and the receptionist confirmed the appointment and handed over a form for her to fill in.

Hillary sighed and took it to a chair. She was sure, when you finally kicked the bucket, you'd probably be required to fill in forms at the pearly gates. Probably not at the other place though?

This particular form wanted to know what medical problems she had, what medication she was on, and if she had any stray bits of metal lodged within her person. She didn't, luckily. The bullet that, some years ago now, had penetrated perilously close to her backside had been duly removed by a surgeon and now probably sat in some evidence bag somewhere in the basement of an anonymous-looking police storage facility. And she had no piercings. The form also asked her, if she was wearing a bra, jewellery or any other form of clothing comprising a metallic fastening to remove them. The receptionist, along with the form, had handed her a key to a locker where she could safely leave her belongings whilst she was having her scan.

Hillary checked her watch as she signed and dated the form and realised that she still had ten minutes or more to wait, providing the system was running on time. Which she doubted. Call her a pessimist.

She duly removed her watch and put it in her bag, handed the form back to the receptionist and out of some weird masochistic urge, decided to tour the various posters and see what other ominous diseases she might have contracted all unawares. She was fairly sure she didn't have Lyme disease. Or Legionnaires'. And the tetanus information had her eyes watering.

She paused in front of a post-natal poster showing a picture of an obviously newborn infant, umbilical cord still attached. It was covered in blood and gore, little eyes screwed tightly shut as it screamed lustily, whilst being held in a pair rubber-gloved, safe hands. The poster was clearly designed to encourage mothers to have their offspring in hospital, rather than at home, because the wording underneath said boldly *DID YOU KNOW, THE FIRST THREE MINUTES OF YOUR LIFE CAN BE THE MOST DANGEROUS?*

50

'The last three can be a bit iffy too,' Hillary muttered to herself, and then nearly jumped out of her skin as a pleasant voice behind her said, 'Ms Greene?'

Hillary turned to look at a pretty Asian woman, dressed in the usual top-to-toe hospital kit, who smiled at her brightly. 'If you'd like to leave your things in the locker and follow me?'

Hillary Greene suddenly realised that there was nothing in the whole wide world that she'd like to do less, and said pleasantly, 'Of course.'

* * *

In Headington, whilst Hillary Greene — sans anything metallic — was being mechanically slid into a white plastic-looking tunnel, in the pretty Wiltshire town of Malmesbury, Peter Cornwallis was sitting at his kitchen table.

From his window, he had a partial view of the back of the beautiful Malmesbury Abbey, but it had become so familiar to him that he rarely bothered to look at it.

At the age of seventy-two, he was still dressed in his pyjamas, housecoat and slippers, and although the morning was well advanced already, probably wouldn't get properly dressed for another hour or so yet. What was the point when you had nowhere you needed to be?

He had just made himself his morning cup of tea and had poured out the milk over his bowl of cornflakes and was looking forward to nothing more than another of his usual leisurely, humdrum days.

Like many of his generation, he wasn't much up on modern technology, and still enjoyed reading an actual newspaper. And although he'd not lived in Oxfordshire for quite some time now, he still liked to keep up with the *Oxford Mail*, along with other, national papers.

He was halfway through his cereal and had just finished the first page of the Oxford newspaper, when he turned it over and spotted the headline on page three.

Slowly, he lowered his spoonful of forgotten cornflakes back into the bowl, and swallowed hard.

The small headline wasn't particularly dramatic. And the resultant small piece that went with it wasn't particularly informative or sensational. It simply stated that the thirty-year-old murder of a vicar in Lower Barton was being reviewed, under the aegis of a retired former DI Greene — who had a formidable record of success — and was now acting as a consultant in a cold case team.

The reporter went on to speculate that the relatives of the dead man, as well as the inhabitants of the village who still remembered the Rev. Keith Coltrane, would no doubt be happy to help the police with their inquiries. And concluded by asking anyone who lived in the village or knew the victim or who had any information that they thought might be pertinent to get in touch with the newspaper.

With shaking hands, Peter Cornwallis let the paper fall onto the table and pushed his now unwanted bowl of cereal away. His heart thumped uncomfortably in his chest, and before he could stop it, his mind leapfrogged back over the decades to the first time he'd met Lower Barton's newest vicar.

Keith.

And with some wonderment, Peter realised that he hadn't thought about Keith for some time now.

At first, of course, he'd thought about him all the time. How could he not? Given all that had happened, and the upheaval it had caused in all of their lives. But as the years had passed, and he'd slowly withered down to become the old man he was now, complete with a slightly dodgy hip, failing hearing and false teeth, Keith had finally, wonderfully slipped away and almost completely disappeared into nothingness.

And now, out of the blue, brutally and without warning, the memory of Keith had come back again. Here in this small, neat, semi-detached house, miles away from where he'd lived and died. Back, and, it seemed, ready to haunt him all over again.

Peter got up feeling odd. His feet seemed to have migrated a long way from his head and his limbs felt unco-ordinated. Nevertheless, he forced himself to go upstairs and dress absently in yesterday's clothes. That done, he sat wearily on the edge of the bed and felt himself weeping.

It was embarrassing. He tried to stop but couldn't, and so he simply sat and let the tears fall and wondered. What could he do? What *should* he do? Should he even do anything at all? What was for the best? What would keep him, and those he loved, safe?

Should he phone Trevor? Would his son even have seen the piece about the reopening of old wounds? He doubted that Trevor would read the papers much — and he didn't know if the story would have made it onto the internet. He knew next to nothing about the virtual world everyone else seemed to live in.

Should he phone him? Tell him? *Warn* him?

But the thought of doing so made Peter shrink back inside himself. What could he say, exactly? It wasn't as if they were close. He hadn't spoken to his son for quite some time — probably not since last Christmas, and he knew Trevor would not welcome the contact.

Although they might see each other occasionally, some-times on Peter's birthday or his own, his son, without ever actually saying so, had made it clear that he wasn't anxious to have a close relationship with his father.

And who could blame him?

If it wasn't for his daughter-in-law, Karen, keeping in touch and phoning every fortnight or so with news of his grandchildren and the latest family holidays and ups and downs, then the two might not ever actually meet up from one year to the next.

But surely this was different? After all, he was not trying to insinuate his way back into his child's life with a lame excuse, or turning up with puppy-dog eyes and putting moral pressure on his son to take him in and feed him Sunday lunch or something.

This was . . . dangerous. And urgent. If the police came calling, asking questions — and they just might, if the reporter was right about this Greene chap being so good at his job — well, then he and Trevor needed to make sure they had their stories straight, right from the start. Any inconsistencies or gaps could spell disaster. Even thirty years later.

He wiped his wet face with the back of his hand and wandered disconsolately into the bathroom. That was the thing with being old — you needed to pee every hour or so, no matter what else life threw at you.

The thought made him laugh, and after he'd finished his business and was fastidiously washing his hands in the sink, he caught his reflection in the small round shaving mirror that rested on the windowsill.

He saw a thin face, topped with still abundant, if white, hair, and deep-set, pale grey eyes. Without vanity, even at his age, he knew that he was still considered to be a good-looking man.

But then, so had Keith been — even more good-looking, if he was being honest. And what good had that done him?

With a sigh, Peter went back downstairs and sat beside his house telephone. He knew his son's number off by heart, even though he never called it. But somehow, he just couldn't work up the courage to lift the receiver and dial.

No, he decided abruptly. This would have to be done face to face.

He still retained a small car, though he seldom drove it much these days — and when he did, it was only short distances, to local places. The garden centre for some spring bulbs. The centre of town to do some shopping or have a cup of tea and a piece of cake.

Perhaps he should take a train? Alas, the town's railway station had disappeared back in the 1960s, along with so many other useful branch lines. Which meant he'd have to drive further afield. Maybe there'd be bus routes he could take?

But still he sat and stared at the telephone, unmoving. Even the effort of trying to find out bus schedules seemed daunting right now. You could never get a human being on the phone, only an automated voice giving you options and telling you to press this button or that, depending on what you wanted. And then, when you'd done it, nine times out of ten, you found it wasn't telling you what you needed.

When had he become so weak, and tired, and generally unable to cope with life, he wondered miserably? And if this was what it was like to be old, perhaps Keith had been the lucky one after all. Dying young and still beautiful and wanted?

Before a wave of familiar self-pity could wash over him, Peter reached determinedly for the phone.

Like it or not, he would have to try and regrow some of his backbone. Because experience told him that he was going to need it.

As he dialled, he tried to curse the day he'd ever set eyes on the Reverend Keith Coltrane. And then felt a wave of guilt and shame wash over him at this latest, silent betrayal.

* * *

As Peter Cornwallis sat in his home, planning a journey, Hillary Greene slid out from under her white tunnel, and was cheerfully told she was 'all done' and could put her shoes back on and leave, and that her GP or consultant would get the results of the scan shortly.

Hillary left with all the speed and grace of a scalded cat.

Once back inside Puff, she sat behind the wheel, breathing hard and trembling, just ever so slightly. She wasn't in any way claustrophobic and hadn't felt any sense of impending panic whilst inside the contraption she'd just left, but for some reason, now that she was back out in the open air and broad daylight, she felt as if she'd just survived something nasty.

Which was absurd. All she'd done was lay there, as still as a statue, whilst a machine had eyed her insides.

She swore at herself for being so bloody feeble, turned the key in the ignition and heard nothing at all from Puff. Not even a cough or splutter.

So she swore even more graphically at her car.

Fortunately, Puff wasn't one to take offence, and at the second time of urging, started up as if nothing had happened.

Hillary pulled out of the parking lot, paying — with a bitterness that she could almost taste — the exorbitant parking fee, and set off back towards work.

A glance at her newly attached watch, as she waited at a red light, showed that it was just approaching eleven o'clock. Which meant that she'd have to work through until seven to make up for the time off. Which was excellent. The last thing she wanted to do was sit alone in her narrowboat as the evening darkened around, feeling woebegone.

Sod that for a game of soldiers.

She'd far rather concentrate her efforts on finding out who had murdered a man thirty years ago.

If Hillary had been prone to introspection, she might have paused to wonder just why it was that somebody's else's life, long since extinct, was more important to her than contemplating the possibility that her own life might be facing the same, inevitable extinction.

But luckily for Hillary, contemplating her own navel — and any fluff that it might have accrued over the years — had never been a favourite pastime of hers.

So when she walked into the communal office twenty-five minutes later, she cast an eye over its two occupants and gave a small nod. 'Gareth — I want to go and interview Max Walker. Feel up to plodding over muddy fields in the rain?'

It wasn't a rhetorical question. She knew that his injuries probably played him up more in chill, damp weather. But even as she asked it, he was already rising, and reaching eagerly for his coat.

Claire watched her leave without comment, but with speculative eyes. For she had spotted the slight bump under the sleeve of Hillary's left arm that indicated that a little pad of wadding had been placed there. The kind that you had taped to you whenever you'd just been given an injection or had blood taken.

* * *

As Hillary drove Puff back towards Lower Barton, where, according to their research, Max Walker still resided, Anthea Ramsey, formerly Greyling, was unknowingly mirroring Peter Cornwallis's actions by reading the *Oxford Mail*.

In her case, however, the paper was still technically her local, for although she had long since moved out of Lower Barton — people could be so unkind — she hadn't gone all that far. Only, in fact, to the village of Hampton Poyle, less than five miles from the heart of the university city.

And just like Peter Cornwallis, the report of the new investigation into the thirty-year-old murder of a country vicar had instantly caught her eye.

Also like Peter, her heart began to accelerate uncomfortably. Unlike the man in Malmesbury, however, Anthea's house was hardly a modest semi, or even a modest detached, come to that, but was instead rather a splendid house, sitting in a large plot of well-tended gardens. It had the generous and effortlessly elegant Edwardian proportions of most large country houses of that period, with high ceilings, square, simple, pleasant rooms and plenty of them.

And every other year, she had interior decorators come in to make sure that she was up to date with the latest trends and colour choices.

After devouring every word of the article, she slowly put the paper aside, where she'd been reading it at the onyx-topped island in the middle of her vast kitchen, and slipped off the high breakfast stool with ease. Although she was now sixty-five, she'd been careful to take good care of herself and had few of the aches and pains that beset many of her age.

Her once naturally red hair was still red — if with the help of the best hairdresser in town. Her slender figure was still slender — if with the help of the best personal trainer in town. She dressed well, and lived well, and supposed, cynically, that that was probably the best revenge. Isn't that what people said?

Of course, it was somewhat spoiled by the fact that her ex-husband Dustin, not to mention the former bitchy inhabitants of Lower Barton, were, by and large, unaware of just how well she *had* done for herself. But then, life was often like that, wasn't it?

She'd remarried barely two years after Dustin had divorced her, after stumbling quite by accident upon a man fifteen years older than herself, who had a thriving and inordinately lucrative business and no children to inherit it. Clive Ramsey, the owner of a whole string of low-rent boarding houses and residential hotels in Birmingham, had been something of a lifeline. A fat, florid, cheerful self-made man, he'd had the taste to appreciate her patrician good looks, upper-middle-class education and natural elegance.

But by far and away the most desirable thing of all about her, from his point of view, was her wryly sophisticated and genuinely willing ability to turn a blind eye whenever he occasionally dallied with the odd nubile blonde or two.

This was no hardship for Anthea, who was merely fond of him, and thus totally unburdened by the love and jealousy that so often came with it. And since Anthea had nothing to quibble about when it came to Clive's financial generosity, the pair had suited one another admirably. She'd host his parties or attend business dinners, flirting mildly with the money men that he wanted charmed, all the while looking the epitome of an attractive, intelligent and charming wife.

Contrary to some people's nasty-minded expectations, their marriage had been a long and contented one, and they'd been fast approaching their silver wedding anniversary when Clive had abruptly departed from the world, in the middle of a golf game on Oxford's prestigious green, of all places. It had, she'd been reliably informed by the captain of the golf club at Clive's funeral, put off a pair at the seventh hole, who had a substantial bet laid on as to who could hole their ball first. But then, as the captain had gone on to generously agree, you couldn't expect a massive heart attack to be considerate of other people, could you?

Anthea made herself a cup of coffee at a very expensive coffee machine and glanced at her gold-and-diamond lady's wristwatch as she did so. She had a lunch appointment soon in a Summertown restaurant with a friend — well, she *supposed* Sofia could be classed as a friend — but wondered if she should cancel it. Sofia had always been very astute, and as curious as a cat, and she would quickly pick up on it if she, Anthea, was off her form.

And with the news of the reopening of Keith Coltrane's case, she was feeling decidedly unnerved. In fact, distinctly upset. But then, she always had lived on her nerves. Her mother had always said she was the most highly strung of all her children.

Now, the thought of Keith made her pale, cosmetically enhanced face crease into a gentle smile.

Even now, just the thought of the man had the power to reach across time and make her heart skip a beat. She sighed heavily. It had been such a pity that they had never been able to get together.

Thirty years ago, she had been so desperate for that to happen and totally convinced that they were destined to be a couple. But there had just been so many frustrating obstacles. Dustin Greyling, her husband at the time, being just one of them. Dustin, with his nasty suspicious mind and petty jealousies. If only he would just have agreed to a discreet divorce and hadn't been so silly about everything, it might all have been so different!

But then, it was not just Dustin who'd been determined to put obstacles in their way. There were the village mafia to cope with as well — that coterie of bitchy ladies, and some men, who gossiped like vipers and delighted in spreading their malice about like so much thick and sickly marmalade. It made it totally impossible for Keith to admit to her that he felt the same way that she did.

And although she had longed for him to do so, she had never blamed him for keeping her at arm's length. After all, when you knew the entire village was watching your every move with knowing, mocking eyes, how could he have ever dared to openly show her the affection she knew he felt for her? It would have been bound to get back to his bishop, and he'd always been too devoted to his calling to cause his diocese embarrassment.

Then, too, there had been the very nature of Keith's job. A job that she had hated, a job that had placed so many hideously unfair restrictions on him. He wasn't ever able to drink more than a glass of wine, or swear even mildly at anyone or anything, no matter what the circumstances, or do anything, it seemed to her, remotely human! And when she'd commiserated with him and tried to show him how much she admired his forbearance and sacrifice, he would only smile blandly and shrug modestly, and stress that it was his duty to set a good example for others.

Anthea sighed heavily now. The man had been practically a saint. Just like that saint he'd always admired so much — the one the church had been named after.

Now, Anthea swore aloud, happily conjuring up as many ugly words as she could think of. If only Keith had been anything but a vicar! A telephone repair man, a second-hand book seller, a dog walker. Anything else, anything at all, and she just knew that her life would have turned out so differently.

Oh, she might not be in this fancy house — but she'd have been with the man she adored.

But this was pointless, all this wallowing in nostalgia. What good did it do you? She sighed and moved into the hall, where a wide, sweeping staircase allowed her to move upstairs.

At the make-up station in her master bedroom, Anthea sat in front of her dressing-table mirror and gave her face its usual, clinical inspection. She'd need to get her eyebrows re-dyed soon. And another nip-and-tuck under her chin

— maybe in the new year? She knew a clinic in Switzerland that worked wonders.

Of course, she couldn't cancel the lunch with Sofia, she decided. She had to carry on as if everything was normal. Her pride demanded nothing less. Determinedly, she reached for the face cream and began to smooth it on. But her hands were trembling, just a little, and afterwards it took her longer than usual to 'put her face on' as she had to reapply the eyeliner — twice — and botched the outline of her mouth with the lipliner.

'It's all your fault, Keith, you lovely, exasperating, dreadful man,' she said softly, staring morosely at her reflection. And again, felt her heart give a little leap. How odd it was to think that not even three decades had been enough to defeat him.

She could still see his face now, as clearly as she could see her own in the mirror's reflection. His mass of thick, dark, almost black hair, that tended to get so poetically windblown with the slightest breeze. The depth of his blue eyes. The smile. And his voice — if she closed her eyes, she knew she could summon it without any effort at all.

'Yes, you were the one, weren't you?' she murmured at her sad-eyed reflection. 'The love of my life.'

The one who had got away.

She grimaced at herself and packed her paraphernalia away, glancing again at her watch. She'd have to get a move on, or she'd be late. And she'd had enough of being maudlin.

She ran a nippy little modern sports car that, to her mind at least, had none of the style and elegance of, say, an E-type Jaguar, but which still turned envious heads whenever she took it out for a run. She'd take that instead of calling for a taxi. She felt like cutting a dash today.

As she returned downstairs and began to search for her car keys, she wondered if the police would be calling on her about Keith. And if so, what should she say to them?

The thought was not a pleasant one. That horrible little man who'd run the initial investigation had been downright rude to her — smirking at her, hinting at her reputation in the village and intimating that she'd made a nuisance of herself with Keith. The bastard!

She didn't like the thought of having to go through all that again. It had been so humiliating. And all whilst she'd been grieving and having to deal with Dustin and his silly divorce too! How she'd coped, she didn't know. Looking back on it from this safe distance now, she could only admire her courage and fortitude.

Well, it couldn't possibly be as bad this time, could it? After all, that horrible man — DI Keating, that was his name! — wouldn't still be in charge, making it clear that she was a suspect in Keith's murder. *Her!* The sheer bloody cheek of it. The stupidity and arrogance of it! Who did he think she was?

Apart from anything else, it annoyed her how he, the rest of the village — and even Dustin — had treated her as if she were a joke. She'd gone to Cheltenham Ladies' College, damn it, and could have gone on to Oxford or Cambridge if she'd been so minded. But people took one look at a pretty redhead and assumed they had cotton wool for brains.

At this, Anthea Ramsey, formerly Mrs Greyling, smiled complacently to herself. Let people think her a bimbo. She knew better.

She took a satisfied look around her lovely home and headed into the hall. As she did so, the postman rattled some offerings though the letterbox, and she bent to pick them up.

A cruise-ship catalogue that she'd sent off for — she quite fancied a nice getaway, maybe to go and see the midnight sun or something equally spectacular? — a couple of bills, and a plain, printed envelope with a stamp on the corner, instead of a franking mark.

As she held it and looked at it, she frowned. There were no markings on it, as with so many business or commercial letters nowadays, and apart from the printed address, it had the look and feel of an old-fashioned, personal letter. In this electronic age, she couldn't remember the last time she'd received such a thing!

She shrugged and thrust all the mail onto the black Italian marble console table that stood beside the front door. She had no time to deal with that now. She'd look through it later.

With a sigh, she opened the door and looked out suspiciously. It had been drizzling earlier, and although the sky was still overcast and grey, some weak sunlight was now trying to filter its way through. Even so, Anthea reached for an umbrella. Her last interior designer had found an authentic Victorian umbrella and stick stand, and it pleased her to use it.

As she stepped out into the inclement September morning, she cocked a mental snook at her ex-husband and the inhabitants of Lower Barton. Most of them were probably dead and gone now anyway, she mused with satisfaction.

And none of them could touch her anymore.

With a confident stride, she set off towards the garage, and her nippy little car. Perhaps she'd have the lobster today, if it was on the menu.

And wondered. Would Keith have liked lobster? Or would he, as a humble vicar, have felt uncomfortable eating such an expensive dish? He'd been so wonderfully *righteous* about some things. It was one of the things that had made him stand out from all the other men she'd known.

But then, Keith had always been special. In so many ways. That had been his problem.

CHAPTER FIVE

'So, how's it going with the electoral roll?' Hillary asked Gareth, as she negotiated the small country lane that separated Little Tew from Lower Barton. A red kite rose from its spot on an unfortunate roadkill, and its big wings and wedge-shaped russet tail caught a stray shaft of sunlight. The majestic sight of it lifted her spirits and she slowed down to watch it go out of sight.

Luckily there were places where the lane widened, allowing passing room for larger vehicles. And it was as she was pulling into one of these, to let a lumbering tractor coming the other way pass in safety, that Gareth grunted in response to her question.

He'd been given the task of finding how many villagers, still resident in Lower Barton, had also been living there during the time of the murder.

'Not much luck, ma'am, as you'd expect. Most of the older residents at the time of the murder have since become deceased. And with the latest trend of the more well-off fleeing the cities and relocating out here in the countryside, a lot of the housing has been sold off to newcomers.'

Hillary nodded. You couldn't blame the villagers, really. Cash-strapped people who'd inherited property from relatives, and whose ancestors had lived in the villages for generations, now couldn't afford to live in those same villages. The incomers priced them out of the market, along with the rising cost of living. Ironic, really, when you realised that, not so long ago, these very desirable rustic cottages were considered 'poor' dwellings primarily for farm labourers. Now they housed upwardly mobile professionals or second-home owners, who gushed over 'original features' and mostly only ever occupied their country escapes at the weekends.

So when grandma's poky, dark and probably damp little cottage could be sold at a price that would allow you to buy a roomy three-bed detached new-build way up north somewhere, what could you do?

'But there must be some people who've stayed put?' Hillary complained, pulling back out onto the lane, and remembering the old lady she'd met when she'd first checked out the village. She at least had sounded like a lifelong habitué of Lower Barton.

'Yes, ma'am, there are some,' Gareth confirmed obligingly. 'I've made a list. Most are elderly though. Their memories might not be the best.'

Hillary sighed, knowing that if she couldn't dig up anything new within the next few days or, she might well have to call on them anyway. Just in the hopes that she could dig up, from amongst their joint recollections and memories, that one little golden nugget of information that might lead her to something that the original investigation had missed.

And that reminded her: when she got back to the office, she'd have to ask Claire to go through the files again and highlight anything — even if seemingly insignificant — which Ben Keating hadn't deemed worthy of following up at the time. It was one of the few benefits of working a cold case, that she could afford to take the time and effort to follow up even the most unpromising angles — a luxury that a DI working a current case could only dream of.

And who knew? In the manic activity of the first forty-eight hours of a fresh criminal investigation, many things had to be downgraded, according to priority. And in one of those overlooked long shots, or unpromising avenues that had been neglected due to time pressures or staff shortages, she might just find her first real whiff of the killer.

'Nice place,' Gareth said, as the first of the thatched, rose-bedecked cottages of Lower Barton came into view. The mellow stone dwellings were so beloved of calendars and postcards, and the village even had a picturesque ditch that ran alongside the road, and probably flooded in times of heavy rain. The village green, which consisted of a wooden bench, a cheery red postbox at one corner and, at the present moment, a pair of waddling ducks, formed a square around which several large Cotswold-stone houses stood guardian. Leading off from one side of this square, as she knew from her previous visit, was Church Lane.

She subsequently veered off to the left, and parked under a weeping silver birch planted in the grounds of the local manor, which had been built right next to the church. This was typical, she knew, because in days of yore, the squire of the manor wanted to keep a beady eye on the peasants and make sure that everyone attended church on a Sunday. And woe betide backsliders. These days, she suspected the squire no longer existed, or if he did, had fallen on hard times, for the manor, she noted, was advertising B&B facilities.

'My my, how the mighty have fallen,' she said dryly, causing Gareth, who hadn't noticed the sign, to look at her curiously.

She alighted, and then waited patiently whilst her passenger got out of Puff with the aid of his stick. The two of them then set off past the church, heading to where a group of barns, originally belonging to the village farm, had long since been converted into desirable residences.

It was here, according to Gareth's research, that Max Walker now lived.

Hillary eyed the tiny settlement of barns, byres, piggeries and outhouses, and frowned. She had a vague feeling that, when she'd read the files before, the address given for Max Walker at the time of the Reverend's death hadn't been Church Lane.

'He didn't live here originally, did he?' she asked, a shade elliptically, but her younger colleague had no trouble following her train of thought.

'No, ma'am. He lived in one of those terraced cottages on the road leading out to Great Tew. He bought this place . . .' Hillary waited as the inevitable gadget came out, and Gareth consulted it diligently, '. . . in 2001. The barns, up to that point, were still in use for agricultural purposes. But the farmer sold off the land then, and these barns were snapped up by a property developer.'

Hillary nodded. It figured. She only hoped the farmer had retired somewhere nice and wasn't haunted by visions of abandoned sheep or deserted cattle. Or his angry-faced ancestors who'd probably been farming the land when mammoths still wandered the plains.

'And the field surrounding the church? The one he and our vic both wanted to claim?' she asked.

'Sold to our Mr Walker a year and a half after the murder, ma'am.'

'Hmmm. So without Keith Coltrane to fight for it as a cemetery, the church didn't bother to do so either?' she said thoughtfully. And wondered. Was that significant? 'Do you know if the vote not to buy the land was close? Or does the bishop or whoever simply decide?'

'No idea, ma'am. Do you want me to find out?'

Hillary sighed. 'You might as well.' Though she doubted that it would amount to much. And wondered what she'd do even if they discovered that the dead reverend's bishop had never been keen to raid the coffers, and the gossip amongst the clergy had it that he'd been secretly relieved when Keith Coltrane's nagging had finally stopped. Should she storm the bishop's palace and demand an interview? Come right out and accuse one of the dog-collared brigade of 'ridding him of this troublesome priest'?

Somehow, she didn't think Rollo Sale would be happy with her if she did!

'Says here the field is now called the Green Valley Glamping Site and has facilities including shepherd huts, yurts, static caravans and unique accommodation experiences, including a bespoke railway carriage and a double-decker bus fitted with all mod cons.' Gareth was reading from his gadget again. 'There are luxurious on-site shower and toilet facilities for those who prefer actual canvas, plus a chance to walk the alpacas. Hang on, that can't be right, can it?' Gareth asked, his voice rising an octave in disbelief at the last statement.

'Well, the site must be close by the church, mustn't it?' Hillary reasoned. 'Let's go see.' She was amused, and in the mood to be distracted.

As she'd predicted, the meadow in question wasn't hard to find. A big acreage of fenced, predominantly flat land, it was graced by a small copse of mixed and native trees at the far end. The various huts, tents and unique accommodations were scattered around with generous spacing in between. Over in one corner, a long, low wooden chalet-type structure probably housed the shower block. And in the neighbouring field past the well-maintained fence were, indeed, alpacas.

They raised their curious woolly heads as Gareth and Hillary leaned on the five-barred gate enclosing the site, then, when they didn't enter, went back placidly to their grazing.

'And, what, you just walk them? Like you would a dog?' Gareth asked, staring at them and shaking his head.

'Presumably,' Hillary said.

'And pay a fortune for the privilege too by the looks of it,' Gareth added sourly, staring down at his phone again. He held it out for her so that she could see the costings for herself. 'Do you see the price of just a three-day weekend staying here?'

Hillary's eyes widened. 'Seems our Mr Walker has done well for himself. No wonder he can afford to buy a fancy new barn conversion.'

As they retraced their steps, Hillary eyed the ancient Norman church thoughtfully. And wondered. What would the Reverend Keith Coltrane have made of having alpacas and more-money-than-sense holidaymakers right on his doorstep? Would he have congratulated the ambitious Max Walker on the success of his diversification?

Hillary also found herself wondering where his parishioners had to be buried, now that the churchyard was full.

* * *

Max Walker's particular barn, named 'Yew Tree Barn' — in spite of the fact that there wasn't a species of that tree in sight — was in the middle of the small complex, and like the rest of it, made mostly of ironstone, a lovely rust-coloured stone that was prevalent in the north of the county. It had some timber extensions, and a vast dark grey slate roof. In the middle of the main building, there was a big arch set in the middle of the wall, presumably where shire horses would once have entered, to either be stabled or, if the place had once served as a forge, to be shod.

Now the arch was glassed in, in the modern way, and gave the inhabitants of the domicile an uninterrupted view of the paved courtyard outside. It was probably the only outdoor space it had, but the inhabitants had made the most of it with a bubbling if generic-looking fountain, the usual garden furniture, and plentiful hollyhocks, now devoid of much of their summer glory, lining a tall wooden fence.

The main door to the house had had a recent grey slate porch built over it to protect the homeowners from the inclement weather whilst they searched for house keys, and when Hillary pulled down on the black wrought-iron bell pull beside it, she heard a discreet clanging echo from within.

Very tasteful, she acknowledged.

Anyone wanting to enter the *Mollern* had to bang their bare fists on the metal hatchway and hope their knuckles didn't swell up later.

She supposed that, September being the tail end of the tourist season, they might be lucky and find the master of the house at home. And they were. The woman who answered the summons was an attractive fifty-something with lush brown hair just turning grey and was dressed in a no-nonsense pair of clean jeans and a ribbed cream sweater that she somehow managed to make look the epitome of elegance. Her large grey eyes widened as Hillary and Gareth showed their ID.

'Police? I hope we haven't had any trouble with vandals? Max never said.'

'No, Mrs . . . ?'

'Oh — Walker. Sandy Walker, Max's wife.' The woman looked puzzled. 'We've never had problems on the site before. Has something happened?'

'No, Mrs Walker, nothing like that. Is your husband home?'

The grey eyes went from Hillary to Gareth, and back to Hillary. 'Yes, yes, he's in the study. Shall I . . . ?' she waved a hand and pulled the door open, and Hillary shot her a pleasant, bland smile as she sidled past.

'Thank you, yes, if you don't mind. We're in the area gathering information about something that happened long ago,' she explained, keeping it deliberately vague. 'Have you and your husband been married long?' she asked, careful to keep her voice conversational.

'Fifteen years next month,' Sandy Walker said proudly, and Hillary gave a mental nod. So, unless she was a native of these parts — and Hillary's radar didn't think that she was — she would probably be of no use to them.

'Well, please, come this way then,' Sandy said, a shade awkwardly, and led them into a vast open-plan space. Above them, rafters sailed to a double-height ceiling, exposing an arched roof, which gave the room the somewhat odd appearance of a nautical dwelling, as if they were aboard some vast schooner or yacht. A mezzanine level, accessed by wide oak side stairs, led off at one end of the building, presumably to a master bedroom and en-suite.

Along the entire side of one downstairs wall was a galley-style kitchen, fitted with every mod con. Opposite it, two massive sofas sat guarding a huge inglenook fireplace that must have been either an aberration of the property developer, or else the place *had* been a forge, and that was where the original blacksmith had stoked his fires.

'Max is in the office,' Sandy said, leading them through all this vastness to the far wall, where she knocked — rather timidly, Hillary thought — on a discreet door that was recessed into a set of bookshelves. She pushed it open just a few inches and looked inside.

'Maxie, there's some people here to see you,' she said quietly. 'They're from the police,' she added, her tone a mixture of curiosity and unease.

Hillary heard a masculine voice rumble something, and then Sandy Walker withdrew her head and smiled, opening the door wider for admittance. 'Would you like some tea or coffee?' she asked as they passed, but Hillary politely declined, and Gareth followed her lead.

The room seemed small after the vastness of the main event, but it was still big enough to house a decent-sized oak desk, some old-fashioned grey metallic filing cabinets, and a few prints –Manet? Monet? — on the walls.

The man, who hadn't deemed it necessary to rise from his chair behind the desk, watched them with an expressionless face.

At the time of the murder, Hillary recalled, this man had just turned thirty, and had become bored with his office job and the big city. Now — at double that age — he hadn't changed much in appearance from the photos taken of him thirty years ago, which still resided in the original case files.

He was still florid of face, still had a good head of mainly brown hair, and large, almost cow-like brown eyes. He had thickened a bit, rather than run to actual fat, and Hillary could see why someone as attractive as Sandy had married him.

On his desk was a picture of their wedding day, but no photos of children.

'Yes?' he said, and Hillary moved forward, ID at the ready. He read it, grunted and nodded to the generic office chairs in front of his desk. 'Have a seat.'

As Hillary nodded her thanks and pulled them out for herself and Gareth, she saw that there was dust on them, and doubted that the chairs were ever used. Not surprising, perhaps. For all its money-generating income, Max Walker's business had the air about it of being a one-man show. Oh, he probably employed casual labour to clean, mow, tend to the animals and so on. And an accountant to try and keep the tax man at bay. But she had the definite impression that this man ran his empire single-handedly from here.

Hard to believe that thirty years ago he'd been an anxious newcomer, desperate to succeed in his new venture, and at loggerheads with the popular village vicar.

'So what's this about then?' Max demanded. Like his wife, he was wearing jeans and a sweater, but on him the clothes hung rather drably.

He was obviously not a man to shilly-shally, and that suited Hillary just fine. The direct approach was always easier than the oblique. 'We are taking another look at the murder of the Reverend Keith Coltrane, sir. And as a person of interest at the time, I'd like to ask you a few questions.'

Max Walker didn't look surprised. Or upset. And Hillary, who hadn't yet seen the local papers, wondered why. If she'd known that there was a possibility that he had been forewarned, she could have saved herself the mental cogitations.

'Right. Well, ask away then,' Max said indifferently.

'I understand, at the time of his death, that you and the Reverend were locked in a dispute over the usage of the land bordering the church?' Hillary got right down to it, aware that Gareth was recording the interview on his phone.

'You might say that. He seemed to think that the dead should have priority over the living. I didn't.'

'By "the living" you mean you, and your business plans. I doubt that your glamping business has benefited the locals much? Your clientele, I imagine, are mainly city dwellers coming here to de-stress, and romantic couples wanting some peace and privacy?'

Max Walker's somewhat thick lips twisted into a near-smile. 'They are. But I employ local carpenters and plumbers and vets and cleaning agencies. They don't complain, I assure you.'

Hillary nodded. It was a good point. But she was not here to discuss local politics or economics. 'But the Reverend Coltrane wasn't swayed by that argument?'

Max grunted. 'Not he! He was only interested in the "souls" of his parish.'

Hillary's own lips twitched. 'How dare he?' she said.

Max Walker stared at her for a moment, then reluctantly grinned. 'Yeah, well, he had his job to do, I suppose,' he acknowledged grudgingly. 'But like I told him at the time, burying people in the ground is unsustainable. Even back then. And I was right — nowadays people prefer to be cremated, or go green. You know,' he added, when Hillary cocked her head questioningly, 'get buried in a cardboard biodegradable coffin only a few feet down in forests and pastures and whatnot and let Mother Nature take its course.'

Hillary nodded, trying not to think about it. 'Ever thought of going into that area yourself, sir? You have the land for it now, and your new customers would be less likely to complain about the facilities, as I imagine your current ones inevitably do?'

Again Max Walker grinned. 'Oh, inevitably. There's always some who come to the countryside in search of the outdoor experience and then complain about the sound of distant cows mooing, or wasps at their picnic. And as for providing an eco-friendly place of eternal rest — now there's a thought! But Sandy wouldn't like it. It'd give her the shivers. Besides, as an income stream it would eventually hit a bit of a dead end, don't you think?'

'Very good,' Hillary muttered at the atrocious and intentional pun. But he had a point. Once you were dead and buried you were hardly in any position to provide repeat custom.

She wondered what the dead vicar would have made of the land he'd fought for being used as a more upmarket and trendy cemetery after all. Had he had a sense of humour?

Thoughts of Keith Coltrane brought her back sharply to the business at hand. 'Did you see Reverend Coltrane on the day he died, sir? This would have been only two days before Christmas Day,' she reminded him.

'I know what day it was,' Max grunted. 'DI Ben bloody Keating wouldn't let me forget it. And I'll be happy to tell you what I told him. Yes, I saw him that day. Out and about and looking like a busy bee. Organising this, that, or the other. But not to speak to.'

Hillary nodded. She knew all this from the original files of course. 'Apart from yourself, do you know of anyone who might have had a reason to resent the vicar?'

'Dustin Greyling,' Max said at once, with a small frown. 'Poor sod — that wife of his was enough to drive anyone to file for divorce.'

'Yes, Inspector Keating's notes made it clear that it was generally acknowledged that Mrs Greyling was, er,' she paused delicately, '. . . a fan of the vicar.'

'Besotted is the word you're looking for,' Max said dryly. 'Mind you, she wasn't the only one, to be fair. Half the female population of the village gushed over him.'

'Good-looking was he?' Hillary asked.

'Suppose he was, yeah,' Max admitted readily enough. And seeing her slightly surprised look, shifted in his chair a bit. 'Look, apart from the fact that he was trying to get in the way of my business, I had nothing against the bloke. I know a lot of the men in the village didn't like him much, because of the fuss their wives or sisters or daughters made of him. But from what I could see, that wasn't *his* fault. And before we got into all that argy-bargy about the land, I got on well enough with him. He seemed a decent enough sort, you know, for a vicar. Down to earth, like. I think all the attention he got embarrassed him more than anything.'

'You don't think he encouraged them at all then?' Hillary asked, careful to keep her voice neutral.

'Not from what I could see. Not that I took much notice, you understand. But from the few times I saw him with his "fan club", the bloke seemed to go out of his way to try and damp them all down. You know, stay friendly whilst trying at the same time to stay aloof.'

Hillary nodded. Now that was interesting. Here was someone that you might expect to have nothing nice to say about the dead man, yet he was practically defending his honour!

'Did you get the impression that was because he had a particular favourite amongst them?' Hillary tried next. 'Maybe someone who'd become special in his life?'

But this was going too far. 'How should I know?' he asked impatiently. 'Like I said, I never paid that much attention. Why would I? I just overheard the odd bit of grumbling in the pub of an evening sometimes, when some bloke or other was complaining about his wife spending too much time at the church, and not enough time cooking his dinner. That sort of thing.'

'When you heard that Keith had been murdered, you must have been surprised?'

'Of course I bloody well was! We all were. We were shocked. It's not the sort of thing you expect to happen in a place like this, is it?' he said, waving vaguely at the view from his window.

'You must have thought about it at the time,' Hillary pressed. 'Mulled it over in your mind and all that. Try and think back — when you first heard that he was dead, did anyone in particular spring to mind as a likely killer?'

Max sighed. 'I suppose I thought first of Dustin Greyling, we probably all did. He'd just served that daft wife of his with divorce papers, and then it turned out that someone had seen Dustin and Coltrane having "a talk" on the day the vicar was found dead. But it quickly turned out that Dustin had gone off somewhere else, and had an airtight alibi. So . . .' he shrugged.

'So who took his place as the frontrunner?' Hillary persisted. 'Somebody must have.' She knew how small communities worked!

75

'The wife, I suppose. Mrs Greyling . . . Anne, was it? A woman scorned, all that sort of thing. And for a while, that DI of yours seemed keen on her too, but nothing seemed to come of it.'

'And being on the skids with the Reverend as you were, you must have earned yourself some funny looks as well?' Hillary said softly.

Max grunted a laugh. 'Oh yeah, plenty. Water off a duck's back,' he added, as he saw her eyebrow rise in query.

'But you must have been a *little* worried,' Hillary challenged. 'Being a suspect in a murder case. It's not nice, is it? Couldn't have done your nerves any good?'

Max's smile widened. 'Nothing wrong with my nerves, I assure you.'

No, Hillary mused. She could see that. 'So, is there anything you want to add?' she asked, surprising him a little.

'What do you mean?' he asked cautiously.

Hillary spread her hands in a vague gesture of appeal. 'It's been thirty years, sir. The wounds are no longer raw. You can speak more freely than you could then. Half the people involved are probably dead now, or long gone from the village. You owe nobody any loyalty. I want to find out who killed Keith Coltrane and why. And if you didn't do it, you might want to try and help me. So — is there anything about the Reverend you can tell me that you think I should know?'

Max Walker looked at her for a long while, in perfect silence, clearly thinking over what she'd said. And she felt her hopes begin to rise. For all his laconic demeanour, she had the feeling that this man might actually be made of the right stuff.

Beside her, she could sense Gareth becoming tense, but she herself was content to let the man cogitate. Because something told her that, if he did choose to speak, what he said might be worth listening to.

Eventually he stirred. 'A lot was made of him being a focus for the ladies. But he was quite friendly with some of the youngsters too. And no, I don't mean like that,' he added at once, as her eyes sharpened. 'I'm not suggesting anything was *going on*. Nowadays, we're all conditioned to think the worst, aren't we? So no, I'm not saying for one minute the man was a paedophile — that's not what I mean. I just mean that a few of the teenagers in the village at the time seemed to like him. Which I thought was unusual. When I was a teen, the last thing I'd want to do is make the acquaintance of the local God-botherer. But he seemed to have a real rapport with them.'

Now it was Hillary's turn to be still and silent for a while, whilst Max waited patiently for her to process his observations.

'Do you remember their names?' she asked finally.

But here Max was unable to help her. 'Can't say as I do. It was thirty years ago, after all.'

Hillary nodded gloomily. That was a phrase she was sure she was going to hear many times before this case was through.

'Well, thank you for your time, Mr Walker,' she said, meaning it. As she rose, the landowner did the same.

'I hope you find out who did it,' Max said.

Hillary smiled blandly. 'I intend to give it my best shot, Mr Walker.'

Max watched them go, and when the door shut behind them, and he heard his wife's voice fading into silence as she ushered them away, he slowly sat back down in his chair.

For a moment or two he sat quite still, and then, slowly, he reached out to the top drawer of his desk and brought out that morning's mail. Amongst which was a plain white envelope that bore no business insignia or franking marks, but a first-class stamp.

Although he could now recite its contents by heart, he opened it up and read the few short, printed sentences again. And his lips tightened ominously.

CHAPTER SIX

Friday was a better day, with not a rain cloud in sight. The sky was that lovely cerulean blue that only late summer or early autumn could produce, and the elderberries lining the towpath were fattening up into their annual small, burgundy-coloured orbs. Just to add his touch to the proceedings, a cock chaffinch gave his descending tonal trill from amongst their pinkening leaves.

The sun was out, though not particularly warm first thing, and Puff started without a murmur. All the auguries seemed promising. Once at the office, Hillary set about going through the murder book to make sure that she was up to date on all the research and paperwork that had been done, then assigned Gareth and Claire their latest tasks. In a case over thirty years old, a lot of the legwork had to be done in the office, mostly on the computer. But she promised them plums further down the line, and only hoped she could keep her promises.

She then went to her stationery cupboard — only when she was in a super-good mood did she think of it as her office — and set about making her own to-do list. Above and around her, she could sense the massive building gearing up for another day, with the night shift leaving as the day shift trickled in. Patrol cars were taken out to set up speed traps or to deter the maniacs doing 100mph on the motorways, whilst solicitors summoned by their clients arrived to try and get them out their various messes.

In other words, it was just another normal day.

But over in the very attractive and desirable town of Eynsham, Trevor Cornwallis's day wasn't turning out to be quite so normal.

A tall, lean, dark-haired man, he was up at his usual time, as was his wife, Karen. With his fiftieth birthday looming on the horizon in three years' time, they had been discussing taking a long cruise to mark the big 5-0, and as they sat eating breakfast, they discussed the various merits of the Caribbean over the Med. Karen had a yen to see the ancient wonders of Greece. Trevor, the modern wonders of a Caribbean beach and beach bar.

Their two kids, who had both now left home but were, as yet, unencumbered with lifelong partners of their own, were half-jestingly threatening to come along on the adventure too.

He was just scraping marmalade onto his second piece of toast when his mobile phone trilled Darth's Vader theme tune. This had been suggested by one of his colleagues at work — a joke, he was assured — and even now it still raised a smile whenever he heard it. As a manager of a large furniture depot in Banbury, he was not sure that the triumphant but doom-laden music was particularly appropriate, but it kept his staff happy.

Glancing at his watch, he wondered who would be calling him this early. He reached for his phone and was surprised to see it was his father.

'Hello, Dad. Is anything wrong?' As Trevor spoke, he saw his wife turn and look at him questioningly. She knew as well as he did that phone calls between father and son were rare, and never casual.

'Hello, son. No. Well, yes. But . . .' Trevor heard a soft sigh and waited patiently. It was typical of his father to beat about the bush. 'Trevor, I need to talk to you about something.' There was a brief but definite hesitation for a moment, and then he said diffidently, 'Can I come over? Or, if you prefer, you could come and see me?'

'Can't we talk now, Dad? If it's urgent, I mean?'

He could picture his father as he spoke, ageing, dithering and distant, perhaps sitting in his kitchen with a crossword puzzle on the go, and next-door's cat kipping on his windowsill. A nice, respectable man, who was universally well liked by all his neighbours, friends, and acquaintances. And his desire to go and see him was absolutely zero.

'It's not urgent, exactly. Well, it *is*, but . . . perhaps *important* is more the case.'

Trevor sighed. Again, this pointless pedantry was typical of his father. The man was like a reed, blown about by the wind, and about as useful. But he could sense, this time, a palpable unease coming over the telephone line that was, in turn, making him feel uneasy also.

'Important?' he echoed cautiously. A quick movement in his peripheral vision caught his eye, and he turned to see Karen waving a hand at him frantically, in a bid to catch his attention.

'Invite him over for lunch this Sunday,' she said, much more loudly than was her wont, obviously intending that her father-in-law should hear the invitation and ignoring totally the frown her husband gave her in return.

Karen came from a large and loving family. She had two sisters and two brothers, and she was close to all of them. They regularly met up with her parents, nephews and nieces. She had, Trevor knew, never understood the hands-off relationship that he shared with his father, and certainly didn't approve of it. To her, family was a very real buffer in an uncertain world, and a source of closeness and familiarity, and she couldn't understand why he didn't feel the same way. Thus she was always trying to mediate closer ties between them, and love her though he did, he heartily wished that she wouldn't.

His father must have heard Karen's invitation and now Trevor couldn't, with any grace, do anything but repeat it. So he sighed and said dutifully, 'Karen says you should come over for Sunday lunch. How does that sound?'

'Fine, fine. I was going to come by bus, but if it's a Sunday I'll bring the car. There won't be so much traffic, will there? All right, I'll be there around elevenish?'

'All right, Dad, that's fine. See you then,' he added reluctantly, and ended the call.

'Well, that'll be nice. It's been a while since we saw him,' Karen said, her voice determinedly cheerful.

Trevor grunted over his cornflakes. Karen, her mission successfully accomplished, tactfully changed the subject.

But as Trevor finished eating, then took his shower and changed into his usual business suit, his mind continued to be restless.

What did his father want to talk about? What could possibly be so important?'

Uneasily, he called a number and checked on his mother, but her situation hadn't changed. Which meant that it couldn't be about her. Could his *father* now be ill? He was — what — seventy? Seventy-two? Karen would know, she always sent him a birthday card and made sure he had a hamper delivered with all his favourite treats included in it. She always punctiliously signed the gift in both their names, of course.

Trevor wasn't sure how he felt about the idea that his father might have something seriously wrong with him. On one level, he was sure that it wouldn't change his life much. How could it? They hadn't been close for thirty years. And yet, he still felt unnerved. For all that he'd never been a real presence in his adult life, Trevor had always been aware that his father had been *there*. Available. Just in case.

As he did up his tie, he scowled at his reflection in the mirror. Just in case of what though, he wondered grouchily. When had his father ever done anything for him? In fact, when had he ever been anything but a liability?

81

Although he himself had only just turned seventeen when Keith Coltrane had died, he'd instinctively known just how close they'd all come to disaster. And they said that the young had no real sense of danger — not like adults, who had accrued enough experience of life to learn the merits of caution!

What's more, now that he was a parent with children and had acquired wisdom of his own, he had indeed duly learned the necessity of keeping your head well down below the parapet. Which accounted for his determination to keep his father at arm's length.

No two ways about it, he'd be glad when the upcoming visit had come and gone, and they'd put to bed whatever it was that was so 'important'.

He trotted downstairs and reached for his car keys, kept in a ceramic dish on the console table in the hall.

Karen obviously heard him, for she called out from the kitchen. 'Trev? Trev, didn't you used to live in a place called Lower Barton?'

Her words froze him to the spot. He saw his hand, fingers starting to curl in anticipation of grabbing the electronic key fob, stop their movement. His heart did a funny little skip. He had one of those weird 'twilight zone' moments, when the ordinary and everyday did a fandango slide into surrealism, leaving him feeling otherworldly. His ears seemed bunged up, like when you had a bad cold, and he felt his mouth fall open as he fought for air.

Then he got a grip, swallowed hard, and forced himself to turn and go into the kitchen, plastering an attempt at a faintly curious smile on his face.

'Why do you ask?' He hoped his voice sounded casual. But his mind was racing.

Karen was seated at the table, reading her tablet. Although she too worked, she didn't have so far to travel, and always left the house about twenty minutes after her husband.

Now she looked up and smiled vaguely at him. 'This article — it just caught my eye. I am right, aren't I? Your family came from Lower Barton before you all moved to Thame for a few years?'

'That's right.' Trevor forced his reluctant legs to move a little closer, telling himself he was being silly. But even now, just the mention of those bad old times in the Cotswolds village was enough to bring him out in a cold sweat.

Although, paradoxically, the last thing he wanted to do was know what had caught her attention, he had to fight off the urge to grab the tablet from her so that he could read the article for himself. Instead, he lounged against the sink, and hoping that his voice still sounded casual and insouciant, asked, 'What article is this? Did the WI ladies come to blows at the local flower show over who'd baked the best gooseberry pie or something? I can't think what else could have made the headlines.'

'Clown,' Karen said fondly, but not looking up from the table. 'Actually it's quite interesting. It says here they're taking another look at some man who was murdered there ages ago. A vicar, they said. Can you believe it? Who'd want to do something like that — the poor man.'

Although Karen's voice kept on making sounds, it became reduced to a mere drone in his head, like the distant buzzing of a big bumble bee. Because Trevor wasn't listening any longer.

For Trevor now knew what the 'important' thing was that was bringing his father to his house.

And he was right.

They did need to talk.

* * *

As Trevor Cornwallis drove very carefully into work, aware that his hands felt cold and the pedals under his feet felt weirdly as if they were too far away from his head, Hillary Greene had read the last of her emails and was just typing up her notes to add to the murder book when there was a tap on the stationery cupboard door.

'Yes?'

The door opened and Claire stuck her head in, an excited sparkle in her eye. 'Guv, we've just had a call from Anthea Ramsey. She says she needs to speak to us urgently. Intriguing or what?'

'Who?' Hillary asked blankly, then smiled as Claire gave herself a comical smack on the forehead with the heel of her hand.

'Sorry, guv, I meant to say. Anthea Greyling. She's now Mrs Ramsey. She remarried not long after her divorce from Dustin. Now a widow. I've just photocopied the dossier I've been working up on her for you.'

She stepped forward — literally, just a single step, which had brought her straight to Hillary's neat, but laden, desk — and handed over a slim beige folder.

Hillary didn't bother reading it then and there. 'Did she say what she wanted to see us about?'

'No, guv, but she sounded tense. Excited. Nervous. Take your pick.'

Hillary nodded, leaned back in her chair, and absently twirled a pen between her fingers. 'Had you made contact with her yet to set up an appointment? Before she phoned, I mean?' She was pretty sure that she hadn't given any such instructions concerning DI Keating's second-best prime suspect, intending to see her first thing next week and to hopefully catch her unprepared.

'No, guv,' Claire promised. 'She just called us out of the blue. Asked the front desk to be put in touch with someone in the CRT, and the switchboard passed her on to the computer boffins for some reason, and they shuffled her over to me.'

'She asked for the CRT specifically?' Hillary asked, slightly puzzled by this. As a rule, the general public had little concept of their department, or what it did.

'Yes, guv, but I expect the article that's gone out about the case in the local paper is behind *that*,' Claire said with a grimace. 'They probably gave us a mention. Since cold cases have become a "thing" on television, our profile is riding high. Apparently. Ah, fame!'

Hillary's brow cleared, but she sighed heavily. She hadn't asked for any press release about the reopening of the case to be issued, preferring to catch any witnesses they could track down unaware. She'd found it usually paid off if you could spring questions on people out of the blue, before they'd had any chance to muster their defences or plan beforehand what they would say.

She *had* planned on asking for the press's help only as a way of appealing for any witnesses from thirty years ago to get in touch, and even then only as a last resort.

'I'm surprised they got on to it at all, let alone so quickly,' Hillary said grumpily. 'It's not as if a thirty-year-old murder is hot news, is it? And I can't somehow see the reporters on our local papers being so industrious or ambitious that they actively went out and dug the story up. So how did they even know about it?'

Claire shrugged. Now that her boss had pointed it out, it did seem odd. 'One of the people we've already talked to must have leaked it?' she offered tentatively.

Hillary nodded. She'd already come to the same conclusion herself. 'But who? I can't see Max Walker being interested in publicity. He might be running a business that relies on word of mouth, but he's hardly likely to benefit, is he? If the story gains momentum, he knows he's likely to be named as one of the persons of interest in the original case. And who's going to want to camp in a field when their host might be a murderer?'

'Goths?' Claire offered, making Hillary gurgle in appreciation.

'DI Keating isn't likely to have approached them either,' Hillary swept on, once her mirth had passed. 'He's not going to want his . . .' she stopped to cough, 'failures dragged into the limelight.'

She reached into her bag for a tic tac and popped one into her mouth.

'That only leaves the sister then,' Claire said, doing a rapid mental calculation of everyone they'd talked to so far. 'Unless you've spoken to someone else?' And if so, Hillary hadn't yet put it in the murder book, was the unspoken reprimand.

But Hillary was already shaking her head. 'Do you think Moira would want the press sniffing around her? With her background? If she is still using off and on, the last thing she's going to want is reporters pestering her. I can't see her supplier being pleased about something like that either. Being in the spotlight isn't their happy place.'

'Hmm,' Claire muttered, for her boss was right. People who lived Moira's kind of life liked to keep well in the shadows. 'Well, *somebody* must have blabbed.'

Hillary sighed and shrugged. 'Well, no use crying over spilt . . .' She coughed again, and when she'd finished, added laconically, 'milk.'

Claire smiled, but her heart wasn't in it. 'The new antibiotics not doing the trick yet then?' she asked casually.

For a moment Hillary stared at her blankly, wondering what she was on about, then remembered that she'd told her team that her GP was giving her new pills for her 'chest infection'.

'It'll take three to four days before I see any improvement, so they say,' she lied glibly. 'Well, if Anthea Grey . . . er, Ramsey, wants to see us, I suppose we should oblige her,' she rapidly brought the conversation back on track. 'It'll be interesting to see if her version of events has changed any since she gave her original statement thirty years ago.'

Hillary got up, slipped her jacket off the back of her chair and put it on, whilst simultaneously rummaging under her desk for her bag. 'She's certainly eager, isn't she? If she *has* seen the article, she's not hanging around and waiting for *us* to come to *her.*'

'Hmm. It's not often we come across people so keen to help us out is it,' Claire agreed cynically.

Hillary's lips twisted. Wasn't that the truth?

* * *

'Wow, nice place,' Claire hissed, barely five minutes later. Although the village of Hampton Poyle was on Kidlington's doorstep, so to speak, the contrast between the huge village and the small one felt poles apart.

Here elegant weeping willows lined an attractive road-side ditch — probably called a stream by the inhabitants — and picturesque, if concrete, bridges spanned this water-course, giving some of the residences a 'moated' feel. Here there were no traffic lights, traffic congestion, fumes or noise. Here there were no rows and rows of similar-looking hous-ing, or shops, or shoppers, or man-made noise of any kind. Only, in the distance, the sound of a tractor ploughing over the remnants of harvested wheat, accompanied by flocks of raucous seagulls.

'How the other half lives or what?' Claire continued her theme, as they walked down the small 'main' road in search of Holly Lodge, the address Anthea Ramsey had given to Claire over the phone.

The 'lodge', it turned out, bore no resemblance to any lodge that Hillary had ever seen, but was rather a large Edwardian edifice of Cotswold stone with big sash windows, large well-maintained grounds, and the groomed, smug look of a property that had always been pampered.

'She remarried well,' said Hillary.

'Didn't she though,' Claire agreed enviously.

When they passed up the path, lined with brightly coloured asters and dahlias, and rang the bell set beside a large oak door, the woman who answered the summons looked every inch as pampered as the home in which she lived.

Dressed in dark grey satin slacks, with a dazzlingly white blouse to offset it, both garments made the most of her strik-ing red hair. A platinum and mother-of-pearl pendant hung discreetly at her neck. Diamonds sparkled on three ring fin-gers, and her make-up was flawless.

Hillary wondered if she'd made this much effort as a form of armour, knowing that a call from the police was imminent, or if she dressed like this habitually. She thought, on balance, that it was probably down to the former. Although it had been thirty years ago now, she could imagine that DI Keating had put this woman through the wringer, and something like that was probably never forgotten.

And although, this time, *she'd* been the one to invite them in, psychologically she probably still felt the need to be as in control as possible.

Hillary and Claire produced their IDs but Anthea Ramsey merely glanced at them. 'Thank you for coming,' she said, opening the door wider for them to slip by.

She led them to a lovely front room, done out in jade green and rich shades of cream. French windows gave a view of the weeping-willow-fringed stream at the bottom of an equally immaculate garden.

'Please, sit down,' their hostess said, indicating four cream leather armchairs, grouped around a large mother-of-pearl-inlaid table, which was a genuine antique, Hillary noted, or she was a Dutchman's uncle.

And she wasn't.

On the table rested only a plain white envelope, and nothing else. It was set square in the middle and the lack of magazines or potted plants gave it a portentousness that immediately drew the eye.

Seeing Hillary duly notice it, Anthea too looked at it with disdain. 'I'm glad you're here. *That* came yesterday,' she said grimly.

Whatever this woman's opening gambit might be, Hillary hadn't expected this. She'd been prepared for the formerly besotted fan of the dead vicar to be polite, or demanding, or ingratiating. She'd been prepared for her to try and probe them for information about how the investigation was going, or present them with a pre-emptive strike, coldly informing her that if she was bothered by them in any way that she'd sue for harassment.

She wasn't expecting a simple, apparently random statement about her mail.

She saw that Claire was staring at the item in question with equal bewilderment and quickly mentally regrouped. Leaning back slightly in the chair, Hillary regarded the older woman carefully. Only her hands betrayed her true age of a woman in her mid-sixties, for her face was free of wrinkles, sags and blemishes.

This was a woman determined to hold on to her youth and beauty, a woman who had picked herself up after a tragic event and a messy divorce, and had done well for herself.

Her eyes, though, were at odds with this assessment, and were telling Hillary a different story. Stormy grey, they looked . . . what? Angry. Frightened. Excited. A mix of all three?

'Go ahead, read it,' Anthea said, her voice halfway between a demand and an appeal, snapping Hillary out of her analysis.

'I'm sorry, Mrs Ramsey,' Hillary said, making no move to take her up on the offer. 'Am I to understand that you called us over here specifically to read this?' she waved a hand at the envelope sitting in the middle of the table.

Anthea nodded emphatically. 'Yes, I did.'

Beside her, she felt Claire give her a quick, nervous glance and could take a good guess at what she must be thinking. For she was probably thinking the same thing.

From the case files, Ben Keating had, once or twice, questioned the stability of this woman's mental state. He and other witnesses, including her soon-to-be ex-husband, had described her variously as 'highly strung', 'besotted', 'spoiled', 'away with the fairies', 'hysterical' and 'all over the place'. And now they were both wondering if all that still held true.

Not that Hillary was in the habit of taking the original SIO's assessments on any of her cold cases as being sacrosanct. She liked to make up her own mind about such things, after doing her own interviews. But from this showing, it was at least clear to her that Anthea's behaviour was somewhat unexpected. Perhaps, even after a period of thirty years, she was still a woman who lived on her nerves and emotions?

After all, when a married woman fell so headlong and inappropriately for a vicar, who by all accounts had never encouraged her or matched her ardour, it had to indicate, at the least, a woman with an obsessive streak. A fantasist perhaps? Someone with a personality disorder that left them with the need to be perpetually in the limelight? A drama queen who had to be the centre of attention. Or maybe she'd simply been addicted to the feeling of falling in love? There were women, Hillary knew, who married up to a dozen times in their lives because of it.

Then again, she might have even more acute mental issues than that which they didn't yet know about.

And, of course, there was always the very tricky possibility that Anthea Greyling, as she'd been then, was the one who had killed Keith Coltrane all those years ago and had got away with it for over thirty years. In which case, any mental issues aside, she'd been clever enough — or simply lucky enough — to do so without being seen in the church that day.

The old adage about leopards and spots had Hillary raising her alert level a notch.

She would need to tread carefully, in case this woman had indeed read about Keith's case being reopened, and it had led to old traumas resurfacing. The last thing Rollo Sale would thank her for would be new headlines about how 'insensitive police officers' had 'badgered a mentally vulnerable witness'.

And there were protocols in place, for good reason, when it came to dealing with such scenarios. Maybe this was one of them? If so, they needed to get out of there fast, and then arrange to reinterview this witness with medical professionals present, or at the very least, a friend or family member.

The question was — was this such a case? Or were they getting played by a very clever killer?

'Mrs Ramsey,' Hillary began gently, 'you do *know* who we are, yes? We have been given the task of taking a second look at the murder of Reverend Coltrane.'

Anthea Ramsey nodded impatiently. 'Yes, yes, I know. That's why I called you. Did they not make that clear? I *asked* for the person in charge of Keith's case to come and see me.'

Hillary sat up a little straighter. Right now, her witness didn't sound confused, or vulnerable. In fact, she sounded more miffed than anything. The older woman pointed imperiously at the envelope on the table again. 'So just read the letter, will you? It's vile. Disgusting. And I won't have it! I'm telling you, I won't stand for it.' Her voice, it was true, had now become a little shrill, but for all that, to Hillary, she didn't look like a woman at the end of her tether.

'All right, Mrs Ramsey. But are you sure you want me to read your private mail? It's none of my business what—'

But she didn't get the chance to finish.

'Hah, that's what you think,' Anthea interrupted. 'It's your business all right. Oh, just read the damned thing, will you? I've spent all night tossing and turning and wondering if I should just burn it but decided that would be silly. So this morning, I vowed that I wasn't going to be bullied. After all, that's what the police are for, isn't it? To catch criminals? So read it, then I want to know what you intend to do about it,' Anthea said, and now there was no mistaking her primary emotion.

It was anger. But tinged, Hillary was sure, with apprehension.

With a shrug, she studied the item in her hand. It was a plain white envelope with a printed label and a stamp. It had been opened neatly, with a sharp letter opener, she assumed, for there were not tell-tale ragged tears.

She withdrew the single A4 sheet of standard copying paper.

The typed message inside was taunting in nature, but to the point. As she took in its contents, Hillary felt a surprised gasp slip from between her lips before she could stop it.

And then felt a familiar urge to start coughing — which had no doubt been triggered by her sudden change in breathing. Only by an immense act of will did she manage to stop herself from doing so.

She did have to clear her throat though.

Once she'd reread it, she reached calmly into her handbag for a clear plastic evidence bag and slipped it inside. Only then did she pass it to Claire, who eagerly read it with widening eyes.

CHAPTER SEVEN

Did you know the police are investigating Keith Coltrane's murder again, Mrs Greyling? Or should I call you Mrs Ramsey now? You certainly did all right for yourself after your husband dumped you, didn't you? I admire that.

You probably wouldn't remember me, even if I told you my name, but I remember you all right. Made a bit of a fool of yourself with the handsome vicar didn't you? We were all laughing about it.

But let's get down to business. Now that you've done all right for yourself, you won't want to spoil your lovely way of life by going to prison, will you, Anthea?

So if you want to carry on living the good life, get together £10,000 in cash. I know that shouldn't take you long, so I'll get back in touch very soon. Once you have the money, I'll send you instructions on what to do with it.

And why should you do that, you may be thinking? Well, I'll tell you. Or rather, I'll tell the POLICE, if you don't. Tell them all about how I saw you that day when the poor vicar got his head bashed in. How you were in the porch and making your usual fool of yourself with the poor man. Pawing away at him, begging him to shag you, were you? I'll tell them what a temper you have when you don't get your own way as well. I'll tell them that the spade that killed poor Keith was right there, leaning against the wall within touching distance of you.

Get the picture now?

And, if you don't pay up you know what you can expect. A call from the cops. And won't that ruin your whole day? What will all your friends think of that?

It goes without saying, it was unsigned.

Wordlessly, Claire handed the letter back to Hillary, who stowed it away in her bag.

The few moments that it had taken Claire to absorb the threatening letter had given Hillary time to do some very quick thinking and roughly plan out her strategy for the next few minutes.

This surprising new development needed to be handled just right if she was to gain maximum advantage of it. And with a witness she couldn't quite get the measure of, downplaying it seemed to be the way to go.

So it was that when she looked across at Anthea Ramsey she only said mildly, 'You said this came yesterday? That must have been distressing for you?'

Anthea's lips, which had been painted in a carefully chosen dark burnished red so as not to clash with her Titian hair, twisted in a parody of a smile. 'It was a bit of a shock, as you can imagine. And yes, it upset me. Wouldn't it upset you?' she challenged.

Hillary supposed, if she'd been in this woman's shoes, that yes, it probably would have.

'Well, I'm glad you didn't destroy it, Mrs Ramsey,' she complimented her cautiously. She was still not quite sure what she was dealing with here — either with her witness, or with this sudden twist in her case.

And whilst the blackmail letter certainly gave them a fresh avenue and a very hopeful new and original lead to follow, experience had taught her not to count any of her chickens until they were well and truly hatched.

And preferably, clucking contentedly.

'So am I. Now,' Anthea admitted. 'At first, like I said, I wanted to just rip it up and burn it. As you can imagine, that time in my life, with Keith and all that happened, was so painful. I thought I'd never get over it. But what can you do? Life goes on all around you, and you have no alternative but to just get back on your feet. And so I did.' Her slim shoulders shrugged elegantly. 'And after all this time I thought I was over it. I could go for months at a time without thinking about it. But then *that* thing arrived through my letterbox and brought it all back. Can you imagine how I felt?' Barely pausing for breath, 'I cried buckets,' Anthea swept on, making it clear that her last question had been strictly rhetorical. 'I found myself grieving all over again. I was a mess! But then, after a while, it just started to make me feel angry. Furious in fact. How dare someone invade my life like this? Turning me upside down. How bloody *dare* they? It made me so angry I could have killed them.'

Hillary wondered if the woman even realised, given the circumstances, the sheer impropriety of her choice of words, but didn't think, on the whole, that she did. She was still too caught up in her own melodrama, for she continued to plough on, the words pouring out of her.

'I paced about the kitchen like a wild animal, I was so furious. And I felt so helpless! But what could I do? I didn't know who'd sent it, so I couldn't even give them a piece of my mind!'

Anthea was panting a little now, and Hillary hoped she wasn't going to work herself up into a frenzy — the last thing she needed now was fit of genuine hysterics. On the other hand, trying to step in and calm her down would be counterproductive. Most witnesses let the truth slip when they were at their most emotional. And she was still waiting to see where Anthea was going with all this.

'I was in despair, thinking another nightmare was going to start up all over again . . .' Anthea continued, seeming to calm down just a little. 'And I know what people are like,' she added bitterly. 'If it did start up all over again, people here would start to look at me funny, and oh . . .' She put her hands over her face. 'I just couldn't bear it.'

Hillary was about to say something soothing, but then the hands were removed from the face, and Anthea was off again.

'And then I suddenly realised something. Blackmail is a crime, isn't it?'

'It certainly is,' Hillary acknowledged, with something of a grimace. Because it meant that Rollo Sale would now have to bring in a sergeant to investigate it. Her remit was cold cases only. Anything current had to be dealt with by a 'genuine' police officer.

And although she understood it, the idea of it still annoyed her thoroughly. To have this tasty morsel snaffled from under her nose was gut-wrenching. But she'd deal with that when the time came. Right now, she needed to regain control of this interview.

'I take it you want to file an official complaint then?' she asked, going by the book.

'Yes, I do. I most definitely want to file a complaint,' Anthea nodded firmly. 'How dare they, whoever they are, threaten me like this? Who do they think they are?' she swept on, her anger levels slowly escalating again. 'To come into my life and try and get money out of me? Well they won't get it. Not a penny. Not a damned penny, do you hear?'

Since she was now shouting, Hillary suspected the people in the next village could probably hear her.

'I take it then,' she said, careful to keep her own voice quiet and calm, 'that you're denying the contents of this letter to be true?'

For a second Anthea opened her mouth to respond, but then slowly closed it again. The angry flush that had suffused her face receded, leaving her paler and more in control.

Now she looked wary.

'What do you mean?' she said cautiously, and much more quietly. 'Of course I deny them. I wouldn't want you to catch the blackmailer if what they're implying is actually true, would I? That would be stupid! I loved Keith — I wanted to spend the rest of my life with him. Why on earth would I kill him? I didn't even get the chance to say goodbye to him, because I never even *saw* poor Keith the day he was killed. Even the inspector in charge of the case finally had to admit that. Oh, I know what he thought. He'd listened to all the village gossip and the spiteful cats who were only too happy to put the knife in. But it wasn't like that.'

Hillary nodded soothingly. 'So tell me what it was like,' she invited, her voice gentle.

Anthea, for the first time since their arrival, leaned fully back in her chair and let her shoulders slump a little. She let out a melancholy sigh.

And Hillary still didn't know whether the emotion was genuine, or whether she was watching a very good actress, giving a very good performance.

'I loved Keith — genuinely *loved* him. That's what nobody seemed to understand! Not my husband, not the villagers, maybe not even Keith himself,' she added, then looked surprised, as if she hadn't meant to say that last bit out loud. Hastily, she carried on. 'It *wasn't* an infatuation. And I *wasn't* some silly bored housewife, like Dustin said,' she insisted resentfully. 'And Keith loved me too. Oh, I know he could never openly say it, or act like it,' she added, as if expecting Hillary to demur at that point. 'But that was because I was married at the time, and he was the vicar. We knew we had to wait and be careful.'

'This was Dustin Greyling you were married to, yes?' Hillary clarified briskly, wanting to put a dimmer switch on all the self-pity and self-justification going on. She had a feeling Anthea could go on in this vein all day, if she was allowed.

Anthea sighed. 'Yes. Poor Dustin. He always was an insecure, jealous sort of man,' she said sadly. And just like that, her focus changed instantly, like quicksilver, and she had gone from wronged, misunderstood lover, to sad, weary wife, contemplating her spouse's shortcomings.

Once again Hillary felt the ground shift beneath her a little. But she had no time to try and untangle the reasons behind Anthea Ramsey's convoluted personality, because she was off and talking once more.

'Trust him to make things difficult! If only he'd behaved in a more sophisticated, seemly way, things wouldn't have become so ghastly. All those villagers sniggering at us behind our backs. If he'd just taken it like a man, and left the house and agreed to give me a quiet, civilised divorce . . . but oh no. He had to make a song and dance out of it.'

Anthea shook her head now. 'I should have known he would, I suppose. Dustin was always so . . . *ordinary*. And Keith was so *extra*ordinary in every way. Keith was hand-some, spiritual, so . . . so . . . oh, I can't really explain it. And Dustin was so pedestrian. So utterly drab and predictable. Do you know he actually went to see Keith that day and demanded to know what was going on?'

Hillary did know — it was in the files. But since Dustin Greyling had since died, Hillary would have no chance to hear his version of this love triangle.

'Perhaps, as the wronged spouse, he thought he was owed an explanation?' Hillary asked, deciding to see what happened if she abandoned her softly-softly approach, and began challenging Anthea Ramsey's rose-tinted version of events.

But all she did was sigh and make a somewhat surprising admission. 'Yes, I suppose he did.'

This was the first time Hillary had heard the woman put herself in someone else's shoes and consider the situation from a position other than her own.

But it didn't last.

'I only hope he didn't upset Keith too much,' Anthea said, back on form. 'At least Dustin had enough about him to make sure that they were alone when he started being so vile.'

Hillary didn't quite know how to respond to that piece of sophistry, so she merely mentally filed it for future refer-ence, and changed the subject.

'Do you have any ideas yourself about who killed the Reverend Coltrane?'

Anthea swallowed hard, and Hillary saw that her eyes were brightening. Tears, she knew, weren't far away. She always travelled with a packet of tissues for just such occasions as these.

'No, not really. Not unless it was that mixed-up wreck of a sister of his,' Anthea said listlessly. 'It was just like Keith not to abandon her. He was always trying to get her well. Taking her to clinics and getting her on programmes to try and cure her addictions. But you could tell she was too far gone. And, oh my, did she *resent* him for it. I overheard them once, and she was shouting at him like a banshee, threatening all sorts.'

'To kill him?'

'Oh yes. Often,' Anthea agreed airily. 'She used to rant and blaspheme and even physically attack him. I was sure he had a black eye once, after one of their sessions. He said he walked into the vestry door. I ask you! He was never clumsy — he had the grace of a dancer. But that was Keith — always protecting everyone, taking the weight of the world on his own shoulders. He was a saint. Like his beloved Saint Anthony.'

Hillary nodded, remembering that the church at Lower Barton was dedicated to that particular saint. He wasn't one that she knew anything about, but since so many of her witnesses had remarked about the dead man's devotion to him, she made a mental note to look him up sometime.

'But apart from his sister, you don't know anyone who had a grudge against him? Apart from your husband Dustin, that is?'

'Well, there was that awful man who wanted to poach the fields next to the church for his ghastly tourist business. What kind of a man steals from the dead?'

This made Hillary blink a bit, but thankfully no response was required of her, for her witness was already elaborating.

'It just highlighted how wonderful Keith was. He wanted the land for his parishioners' last resting places, so their souls could rest in peace and family members would have graves to visit and tend. And that awful . . . Williams man — Wilson . . . Something beginning with a "W" anyway, *he* just wanted to bring noisy tourists to the village, clogging up the village streets with their cars, and creating noise and mess.'

'Yes. He does now own a glamping business on that site,' Hillary murmured, amused when Anthea Ramsey shuddered graphically.

'Ugh! Well, all I can say is, I'm glad I left there now. Mind you, I'm rather pleased that the village got what it deserved! They were all obnoxious people. They treated me abominably.'

Hillary nodded. Yes, Anthea Ramsey certainly had narcissistic traits all right. Did she really imagine that Lower Barton had been preserved in aspic, and after thirty years, all those gossiping, disapproving residents still lived there, or cared tuppence either for Max Walker's glampers, or Anthea Greyling's thoughts and opinions on the matter?

Hillary suddenly realised she felt bone tired. She hadn't been sleeping all that well recently, and now this woman's emotional baggage had worn her out.

Deciding they had enough to be getting on with for now, she made the decision to call it a day. Of course, a second interview would probably be necessary quite soon, but for now, she'd had enough of Anthea Ramsey.

'Well, thank you for calling us, Mrs Ramsey. I'm going to take the letter to my superintendent, and we'll be following up on it, rest assured. You'll be asked to sign a statement about it at some point, but in the meantime, I want you to call us the moment you get the second letter with further instructions on how to drop off the payment.' So saying, she handed over one of her cards. It was a bit naughty, she knew, given that another acting officer would have been assigned the blackmail case by then, but this way, she would at least be kept in the loop and be amongst the first to know of any developments.

'Fine, I can do that,' Anthea said crisply, and in yet another abrupt change of mood, rose and held out a cool hand.

'Thank you for your time.' She was now the epitome of a superior class of woman, dealing with minions.

Hillary, a little *be*mused but also a little *a*mused, indulged her, and gave her a cool handshake and an ultra-polite smile in return. Claire, it seemed, had been forgotten altogether by the lady of the house, for Anthea didn't even acknowledge her as she turned and showed them out.

Once back on the front path, Claire let out a long, slow breath. Hillary would have followed suit, but she suspected it would set off another coughing fit.

As they walked back to the car, both women were thoughtful. Finally, Claire roused herself enough to say, 'Well, that was interesting.'

Hillary's lips twitched. 'I'll give you that. It certainly was.'

Once they'd regained the car — they'd come in Claire's, who now took her seat behind the wheel — Hillary fastened her safety belt and stared out of the window. Claire made no attempt to turn on the ignition but followed suit, and the two women absently tracked the progress of a big ginger-and-white cat as it strolled in the grass, searching for unwary field mice. 'So, do you think the blackmailer actually saw her that day, guv, or are they just trying it on?' Claire finally asked.

'Not sure,' Hillary said.

'Do you think Anthea has genuine bats in her belfry, or is just a bit muddle-headed?'

'Not sure.'

'Do you think she's the killer?'

'Not sure.'

Claire laughed. 'So what are you thinking, guv?'

Fighting off the urge to repeat 'not sure', she shrugged. 'Lots of things,' she said instead. 'But chief amongst them, I'm wondering about that letter.'

'Well, it seems to be obvious enough on the face of it,' Claire said. But she'd learned to be cautious around Hillary Greene. Her guv'nor didn't have the best solve rate at HQ for nothing, and she'd seen Hillary pull enough rabbits out

101

of the hat — and too many times — to risk looking a fool by sounding too confident of her own conclusions. 'The writer probably saw the same newspaper article everyone else has and thought now was a good time to capitalise on it.'

'Yes. Maybe,' Hillary agreed absently. 'But ten thousand pounds is an interesting figure, don't you think?'

Claire, who hadn't thought anything of the sort, nodded judiciously.

'It's not peanuts, but it's hardly a life-changing sum either,' Hillary said, continuing to stare straight ahead of her, but blind to the village's bucolic charms. 'If it's genuine, it has to be just the opening gambit. And once Anthea had paid up, the demands would become more regular. Probably for the same amount, say every two to three months? Ten grand is a small enough amount for someone of Anthea's obvious wealth to pay, just to avoid the hassle; not *too* much to eventually make her baulk and decide to call their bluff and stop making the payments. If it *is* a bluff, of course.'

Claire nodded. 'Blackmailers. All they want is an easy mark and an easy life. Bastards!' Like most cops, Claire had a special hatred for blackmailers. Then, a little belatedly, something her boss had just said registered.

It paid, Claire had learned, to listen closely to what Hillary Greene actually *said*.

Now she echoed, 'What did you mean — "if it's genuine". How could the letter have been a fake?' she asked, puzzled.

Hillary sighed. 'I was just wondering if Anthea herself had written it.' But now that she said it out loud, she didn't like the sound of it.

'Huh? Why should she do that?'

'To be the centre of attention? She struck me as someone who lived off heightened emotion.'

'Ah,' Claire said. 'Yes, she does rather fancy herself all right. But it's a dangerous game she's playing, if she wrote it herself. It *does* name her as the killer, after all. Even if she is super confident that we won't be able to nab her for the

Reverend's murder after all this time, it's still putting her head in the noose unnecessarily.'

'Yes. I'm not saying I'm convinced she *did* write it. Just that we need to bear it in mind.'

Claire nodded. 'Fair enough. Back to HQ?'

'Yes. I need to update Superintendent Sale on this new twist in the tale,' Hillary said reluctantly.

* * *

'I'll have to assign someone from upstairs on it, of course. You know that?' Rollo Sale said, the moment Hillary handed over the plastic-encased blackmail note and had finished giving him her report on her interview with Anthea Ramsey. Complete with her thoughts about the surprise twist in the Coltrane case.

Hillary nodded glumly. 'Yes, sir.'

'I'll make it clear that whoever is assigned to it keeps us in the loop,' he said, a twinkle in his eye.

Hillary's lips twisted. She could well imagine how they'd feel about that! As far as they'd be concerned, they were being handed an interesting case — blackmail being rarer and a definite step up from the usual fare of burglaries and common assault — which was guaranteed to be a significant notch on their truncheon. And reporting diligently to a former DI, put out to pasture on a thirty-year case, would not exactly be high on their list of priorities.

Still, Hillary mused, there were always ways and means around recalcitrant colleagues, and she knew them all. She was already compiling a mental list of people who owed her favours. And if the odd document from the blackmail case somehow mysteriously found its way onto her computer . . . well, snafu's happened right?

Rollo Sale, who had followed her mental reasoning — almost word for word — now smiled at her conspiratorially and leaned back in his chair.

'So, what's your thinking on the case so far? I take it the two main suspects couldn't be more different? What with the sister spitting in your face without saying barely a word, and the would-be besotted lover falling on your neck and emoting as if auditioning for RADA, by the sounds of it,' the superintendent grinned.

Hillary's lips twitched. 'I could have sold tickets, if I'd known.'

Rollo nodded, but his smile was already fading. 'So is she playing games with us? Do you think the blackmail letter really is a fake?'

Hillary shrugged. 'I can't say I'm all *that* enamoured of the idea, sir. Just that, given Mrs Ramsey's, shall we say, effervescent personality, I think it would be wise just to bear it in mind.'

'I'll be sure to pass that on to whoever gets the case. Whoever it is won't be happy if she's leading us on a wild goose chase.'

Hillary nodded. Then, knowing she had to get it over with, said abruptly, 'I'm sorry, sir, but it's likely I may have to take some medical leave in the near future.'

There was a moment of tense silence, then Rollo slowly nodded. 'I'm sorry to hear that,' he said quietly. And he was. He'd had his suspicions for some time that there was more to Hillary's 'chest infection' than she was letting on. And he felt not only concern for her on a personal level, but the news that his top investigator might be out of action for a while gave him a fit of the professional heebie-jeebies as well. 'Have you any idea how long?' he probed delicately.

Hillary shrugged. 'I'll be in a better position to answer that soon I hope, sir. I'm awaiting results,' she added, her tone and level gaze warning him in no uncertain terms that he'd better leave it there.

Superintendent Sale left it there.

Superintendent Sale was not an idiot.

So it was that just a few minutes later, Hillary left, making Claire's day by popping her head into the communal office and saying that she'd type up the notes of the Anthea Ramsey interview from memory, if Claire could just edit them and add anything she'd missed from her own, more reliable notes.

* * *

As Hillary sat down to tackle the not inconsiderable task of reducing Anthea Ramsey's evidence into dry, constabulary English, Sandy Walker watched her husband leave their home with a small frown on her attractive face.

Ever since the post had arrived yesterday, she'd noticed Max was acting a little differently. Oh, it had been nothing startling, nothing overt. There had been no snapping at her, which might have indicated stress, nor awkward silences caused by obvious distraction. But still, he was unhappy about something. Annoyed perhaps. Tense, possibly. She could just tell.

Sandy had always been intuitive and observant, two traits that had always stood her in good stead, both in the workplace and in the home. And perhaps unlike some wives, she had always been fully invested in her husband, still loved him after so many years of being together, and genuinely wanted to make sure he was well and contented.

Now, as she heard his Land Rover start up and pull away from the house, she went to his study and sat briskly behind his desk. She knew where he kept his mail, and she knew his filing system. In fact, there was very little about him that was unknown to her.

But after ten minutes of dedicated searching, she had to admit defeat. The plain white envelope that she had picked up from the hall mat yesterday, along with all the other brown and business mail which she habitually dropped off on his desk, was nowhere to be found.

Which meant that he'd either destroyed it or taken it with him. And both options would be a departure from his usual practice. He always filed *everything*, almost religiously, ever since a spot-check audit seven years ago had caused no end of problems for him when he wasn't able to produce every last scrap of paperwork that HMRC's tax inspector had demanded.

The only thing he binned were circulars and requests for charitable donations. But she'd already checked the wastepaper basket, and it held only the usual rubbish. Which meant that he must have slipped it into his jacket pocket, and presumably now still had it on him. But why?

She was sure that he had no idea of how aware she was of his moods and activities. Men just didn't notice things like that, did they? So she didn't think he was deliberately trying to hide it from her. So what was so important that he wanted to keep it close to him? Or perhaps she was being over-sensitive?

With a sigh, she left the office and wandered into the kitchen. There she made herself a cup of coffee and tried to convince herself that she was reading too much into things. Even though, twice yesterday when she'd looked in on him to see if he'd needed anything, he'd been staring diligently at a sheet of paper, with the offending plain white envelope resting empty in front of him. And it was not like Max to brood.

But just as she was finally managing to shrug the incident off, twenty minutes later, as she sat in the lounge reading her latest crime novel — she was addicted to the things — her phone pinged with a text message from her bank. And as she read it, she felt her unease ratchet up another notch.

Between them, they had many different bank accounts — some dedicated business accounts, some individual joint and savings accounts, and a few fixed bonds.

And whenever a large amount was taken out of one of the joint accounts, an automatic text message was sent to them both, as a form of security, and to make sure that they were aware of the change in the balance.

Normally, she wouldn't have given the notification of a large withdrawal much thought. She nearly always knew what Max was spending his money on and why.

But this time, she didn't. She stared at the message for some time, wracking her excellent memory for an explanation, but couldn't find one. She simply could not think why Max needed £10,000 in cash.

If he was buying a new yurt, or camping equipment, he wouldn't pay with cash. Nowadays, hardly anyone used cash. No. This was out of the ordinary. And things that were out of the ordinary worried her.

Normally, Sandy Walker's life went along at a pleasant, comfortable pace, with very little to ruffle her relaxed, country lifestyle. And she was perfectly happy with boring but nice.

But right now she could feel the chill of impending trouble. Why was Max hiding things from her? And why did he need so much ready money?

And what should she do about it?

Most wives would probably confront their husbands, demanding explanations. But Sandy Walker wasn't most wives.

The last thing she wanted was to cause serious ructions in her marriage when she was very happy with it just the way it was. Besides, Max, when pushed too far, tended to just lose his temper anyway, and dig his heels in.

No, she would have to be far more subtle than that.

Putting the crime novel aside, Sandy began to pace. And think.

CHAPTER EIGHT

Hillary finished typing up her notes on the Anthea Ramsey interview and emailed them to Claire for her additional input. By the time she'd finished reading the latest reports from her team she was ready to call it a day.

Since it was POETS day she decided, for once, to add herself to the number of workers who left work on a Friday a good half an hour or more early. After cheering on her team, and promising that next week they'd have broken the bulk of the hard slog, she made her way wearily home.

A coughing fit just as she'd parked Puff and was climbing from out behind the driver's seat only added to her general feeling of ill humour. Eventually the fit passed, and she was able to walk, a little weak-kneed, back to her boat, and clamber on board.

Once inside the *Mollern*'s cosy interior, she practically collapsed onto the two-seater built-in sofa and simply sat, with her eyes closed, listening to the sound of this year's nearly grown moorhen chicks calling for their parents and enjoying the mild rocking of the boat whenever another vessel passed her mooring. She was too tired even to remove her shoes.

Although, like most people who'd seen their fiftieth birthday come and go, she had been vaguely aware of a very slow loss of energy and some mental agility — crosswords took her ten minutes instead of five nowadays to complete — she hadn't ever really given any serious thought to the idea that she was actually 'growing old'. Apart from the occasional memory lapse and the growing acceptance that she'd need to get glasses at some point, it had always seemed something that was still on the distant horizon. Always something that didn't need to be thought about *just yet*.

And, she mused, opening her eyes with a snap and forcing herself out of the sofa and into her bedroom to change and briskly shower, she was buggered if she was going to do so now!

It was the weekend, and her leisure time started as of this minute. She was going to read her favourite Gothic novel, buy her favourite chocolate bar when she did the grocery shopping, and was going to enjoy the sunshine the weather forecasters were promising over the next few days by taking the deck chair out onto the towpath and finding the sunniest spot.

And work, whatever it was that was growing in her lungs, the identity of the killer of Keith Coltrane and everything and anything else could go suck on a lemon

* * *

Saturday dawned with the promise of a sunny spell looking, for once, as if it was going to be fulfilled and not veer off over France's way at the last minute.

But as Hillary Greene shopped and bought *two* of her favourite chocolate bars and, after some hesitation, a packet of hair dye that looked on the packaging to be a good match for her dark auburn shade, Max Walker was busy doing something very different.

His wife had left the house earlier citing various errands to run, and he was closeted in his study, collecting various items of stationery around him. Now an A4 padded envelope, a pair of scissors and some sellotape lay beside a stack of Sandy's out-of-date magazines, consisting mostly of *Cosmopolitan*, *House & Garden* and *National Geographic*.

Carefully he tore pages from the magazines, placed two or three pages together, then using a sharp pair of scissors, cut them into rectangles roughly the same shape and size as the stack of twenty-pound bills that he'd withdrawn from the bank yesterday.

Every now and then he'd pause in his cutting to bundle them up and put an elastic band around them. When he had finished, he lined up the actual cash against the cut-up paper facsimiles and checked the size and weight.

Not that he expected anyone would be able to tell the difference in weight once the fake packs were placed in an envelope, but Max just liked doing things properly.

Mind you, if he was lucky, the little scrote who'd written to him demanding money — unless Max wanted the police to hear some very interesting 'eyewitness' testimony that would put him in the frame for Keith Coltrane's murder — was going to be in for a big surprise. And he wasn't thinking only of the false payoff.

The blackmailer might confidently be expecting to have to deal with a cowed and anxious victim, but they would soon find out very differently! Because if, when Max received his final instructions on where and how to leave the 'money', he could think of a way to turn the tables, he was bloody well going to do so. And once he got his hands on them . . .

Max had always been a big, fit man, and one, moreover, who was prone to losing his temper when pushed too far. And although he was as capable of clear and logical thought as the next man, by nature, he preferred action. And right now, he was just in the mood to do some damage to a certain cocky correspondent.

He smiled a little at this delicious thought, then walked to the safe which was concealed behind what looked like a small display cabinet. Made of mahogany and sturdy glass, it did indeed contain a collection of natural crystals — mostly amethysts and agate. But when he reached inside and pressed a hidden button, it allowed him to slide the whole cabinet along the wall on concealed tracks, revealing the safe in the wall behind it.

He stashed the real cash safely in there, and then returned to the desk. He'd gone to the trouble of taking out the cash in reality just in case he was being observed. If he was dealing with someone as careful as himself, he wanted to look as if he was meekly complying with the instructions and buckling down under the threats.

But once this little hiccough was resolved, the cash would go safely back into the bank.

Back behind his desk, he arranged the various stacks of cut-up paper into a tidy shape inside the padded envelope and then sealed it shut with sellotape. He took a rather juvenile pleasure in taping up not only the flap, but also in wrapping the envelope around and around with the clear tape, knowing how hard that would make it to open without using a sharp knife or pair of scissors.

It amused him mightily to think of a would-be blackmailer struggling to open the envelope, all hot and sweaty and greedily eager to get at the cash, only to find the multiple pieces of paper within.

Once the envelope was sealed, he stowed it carefully away in the bottom drawer of his desk, which he then locked, then scooped up the remains of the magazines and swept them into the bin.

Where Sandy, his wife, would find them a few hours later and retrieve them with a puzzled frown. A frown that would slowly grow more and more dark and troubled.

* * *

Miles away, Max Walker's would-be blackmailer was also busy with *their* paperwork, but in their case, it involved simply printing off a set of instructions onto a single page, then slipping it into a plain white envelope and adding a first-class stamp.

A quick stroll to the nearest post box, only stopping to make sure that it was in time for the first collection, thus ensuring it would get to the Walker residence first thing on Monday morning, and their work was done for the day.

The blackmailer was feeling in a good mood for once. Times were tight, and a double income stream from two separate sources which — if all went well — could continue for some time to come was very welcome indeed.

Had the individual concerned known of Max Walker's plans, perhaps their mood wouldn't have been quite so jolly . . .

* * *

By three o'clock that afternoon, the late-summer sunshine began to lose some of its warmth, and Hillary, who was indeed sitting in a deckchair in a veritable suntrap in front of a hawthorn thicket, finally roused herself.

She'd read three chapters of her novel and eaten one of the chocolate bars. A blackcap, that had been keeping her company for the last five minutes or so, flew off in alarm when she suddenly rose and folded up her chair.

Once back in her boat, she stood in the small galley, inspecting her meagre cupboards for inspiration. She'd just decided that she'd treat herself to a meal in the Boat pub, which was literally just a short stroll away, when she heard the ping on her phone, denoting the arrival of a text message.

She'd deliberately left the demanding little pest behind her on the boat, and now she sighed, answering the demanding siren call of modern technology.

There was a message from her GP.

Hillary's whole body froze.

And instantly it reminded her of a time when, as a child, she'd been out picking damsons with her father.

They'd been out and about one day and had found a rich source of low-to-the-ground bounty clustered between two blackthorn hedges, courtesy of a farmer who had the good sense to cut and lay his hedges properly.

She'd been about ten, maybe eleven, and whilst her father plucked the small black plum-like fruit from the top of the hedge which he could easily reach, she had squatted down on her haunches to pick the fruit at the bottom.

She'd been happily picking away, adding to her growing bag of rich blue-purple bounty, and was reaching for one particularly luscious specimen, hanging so low it was half-buried in the grass.

It had been a day very much like this one — warm, late summer, early autumn, with golden sunshine and the drone of dozy wasps buzzing around her.

The hedge had lined a ploughed field, and the farmer, over the years, had haphazardly tossed stones kicked up from multiple ploughings into the ditch at the bottom of the hedge. These stones now caught some of the sun, warming them up, and as the ten-year old Hillary had put her hand out to pick the damson, she had seen two red spots in the darker area under the hedge.

And instantly peed herself, just a little. For the red spots were eyes. And as a country girl born and bred, she knew there was only one creature that she might encounter sunning itself and warming its cold blood on a warm, sunlit stone. And that was Britain's only venomous snake — the common adder.

And sure enough, now that the red eyes had given away its location, Hillary had been able to make out the rest of its coiled dark body, with the iconic black zig-zag stripes. The near-black colour told her it was a male, not a female.

Her father had always been a countryman of the old order and had quickly introduced his daughter to all the nearby badger's setts, and taught her how to find the scrapes in the soil where hares would lie in their forms, out of the worst of the wind during the winter storms. He'd explained which birds like to nest where, and why, and regularly found nests where she would then be lifted up in his arms so that

113

she could see — but never touch — the pale blue or speckled eggs of the various birds within.

So as she froze to the spot, her heart beating suddenly loud and fast in her chest, she was already remembering what her father had told her about snakes. And what he'd told her was that adders — in fact, most snakes — were far more afraid of humans than vice versa. That they used their venom to catch small prey to eat, and so they had no reason to want to bite a human. And that they only did so in self-defence, when disturbed, and before they'd had a chance to slither away.

And most importantly of all, that they reacted to sound and vibration, and so it was best to keep quiet and still if you ever stumbled upon one, and just back away slowly and carefully.

And so, after her initial fright, she slowly withdrew her hand, and backed away.

She'd left the damson unpicked and had gone back to tell her father about the snake, proud of herself for finding it, and wanting his approbation.

But by the time she'd taken him back to show it off, it had gone, of course. Her father hadn't been at all surprised, and told her that she'd probably frightened *it*, far more than *it* had frightened her!

And although that meeting had never been a traumatic experience for her, that very first moment when she'd spotted those weird red eyes in the undergrowth had been ingrained in her memory ever since. Along with the sensation that followed, when her blood had seemed to run as cold as that of the reptile itself, and her breath had lodged, un-expelled in her throat and her fingers had tingled in expectation of fangs piercing into them.

And now, so many years later, she felt that same feeling once more.

This time though, she was an adult, in her boat, and it was the sight of a text message from a very nice woman and a friendly, hard-working doctor that had presaged it.

Firmly she scrolled down to it and opened it with a jab of her finger.

The message was short and clear. An appointment had been made for her to see her private health specialist on Monday morning, at a clinic in Headington, not far from the Nuffield Hospital, in order to discuss the results of her scan.

Hillary texted back the 'Attend' option and sent it.

She then went to her bedroom and changed into a favourite velvet skirt with a complementary, floaty flowery top, added a squirt from her second-best perfume vial, and took herself to the pub.

There she ordered a slap-up meal and drank just a little — just a very little — too much of a very fine Chardonnay.

* * *

Fairly early on Sunday morning, Peter Cornwallis drove his car — a well-mannered navy-blue Skoda — out of a sleepy-looking Malmesbury and set off for Oxfordshire.

He drove with slow care, not just because driving wasn't a favourite activity any more, but more because he didn't want to arrive at his son's house too soon.

All night long he'd been tossing and turning, running over various scenarios in his mind about how this day might go. As for the conversation he knew that they must have, Peter could only pray for the best. He knew what he wanted to say — *needed* to say — but he was not confident he'd manage it with any finesse. But then, he and his son had become masters, over the years, of getting a message across to one another without *saying* much at all. And he hoped today would be no different.

Because today, the message he needed Trevor to understand was vital.

He began to sweat a little as he got nearer to his destination, but by the time he'd pulled up outside his son's home he'd convinced himself that he was feeling better, and climbed out of the car with a small smile stuck determinedly to his face.

Karen, who'd been watching out for him, was at the door and opening it before he even had a chance to ring the bell.

'Peter! How lovely to see you. I've cooked a leg of lamb, your favourite, and plenty of roasties. I know how you men like your roast potatoes.'

'Sounds absolutely delicious,' Peter said, with genuine affection. He'd always liked his son's choice of bride, and asked hopefully, 'Are the kids here?'

'Sorry, both of them had other plans and it was too short notice for them to cancel,' Karen said, her eyes flickering just a little as the lie left her lips.

In truth, Trevor had insisted that their adult son and daughter weren't told that their grandfather would be over today on one of his rare visits. Which meant that they were now happily contemplating a quiet dinner with their respective friends and oblivious to Peter's proximity.

To make matters worse, she was sure, from the look of resigned disappointment on his face, that Peter had guessed the truth of this, and so made a big fuss over him, taking his coat and showing him into the living room, all the while chatting brightly.

'I'll put the kettle on then, shall I?' she asked rhetorically, sweeping out of the room as her husband rose from his place on the sofa, and nodded across at his father.

'Hello, Dad,' Trevor said, giving back the same, meaningless smile that closely resembled that which was still sticking stubbornly to his father's face.

'Son.'

The old man felt a sharp pang of pain as it hit home, yet again, of all that they had lost over the years. The shared moments with his growing grandchildren that had never happened. All the normal, wonderful, everyday things that most families enjoyed. All the things that Keith Coltrane had cost them.

There was the usual awkward, tense moment of silence, and then Trevor nodded to an armchair by the unlit fireplace. 'Well, sit yourself down. How was the drive?'

'Fine, not much traffic about, just as I like it.'

Trevor nodded, then sat down himself. He carefully folded the Sunday paper he'd been reading and put it on the coffee table separating them.

They both knew from past experience that Karen wouldn't be in any hurry to disturb them with the promised tea. She always liked to leave them alone for a while, in the fond but forlorn hope that they'd start chatting and enjoy each other's company.

Now Trevor cleared his throat. He saw no sense in prolonging the inevitable. Best, he'd decided, to just get right down to it. Consequently, he took a long but shallow breath, and let it out slowly. He'd learned the technique from his first girlfriend at college, when he'd been having his panic attacks. Her brother, too, had been prone to them, so she knew the routine.

'I think I know why you're here,' Trevor said. 'I saw the article in the local paper too.'

'Oh. Yes. Er . . .good,' Peter said, relieved that there was one less hurdle he would have to negotiate. 'It didn't say much, did it?' he added lightly, looking down at the knuckles of his slightly arthritic hands that were resting in his lap.

'No. It was rather short,' Trevor agreed. Then cleared his throat. 'I daresay it came as a bit of a shock?'

'Yes, it did rather,' Peter heard himself say, then winced. They were talking like chance acquaintances, meeting up unexpectedly on a holiday beach somewhere, and fumbling for something interesting to say. Instead of discussing something that had ripped them apart once, and now had the potential of finishing them off entirely.

It made him want to cry. But he ruthlessly quashed such sentimentality. It would never do to let his son down now, at a time like this. Summoning up his courage, he stared fixedly down at his hands, and then launched right into it.

'That's why I wanted to come and see you, son, to reassure you that it's going to be *all right*,' he said with a fierceness that took Trevor by surprise. 'I mean, it's just a standard review, as far as I can tell,' he went on, his tone reverting back to its normal, slightly wavering baritone. 'I've been doing some research in the library, and it seems that unsolved murder cases are sometimes opened and looked at again periodically. I think it may be a bureaucratic requirement or something. It doesn't necessarily mean that anything *new* has come up. And it's not even a "real" investigator this time around anyway, but a retired police officer who's just a consultant or something. So you see, it's almost bound to be just an exercise in dotting the i's and crossing the t's in order to tick some box on some form or other.'

Peter could hear his voice droning on, and when he risked a glance at his only child, saw that Trevor was staring blankly at the dried flower arrangement in the hearth.

Peter quickly dragged his gaze back to his own hands, folded neatly in his lap. 'After thirty years, I'm sure there's nothing that we need to worry about,' he concluded, feeling suddenly exhausted by the effort.

'I'm sure there isn't,' Trevor agreed quietly. And hoped he was right. But he knew that his father was not the most competent of men. For all that Peter had earned his living as a structural engineer and surveyor, and thus supposedly had a tidy, scientific mind, Trevor had always known that his father was a bit of a muddler.

The kind of man who forgot to stock up on spare batteries in the winter, or went out with his wife's shopping list and returned with less than half the needed items. The sort of man who booked holidays that always proved to be inadequate in some way and couldn't even get a car in for its MOT on time.

It was no wonder that his mother, Dot, had tactfully taken over all the important chores. Now, of course, she was immune to such things. Safely ensconced in a pleasant nursing home, her mind blithely wandering back further and further into her past, she was at least spared the day-to-day worry of keeping her family and home life together.

Trevor shifted uneasily on the sofa, but still didn't remove his gaze from the fireplace. 'Have the police been to see you yet?' he asked, knowing how vital it was that he kept himself informed.

'Oh no. And I doubt that they will. I mean, why should they?' he asked casually, but Trevor heard him swallow hard. 'After all, I was only questioned, along with everyone else in the village at the time, and then never heard from them again.'

At this, Trevor felt some of the tension leave him. Because that was true enough. He knew this to be so, not because he trusted his father to tell him the truth. No. Thirty years ago, he'd learned a very valuable lesson indeed about his father's surprisingly adept abilities in the lying department.

But he could remember those days for himself, along with the police constable who'd come to their house that evening when the entire village had been abuzz with the news that someone had murdered Keith. He could still picture the policeman in his mind — not that many years older than Trevor himself had been at the time. Maybe twenty-one or two? Tall, with short fair hair and a spot on his chin. He'd had big, bony hands, Trevor remembered. What an alien presence he'd been, in his police uniform and with his notebook out and asking awkward questions.

He could recall in detail how his mother had shown him nervously in, and offered him tea or coffee and biscuits, all of which he'd refused. How they'd all sat on the sofa and been asked in turn if they'd seen Keith Coltrane that day. And how they'd all said in turn that they hadn't. And then how they were next asked if they'd seen or heard anything strange that day, centred around the church. Strangers, or unknown cars, or shouting. And again, how they'd all said they hadn't.

And that really had been that. In spite of the unbearable tension he'd endured, waiting for that knock on the door that would bring a more senior officer, demanding more difficult answers from them, it had simply never happened. And by then, Trevor had been playing very close attention to his father and his doings and would have known if the police had been taking an undue interest in him.

Or in Trevor himself.

But slowly, over the days that then turned into weeks, which in turn finally became months, the young Trevor Cornwallis had finally begun to believe that they were, indeed, safe.

So, perhaps, for once, his father was right to be optimistic.

'Has anyone contacted *you* yet?' Peter asked. 'I mean, from the police?'

'No. Like you, why should they want to talk to me?' Trevor asked, with heavy, almost vicious, irony.

'Yes, yes, of course,' Peter agreed hastily, backing off at once as he sensed the challenge in the question, and the growing anger behind it. 'So that's all right then, isn't it?' he added brightly.

Too brightly, as it turned out. For it instantly made his son worried, reminding him of Peter's annoying propensity for burying his head in the sand instead of meeting trouble head on and being sensible about it.

'Dad,' Trevor said urgently. 'You *have* destroyed the . . . er . . . I mean, you haven't kept anything . . . I mean, there's nothing you've kept *safe* from that time, is there?' he asked, for the first time looking his father in the eye.

Peter Cornwallis flushed with guilt, then swallowed hard. 'No, son, there's nothing you need worry about, I promise you that,' he pledged. Then, very unexpectedly, he leaned forward and in an unprecedented action, put his gnarled hand over that of his son's and squeezed it comfortingly.

Trevor looked down on their grouped hands in total surprise.

'Trevor, you know, I'm an old man now. I've had my life, so nothing much can matter to me now. If things start looking black — well I can take care of it. And with your mother safely settled — the nursing home bills are paid automatically from my pension, you know, so there would be nothing that would need doing if . . . well, if something were to happen. To me, I mean. Nothing will happen to *you*, of course, I won't let it. So you see, everything would be all right. It's important that you *understand* that. You wouldn't have to do a thing. That's really what I wanted to come here and explain to you. So that you won't be worrying. You can rest assured that I'll make sure everything is all right.'

Trevor Cornwallis slowly removed his hand from under that of his father's, the gesture making the old man go pale and hastily withdraw his own hand. But for all that Trevor's gesture might have looked contemptuous, his son's voice was quiet and almost gentle as he said, 'Yes, I know that Dad.'

Relieved, Peter Cornwallis sat back in his chair, his shoulders slumping a little now that the worst of it was over. He'd done what he'd set out to do and was confident that his son had understood the message. Namely, that Trevor would be safe. Always. His lovely wife, his kids, his home life, his bright future, everything could go on as always. And that if, by some freakish chance, the police did come calling, then he, Peter, would make sure that everything would be all right.

Karen chose that moment to arrive with the tea tray. She glanced from her husband to her father-in-law and saw the same small, meaningless smile on both their faces as they looked at her and sighed a little.

But as she sat down beside Peter and poured the tea, and pressed her home-made strawberry shortbread on him, and chatted about the children, Peter smiled and nodded and felt much better.

The same could not be said for his son, however. For Trevor Cornwallis, although he believed his father had good intentions, was not at all optimistic that things were going to be all right.

Not at all.

CHAPTER NINE

That Monday morning, three people prepared for the day in various states of heightened tension, excitement or anger.

Clara-Jane Coltrane was undoubtedly excited but also a little tense. As she pulled her scruffy second-hand car off the side of the single-track lane and onto a wide grass verge, she glanced around thoroughly, glad to see that the place was as deserted as she'd expected and hoped.

This was not surprising, as she'd chosen the spot very carefully, after much scouting around. Way out in the sticks but not three miles as the crow flies from Lower Barton, the nearest B-road was even further away. She'd taken gradually narrowing lanes until now she was the sole occupant of a sin-gle-lane byway used mostly by the farmers of the surrounding land, lazy hikers who didn't want to tramp cross-country too much, or extremely lost tourists.

On one side of the copiously pot-holed lane was a large copse of native shrubs and trees, and on the other, a recently ploughed field that was attracting the attention of a lot of landlocked seagulls and argumentative jackdaws.

A noisy rookery, set up in a stand of trees a mile away, provided a soundtrack as she drove the car carefully under the low, overhanging boughs of a lime tree, and climbed out.

Once on her feet, she carefully pulled up the concealing hood on her black hoodie and tied it firmly under her chin before opening the boot of the car. There, she lifted out of it her old racing bike, originally bought to help her keep in shape.

Clara-Jane had had her fortieth birthday a few years ago and hadn't liked it much. It had made her feel robbed of her youth and her resentment had been growing ever since. It was a trait that she knew she shared with her loser of a mother, Moira, and that moment of self-awareness hadn't improved her mood either.

Although for a while, back in her halcyon days, her life and future had seemed bright and promising enough, that, too, had somehow inexorably faded.

With the death of her uncle Keith, her mother had become her grandparents' only child. But given her addictions and inability to look after herself, let alone her offspring, her grandparents had tied up their money carefully — and were wise to have the foresight of doing so.

So it was that Clara-Jane and her brother had found themselves the happy recipients of trust funds, which released the cash in monthly payments, starting on their respective twenty-first birthdays. Both grandparents had died some years before, passing in close succession following the death of their beloved son.

The amount of money paid — when shared between the two of them   hadn't been huge enough to buy them a house each or anything like that, but still. After a childhood of upheaval and wearying poverty, it had felt like winning the lottery.

The day after she reached twenty-one, she chucked in her dead-end job at a supermarket, said goodbye to her bedsit, and began to thoroughly enjoy her Cinderella moment.

According to the arrangements her grandparents had set out, she had a guaranteed and regular income for the next twenty years, at which point, the funds would be exhausted. Naturally, the Coltranes had hoped, by this time, their granddaughter would be properly settled and living a comfortable life.

But to a young Clara-Jane, twenty years had felt like a lifetime, and she saw no good reason why she should plan for when she was old and wrinkled. Subsequently, her twenties had been spent living it up with two good holidays every year, endless parties, idleness and having a laugh with her mates. She moved into a nice rented flat in the centre of Oxford and amused herself with love affairs and a spot of gambling.

In her thirties though, she'd begun to wise up. Just a little. One morning, it suddenly impinged on her that she no longer had a 'lifetime' of the dolce vita ahead of her, but only ten more years. And it had slowly begun to sink in that she couldn't live like she had been without making some plans.

Although loath to do it, she'd finally found a part-time job, and cut out the gambling altogether. Instead of buying the latest fashions every year, she bought a few good pieces and learned the art of accessorising. And for the first time ever, began to actually save some of her monthly payments for a rainy day.

But even she hadn't expected the rainy day to come so soon. As her thirties counted down and she began to feel the remorseless march of passing time, she looked around for a rich lover, but they were few and far between. Although she'd inherited her uncle's good looks, she was not young enough, it seemed. Or quite sophisticated enough. Or quite . . . *something* . . . enough to suit the rich men that she sought out.

When she'd finally hit the dreaded big four-oh, the part-time job had to become full-time. She had to take out a mortgage on a poxy flat in Cowley overlooking a MINI car production plant, because she could no longer afford the luxury of renting. She'd had to forget about the holidays and face the facts. She was middle-aged, alone, and by no means well off anymore.

She wasn't happy about it, and the likelihood of her being able to do anything constructive about it had become remote, and so she'd been in her usual state of vague depression and savage resentment at the state of her life, when she'd heard from Sara Reese, her mother's neighbour.

When she'd been growing up, she supposed she'd been quite close to Sara. Foul-mouthed, funny, perpetually skint but warm-hearted Sara, who'd at least seen to it that she and her brother were fed when Moira spent the grocery money on dope or booze.

Over the years, the two women had kept in sporadic touch, mostly to slag off Moira behind her back, and enjoy sharing a few ciders together. Clara-Jane always buying, of course.

So when she'd seen Sara's number appear on her phone the other day, she'd not been particularly enthused but had answered it anyway, since she'd had nothing else to do but sit in front of the telly and watch *Emmerdale*.

But Sara had had something interesting to say this time, about her mum's visit from the cops — which in itself wasn't exactly an unheard-of event. But the reason behind this particular visit definitely had been. And when she heard that her murdered uncle's case was being reviewed, Clara-Jane had begun to take a definite interest.

As Sara's voice had droned on and on, Clara-Jane began to do some thinking. And long after Sara had rung off with vague promises to meet up some time in the future, Clara-Jane had continued to think long and hard indeed.

And the more she thought about it, the more she realised that life, at last, might have just presented her with an opportunity to do something about the pitiful state of her existence.

She'd been twelve when her uncle Keith had been murdered, and living, for a while at least, with her mother in a fleapit in nearby Banbury.

Naturally Moira, being Moira, had been in the habit of sending her off on the bus to the village where her uncle was the vicar, so that he could have the pleasure of minding her until Moira eventually finished doing whatever it was she was doing, and rang and asked Keith to drive her back.

To Clara-Jane, Keith had been an odd combination of an embarrassment — he was a vicar, for Pete's sake — and, because of his good looks, intelligence and kindness, a bit of a romantic hero figure also. A lot of her friends thought him dishy, for instance, and some had even volunteered to go with her for the day, willing to trade the dullness of a day out in the boring sticks for the chance to be one of Keith's little helpers.

So when her mother had casually, one Christmas, told her that someone had 'bashed in your uncle Keith's head' she'd been surprised, and sorry. But it had not, in truth, impacted on her life that much at all.

But now, thirty years later, Clara-Jane was feeling far more kindly towards her dead, saintly uncle. Because, thirty years after his death, he was going to help her get back her sorely missed dolce vita and secure her a comfortable future once more.

Now she quickly checked her watch again, made sure that her car couldn't be seen by anyone passing along the track, and pushed her bike carefully across the damp grass and onto the lane, before mounting it and pedalling a quarter of a mile or so to her chosen rendezvous point.

She was an hour early to keep her appointment with Max Walker. She wanted plenty of time to take a good look around and make sure that everything was just as she needed it to be. The last thing she wanted were unexpected witnesses or any nasty surprises.

But so far, things were looking good. There were no late-summer hikers or bikers, and no tractors toiled in any of the fields. Only the rooks from the rookery called raucously, as if mocking her attempts to recapture past glories.

'Noisy sods,' Clara-Jane muttered as she propped her bicycle against a tree and withdrew a cheap pair of binoculars from the saddlebag.

She'd bought the bike during her search-for-a-wealthy-man phase. Although she'd always been slim, middle age had threatened to put a little weight on her hips and belly — and no man liked that. Hence the bike. Plus it saved her money on petrol to do most of her travelling on two wheels, and Oxford, at least, was the ideal place for that mode of transport.

Now, she'd let her long black hair grow out — why pay a hairdresser? — and the clothes she was wearing were strictly utilitarian. Jeans and a dark knitted sweater under the black hoodie were ideal for this morning's activities.

A quick check on her watch — they were cheap as chips in charity shops nowadays — told her that she had less than half an hour now to wait. If Max Walker followed the instructions in the letter she'd sent him, he'd be arriving soon.

And with the cash. All that lovely cash.

Clara-Jane smiled wolfishly at the thought of it. Ten grand would be just the start of course. Once he'd paid up, and she knew she'd got him running scared, she'd touch him for the same amount as and when she fancied.

And then, of course, there was dear, batty old Anthea. Even as a twelve-year old girl, she'd known there was something squirm-making about the way Mrs Greyling fawned over her uncle.

So when she'd been thinking of people who might be willing to shell out to keep their names out of a second murder investigation, hers had definitely been on her radar. And in this age of technology, it hadn't taken her all that long to not only find out where Mrs Greyling was now living, but also to realise that the old bat had done very well for herself in the meantime — maybe even better than Max, with his 'glamping' empire.

Clara-Jane intended to post Anthea's instructions later today. And once the besotted widow had paid up too — another ten grand — then between them, her two benefactors would be providing her with a tidy sum indeed.

And tax-free this time, of course, Clara-Jane thought with a grin, for she certainly wouldn't be notifying his majesty's tax inspectors.

Yes, it would be nice to have the comfort and security of a 'trust fund' again. And she could jack in her job once more, and find a decent place. Lease a flash new car — a Merc maybe. And then she could look around for a toy boy! This time, she'd be the picky one. He'd have to have pecs, and a washboard stomach, and long hair. Dark or fair, she wasn't fussy.

As she lurked under cover in her chosen spot, Clara-Jane began to dream of the good times ahead.

* * *

Max Walker, the second person that morning who was operating in a heightened state, walked to his car and deposited the envelope of cut-up magazines onto the passenger seat.

Unlike Clara-Jane Coltrane, he was not feeling excited so much as angry. Very angry.

He turned and waved briefly to his wife, who he knew was watching him leave from her position by the study window. He'd only just been in time to hide that morning's letter from her as she'd brought him his usual morning cup of tea.

Now Sandy smiled brightly back and waved him off, and Max never gave her another thought as he drove away. He was too busy thinking of what he was going to do in the next half an hour or so.

The instructions for the money drop had been in that morning's post, and from the moment he'd read them, he could concentrate on only one thing: getting his hands on a dirty little blackmailer.

And when he'd read where and when the drop was to be, he'd begun to grin in growing anticipation. Because, being so close to the village, he knew that area fairly well. He'd driven down the back lanes often enough — whenever the main roads had been blocked by accidents or roadworks — to have a good idea of where the drop was.

And it had given him an idea.

* * *

In contrast to the excitement and anger being experienced by Clara-Jane and Max, Hillary Greene felt only nervous as she drove Puff past the Headington roundabout and headed towards the clinic and her appointment with her specialist.

Right from the time when her symptoms had first started and she'd consulted her GP, she'd told herself that anticipating trouble was pointless. And had thus made a prolonged and concerted effort not to brood on things or speculate too gloomily; and with a few backsliding exceptions, she thought she'd managed rather well.

Now though, with the preliminary tests done and the judgement of the medics imminent, she had to admit to feeling a slight case of the wobblies. Which pissed her off enormously. So as she parked in the clinic's parking lot, for once unable to fully appreciate the sheer luxury of not having to cruise around for off-street parking, she told herself to knock it off.

The clinic, a sprawling, single-storey new-build, had that freshly painted, featureless look common to such places. But at least the reception area was free of that antiseptic smell that most people who hated hospitals objected to so much.

Hillary walked across the hard-wearing grey carpeting to give her name to the receptionist, who smiled, logged her in and then indicated the mandatory area of low coffee tables, beige chairs and uninspiring reading material.

A vase of gladioli — real, not fake! — stood on the windowsill of one of the windows, and over in one corner, a television was turned on, but set to mute. It was showing a perpetual news channel with subtitles, which Hillary studiously ignored.

The last thing she felt in the mood for right now was more doom and gloom.

A glance at the wall-mounted clock showed her that she was a good twenty-five minutes early for her appointment. But that was the trouble with traffic in Oxford — you had to factor in so much time for rush hour that, on the rare occasions when it wasn't as bad as usual, you were left with time on your hands.

And right now, Hillary could have done with just walking into the appointment and getting down to it. Once she knew what she was facing, she'd be able to do something. It was the waiting around in ignorance that she was finding hard to take.

Restlessly, she got out her phone and began to trawl the internet in search of distraction. After a few futile minutes of that, however, her conscience stirred itself and told her that if she had that much time to kill, she could bloody well do something useful with it instead.

For a moment she wracked her brains, going over the Coltrane case, trying to come up with something that she could usefully research. And finally remembered that she'd made a mental note, at some point, to learn more about Saint Anthony, whom Keith Coltrane had so admired.

She typed 'St Anthony' into the search engine, and, as usual, up shot multiple hits that made her eyes cross. For a start, there was more than one St Anthony, but after scrolling through them for a bit, she was confident that the one she wanted was most likely to be St Anthony of Padua.

Born in 1195 in Lisbon, Portugal, he had died at the age of thirty-five, which gave her a tiny mental jolt, as she remembered that Keith Coltrane had been the same age at the time of *his* death. And although life was littered with such peculiar little coincidences, right here and now it struck her as particularly odd that the murdered vicar had lived exactly as many years as the man he'd so admired.

She told herself to knock it off with all this spooky stuff and keep her mind on the work. Determinedly, she continued reading and absorbing the information on offer, all the while trying to ascertain what it could have been about the long-dead saint that had made him such a hit with Keith Coltrane.

A Franciscan preacher and teacher, he was the patron saint of lost or stolen articles. But try as she might, she could see no good reason why that fact should have impressed a twentieth-century vicar. And there'd been nothing in the files about the Reverend having any teaching ambitions. Maybe he'd lost a favourite toy as a kid, and had suffered psychological trauma thereafter?

She gave herself a mental head-slap and ploughed on.

She paid close attention when she typed in 'miracles attributed to St Anthony' hoping to find *something* that would account for Keith's loyalty to his favourite saint, but wasn't sure, after she'd finished browsing, that she'd altogether succeeded.

St Anthony, she was informed, had at one point in his life had his sacred book of psalms stolen by a novice. It had probably been written on slate, the literary part of her brain butted in, and kept bound in some sort of animal skin for safety. She then promptly discarded this interesting but useless snippet of knowledge, and again tried to concentrate.

But her eyes kept lifting from the tiny screen and checking out the closed doors around her. How much longer was she going to be kept waiting? A glance at the clock told her she still had another ten minutes until her appointment. She took a deep breath, then waited for the almost inevitable urge to cough that usually followed such a reckless procedure.

Ironically, now that she was *here*, her lungs were behaving themselves.

With a twitch of her lips, she bent her head once more to her phone, and continued to read.

St Anthony, after saying many prayers for the return of his precious book, was rewarded when the novice returned the book to him, claiming to have heard voices from God urging him to do so. What's more, the novice was so repentant that he re-joined the brotherhood.

Hillary gave a little 'huh' and leaned back in her chair. As a vicar, she supposed she could understand why Keith Coltrane might have found this appealing and satisfying.

Another glance at the clock told her she still had five minutes to go. And doctors, she reminded herself, always seemed to run late.

With a sigh, she ploughed on with her research.

St Anthony was also reputed to be very good at finding missing people.

As she read this, Hillary's lips twitched once more. By the sounds of it, they could have done with him in the Missing Persons unit.

Reaching the end of the information on offer, she began to read about the manner of St Anthony's death.

Along with two other friars, St Anthony had sought retreat to a woodland in Camposampiero, but had died on the return journey back to Padua. Unfortunately for him, he succumbed from something called 'ergotism' in 1231. This was a disease that killed millions during the Middle Ages, and came about from eating rye bread that had been infected with the ergot fungus.

The symptoms of which, she read, were frankly horrifying and included vomiting, muscle pain, itching, numbness and rapid or slow heartbeat. It could then progress to gangrene, vision problems, confusion — including hallucinations — spasms, convulsions and finally death.

The disease was also known as 'St Anthony's Fire' although, confusingly, this seemed to be attributed to a different St Anthony.

By this time, Hillary was heartily wishing that she'd stuck with the magazines on offer on the coffee tables.

She had just switched off her phone with a decisive stab of her finger, when she heard her name being called, and looked up to see a pretty young girl approaching her, saying that the doctor could see her now.

'Wonderful,' Hillary muttered under her breath.

* * *

As Hillary sat down in a comfortable chair, in a pleasant office, opposite a pleasant-faced man who began to speak to her in a soothing professional voice, Max Walker slowed his car to a crawl. He was now less than a quarter of a mile from the rendezvous point, and as he crept along at a snail's pace, he peered carefully to his left and his right.

Eventually his faith in his memory was rewarded by the sight of a large, five-barred metal farm gate, set in the middle of a hawthorn hedge, which in turn was practically growing right up to the edge of the narrow lane.

He grunted in satisfaction that he'd remembered correctly, and pulling over a few yards ahead of it, got out and walked back to the gate. Peering into the field beyond he was relieved to see that it wasn't currently in use for livestock, and with a relatively clear conscience, he unlatched the heavy gate and pulled it out to its full length, which, he was pleased to note, blocked more than a good three-quarters of the narrow lane.

By hunting around a bit, he finally found a large piece of ironstone, which he wedged under the bottom bar of the gate, leaving the lane effectively blocked off to any passing traffic. Anyone approaching it in a car would have no other choice but to get out and move the gate back into its original position.

And given that hardly anyone used these roads, he thought he had a good chance of the barrier remaining in place long enough to give a certain blackmailer a very bad time of it indeed.

Driving on, he turned a few twists and bends in the road until he arrived at his destination. As instructed, he pulled the car to a halt, got out, and walked up to the dead tree mentioned in the letter. It was, as the blackmailer had described, very visible, since its trunk and dead branches had been bleached almost white over the years, so much so that it stood out against the various greens and browns of the surrounding countryside like the proverbial sore thumb. And sure enough, about three feet off the ground, there was a bole on the bare trunk, which itself contained a hollow cavity.

Without so much as even glancing around, he shoved the package of magazine strips into the hollow, got in his car, and drove off. Once he thought he was out of earshot of anyone who might have been watching him from cover, he stopped, did a rather ragged and very tight three-point turn and sat in the car, with the vehicle now facing the way he'd just come.

And once again, his memory of the place had served him well. For in this stretch of the track, the road bent once and then, after just a hundred yards or so, bent back again on itself, giving him a straight view between the gaps in the two bends of the farm gate that he'd just moved. Although it was a fair distance away now, its metal was helpfully shining in the sun, almost as if it was winking at him conspiratorially.

Satisfied, Max then pushed the button which lowered his windows and waited, ears strained for the sound of an approaching car engine. Because, sooner or later, someone would have to collect that package, and to do so, they could only get to — or leave — the site in one of two ways. They might approach on the road behind him — in which case, he'd be blocking their way, giving him a chance of getting their number plate if nothing else. And given the narrowness of the road, the blackmailer would either be forced to reverse back a long way — and in a flaming hurry! — or else risk a hasty turning manoeuvre. And Max had just seen for himself how hard that was on this narrow track. Either option would give him a fair chance of catching the swine before he could make a getaway.

Or else, they would come to the drop-off point from the road ahead — in which case they'd have to get out to move the gate in order to proceed. Allowing Max to race ahead and with luck catch them whilst they were out of their car and on foot.

Of the two options, he was hoping for the latter.

But either way — he'd given himself a fighting chance of getting his hands on the bastard! And woe betide them when he did.

CHAPTER TEN

From her position behind a large sycamore tree, Clara-Jane Coltrane watched through her binoculars as a car approached the conspicuous dead tree and stopped. It was, she knew, Max Walker's car, because she'd made it her business to find out what make and model he drove.

Unluckily for her, however, the tree that had hid her body from *his* view had also hidden from her Max Walker's business with the farm gate, otherwise she might not have been feeling quite so upbeat.

As it was, her heart began to pound in anticipation and excitement. This was it. This was actually, really, happening! And as she watched the man walk to the tree and stuff something inside the hole in the trunk, everything began to feel just a bit weird.

Before, when she'd been putting the plan together, printing off the letters and scouting around and coming across this isolated spot and the dead tree, she'd felt like a character from off the telly. As if she was living in a film or thriller novel or something. It had almost felt playful, like her games of make-believe as a child.

But now it suddenly felt very real. This was not a game. This was her life, and she was watching it change for the better again right before her eyes! All she had to do was keep her head and she was in clover.

Ever cautious, she watched as the car drove away and then listened carefully to the engine slowly fading into total silence.

So he'd knuckled under after all. She had, in her darkest moments, wondered if he'd simply ignore the letters, leaving her standing on her own in the deserted countryside and feeling like an idiot.

But her gamble had paid off!

She tried to push her bike over the ploughed field separating her from the dead tree, but it kept snagging in the ploughed ruts, and eventually she just lifted it and carried it. Luckily she didn't have to carry it far, but she was still puffing a little, and swearing softly under her breath by the time she reached the lane.

Once she had arrived at the dead beech tree, she propped the bike against its pale trunk and reached gingerly into the hole. There was always something atavistic about putting your hand into a cavity created by nature. Your inherited survival genes were always warning you that there might be something nasty lurking inside, with teeth, just ready to take a bite out of you. So she couldn't help but feel a little shiver of unease claw its way up her spine as she put her hand into the darkness, but she needn't have worried. There was no squelching nest of cold slimy slugs for her fingers to delve into, nor a family of spiders getting ready to run, eight-legged, onto her hand and along her arm.

Instead, her questing hand found only the smoothness of the package, which she at once dragged out, her mouth dry in anticipation, her heart going like a jackhammer in her chest.

The package, she quickly realised, was a brown envelope, folded and swathed all about in tape. She wanted to rip it open there and then, and look at all the lovely lolly it contained, but she restrained herself. Time to do that later. Right now, instinct was screaming at her to make herself scarce.

She unzipped her hoodie just enough to stuff the package securely against her breasts, where it felt warm and snug, then zipped the hoodie right up to her chin to make sure there was no chance it could fall out. She then mounted her bike and began to pedal rapidly away.

Very luckily for Clara-Jane, she'd left her own car on one of the many little by-roads which led from the track she was now on, and in the opposite direction from where Max Walker now sat, avidly watching the road.

As she pedalled, she began to laugh.

In his car, Max Walker kept his eyes fixed on the shining metal gate.

It was a bright day, and the leaves were beginning to turn. And for the first time in a long time, the woman on the bicycle felt able to appreciate the small, pleasing things in life — now that she had money to spend again!

So she smiled benevolently on the blue sky and the chirping hedge sparrows, and as she negotiated one of the many bends in the road, she was already mentally spending the money. A trip to the Maldives, first. She needed a break. And then . . .

Ahead of her, a farm gate was blocking the road — or almost all of it; there was, she saw, just a small gap on the far side that she could slip past. Instinctively, though, she hit the brakes, her mind trying to make sense of what she was seeing.

Why the hell was a gate blocking the road?

And then, behind her, in the distance, she could hear the racing approach of a car engine.

And instantly understood.

Adrenalin rushed into her bloodstream, her heart gave a massive lurch, and with a cry of alarm, she shot forward, running her bike wheels almost onto the grass verge as she swept past the small gap between the gate and the hedge on the other side. Her legs pumped up and down as they'd never pumped before, even as a kid, when she'd liked to ride her bike as fast as she could.

Behind her, fast approaching now in his car, Max Walker shouted in outrage as he watched the black-clad, hooded figure on the bicycle dodge around the gate and disappear around the next bend.

When he'd first seen the figure on the push bike approach the gate, he'd almost not realised the significance of it. He'd been so focussed on waiting for a car or van that he hadn't even considered that the blackmailer might use another mode of transport. By the time he'd realised that he was actually witnessing the blackmailer making their getaway, he'd lost a precious few seconds to sheer disbelief, before turning on the ignition and gunning the engine.

He had covered the distance between him and his quarry rapidly enough, but then was forced to brake in order to get out and move the gate out of the way. Ironically, the booby trap that he'd set up so carefully to trap his tormentor was now costing him valuable time! As he kicked out the stone from under the metal grid, he was swearing savagely. Although the irony of it was not lost on him, he wasn't in any mood to appreciate it, and as he tugged the gate away from the road, his head was almost throbbing in frustration and rage.

The only consolation was that he would now soon catch up with the man on the bicycle. For whilst the push bike had enabled him to sweep past the gate without stopping, pedal power over a longer distance was definitely no match for horsepower, and the advantage now lay firmly with Max.

Unfortunately for Max Walker, Clara-Jane, after her initial moments of panicked flight, had also worked that out. And the first thing she'd done was screech to a halt at the first gap in the hedge and drag herself and her bike through it. She'd then abandoned the bike after lying it on the ground out of sight behind the hedge, and using the hedge for cover, made for the copse of trees where she'd left her car on foot.

If she could just reach her car, she'd be safe.

She wasn't aware of it, but she was sobbing with tension and fear as she crouched and ran, and when she heard an engine roaring along the road behind her, she immediately dropped down into a tight ball behind a stand of rust-coloured dock — the only place of concealment nearby. She was panting so hard as Max Walker's car shot ahead of her and disappeared from sight that she was in danger of hyperventilating.

Now free to run hell-for-leather, Clara-Jane did just that, and made it to the copse of trees with only a little time to spare. For, as she dashed along the small deer-path that she'd found on her initial scouting of the area, she heard a car coming back in her direction.

Max, after driving for a few minutes but seeing no sign of a cyclist, had realised what must have happened. And swearing and still raging, had done another messy three-point turn, and was now coming back along the lane, eyes peeled for any signs of where the blackmailer had left to the road and taken to cross-country cycling.

In the trees, Clara-Jane, still sobbing and swearing herself now, ran as fast as she could, ignoring the stitch in her side as she pushed herself on. She could almost have kissed her scruffy, down-market car when she first caught sight of its sad paintwork glinting intermittently in the patchy sunlight filtering through the trees.

She almost fell into the driver's seat, and her hands were shaking so hard she had trouble fitting the key into the ignition. When she did, she had that moment of panic when she wondered if the engine would start. How many times, when watching horror films on the telly, did the heroine try to escape her pursuer and make it to the car, only to find it wouldn't go?

But that was in the films, and when she turned the ignition, her car started as normal. She wasted no time in hitting the road, and took the very first turn she came to.

Max Walker, she knew, would be prowling around the twisting back lanes for some time looking for another vehicle, and she wanted to be long gone!

She took the next turn left, which she knew would bring her out onto the B-road within three miles. She drove too fast and had to keep wiping the tears out of her eyes as she did so, in order to see. Had she met a farmer on a tractor, she'd probably have killed herself, but her luck held.

Every few seconds, she kept obsessively checking her rear-view mirror for the sight of Max's car bearing down on her, but it never appeared.

It was only when she saw traffic streaming left and right beyond a hedgerow in front of her, and knew that the main road was now within sight, that she felt the paralysing grip of fear and tension slowly release her.

She forced herself to sit and wait patiently at the T-junction for a gap in the traffic, then pulled out and drove sensibly away, and at a reasonable speed. And slowly, as she put more and more miles between herself and near disaster, she began to calm down.

But then, without warning, reaction set in, and she had to pull off onto the side, and stagger from her car to be spectacularly sick in a stand of cow parsley.

* * *

As Clara-Jane Coltrane was losing her breakfast, Hillary Greene concentrated on what Mr Kurt Winstanley was telling her.

As a consultant, he was not addressed as Doctor, but this piece of confusing pedantry barely registered with her as he explained the results of her scan.

A man in his early forties, he had a shock of fair hair, pale blue eyes, and was wearing a dark blue suit. He had hands with long, thin, tapering fingers, and Hillary found herself slightly distracted by them as he indicated the image on the screen of his computer.

'As you can see, Mrs Greene, there is a small anomaly just here.' With the tip of a pen, he pointed to a spot on the screen.

When her consultant had first pulled up her results, she'd been able to make out very little of it. She was not a doctor, and had no idea what human lungs looked like, especially when shown as a CT image. To her, she was looking at vaguely amorphous shapes, in various shades of greyish-green, with some obvious features — veins, arteries? — and splotches that stood out.

It was almost impossible to believe she was looking at her own insides. But when Mr Winstanley's pen pointed to a small, solid-looking object, that looked to her to be about the size of a child's marble, she admitted that, even to a lay-person like herself, it didn't look as if it belonged in a human body.

'Your GP notes confirm that there was a rattle in your breathing, and this is the culprit I'm afraid,' Kurt went on.

'Right,' Hillary said flatly, staring at the small round blob of green. So that was the little sod that had been causing her so much aggro. For some reason, she decided then and there that it needed a proper name; for something that had caused her so much turmoil, thinking of it as just 'that green blob' didn't seem adequate somehow. And after a moment of thought, decided to call it Butler.

One of her father's favourite television comedies back in the sixties or early seventies was a programme called *On the Buses* and in it, one of the main characters had a running feud with a bus driver named Butler. And his most famous catchphrase was 'I hate you, Butler!' And for some weird reason, it was this memory that popped into her head as she was staring at the screen.

Telling herself not to be so daft, she glanced away from it and to Kurt Winstanley, and asked, without preamble, 'Is it cancer?'

'I can't say for certain at this point, but I think it unlikely. Your GP notes say that you've never smoked?'

Hillary nodded. 'That's right. So if it *is* cancer, I'm warning you now, I'm going to feel seriously ticked off and short-changed.'

She was not about to let him get away with dodging her question, and the gaze she levelled at him was her best dead-eyed cop stare.

Under it, even the seasoned consultant shifted slightly in his seat, but the next moment, the gentle smile came back into play once more. 'I understand your need for a quick and definitive answer, Mrs Greene, and we're going to do our best to oblige you. And in order to do that, I'm going to arrange for you to have a bronchoscopy. Have you heard of this?'

'Isn't that where you get a tiny camera shoved down your gullet?' Hillary asked, beginning to feel just a little light-headed. Although the idea of undergoing something that sounded so outlandish didn't sit easily with her, she knew that she was going to have to become inured to such things.

Kurt Winstanley's smile widened just a little at this rather warts-and-all — if accurate — description of the pro-cedure and casually turned a page over on her paperwork, in order to remind himself of her personal details. For he was getting the distinct impression that kid gloves were not going to be the best way forward with this particular patient.

When he read that she'd spent her career in the police, retiring at the rank of inspector, he gave a mental nod. That explained a lot.

'Yes, that's basically it,' he let the page fall back on itself, and turned to face her. This time he didn't bother with the soft-soaping smile. 'While we're having a look at what we're dealing with, we'll also take a sample of it.'

'A biopsy?' Hillary clarified.

'Indeed. Now, what a lot of people don't understand is that a CT or MRI scan is so all-embracing, as it were, that it gives us vastly more information than an X-ray. And because it shows up so many tiny anomalies, a vast number of them are irrelevant. Only a very small percentage are malignant.'

Hillary, for a split moment, wondered if she'd heard him correctly. Because cancer was such a well-known condition, and she heard so many times over the years how it affected one in two people, she had assumed, without ever really put-ting it into words, even in her own mind, that she was one of the unlucky ones.

Dorothy took a sip and grimaced. 'Hot.' She stared at her pink biscuit and then scowled. 'I won't let him be taken away. Not right. A vicar. Not right.'

'No, of course it isn't, lovey,' Susan said, with just a small sigh. So Dot was having one of her 'vicar' days then. Often her patients became fixated on one thing. With Mr de la Mare in 'Tulip' it was glass for some reason, and during one of these spells they had to make sure to keep him away from the windows, whilst with poor Miss Golder in 'Lupin' it was leeches. Always convinced she had leeches on her legs.

At least with Dot it was a phantom clergyman lover that occupied her poor, wandering mind. Which, Susan thought with a smile, was a much nicer thing to have on your mind, wasn't it?

She held the cup back up to her lips. 'Nearly finished, Dottie. Just a few more sips,' she encouraged gently. She needed to keep her charges hydrated.

'Hot,' Dot said again, pushing the cup away in disgust.

Susan patted the back of her hand, and then gently removed the unwanted pink wafer from it. She put the sugary treat on a plate and left it on the table beside the chair so that she could have it later.

Then she pushed the tea trolley back to the door and somewhat awkwardly manoeuvred it out. By the time she'd turned back to close the door, she could see that Dot was asleep again.

With a smile, she left her to her dreams and went on to her next resident.

CHAPTER ELEVEN

Hillary arrived back at HQ, pleased to have missed only two hours from the start of her working day. She poked her head around the door of the communal office to say a brief hello, then went on to her stationery cupboard.

She'd barely begun to catch up on the latest news coming in about her case, however, when the phone rang, and she was informed that she had a visitor. It wasn't often they had a member of the public who came to the station unasked, especially when the crime in question was thirty years old.

And she could sense from his tone of voice and manner in which the desk sergeant had summoned her that he was both intrigued and amused by something.

As she walked back up the stairs and into the main lobby, she was therefore on the alert for some kind of joke about to be played on her. Desk sergeants were notorious for their so-called practical jokes and sense of humour, which were usually on a par with that of a precocious five-year-old.

But the moment Hillary saw the man waiting for her in reception, she understood the source of her colleague's amusement. For an elderly man in full and colourful clerical gear looked at her hopefully as she emerged from the depths of the basement and smiled uncertainly. He was in his mid-to-late sixties and had the wispy white hair and slightly myopic mild blue eyes so beloved of characters from a certain type of novel. A P.G. Wodehouse bishop, perhaps, about to visit an ancestral pile, and run foul of Jeeves or Wooster on one of their capers.

Even his voice, as he said, 'Good morning, I'm awfully sorry to call on you unexpectedly like this, but I really *was* just passing,' sounded distinctly upper class, academic and dry as dust.

'This is DI Hillary Greene, sir, the lady you want,' the desk sergeant informed him helpfully and with a definite grin in his voice. Like a lot of the rank and file at the station, he still used her former title, partly out of respect for her, and partly out of sheer laziness. It took too much effort to explain her former DI status — now reduced to civilian consultant — to the general public, and this particular visitor certainly looked less with-it than most.

Now the sergeant watched this meeting of two such divergent characters with a glee that was almost palpable.

'I was on my way to a conference in Oxford, and my conscience simply wouldn't let me pass by without stopping off. I promised the bishop I would, you see,' the newcomer remarked.

Hillary didn't see at all, but she wasn't about to admit it for the further entertainment of the desk sergeant. He was already getting his money's worth as it was. 'Certainly, er, Reverend . . . ?'

'Bulstrode,' the man said happily. 'Right Reverend, actually, not that it matters much. I don't insist on it, because . . . Oh dear, I'm wittering on like this because I'm nervous. I've never been inside a police station before. Shameful, I know, in these modern times, when we churchmen are supposed to be rubbing shoulders with criminals every day and getting our hands dirty and all that. But I've always been more of an administrator than a robust soldier of Christ.'

By now the desk sergeant was openly grinning, and Hillary was careful not to catch his eye, because she knew she'd only start grinning too. 'Is there something I can do for you, Reverend?' she asked firmly, lest he carry on confessing to the inadequacies of his CV.

'Oh yes. That is, I hope *I* can be of service to *you*. I'm here on the behalf of the bishop; well, former bishop — he's in his nineties now, but although he can't get out and about, he's still as sharp as a tack up here.' Here the Rt. Rev. Bulstrode tapped his forehead significantly with a bony finger. 'And when I told him yesterday that I was coming out this way today, he made me promise to come in and talk to you about poor Keith Coltrane.'

At this, Hillary instantly came to attention. 'In that case, Reverend, please follow me,' she said, with a business-like smile. With a bit of luck, if she could set the tone as being a bit brisker and more formal, she might be able to steer her potential witness into keeping to the point.

She indicated the top of the stairs, and as the clergyman passed by her, Hillary half-turned and gave the desk sergeant a quick and cheeky two-fingered salute which had him shouting with laughter.

The Rt. Rev. Bulstrode looked vaguely back over his shoulder at this sudden and unexpected snorting sound, but already the desk sergeant had his head well down over his computer, though his shoulders were shaking suspiciously.

As she led her unexpected visitor down the thankfully wide and shallow steps, she was mentally reviewing her options. It simply wouldn't be possible to interview the man in her stationery cupboard. They'd practically have to sit in each other's laps, and she wasn't sure the old boy could stand the strain. Whichever way they went about it!

And he might find it a bit overwhelming in the communal office. He didn't strike her as the type who'd find the face of modern policing particularly agreeable or even interesting.

So it was that at the bottom of the steps, she turned firmly towards her superintendent's quieter and more spacious office, and tapped on the door, barely pausing to wait for a summons before opening it.

Rollo Sale looked up, smiled, and opened his mouth to speak, then closed it again abruptly as he saw the man entering behind her. Dressed as one of his visitors was, in purple robes and other miscellaneous and rather splendid ecclesiastical regalia, it was not surprising that Rollo Sale felt his jaw drop just a little.

Seeing his consternation, the Reverend Bulstrode became flustered once more. 'I'm sorry to interrupt everyone when they must be so busy. And please forgive . . . er,' he indicated his attire with an apologetic gesture of his hand. 'I don't usually come out dressed like this, but as I was saying to Inspector Greene just now, I'm on my way to an ecclesiastical conference at Oxford, and you do rather have to keep up appearances in such circumstances, don't you?'

'Er, yes, I'm sure you do,' the superintendent agreed, though in fact, he'd never attended an Oxford ecclesiastical conference in his life.

Hillary took pity on her boss, and said succinctly, 'The Right Reverend Bulstrode was asked by his bishop to stop by and discuss the Keith Coltrane case with us, sir. And I thought,' she glanced around the more spacious office tellingly, 'that the Reverend might be more comfortable in here than in an interview room.'

Instantly, the superintendent caught her drift. 'Ah yes, quite right,' he said, rising urbanely. 'Would you care to take a seat, Reverend?' The super's office, apart from his desk and chair, contained two more comfortable chairs and a low coffee table, both of which were practically never used.

Hillary ushered their visitor to one such chair and took the other herself, knowing that Rollo would prefer to watch and listen from his desk, rather than take an active part in proceedings.

'Well, sir, what can we do for you?' Hillary asked, taking out an ever-present notebook and small pen from her jacket pocket and looking at him expectantly.

'Oh yes, right.' The clergyman tried to look efficient and composed and failed charmingly. 'Well, you see David

— that's the bishop — was Keith's mentor, I suppose you'd say, as well as his bishop. He got to know the poor man quite well. I was abroad at the time of the terrible events that befell poor Keith, but I *did* meet up with David a year or so afterwards, and I could tell that the tragedy had hit him hard.'

'Not surprising, Reverend,' Hillary said quietly. 'It must have come as an enormous shock to him.'

'Oh yes, absolutely. To us all, naturally, in the Church. And Keith was such a lovely chap too,' Reverend Bulstrode said sadly. 'Even though I didn't know him anywhere near as well as David, he always struck me as being very *genuine* you know. A properly *spiritual* man, as well as a practical and kind one. He was just the kind of cleric that the Church needs, but . . . well . . .' he shrugged helplessly. 'I'm afraid they are few and far between. And getting even rarer nowadays.'

Hillary, who could only guess at how unpopular theology had to be as a career choice, could sympathise.

'And the bishop urged you to come here today . . . ?' she coaxed.

'Yes, that's right. He'd read online that the police were looking into Keith's case again. Despite his age, David loves computers — he's very competent with them. Marvellous, really . . . Er, yes, sorry, I must keep to the point,' he said, making Hillary aware that she hadn't concealed her growing impatience and frustration as well as she'd thought. 'The bishop will be upset with me if I don't carry out his instructions properly.'

Over at his desk, Rollo Sale, like the desk sergeant one floor above him, was beginning to feel the urge to grin. Already he was forming a mental image of a ninety-year-old, but up-to-date powerhouse of a man, patiently schooling one of his less-gifted colleagues on his appointed mission.

Hillary, however, was keeping her eye more firmly on the prize and refusing to let her winsome witness get the better of her. 'And what were his instructions, sir?'

'He wanted to make sure that you were . . . oh, what were his words. Oh yes, "not setting off down the wrong path". The bishop, you see, for all that he is definitely — oh most definitely — a man of God, has always been, er, well aware of the failings of humanity. That is . . .'

But Hillary, who'd now got the measure of her man, wasn't about to let the Rt. Rev. get into his meandering stride. 'I think I know what you're trying to say, sir,' she interrupted him gently but firmly. 'Would I be right in thinking that the bishop, although very Christian in his ways, isn't the kind of man to have the wool pulled easily over his eyes? And can sum someone up on first acquaintance, and rarely get it wrong?'

'Yes, that's it exactly!' he beamed at her, as if she were a particularly bright student. 'David understands people, you see, warts and all. So, although he loves the sinner, he's never blind to their sins.'

'Quite. So what was it that he wanted you to tell us?' she prompted.

'Well, after Keith was killed, there was a lot of sensational speculation in the press, as you can imagine, as well as a lot of gossip amongst Keith's parishioners. And whilst the bishop put a stop to the village gossip, there was little he could do about the gutter press. Disgraceful behaviour they showed.' The clergyman tut-tutted disapprovingly.

Hillary cleared her throat, but luckily didn't start coughing. 'Yes, I've read some of the headlines of the day. They seemed to imply that the Reverend Coltrane might have been a bit of a ladies' man,' she said blandly, carefully choosing her words.

'Yes! That's just it,' the Reverend said, nodding emphatically. 'And that's what concerned David so much. Because the reporters kept hearing these stories about how all the village women seemed keen on him — especially that woman who made such a fuss of him that her husband ended up divorcing her. Oh dear, such a mess that was! Well, the stories that circulated seemed to take it for granted that poor Keith was some sort of Casanova. I believe "Casanova in a Cassock" or something equally hideous was one headline in a particularly nasty little Sunday shocker.'

'Yes, I wouldn't be surprised,' Hillary agreed dryly. 'Well, I'm afraid that's just how the press works.'

'Oh yes, but David was particularly incensed by it because it was so *untrue*. That's what he asked me to convey to you. He said he didn't want a second investigation being hampered by false trails,' the clergyman said, beginning to look a little flustered. His eyes swept to the superintendent, who looked at him benignly, then back to the rather handsome woman who'd greeted him in the foyer. 'David can be a little forthright you see, especially now that he's officially retired, and he was a little scathing, I'm afraid, that nobody was ever charged with Keith's murder.'

'I can understand that, sir,' Hillary said. 'And we aim to rectify that if we possibly can. So, do I take it that Dav . . . your bishop isn't convinced by the common opinion at the time, that the murder of the Reverend Coltrane was due to the actions of either a jealous lover, or the jealous husband of a lover?'

'Yes, exactly that,' he beamed approvingly, pleased, yet again, by her perspicacity. 'He said I was to tell you that, for all that the Reverend Coltrane was a good-looking and relatively young and unmarried man, he did absolutely nothing at all to encourage the village women in their, er, perhaps somewhat unseemly devotion to him. And,' here the clergyman suddenly leaned forward earnestly, 'I do hope you understand this when I say that the bishop is not a man to be wrong in his assessment of people. If he said Keith Coltrane wasn't a ladies' man, my dear inspector, I can absolutely assure you that he's right in what he says.'

* * *

'So what do you make of it?' Claire asked ten minutes later. Hillary, after gleaning all the second-hand information about their murder victim that she'd been able to from her unexpected visitor, had respectfully shown him out and seen him safely ensconced in his car, before reporting back to her team.

Now she sat in the communal office, sipping coffee and nibbling on one of Claire's home-made brownies, and frowned thoughtfully.

Behind his own desk, Gareth, typically, was keeping silent, but was watching and listening to the two women talk. Since they had decades of combined experience between them, he found it fascinating.

'I'm not sure,' Hillary said.

'Well, first off, you have to allow for them all sticking together,' Claire said cynically, and Hillary immediately nodded in agreement.

'Oh yes. Especially given the recent scandals surrounding the various churches recently, you'd expect them to close ranks. And I can see this retired bishop wanting to try and control things, if possible. And no doubt, damage limitation would be his first priority.'

'Can I hear a "but" coming, guv?' Claire asked, cocking her head slightly to one side, whilst simultaneously dunking her brownie into her tar-like tea.

Hillary shuddered at the rather unappetising sight, and then shrugged. 'Just because the wily bishop might have an agenda of his own, doesn't mean to say that he's wrong about his assessment of our victim. And our visitor's blind faith in his bishop's ability never to be fooled by the wily antics of humanity might well be justified. I've met churchmen like the Right Reverend Bulstrode before, who seem to live totally sheltered lives and have no idea about human nature; and I've also met some who are even more cynical about the depths it can plunge to than I am.'

Claire snorted in disbelief over this, then thoughtfully chewed on her soggy brownie for a moment, before finally nodding. 'It's the confessions that do it, I shouldn't wonder,' she opined. 'They probably hear more hair-raising stuff than we do. Does it get us any further forward though? Let's say, for argument's sake, that all that "randy rev" stuff really was just so much journalistic eyewash to sell papers—'

'And don't forget, so far, we haven't come across any real proof in the case files that suggested otherwise,' Hillary interrupted her to point out. 'And in my experience of village life, if there *had* been anything going on, somebody in that village would have seen something, or heard something, and would have been only too happy to dish the dirt, either to the police or to sell it to one of the journalists.'

'OK. So say he really was squeaky clean and not a ladies' man,' Claire conceded amiably, 'doesn't that set us back, rather than get us further forward? It certainly reduces our suspect list. I mean, if his murder can't be put down to lust or debauchery, what are we left with? He wasn't personally robbed, neither was the church building itself. His financials were normal — he didn't have any undetected gambling debts or what have you. Are we really left with a chance encounter with some passing maniac, or a random visitor to the church with a grudge against clerics in general?'

Hillary shook her head. 'No. It *feels* personal; I think the motive is emotional all right. I'm just not convinced we're looking at it from the right angle, that's all.'

'So we're left with the sister then,' Claire said, somewhat resigned. 'Perhaps DI Keating had it right, and we just can't pin it on her.'

'We were always going to have to go back and reinterview her anyway,' Hillary mused. 'There was something she said in her initial interview that I've been chewing on for some time now.'

'There was?' Claire said, surprised. From her memory of the interview with Moira Coltrane, the woman had practically said nothing at all.

'Hmmm. It may be something. Then again, it might be nothing at all.' As Hillary finished delivering this rather unhelpful observation, she felt a familiar feeling in her sternum, and quickly stood up. 'Right, well, I have to be getting on,' she said abruptly. 'Keep me updated,' she added unnecessarily, and headed quickly out of the door.

As she moved off down the corridor towards her own so-called office, they could clearly hear her coughing all the way.

Gareth and Claire looked at one another, and then without a word, went back to their various research projects.

* * *

It seemed to be a day for out-of-the-blue communications, for back at her desk, Hillary found a note in her mail.

Like Anthea Ramsey's blackmail note, it was printed, anonymous, and to the point — but unlike the blackmail notes, was very different in content.

As she read it, Hillary's eyebrows rose.

You need to talk to Max Walker again. He's in danger.

She immediately checked the envelope the letter came in and saw that it was addressed to her by name. The envelope was probably a total non-starter, having gone through the sorting office of Royal Mail, but she nonetheless reached for an evidence bag and slipped it inside. She then put the letter itself in a second evidence bag.

'Well, well,' Hillary muttered out loud, then took both pieces of evidence through to the communal office. Having not long left it, both Claire and Gareth looked at her in some surprise.

'We're getting anonymous tip-offs now,' she said, waving the bits of paper in the air. 'Apparently, we need to go and reinterview Max Walker.'

She laid the see-through plastic bags on Gareth's desk, and beckoned Claire over. The message was so short, Gareth had read it before Claire arrived, and he turned it to face her for easier reading.

Claire gave a low whistle. And then, 'A crank, guv?' She knew, as well as Hillary, that any mention of an investigation in the papers brought out the cranks, pranksters and publicity hounds.

'Chances are,' Hillary agreed dryly. 'Then again, maybe not. It was posted locally. And I think I know who by.'

Claire, who hadn't gone with Hillary on the initial Max Walker interview, looked at Gareth.

He thought for a moment and then said, 'You think it's from Mrs Walker, ma'am?'

Hillary nodded. 'I think it's from Mrs Walker,' she repeated. She glanced at Claire, then at Gareth. Protocol said it would make more sense to take Gareth with her, since he'd been in on the initial interview. But Hillary didn't always blindly follow protocol.

'Claire, I think you should come with me to the Walker residence. I want a second opinion on our Mr Walker. Gareth, at some point I want to talk to Moira Coltrane again, and I want *you* to come with me on that. This way, both of you get a look at our suspects, and will have a better overall feel for our case so far.'

'Guv,' Claire said happily, already heading back to her desk to collect her coat and bag. Although she was long past the age when chasing around the streets was something to look forward to, sometimes you could have too much of a nice, safe and warm office.

Gareth watched the two women go and wondered what they'd come back with.

* * *

Sandy Walker didn't look surprised to see Hillary on her doorstep when she opened the door to her half an hour or so later, but she did glance at Claire with interest.

Hillary introduced her colleague.

'You want to see Max?' Sandy said. 'You're in luck. He's in. Shall I show you through to the study?'

'In a moment, Mrs Walker,' Hillary restrained her gently by putting a hand on her arm as the woman made to move away. 'First, I'd like to ask you why you think your husband is in danger.'

158

For a moment, Hillary thought Sandy was going to deny it and ask her what she was talking about. Indeed, she could almost see the words forming on her lips. But then the other woman paused, reconsidered, and sighed softly, her shoulders slumping a little as she gave their visitors a rather sheepish smile.

'You *did* write us a note saying as much, yes?' Hillary prompted, careful to keep her voice mild and non-judgemental.

'Yes. Sorry. I suppose I should have owned up to it and just called you but . . .' She shrugged helplessly. 'I don't know. I didn't want Max to get the idea I was spying on him. It felt easier, somehow, hiding behind anonymity. Less disloyal for some reason. You won't tell him what I did, will you?'

Hillary shook her head. 'Not if you tell me what it's all about, no,' she promised.

'That's just it — I'm not sure that I can really. It's a feeling, that's all. It's all so . . . vague. Nebulous, that's the word I'm looking for. It's not one thing, it's a whole series of little things.'

Hillary nodded at Claire to get out her notebook. 'Why don't you just tell us, in your own words and as best you can, what's worrying you, Mrs Walker?' she advised gently.

And so Sandy did. She recounted the tale of the plain white envelope, the cut-up-magazines, the unexpected withdrawal of money from their account, and how her husband had left the house yesterday looking excited, and then came back again, but in a very different state of mind, being both angry and withdrawn for the rest of the day.

'I know it doesn't sound much, but I've always known how Max was feeling and more often than not, what he was thinking,' Sandy concluded, looking from one to the other, 'and I just know something's up. Seriously up, I mean.'

Hillary, who by now could take a pretty good guess as to what was up, nodded at her reassuringly. 'Don't worry, Mrs Walker, we'll get to the bottom of it. Now, you said your husband is at home?'

He was, and Sandy showed them into his study with alacrity, then made herself scarce.

Once in the study, Claire regarded Max Walker with interest — a big, good-looking man, she thought that he appeared both surprised and uneasy to see them. He rose slowly, looking from Hillary to Claire as Hillary introduced her colleague, then, after a momentary hesitation, waved to the chairs in front of his desk.

'Please, sit down,' he said, trying to sound hospitable, when he clearly felt no such thing. 'I have to say, though, I'm a little surprised to see you back again so soon. I don't think there's anything more I can tell you about the old days. I really haven't thought about Keith or the murder for years. So . . .' He shrugged his wide shoulders and grinned apologetically. The grin did little to hide his impatience, though, which made Hillary all the more determined to take her time.

She sat down slowly, and made sure she was comfortable, prayed she wouldn't have a coughing fit, and eyed him curiously. It didn't take her long to come to a decision as to how to play this. Big, hearty men, if you let them, had a tendency to bluff, and then dig their heels in stubbornly when called out on it. What's more, if they were given the chance to let their egos come to their rescue when challenged, they could become downright belligerent.

Best, she thought, to take the wind out of his sails right away and give him no time to think, let alone to bluster.

'We know that, since the Keith Coltrane case has become active again, a blackmailer has been at work. And we know, too, that you've been contacted. And we know that yesterday you paid out £10,000 in blackmail money. Do you still have the original demands, Mr Walker?'

'What? Like hell I paid out ten grand!' Max said, his face flushing instantly in anger. 'No way would I ever let that lowlife. . .' And as suddenly as the colour had come into his face it now drained away, as he realised his mistake.

Hillary smiled at him amiably. 'No, sir, I rather thought you might not have done. You made up a parcel of old magazine cuttings then?'

Max Walker stared at her as if she was a magician. 'How the hell did you know that?' he demanded.

Mindful of her promise not to give away his wife, she shrugged. 'It's what people do, sir. They watch too much television, in my opinion. So, do you still have the original blackmail note?' she repeated, this time allowing a slight impatience to show in her tone and look.

For a moment, Max wavered, temped to lie and say that he'd burned it. But something in the stare from this woman's unwavering, sherry-coloured eyes made him pause. He looked at the other woman, who seemed to be waiting for him to speak, pen poised over her notebook, appearing vaguely bored by it all. A successful and good-looking man, Max was used to female approbation, and now he was beginning to feel uneasily like a child having been caught out doing something naughty by his mother.

Suddenly feeling ridiculous, he slumped back in his chair, opened a drawer and grumpily withdrew two envelopes. Wordlessly, Hillary retrieved another evidence bag from her case and got up, opened it out, and held it over the desk, nodding at him to drop the notes within.

Which he did, albeit with an exaggerated sigh.

'Now, sir,' she began crisply. 'I'd like you to tell us exactly what happened when you dropped off the false blackmail payment. Shall we begin with where the drop-off point was?'

Max gave his best nonchalant shrug. 'It was in the middle of nowhere. Really, I mean it, well out in the sticks. You think this village is isolated,' he waved a vague hand at the rural vista outside his window, 'but this was on another level. A network of barely maintained back roads and farmland, without even a sheep in sight.'

Hillary sighed. 'Directions, sir.'

'They're in the second note, see for yourself,' Max growled.

Hillary sighed again. 'What happened? In detail, please, sir.'

Max shrugged, beginning to feel seriously nettled now. No way was he going to admit to making a fool of himself in front of these two women.

'I drove to this dead tree, put the stash of papers inside, and drove off chortling. What else?'

Hillary looked at him, then slowly looked across at Claire. Sensing the movement in her peripheral vision, Claire returned the gaze, saw one of her eyebrows rise, and caught on at once.

Obligingly, Claire let out a slow sigh, shook her head gently, and glanced back at her notebook.

Hillary sighed yet again, and turned back to Max, who was now flushing angrily.

'You waited to see who would pick up the false payment,' Hillary corrected him. 'Why else would you bother to leave it at all, unless you hoped to catch sight of who was blackmailing you?' Then she held up a hand as he made to speak. 'Please, Mr Walker, I'm really not in the mood for lies and playing games right now. Just tell me what happened. Did you see who picked it up?'

'No, I bloody well didn't,' Max snapped, his failure to capture the blackmailer still a very raw and sensitive subject. 'And I didn't wait around,' he lied. 'I only left the fake money because it amused me. I wanted the bastard to think he was rolling in it, and have all the excitement of picking it up, only to find magazine cuttings. That'll teach the swine to try and put the bite on me.'

His chin came up as he stared at her challengingly. And that, Hillary knew, was all he would say. To her, at least.

Unwilling to waste her breath — or try her patience even further — Hillary rose. 'Very well, sir,' she said, catching Claire a little by surprise, and making her scramble to finish her notes and put her notebook and pen away.

'However,' Hillary added quietly, the moment a look of smug satisfaction crossed his face, 'I feel I should warn you now that I'll be informing my superintendent of these latest developments, and he'll appoint an acting police officer to your case. As you know, I'm a civilian consultant reviewing Keith Coltrane's murder. But an *active* case is something quite different. You can expect a visit from a fully-fledged police officer shortly, and if you refuse to answer his or her questions thoroughly, it's very likely that you will find yourself facing a charge of obstruction, at the very least. So unless you're willing to face a court of law, Mr Walker, I suggest you think long and hard about things. And prepare to be more cooperative.'

At this, both women had the satisfaction of seeing the smile wiped off his face.

'Good day, sir,' Claire said sweetly as Hillary swept out of the room.

Outside, and back inside Claire's car, Hillary did up her seat belt and gave a small grunt. 'So, what do you think?'

'I think he had a go at trying to catch the blackmailer and ballsed it up, guv. He's just the sort to have a go at something like that.'

Hillary nodded. 'Hmmm. That's not the most interesting thing, though, is it?'

Claire blinked. 'Not sure I'm following you, guv.'

'Well, he received a blackmail note, threatening to tell us, the law, that he was in the frame for Keith's murder, unless he pays up.'

'But he has too much ego to pay,' Claire said, still at sea.

'Yes. But what if he *had* killed Keith all those years ago? Do you think he'd still be so keen not to pay up then, and risk a potential witness telling us what they heard or saw?'

Claire slowly nodded. 'I get it. Yes, that might be the one thing that would give him second thoughts. He'd have a lot to lose, wouldn't he, being banged up for murder? The business, the pretty wife. All this,' she indicated the handsome barn conversion and surrounding bucolic loveliness. 'Yes, it would take real guts to take the risk. So, what, you don't like him for the killer then, guv?'

Hillary gave a wry smile. 'Hold on, I wouldn't go quite *that* far,' she said. 'Let's just say I'm putting him towards the bottom of my list.'

Claire started the car, then frowned. 'By that logic, are you ruling out Anthea then? She had a blackmail letter too, and didn't pay out on it. Instead she came to us.'

'Ah, no,' Hillary said. 'Anthea has a very different personality from our Mr Walker.'

'Now that's an understatement, guv,' Claire grinned. 'She's bats, if you ask me.'

Hillary grinned. 'Hmmm. I certainly think she might have killed Keith in some sort of fit of passion, and still feel fearless about defying a blackmailer all these years later. For a start, I have a feeling that she's enjoying being back in the limelight. And I'm not sure that her thought processes are particularly logical, let alone self-serving. On the other hand, she might be as cunning and calculating as a fox who's read Machiavelli. It'll be interesting to see what the officer put in charge of the blackmail case makes of her.'

'Won't it just?' Claire gurgled happily.

CHAPTER TWELVE

Back at the police station, Hillary Greene went straight to Rollo Sale to brief him on the latest developments. He'd need to inform whoever had been given the Anthea Ramsey blackmail case that they now had another victim on their hands.

And for another thing, she needed to tell him she wouldn't be in to work tomorrow.

He listened to her report with interest and confirmed that he'd have a word with 'them upstairs', just to make sure that his team would get first dibs on questioning the blackmailer once he or she was caught. If the culprit really did have information about Keith Coltrane's murder they needed to know sooner rather than later.

When she told him that she needed tomorrow off, he gave it to her without asking for any explanation, for which she was grateful, and then asked her what she intended to do next.

Hillary glanced at her watch and nodded to herself. Yes, she had time. 'I'm going to take Gareth with me and speak to Moira Coltrane again. And this time, she'd better be a bit more forthcoming.'

Rollo smiled. 'Oh, I'm sure you can persuade her,' he said. But after she'd left, he sat looking at the closed door for some moments, a worried frown on his face.

He literally couldn't remember when Hillary Greene had ever taken a day off in the middle of a case — especially one that now had an active, concurrent case running alongside it.

And he didn't like it. It just felt so ominously wrong.

* * *

This time, there was no nosy neighbour on watch when Hillary and Gareth arrived at Moira's flat.

In deference to Gareth's limp, they'd again taken the lift, and she could feel the mustiness of its interior catch the back of her throat. Which meant that she wasn't particularly surprised that she began to cough as she tapped on the door to the flat.

She muttered under her breath something that Gareth couldn't quite catch, but which sounded to him as if she was telling off a Butler.

Which couldn't be right, could it?

As the door opened, Hillary, with an effort of will, fought the urge to keep on coughing, and Gareth, sensing her difficulty, quickly held out his ID and introduced himself, giving her time to recover.

Keith's sister merely glared at him with disgust. 'You lot back again?'

'We have more questions, Miss Coltrane, now that we've had some time to look more deeply into Keith's case,' he said. 'May we come in?'

Moira smiled sourly. 'No point in saying no to you lot is there? Sure, come in, but don't expect a cup of anything. With prices nowadays like they are, I can't afford to waste a tea bag on the likes of you.'

With this less than gracious offer ringing in their ears, they followed Moira into the flat. Gareth noticed her eyeing his limp and damaged hand with a frown of puzzlement. Used, as she was, to dealing with physically fit and serving police officers, she was probably nonplussed by him, and he was relieved when she couldn't even be bothered to comment. Or jeer.

Hillary watched as she slumped down in the same chair that she had favoured before and eyed them warily.

'So, what is it? I told you last time, I've nothing to say about what happened to Keith. I didn't know anything about it when it happened, and I don't now.'

Her hard gaze went from Hillary to the young man, and back to Hillary. 'Well, whaddya want?'

'We've been learning more about your brother since we last spoke, Miss Coltrane,' Hillary began, 'and I wanted to know if your remembrances of your brother fit in with what we've been hearing.'

'Oh yeah? Been hearing what a saint he was from all his adoring *flock* have you?' she sneered.

'We've been hearing from the people who knew him best that for all his popularity with the women of his parishes, Keith himself was not a ladies' man. Do you agree with that assessment?'

Hillary wasn't actually interested in her answer, so much as she wanted to break down her resistance to talking at all, and this was as good a way of going about it as any.

'He was a poof, you mean?' Moira snorted. 'Well, somebody's given you a bum steer there,' she said, then laughed at what she perceived to be her own unintentional wit. 'Bum steer. Get it?'

Hillary smiled obligingly. 'He wasn't gay then?' So far, they'd heard nothing to suggest that he was, but she found it interesting that that was the immediate interpretation the dead man's sister had given to her phrase 'not a ladies' man'.

'No, not our Keith. He liked being admired by women right enough,' Moira said. 'He knew he was good-looking, and he got off on all this holier-than-thou stuff.' She shrugged. 'Takes all sorts, don't it?'

'But according to everyone we spoke to, your brother didn't take advantage of his good looks. That is, we can find no one who believes he encouraged his female fan club, as it were,' Hillary continued. 'Was he celibate then, do you think?'

'Celi-what?' Moira asked suspiciously.

'Being a vicar, he wasn't supposed to have sex outside of the marriage vows,' Hillary helped her out.

At this, Moira snorted with laughter. Then, slowly, a more thoughtful look came over her face. 'You know, now that you mention it, that wouldn't altogether surprise me. It's the sort of thing the daft sod would go and do.'

Hillary nodded. 'Did you ever see your brother in a compromising situation with one of his parishioners, Moira? After all, by your own admission, you used to dump your children on him. Or perhaps one of them might have mentioned seeing him doing something he shouldn't? Kids see and understand a lot more than people think, don't they?'

Moira snorted with laughter. 'Ain't that the truth? But no, I never caught my brother shagging anyone. Happy?'

Hillary thought she could detect the sound of something gleeful or knowing in Moira's voice and decided that now was as good a time as any to expand on what it was that Moira had said, in passing, in their initial interview. Although she had said very little, one thing had stayed with Hillary all this time, and kept nagging away at her, in the back of her mind.

'When we spoke before,' Hillary began, careful to keep it casual, 'you said that your brother was a hypocrite. But now you seem to be saying that you agree he wasn't the type to sleep around. So how was he a hypocrite exactly?'

Moira shot her a dirty look. 'Piss off.'

Hillary smiled. For all her supposed hatred of her brother, could she detect a hint of defensiveness here? A reluctance to speak ill of him? Maybe even to defend him?

She made a show of looking thoughtful. 'Well, let's see. If he wasn't sleeping around himself, then his disapproval of your own sex life couldn't have been the cause of your anger with him. What else . . .' She cocked her head and then nodded. 'It had to be the drink or drugs then, right? He was always trying to get you into rehab and off the illegal

168

substances. Did you catch him indulging in something himself? Drunk as a lord, was he? Or smoking pot maybe?'

'No he wasn't! He was off his head on something though,' Moira said in an eruption of anger and self-righteousness.

Gareth's head shot up from monitoring his recording device at this, and glanced at Hillary quickly, to find her regarding their witness with an unperturbed expression.

'When was this?' Hillary asked calmly.

Moira, sulking a little at having failed to shock her, shrugged impatiently. 'How the hell should I know? It was over thirty years ago for pity's sake!' she huffed. 'It was just one afternoon — in the summer I think. I had this girlfriend who fancied him from afar, and she often used to offer to drive me over there to pick up Clara-Jane so that she could moon over him. But this one time we found this kid in the vicarage garden with my brother, both off their heads and seeing fairies or something.'

'This kid,' Hillary asked, interrupting her. 'Did you recognise him?' She didn't usually like to stop her witnesses mid-flow, but this was vital.

'Nah. Only as someone I'd seen around the village like.'

'How old was he?'

'Maybe seventeen or eighteen. Quite good-looking.'

'Can you describe him?'

'Oh piss off, how can I remember someone I saw once, thirty or more years ago?' Moira scoffed.

'You thought he was good-looking though?'

'Yeah, so what? Tall dark and handsome then! Anyway, my friend asked if we could have some of the good stuff too, but the kid scarpered. I think he was scared we'd grass him up. As bloody if! And when I pressed my saintly brother to share whatever it was he was on, he pretended not to know what I was talking about.' Moira shrugged. 'Selfish sod,' she said bitterly. 'I can tell you, after that, whenever he suggested rehab I gave him the finger, good and proper.' She paused, then frowned. 'Funny thing is, the bastard kept right on denying it had ever happened. Didn't fit in with his own fantasy of him being the supreme goody-two-shoes or something, I suppose.'

Hillary nodded. 'You're sure he was high on something?'

Moira shot her a look. 'Oh *please*. You don't think *I* would be able to tell?'

'What do you think it was? Pills . . . or LSD maybe?'

But now that they were getting into the nitty gritty of it, Moira's bounty was fast running out. And with the realisation that she was, in fact, now 'grassing' on her brother, her belligerence returned. 'Oh, piss off — how many times do you need telling? I don't talk to you lot, and certainly not about drugs. 'Sides, you can hardly run him in for possession, can you?' she jeered.

She waved angrily at the door. 'Go on, piss off, *now!*' she shouted, making as if to rise from the chair and physically turf them out, and Hillary nodded at Gareth and rose from her chair.

Moira watched him use his stick to lever himself up and then limp to the door. She was just about to say something she no doubt thought would be pithy — some comment about how useless he'd been to Hillary, maybe he'd been in a fight or something — but then she caught Hillary's glare just in time.

She smirked and shrugged, but wisely kept silent.

Hillary nodded at her and followed her colleague out.

Once back at HQ, Hillary told him to type up the report for the murder book, and then filled in Claire on Moira's latest revelations.

Claire listened, her eyes widening slightly as the information became more and more juicy. 'So he wasn't a ladies' man, but he *was* into good-looking teenage boys and drugs? Well, well, now we're into something! That opens up the investigation and no mistake,' she said with satisfaction.

Hillary leaned against the doorframe and frowned. 'Ye-es,' she agreed slowly.

Claire shot her a surprised look. 'Why so cautious, guv? Where there's drugs involved, you've got money and dealers in the mix, and where good-looking teenage boys are involved, you've got paedophiles and avenging parents and who the hell knows what else. If DI Keating had known about this, he'd have been on it like a greyhound on a rabbit.'

Hillary nodded. 'I'm not disagreeing with you. I'm just not totally sure that we've got the whole picture yet, that's all. And bear in mind the source. Moira isn't the most reliable witness, plus she has a king-sized grudge against her brother. For all we know, she could just be having fun with us — telling lies to mess up our investigation out of spite, whilst at the same time getting some revenge by ruining her saintly brother's reputation.'

'Hmmm,' Claire conceded. 'So we ignore it then?'

'Hell no!' Hillary said, shocked. 'I want you to find out the names of all the good-looking male teenagers in the village at the time of the murder. There can't have been that many in such a small village. Then track down their current whereabouts. I'll be wanting a word with them. Also, contact any of the locals who were around at the time and see if they can remember if our victim was close with any particular youngster — especially a good-looking teenage boy.'

Claire grinned. 'A brand-new suspect! Just what the doctor ordered.'

At the mention of the word doctor, Hillary's mood deflated, and she abruptly informed them that she wouldn't be in tomorrow and left them to it.

Back in her office, she buried herself in work, and tried not to watch the clock ticking away. But eventually five o'clock rolled around, and she reluctantly shut down her computer and made her way into the car park.

* * *

Bright and early the next day, Sergeant Janet Stebbings made her way not to the top floor, where her usual desk awaited, but across the lobby and down the steps into the basement area.

Before clocking off last night, her boss had ordered her to report to CRT first thing for a briefing and an update from Detective Superintendent Roland Sale. She thought she had a good idea why her presence was really required though. The head of the CRT wanted to assert some rights over *her* new and current case, and Janet wasn't sure how she felt about that.

Although she didn't know the superintendent, she'd asked around about him and discovered he had a reputation as a fair if undistinguished officer, awaiting retirement in his basement department. No doubt supervising the reinvestigation of old and dusty cases was a worthy job, but it wasn't something that Janet had much interest in.

Promotion came with the solving of high-profile and immediate crimes, and she'd been chuffed to be handed the Anthea Ramsey blackmail case as SIO. She hadn't been able to take the reins on many cases so far, and was determined to guard this one like a tigress would her newborn cub.

Although she was prepared to be polite and respectful with such a senior — if rather unimportant — officer, she intended to be firm and stand her ground. She was not going to allow any unwarranted interference in her case even if the station-house legend that was ex-DI Hillary Greene *was* involved in the cold case that had brought to light *her* blackmail scheme.

Janet had transferred to Thames Valley from Kent when she'd passed her sergeants' exams, and the first opening for a new sergeant had come up in this area. It hadn't taken her long to settle into her new county, home and job, and naturally, she'd made it her business to learn all the station gossip and folklore along the way.

She knew all about Hillary Greene. The medal for bravery, the great solve rate when she was an active DI, the dead, bent former husband. And, most intriguingly of all, her odd, not-totally-understood working relationship with Commander Marcus Donleavy.

And although she felt a young officer's respect for an old-timer's undoubted achievements — and as a female officer was well aware that she owed a lot to women trail-blazers like DI Greene — nonetheless, she was determined not to let herself feel overwhelmed by her.

As she descended into the bowels of the building, her shoulders came back and her chin came up and she marched along confidently, eyes scanning the office doors for the name she was seeking. Since she was a tall, lean woman, with short-cropped fair hair and a powerful brown-eyed gaze, she looked like someone that you wouldn't want to mess with.

After a few false turns and starts, she finally found and knocked on the super's door, and promptly answered the summons to enter. She was somewhat surprised to find two others already in the room, sitting in chairs facing the super's desk. One was a plumpish woman somewhere on the wrong side of fifty, with short, curly dark hair and a fair-haired man in his late twenties, early thirties, who was sitting in his chair a little oddly. It wasn't until she got closer that she noticed the cane lying beside his chair and the injury to his arm.

'Ah, Sergeant Stebbings?' the super rose from his desk, a pleasant-faced man, whom Janet — against her better judgement — found herself instinctively liking.

'Sir,' she said smartly. 'I was told to report to you?'

Rollo nodded. 'Yes, please drag up a chair and join us. As you know from your DI, our team uncovered a blackmail scheme whilst working on the murder of a vicar thirty years ago. Your DI informed me last evening that Anthea Ramsey had just received instructions for a drop-off today?'

'That's right, sir,' Janet said, making no effort to disguise the fact that she was consulting her watch. 'It's due to take place in a small park, right here in Kidlington, at three o'clock this afternoon. Naturally myself and my team will be setting up surveillance,' she said, staking her claim right away.

Rollo, hearing it, and understanding at once the reasons for her assertiveness, merely smiled and nodded. 'Indeed. And *naturally*, we don't want to interfere with your arrangements,' he reassured her.

He saw the sergeant relax slightly and then flick a slightly troubled glance towards the two others in the room. The sergeant, so her boss had informed him, was something of a judo expert, and was clearly a very physically fit and capable officer. No doubt she had selected a young and fit team to help her with her case. And the likes of an experienced but definitely older woman like Claire, and a man who clearly had physical disabilities, wouldn't be her idea of 'back-up'. And she was probably worried that he might be about to insist that his team be present at the park.

On that, she need not have worried. Neither Rollo or the powers-that-be had any intention of putting civilian consultants in a position that might pose any physical danger to them. For one thing, the insurance people would have hysterics.

He was only glad, for once, that Hillary Greene wasn't present. She alone might have insisted on having a ringside seat at the action, and he doubted he'd have been able to prevent her.

'I just wanted to make you aware of two things, Sergeant,' Rollo swept on smoothly. 'As you already know, the blackmailer claims to have knowledge of our cold case, which means we want to be able to question him or her at the earliest opportunity.'

Janet nodded. 'I have no problem with that, sir. Although any initial arrest will be for attempted blackmail, and the paperwork done by myself and my team.'

Rollo again smiled and nodded. 'Naturally — it's *your* collar,' he assured her. 'The other thing you need to be aware of is something Hillary Greene uncovered only yesterday. Anthea Ramsey is not the first or only victim of blackmail surrounding the Coltrane case. We've since learned that a man named Max Walker has also received threats and instructions for payment.'

At this, Janet sat up and really took notice, listening intently as Rollo read out the report Hillary Greene had made for him before clocking off yesterday.

'In conclusion,' he finished, a few minutes later, 'Hillary is convinced that Max Walker attempted to capture the blackmailer and has suggested that it would be a very good idea indeed if you were to go back to him and question him yourself. Obviously, you'll want to do that, and I have his details here,' Rollo said, hiding his amusement as the gung-ho young woman in front of him all but snatched the document he handed over. 'Hillary suggests you put the wind up him good and find out all the details you can *before* the drop-off this afternoon. She has a hunch that it might prove very useful to you.'

At this, Janet cast a quick, slightly puzzled glance at the older woman, wondering why Hillary Greene wasn't speaking for herself.

Claire, cottoning on at once, smiled, and said, 'I'm Claire Woolley — a former DS myself, and this is Gareth Proctor, formerly a member of his majesty's armed forces. We're the civilian team who work with DI Greene. Hillary's not here today.'

'Oh,' Janet said, slightly deflated. She'd worked herself up to the point of maybe having to hold her own against a formidable opponent, and now wasn't sure whether to feel relieved or disappointed that it wouldn't be necessary.

'Any questions, Sergeant?' Rollo asked. Janet had none and rose eagerly, ready to get on with things.

'No, sir. And thank you for this,' she waved the paperwork in her hand. 'I'll certainly go and see this Mr Walker right away. And, er, thank DI Greene for me for the tip,' she added stiffly.

The room fell silent as the sergeant left, then Claire sighed gently. 'I can remember, just, being that young and ambitious.'

Rollo Sale grunted. 'Yes, she does seem highly efficient, doesn't she? Don't worry,' he added, reading into her silence, 'we'll get access to the blackmailer as a priority. I've already sorted that out with her DI. Since Hillary isn't here, I'll be doing the interview myself,' he added, less confidently. It had been quite some time since he'd had to conduct an interview with a suspect.

Claire grinned. 'I don't think Sergeant Stebbings is going to be happy about having her prey prised out of her paws and handed over, sir,' she remarked.

Rollo shrugged philosophically. 'Then Sergeant Stebbings will have to lump it, won't she?' he said.

* * *

As Janet Stebbings bearded Max Walker in his home, and did indeed put enough wind up him to drag out of him the whole sorry saga of his failure to catch the blackmailer, Hillary Greene allowed herself to be sedated and wheeled into surgery.

The next half hour or so was something she would choose to forget — and in a hurry — and after snoozing off the effects of the procedure for a couple of hours or so in 'recovery' was relieved to be going home.

As she sat in the back of the cab, with a slight headache and a throat so sore she dreaded her first coughing fit, she wondered what was going on at work.

Luckily, she'd left before hearing the news that Anthea Ramsey's instructions to drop off the blackmail payment had finally arrived. Which meant that she was unaware that as she walked a little unsteadily up the tow path towards the welcoming sight of the *Mollern*, a little over a mile away, in a small park not far from the Moors area of Kidlington, one of her colleagues was lying in wait for a blackmailer.

Having learned the crucial fact from Max Walker that the blackmailer had used a bicycle in their last attempt to collect the money, Sergeant Stebbings had put one of her team on a bicycle. Luckily the constable in question was an avid mountain-biker, and fitter than even the proverbial flea, and she was confident that he'd be able to run down anyone fleeing on two wheels.

She'd also noticed that the park was accessed by one road only, and that off that road, a tiny alleyway led away into a maze of a housing estate just beyond. And that this alleyway's access was cut off to cars by bollards. It was, she'd seen at once on her initial reconnaissance of the area, just the sort of ideal getaway point that a blackmailer on a bike might choose to use. Consequently, she'd put the second member of her team, in a car, parked up on the pavement and right in front of the bollards, blocking access to them.

She herself was jogging aimlessly around in full tracksuit gear, trying her best to look like a bored housewife reluctantly doing her daily exercise.

Right on time, and in accordance with the instructions in her letter, she saw Anthea Ramsey enter the park, walk quickly to a small bench underneath a large weeping willow tree and sit down. As per the instructions in the letter, she then reached down and put a shopping bag on the ground, pushing it a little under the bench, then got up and walked away.

The member of her team Janet had assigned to deal with Mrs Ramsey whilst she'd been unexpectedly delayed talking to Max Walker had later relayed to her the fact that the woman was a 'total flake' and a 'nightmare to deal with' and so she felt some relief that the drop-off had gone according to plan. The last thing she needed at this crucial point was for her victim to muck it up with a display of histrionics or whatever.

Now it was just a matter of waiting.

If she hadn't been forewarned by Max Walker to be on the lookout for a cyclist, she might not have paid the figure, dressed in dark jeans and a hooded sweatshirt, quite as much attention as she did when it pedalled onto the scene a few minutes later.

As it was, she was prepared. Over her radio, she told her team member on the bike to be ready and on the lookout for a figure with a hood pulled up well over their head, riding an old-looking bicycle.

And the moment the cyclist stopped, picked up the bag and pedalled quickly off, Janet felt a swift whoop of glee rise up in her throat. *It was on!*

She went from lazy jogger to full-out sprinter the moment the cyclist had picked up the bag and so was just in time to watch as her team mate on the bicycle crashed into the other cyclist at full pelt. The hooded figure, caught off-guard, hit the ground with a 'whump' and before they could even rise to their knees, her colleague was kneeling beside them and putting on the handcuffs, all the time reciting the usual warning.

Hardly out of breath, Janet quickly joined them on the grass, waving off concerned onlookers with a show of her badge and a warning to stay away.

The figure on the ground began swearing and howling, her voice that of a thoroughly ticked-off woman.

* * *

Hillary carefully ate some soothing ice cream and stretched out on her sofa-cum-daybed. The afternoon was well advanced when she finally telephoned the office, and had to listen, with some chagrin at having missed it all, as Claire filled her in on the day's events.

'And the super's interviewing her now?' Hillary croaked painfully. 'ID'd her yet?'

'Yes, guv. It's Moira Coltrane's daughter, Clara-Jane. We've been listening in, and so far it seems she doesn't know anything of real use to us. She just saw an opportunity to try and make some money. She admitted to doing some research, and apparently Max Walker's healthy business and Anthea's advantageous second marriage gave her ideas.'

'Do you think she's telling the truth?' Hillary croaked, sipping warm coffee in between sentences and hoping her voice didn't go completely.

'I think so, guv,' Claire said cautiously. 'The super's a bit rusty when it comes to his interview technique, but I haven't heard or noticed any red flags. Gareth and me were watching from observation. I think Clara-Jane Coltrane is just a chancer. And mad as a wet hen! Not only did she not get any easy money, she knows she's facing jail time. You should have heard her go on about finding nothing but cut-up magazines in Max Walker's payoff! I thought she was going to go into orbit.' Claire laughed. 'But she sticks to it that whilst she remembers bits and pieces about her visits to her uncle, she wasn't there on the day he died. Which fits, because DI Keating's team had her placed at an arcade in Oxford for most of that day.'

'Hmm. Ask her about good-looking teenagers hanging around with her uncle,' Hillary reminded her. 'She'll have been boy-mad at the time and might give us a better description of likely candidates. Maybe even a name. After all, she should've been there that day when Moira and her friend caught the Reverend and the young lad "off their heads", as she put it — if Moira is to be believed, that is.'

'Yes, guv.' After a pause, 'You sound a bit rough, guv. The chest infection worse is it?' she asked tentatively.

Hillary sighed. 'Probably. Look, I'll see you tomorrow,' she said. 'I want a full report on the interview, yeah?'

Claire sighed. 'Right, guv,' she said, contemplating a couple of hours of typing. 'It's nearly five now. Do I get overtime?'

Hillary, despite her sore throat, had to laugh heartily at that.

CHAPTER THIRTEEN

The next morning, Hillary was relieved to find her sore throat was much improved, but still drank her first cup of coffee cautiously. On her way into work she tuned in to the Radio Oxford news report, and discovered they already had the story of a local woman being arrested for attempted blackmail and hinting at a connection to a thirty-year-old murder case.

As she pulled Puff into the car park and scouted around for a free spot, she wondered vaguely if Max Walker was also listening to the radio, and if so, what he made of the arrest of his would-be blackmailer. Knowing him, he was probably pleased at his adversary's come-uppance, but annoyed that it meant he wouldn't now be able to have a second crack at his tormentor himself.

Before going to her stationery cupboard, she detoured to Rollo Sale's office, where he filled her in more fully on yesterday's events. Although her voice wasn't as croaky as it had been yesterday, it still had enough of a rasp in it to catch his attention, but he was careful not to mention it.

'Sounds as if Sergeant Stebbings did a good job,' Hillary said with genuine satisfaction, when he'd finished briefing her. 'Just a pity Clara-Jane Coltrane didn't have anything for us about Keith's murder.'

'Yes. Mind you, she had one gem for us. Claire passed on your request to ask her about any good-looking teenage boys she might have noticed hanging around her uncle, and she came up with a name.'

'Oh?'

'Hmm. One Trevor Cornwallis. I've already put Gareth on to tracing him.'

Hillary nodded. 'Let's hope he hasn't moved to the outer Hebrides then,' she grunted. 'This is one interview that can't be done over the phone. I need to see his face and body language for myself.'

Rollo nodded in agreement. The possibility of a drugs angle was the only new thing his team had come up with, and it looked promising.

But Hillary was in luck. After sorting out her mail, she popped her head around the door of the communal office only to be informed by Gareth that, not only had he already traced Trevor's whereabouts, but that he lived in nearby Eynsham.

'Prior convictions?' she asked.

'No, ma'am. He seems to be a model citizen.'

'Great. Get your coat,' she said to him. 'Claire, would you mind phoning him and ask him to make himself available in,' she checked her watch, 'forty-five minutes or so?'

'He'll probably be at work, guv,' Claire pointed out. 'And he might not think it worth his while to oblige us.' They had no powers to insist that their witnesses talk to them, and Mr Cornwallis might well think that he had better things to do with his time.

Hillary shrugged. 'Something tells me that he will. If nothing else, I think his curiosity will get the better of him. Ask him to return to his home and we'll meet him there. I don't want him distracted by a work environment, and he'll feel more free to talk without his colleagues knowing that he's brought the cops to the office.'

Claire's eyebrow went up, but, as ever — and not surprising her at all — Hillary's fortune-telling was spot on, for when Claire was put through to his office, and explained her request, Trevor Cornwallis agreed to return to his home at once and assured her that he would be happy to talk to them.

But to Claire's experienced ear, he hadn't sounded happy at all. He'd sounded downright worried.

* * *

Hillary opted to take Gareth's car and so save her the task of driving. Although she wasn't feeling particularly fragile, it made sense for her to preserve her energy where she could. She had a feeling that the upcoming interview with Trevor Cornwallis was going to prove vital, and she wanted to be fit for purpose.

Trevor answered the door almost immediately on them ringing the bell, a sure sign that he'd been looking out for their arrival. Which meant, Hillary deduced, that he was either the sort who craved excitement and was looking forward to being interviewed by the police, or else his nerves were playing up.

And the moment she looked into his wary face, she knew he wasn't in the least excited.

Hillary and Gareth showed their IDs, which Trevor barely glanced at, then followed him into the house to a small but attractive study that overlooked the back garden.

A quick mental calculation on her part put the man in his late forties, but he showed no signs of middle-aged spread. Rather, he was tall and lean with rather a gaunt face. He had dark hair slowly turning grey, and wide grey eyes.

'Please, have a seat,' he indicated several scattered chairs, mostly grouped around a small coffee table, and Hillary opted for the most comfortable-looking one whilst Gareth chose the one farthest away, where he set about unobtrusively preparing his phone to record.

Trevor took a chair next to a small desk but chose not to sit behind it. No doubt a psychologist would have made something of that, but Hillary had no idea what subliminal message it was supposedly conveying. She was just glad it gave her an unrestricted view of her witness.

'Your colleague, on the telephone, said you wanted to talk to me about Keith Coltrane. Is that right?' Trevor began cautiously. He watched Hillary's face as he spoke and seemed to have forgotten Gareth's presence already. Such focussed attention instantly put Hillary on high alert. In her experience, witnesses with nothing to hide didn't usually need to be so in control of themselves, or so invested in trying to pick up every nuance of their interrogator's behaviour.

'Yes, sir. As you may be aware, we are taking another look at the murder of the vicar of Lower Barton thirty years ago. We've now had a chance to talk to a lot of people who were around then,' she exaggerated just a little, 'and your name came up as someone who knew Keith well.'

Trevor shifted a little on his seat. He was wearing a smart charcoal-coloured business suit, with a crisp oyster-coloured shirt and a black, red and grey striped tie. He looked incongruously dapper in his pleasant but everyday study.

'I wouldn't say I knew him *well*, but yes, I knew him. He was a nice man. A good man. What happened to him was appalling and unfair, and it affected a lot of us deeply.'

Hillary nodded. 'Yes, I can imagine. You were only young at the time, weren't you; sixteen or seventeen?'

'That's right, seventeen.'

'Most teenagers that I know tend to avoid anything church-related like the plague,' Hillary mused gently, allowing a smile to creep into her tone. 'Unless, of course, they were raised in a religious household, or became religious.'

She left it as a statement, but Trevor understood it to be a question. He shrugged. 'My family were never devout, Mrs Greene. And no, I didn't go through a phase or anything like that. I just liked Keith. As I said, he was all right.'

Hillary nodded. 'We know the Reverend was a young and good-looking man, and as such, attracted a lot of, er, shall we say, *attention* from his female parishioners. One of them was so devoted to him that it actually led to her husband divorcing her, I understand?'

'That wasn't Keith's fault,' Trevor said quickly, showing his first trace of irritability. 'I remember who you mean — but I can't think of her name right now. But I can tell you, there was nothing in it as far as Keith was concerned.'

Hillary nodded. 'Yes, that's the general impression we've been getting as well,' she agreed peaceably. But she found it interesting that he had abandoned his habit of careful caution to leap to the dead man's defence the moment that she became critical of him.

'Everyone's been telling us that the lady in question was rather . . . obsessed,' she continued smoothly. 'Of course, we've also talked to several husbands who were rather jealous of the vicar's popularity. And DI Keating, the original investigating officer, believed that the most likely cause of the murderous attack on the Reverend was as a result of either a jealous husband, or maybe a lovers' spat that turned vicious.'

She noticed how tense Trevor's shoulders were now, and wondered if he realised how defensive and wary he looked.

As she finished speaking, he forced himself to shrug nonchalantly. 'Well, I suppose the police knew best. But I never thought it likely, personally. If Keith had been playing around, then yes, maybe. But I never believed that he was. It wasn't the sort of thing he'd ever do. Take advantage of people, I mean.'

'And yet, according to you, you didn't know him that well,' Hillary pointed out. 'But for you to be so sure of him, it seems to me that you must have known him very well indeed. So, which is it?'

Trevor's lips thinned, unhappy at being caught out so easily. 'I suppose you could say that I saw a fair bit of him,' he temporised. 'But not just me — there were others — a small gang of us in fact. He was just a nice bloke to talk to you, you know? Interesting, and not at all . . . well . . . vicar-like. He never preached at you, for instance, never tried to lure you over to his way of thinking. He just listened to what you had to say.' He shrugged and gave an attempt at an abashed grin. 'So, a few of us took to hanging around the vicarage sometimes, during the summer holidays mostly. There's nothing to do in a village as you can imagine, and we were bored out of our minds. There was an old tennis court in the vicarage grounds that he let us use — it was a bit manky, but it was better than nothing. And there was an old fruit orchard there as well. It was a good place to meet girls and hang out, and our parents never objected because they felt we were safe there.'

'And were you, Mr Cornwallis? Safe there?' Hillary asked softly.

Trevor looked at her, a small frown of puzzlement tugging at his brows. 'Of course we were.'

Hillary allowed herself a very cynical smile. 'Oh, come now, Mr Cornwallis, we both know there are two sides to every story. A good-looking young vicar encouraging teenagers to hang out at his place, unsupervised. It's been suggested that the Reverend might have had less innocent motives than merely administering spiritually to his young flock.'

Trevor's face immediately flushed an ugly brick-red. 'And some people just have dirty minds,' he growled. 'And a dead man can't defend himself, can he? There's no way Keith was like that. I'd have known. We had nothing to fear from him,' he continued hotly. 'In fact, if anything it was the other way ar—'

Abruptly, he stopped speaking, and then went rather pale.

'The other way around, you were about to say?' Hillary slipped in smoothly, giving him no time to deny that that was indeed what he'd been about to say. 'Now that's interesting, sir. Exactly who was it that the Reverend Coltrane should have been afraid of?'

Trevor swallowed hard, then turned to glance out of the window.

'Sir?' Hillary prompted. 'It was thirty years ago now. If you've been keeping guilty knowledge to yourself all this time, don't you think now's the time to let go of it? Do you have an idea of who might have killed your friend?'

'No,' Trevor said at once, turning his attention back to Hillary, that wary and intent look back on his face.

'But *something* is worrying you,' Hillary urged, holding his gaze challengingly. 'I have to tell you, Mr Cornwallis,' she said quietly, 'that we have a witness who believes she saw you and the Reverend indulging in some sort of illegal substance. Is that true?'

Stunned, Trevor sat quietly for a while, breathing deeply and thinking furiously. Eventually, though, he opted not to lie. He ran a harassed hand through his hair and shook his head. 'It was nothing . . . it was just stupid. A stupid thing that as a teenager . . . I regretted it the moment I did it. Funny thing was, I was trying to be good to him. To give him a gift, almost.'

At her puzzled look, he again shook his head and slowly leaned back in his chair. 'I suppose it doesn't matter now.' He looked at Hillary with his lids half-lowered, then dropped his gaze to the back of his hands, resting in his lap.

'All right, this is how it was,' he capitulated. 'Keith was a very educated guy, you know that right? And not just about theology and all that stuff. He was into history too, and archaeology, and art. Literature too. That's why it was so fascinating talking to him. It wasn't like being at school, listening to some boring and brain-dead teacher regurgitating textbooks, and who couldn't wait for the bell to ring any more than we could, so that he could get away from the place! Keith brought it all to life — whatever it was he was talking about. And one of the things he was really into was the life and times of Saint Anthony. Probably because the church was named after him.'

'This is Saint Anthony of Padua, yes? The one who died of ergotism?' Hillary put in, surprising both men in the room with her recently acquired knowledge.

'Yes, how did you . . . ?' Trevor began, then trailed off as he realised that he might be about to commit a faux pas in showing such surprise at a dumb copper's unexpected intellect. 'Yes, that was the one. Keith had researched a lot about him when he was given a job in a church dedicated to him. He told us all about what life would have been like back then, and how he'd died. How he must have been confused by the illness, suffered hallucinations and whatnot. And how it must have been hard not to lose his faith. He admired him so much that it gave me this stupid idea . . .'

He paused and gave a weary laugh.

Hillary waited patiently.

'I had this friend,' Trevor began, making Hillary fight not to roll her eyes. How many times, over the years, had she interviewed people — victims and perpetrators alike — who'd found themselves in a police station, in trouble, and begun to explain themselves with those very words? Everyone, it often seemed to her, had that one friend who was always capable of bringing about disaster!

'I can't remember their name now,' Trevor added, the lie so blatant that Hillary didn't even bother to call him on it. 'He used to know people who could get all manner of stuff. Bragged about it in fact. So, one day I asked him if he could get me some magic mushrooms.'

He stopped to watch her, trying to gauge her reaction, but Hillary merely nodded wearily.

'We're talking about golden halos, cubes, gold caps, yes?' she said, once more making both Trevor and Gareth look at her with respect. She got out her phone and a hasty search brought up the scientific name for her. '*Psilocybe cubensis?*'

Trevor shrugged. 'Maybe. I can't remember what it was called now. I just know that my friend told me that to get high on them I had to dry them out, as that had a much more powerful effect than if they were eaten raw.'

Hillary's lips twitched. 'I take it, then, that your friend didn't brag in vain? He was able to get you a supply?'

'Yes. And showed me how to prepare it,' Trevor confirmed. 'After drying them out, I crushed them into powder and made a sort of tea with it. It was so bitter, though, that I couldn't stomach it, so I put some into some sweetened hot chocolate instead.'

Hillary sighed. 'All this is very interesting, Mr Cornwallis, but I'm not interested in the drugs you took thirty years ago. What does this have to do with the Reverend?'

'Well, I'm coming to that,' Trevor said. 'I got the mushrooms because I wanted to help Keith get high.'

Hillary blinked. Then blinked again. 'Sorry?' she finally managed. Her throat was beginning to dry out again with all the talking and she hoped her voice would hold out. 'What was it, some kind of practical joke?'

'No, it was nothing like that,' Trevor said, sounding irritated once more. 'Once I learned how Saint Anthony died — of eating some poisonous fungus or what-have-you, I thought it would be interesting to get hold of some of these magic mushrooms that my Uncle Bar . . . er, some old fart who reckoned the sixties were so great, kept droning on about. How it let you see some weird and wacky stuff, and all that freeing-of-the-mind guff. And since Keith was always going on about how he wished he could have lived back when Saint Anthony was alive, and experienced some of the things he did . . . well, he was such a nice bloke but always so *uptight*! You know, always restricted by his job, like, so that he could never properly let go, and I thought . . .'

'You thought it would be funny to let him "trip out" is how I think they put it in the sixties,' Hillary finished for him dryly.

Trevor hung his head. 'Yes. I suppose so. But mostly I wanted him to feel something of what Saint Anthony must have felt, before he died. Maybe he'd have seen . . . I don't know, angels or something. I knew he'd never knowingly take drugs, but I thought if he could just experience it . . . Look, I said it was stupid,' he added lamely, seeing her expression.

'Yes, you did, didn't you?' Hillary agreed. 'Go on then,' she cajoled. 'What happened exactly?'

Trevor shrugged. 'Well, not that much, not really. I made some hot chocolate in a thermos like I said, and added some of the magic mushrooms, then cobbled together a picnic of sorts, and took it to the vicarage. It was a nice sunny day, I remember that, and luckily Keith was in, and so we went out into the garden and ate and drank the stuff and just chatted. And sure enough, after a bit, things got a little fuzzy and weird. I think I saw a unicorn. But not . . . I wasn't off my head or anything. I still knew who I was and where I was and all of that. And I think Keith did too, though he did look kind of weird and a bit out of it. But then somebody came into the garden, some woman, I think, or maybe two women. Or perhaps I was just seeing double, I'm not sure. Anyway, one of the women got really nasty with Keith and started to get so angry that I got spooked and ran off.'

Hillary nodded. This, at least, was confirmation of Moira's story. 'What happened then?'

Trevor shrugged, looking ever more shame-faced and contrite. 'Nothing. I mean, I never mentioned it to anybody, and the next time I saw Keith, he didn't say anything to me about it either. So, I figured that maybe he never even knew what I'd done. I don't think I could have put a lot of the stuff in, because it quickly wore off, and I daresay it was the same for him.'

Trevor paused, then bit his lip. 'I threw the rest of it down the toilet.'

Hillary, again, let the blatant lie pass by without comment. 'And that's it?'

'Yeah, that's it. I'm telling you this because you seem to have got hold of the wrong end of the stick about Keith. He never gave *me* stuff, *I* gave it to him! No way was he a bad guy. In fact, just the opposite. Too trusting and nice for his own good. Innocent. Naïve. Call it what you like. But I tell you this — no way was he any kind of a predator. Of women, or kids or anyone else. And I hope you catch who did it, I really do.'

Hillary continued to press him for a while, but it quickly became apparent that now he'd 'confessed his sins' to her, Trevor had little more to offer.

So it was that an hour later they were back at HQ, where she asked Gareth if he'd also found out whether Trevor's parents were still alive, and if so where they were living. It was a long shot, but they'd lived in the village at the time of the murder, so perhaps they'd be able to recall something useful.

Gareth came up trumps. 'The mother is in a care home somewhere — dementia, I think. But I found the address . . . I have it somewhere. His father's still living in the family home though . . .' he searched through his notes and triumphantly came upon both addresses, which he then wrote down for her.

Hillary regarded the slip of paper thoughtfully. Malmesbury was over in the next county of Wiltshire, and the care home had a Swindon postcode too. She glanced at Claire. 'Fancy a short field trip?'

Claire didn't need asking twice.

* * *

Back in Eynsham, Trevor carefully locked his front door behind him and went back to his car. He was feeling a bit light-headed after his ordeal, and when he opened the car door, his hands trembled a little.

But he was confident that he'd done a good job of talking to the police. And hoped that he'd diverted them enough with his stupid behaviour to sidetrack them away from what was truly dangerous.

He would not have been feeling half so confident, however, had he realised that, as he drove back to work, the very woman who'd just interviewed him would shortly be on her way towards his unsuspecting father's house.

CHAPTER FOURTEEN

Hillary saw at once the strong family resemblance when Peter Cornwallis opened the door to her knock. Like his son, he was tall, lean and gaunt-faced, with almost identical grey eyes to those of his offspring.

She saw, too, the unmistakable look of alarm that crossed his face the moment she introduced herself and Claire, and explained their remit.

'Please, come in,' he stood aside to let them pass, and showed them into a pleasant living room with French doors leading out to a small but well-maintained garden. This time of year, it was full of colourful Michaelmas daisies, dahlias and chrysanthemums.

'Tea or coffee?'

Hillary was about to refuse, but her dry and still sore throat changed her mind for her, and she asked for coffee. Claire asked for tea. He invited them to sit on a comfortable sofa, and when the old man had left for the kitchen, Claire leaned closer to Hillary and said softly, 'Did you see how frightened he was when he realised who we were?'

'Yes,' Hillary whispered back. 'Think he's got a guilty conscience about something?'

'Unlikely, guv. I was sitting opposite Gareth when he called up the man's details. Like his son, he hasn't got any form either. He's been a structural engineer all his life; one marriage, one child, and not even a parking ticket to his name. Your typical honest, hard-working citizen, in fact.'

When the typical honest, hard-working citizen returned with a laden tray he found the two women sitting a little apart, and silent. Both looked at him with a vague smile and accepted their cups and saucers. Peter Cornwallis, Hillary saw at once, would have had nothing to do with common or garden mugs.

Peter sat down on an armchair opposite them, and immediately put his own beverage on a small occasional table beside the chair.

He looked at them expectantly, hoping that he appeared calm and only marginally curious.

'Were you aware that Thames Valley Police are currently taking another look at the murder of the Reverend Keith Coltrane, thirty years ago, in the village of Lower Barton, Mr Cornwallis?' Hillary began conventionally.

'No, I had no idea,' Peter responded.

And that, Hillary strongly suspected, was the first big lie. Not a good start, that. If she'd been feeling a hundred per cent, she might have decided to approach things in a more roundabout, softly-softly kind of way. Take some time in order to let the man tie himself up in knots and then have to try and untangle himself. She didn't think he was the kind who lied well, or even felt comfortable flouting authority, and she felt sure she could break him down by troubling his conscience and demanding that he did his duty to help the police with their murder case.

But her throat was already feeling the strain of her interview with this man's son, and she didn't want to prolong either his agony, or hers.

'We've just been talking to your son, Mr Cornwallis. Trevor—'

At the mention of his son, the colour drained out of the old man's face, and he jerked — literally jerked, as if receiving a mild electric shock — in his chair.

'Trevor? What do you mean? Talked to him when? Why?' The staccato, panicky words tumbled from his mouth before he could stop them, making him clamp his lips firmly together, lest he say even more.

'Earlier today, sir,' Hillary said slowly, watching him closely. Claire, taking notes beside her, had also become more alert, sensing the sudden tension in the air.

'But that's . . . I mean, he was just a child when, when, Keith, er . . . died.'

'Hardly a child, sir,' Hillary corrected him firmly. 'He was seventeen. And the Reverend didn't only die, he was brutally murdered. In his church.'

Under this somewhat brutal recital, Peter Cornwallis looked both appalled and panic-stricken in equal measure. He'd thought, if this moment ever came, that he'd be able to give a good account of himself, and gloss things over. Failing that, he'd do the right thing with at least some dignity and decorum. Yet here he was, with barely a dozen words spoken, and already he felt as if the bottom was falling out of his world.

It didn't help that Keith suddenly seemed to be right here in this room with them, and all of his old grief for the dead man threatened to overwhelm him. Worse still, the fact that the police had already spoken to Trevor terrified him.

What had his son *said*? Surely he'd have been careful?

'I don't imagine Trevor could have told you much about that awful time, Inspector,' he began, and Hillary didn't bother to correct his misconception about her true rank and status. 'Like you said, he was only a teenager. I doubt he even knew the Reverend existed. We were not a very religious family, I'm afraid.' He tried an apologetic smile, but his face felt stiff and alien.

Peter knew he had a bad habit of tapping his feet on the floor when he was agitated or nervous, and the strain of sitting perfectly still was bringing him out in a sweat.

Hillary noticed the old man's forehead had become shiny and sensed that she needed to be careful now. The man was like a powder keg, ready to blow at any second. But she had no idea what would light the fuse, or even what it was that had got him into this condition so quickly.

She began to probe with extreme caution. 'I think you'll find, Mr Cornwallis, that your son was much closer to the Reverend Coltrane than you suppose.'

Peter swallowed hard. 'Oh?' he said, attempting a shrug. 'Perhaps that's so. What, er, has he told you about Kei . . . the vicar?'

Hillary didn't miss the unintentional slip. So, the old man in front of her and the murdered man had been on first-name terms then? Strange, for a family who were not religious.

'He says that he and a small group of teenagers liked to hang out at the vicarage in the old days. Play some tennis. Picnic in the vicarage gardens,' she added carefully, watching her witness's face closely at the word 'picnic' but getting no reaction whatsoever.

If this man had been aware of his teenage son's experiment with drugs, then he was a far better actor than she was giving him credit for. So, whatever was the cause of the man's angst, it wasn't that.

'You knew nothing of this, sir?'

'Oh no. No, I had no idea,' Peter said, unconsciously rubbing his damp palms against the material of his trousers. And unaware that he was beginning to tap his left foot spasmodically.

Claire noticed it though and made a note of it in her notebook.

'Would it have caused you alarm, do you think, if you had known your son was close to Reverend Coltrane?' Hillary asked, pausing to take a sip of her coffee as she felt a warning tickle start up in the back of her throat. If she started coughing now, interrupting her interview just when it was at such a crucial stage, then Butler wouldn't have to wait for an operation to remove him. She'd cough the bastard right up out of her lungs herself!

'No,' Peter said instantly, before having time to think. 'Of course not. Why would it?'

'You trusted the Reverend then? With young people?' she asked, taking another sip of the warm coffee, relieved to hear the croak in her voice recede somewhat.

'Yes, of course,' Peter said, looking genuinely puzzled now.

Hillary nodded. 'Some people might have found the Reverend's closeness to good-looking teenagers suspect.'

As his son had not long before him, Peter scowled darkly. 'That's totally outrageous! Keith would never . . . er . . . he wasn't that sort of a man.'

'And yet somebody murdered him, sir,' Hillary said flatly. 'Hit him over the head with a convenient spade, in the doorway of his own church.'

Peter swallowed hard but said nothing. At that moment, he felt incapable of saying so much as a syllable.

Hillary could see that there were genuine tears in the man's eyes now and rapidly rearranged her thoughts. Slowly, she leaned forward. 'You were very fond of the vicar, weren't you, Mr Cornwallis?' she said, very gently now.

Beside her, Claire stiffened. She knew that her boss was on the scent of something, and was careful to keep so still and quiet that she hardly dared breathe.

'I, er . . .' Peter barely managed.

'It seems to me that many people loved the Reverend, Mr Cornwallis,' Hillary went on, keeping her voice warm and soft, almost hypnotic. 'We've been talking to a lot of people who knew him, as you can imagine, and from them, we have now begun to fit together an overall picture and understanding of Keith. I get the sense of a very caring man, but also a handsome and charismatic one. Some of the women in the village rather lost their heads about him, didn't they?'

Peter shrugged. 'Keith never encouraged them, I assure you. But he was kind to them. Always. Keith was a very kind man.'

Hillary nodded. 'He *was* kind, yes, I think in that you are right,' she agreed, both to keep him on side, but also because she was genuinely coming to believe that that was probably the case. 'He was understanding with besotted women, and honest with jealous husbands. He was a teacher and mentor to young minds and tried to do what was best for his difficult sister. All that was very admirable.'

Peter was nodding now.

'So how was he kind to you, Mr Cornwallis?' she asked softly.

For a moment, Peter blinked. 'Me? Oh . . .' In his mind's eye, Keith was standing right there in front of him now. Smiling. Talking. So understanding, so non-judgemental. So handsome.

'Oh, he never . . . I mean, I never had much to do with him,' he said, feeling an appalling wave of guilt wash over him as he told the massive lie. Never had he felt so traitorous. But he tried to console himself with the knowledge that Keith would understand why he had to do it. Keith would never judge him harshly.

Unfortunately for him, the woman watching him so closely wasn't Keith. And he could tell at once that she knew he was lying. To make matters worse, it was at this point that he became aware that his foot was beating a veritable tattoo on the floor and he abruptly put a stop to it.

As he did so, he felt a trickle of sweat run down his temple. Should he try and wipe it away? Make a casual move with his hand to sweep his hair back, and brush the sweat away with his sleeve as he did so? Or was it best to just leave it? But this sharp-eyed woman must be able to see it?

Like so many times in his life, Peter felt frozen, and utterly incapable of making a decision.

Hillary watched the bead of perspiration trickle down his temple and disappear behind his ear. Slowly, she leaned back in her chair. 'I think, Mr Cornwallis, that you should tell me about Keith. Did you love him?'

Peter blinked. 'Love him?' he echoed faintly. 'Me?' *Of course* he had loved him! Deeply and profoundly. In fact, Keith had been the only man he'd ever loved.

Peter had known almost since he'd hit puberty that there was something amiss with him. His mother had paraded girls in front of him from his eighteenth birthday onwards, whom he'd dutifully date for a while until they tired of his lacklustre courtship and threw him over.

He'd make excuses for his lack of a lasting relationship by insisting that he was concentrating first on getting his degree, and then on getting a good job, and then later still, on climbing the ladder to a better position.

And all the while, the years of his early twenties counted down, and a sense of panic grew stronger and stronger within him that he would be found out. Ostracised. Shamed.

It wasn't until he'd eventually met Dorothy, who at least seemed to be a gentle soul who shared some of his interests, that he'd finally settled matters once and for all by proposing to her. And, to be fair, he'd never really regretted it. They'd had Trevor, much to his mother's delight, but in spite of her hints and prompting, no second child. By then, their sex life had all but dwindled down to nothing.

Dorothy had come to accept this, and had seemed happy enough with her nice home, respectable husband, and handsome, clever son. And life would probably have gone on that way, with him ignoring his true nature and enduring his tame, mediocre and untroubled existence until he'd . . . well . . . become an old man, like he was now.

But then the old vicar at Lower Barton had retired, and Keith Coltrane had come to the village. And everything had changed.

At first, he'd just admired Keith from afar. He didn't attend church services, and their meetings, to begin with, were few and far between. A chance encounter in the village pub every now and then, resulting in the odd game of darts. Rubbing shoulders with him at the annual village fete.

But then he had wangled his way onto Keith's team at quiz nights at the village hall. And somehow, over time, things had begun to deepen for him. He'd start going to the pub more often, when he knew Keith would be there. He joined the squash club, because he knew that Keith played the game. And they began to talk more.

And for the first time in his life, he, Peter Cornwallis, a supposedly happily married and respectable man, had fallen hard and headlong over heels in love.

Stupid. And yet, he thought sadly — and from the safety of all these years later — somehow heartbreakingly inevitable.

Keith had been kind to him. Of *course* he had. Had talked to him, counselled him, tried to get him to see how lucky he was to have an understanding wife and a good child. All the while, gently trying to steer him away from himself.

But Peter hadn't wanted to let him go. He cringed now to think of the letter he'd written Keith — the last, and only letter he'd ever written to him. Asking him to be honest with himself. To admit that he, too, was gay. That he wanted to be with Peter as much as he, Peter, wanted to be with Keith. Asking him to leave the Church, leave the parish, to go away with him somewhere new. Maybe abroad. Promising that he would leave his own wife and son well provided for so that they could live together guilt-free, somewhere tropical maybe.

The thought of it now made him want to both weep and cringe.

'Mr Cornwallis!' he heard his name called sharply, and he was suddenly jerked back to the here and now.

'I'm sorry. Er, what was the question again? I'm afraid I was miles away,' he admitted feebly.

He was about to reach out to take up his cup of tea but realised that his hands were shaking so much that he kept them firmly folded in his lap.

But Hillary, much to Claire's surprise, didn't repeat her question. Instead, she changed course abruptly.

'Did you know your son, Trevor, has admitted to trying to poison the Reverend?' It was, she knew, a misrepresentation of what Trevor had told them, but she said it without a qualm. She had a feeling that she and Peter Cornwallis could play ring-a-ring-a-roses forever if she didn't do something shocking to break through to him.

'What? No, he couldn't have,' Peter squawked, then immediately contradicted himself. 'I knew it! I knew that he'd found out . . .' And then all movement within him abruptly stopped. The sweating dried up. His feet, which had begun to tap again, went as still and heavy as lead. But, perversely, now that the crisis he'd dreaded for most of his life was finally upon him, he felt so much better! At least the awful uncertainty was over.

He gave a slow nod. He felt disembodied and — oddly — even quite safe now somehow; and in this newly acquired and wonderful state of calm, he raised his eyes slowly and looked across at Hillary Greene.

'I killed him,' he said quietly.

The room became utterly still.

'Who did you kill, Mr Cornwallis?'

'Keith. I killed Keith,' Peter said. He cleared his throat. 'Keith Coltrane. I'm admitting that I was the one who murdered him.' He spoke very calmly and deliberately, almost as if dictating for Claire, whom he watched as she faithfully wrote his words down in her notebook. It was as if he didn't trust either of them to understand what he was saying and wanted to make sure they didn't make any mistakes.

'Why did you kill him, sir?' Hillary asked next. Her voice was still casual and calm — almost uninterested.

'Because I loved him. And he didn't love me. Or wouldn't love me. I just lost control of myself, and killed him.'

And there, Hillary thought, was another whopping lie.

'I see. Let me get this straight, sir. As you can imagine, in cases like this, we all need to be very clear about things. You're saying that you killed the Reverend Keith Coltrane, at his church on 23 December 1992?'

'Yes.'

'But weren't you at work, sir?' she asked, cocking her head a little to one side. 'We can easily find out if you were or not, you know,' she added, telling fibs herself now. She doubted that the records of the company he had worked for would still be in existence.

But that didn't worry her. What she wanted to see, for herself, was his reaction to this comment.

And, as she expected, a momentary look of panic crossed his face. At that moment, she would have bet the keys to her narrowboat that, right now, Peter Cornwallis was desperately trying to remember exactly where he'd been, and what he'd been doing, the day the man that he'd loved had died. And the sheer fact that he was doing that told her all she needed to know.

For if this man *had* killed Keith Coltrane he'd know exactly where he'd been. And that was at St Anthony's Church, wielding a deadly spade.

Peter Cornwallis opened his mouth, then closed it again. Where *had* he been? In the office or at a site, surveying something?

He shook his head. He had to risk it. 'Go ahead,' he said, striving to sound confident. 'You'll find that I was nowhere to be seen that day at work. That's because I was in the village. I killed Keith. And I'll plead guilty to that in a court of law,' he added emphatically.

And sat straight in his chair, panting a little, his face as pale as milk.

Hillary sighed. 'Very well, sir. I'm going to ask you now to come back with us to Kidlington, to the Thames Valley Police Headquarters. You might like to get a coat and some toiletries together. Claire, would you accompany Mr Cornwallis upstairs to pack an overnight bag?'

Claire caught her eye, nodded, and followed Peter, who had now risen and was walking, stiff-legged to the door. He looked in a daze, very old and shaken to his core.

Claire was solicitous.

Hillary watched them leave, then reached for her phone and called her superintendent, who answered on the first ring.

'Superintendent Sale.'

'Sir, it's Hillary. We have a witness who has just confessed to the murder of Keith Coltrane.'

There was a moment of stunned silence, and then, 'Who is it?' Rollo asked happily.

'Peter Cornwallis, sir. Gareth can fill you in on his details.'

'Will do. Great job, Hillary.'

'Don't praise me yet, sir,' she said sardonically. 'I'm pretty sure that he didn't do it.'

This time there was another silence, slightly longer, and then she heard her boss sigh. 'Wonderful. A false confession? He's covering for someone then — or is he just a nutter?'

'The former, I think, sir. Can you arrange with the locals for a patrol car to come and pick up Claire and the witness? Whilst I'm in the area, I want to have a word with the suspect's wife. She's in a care home nearby.'

Rollo again sighed heavily. 'Sure, I can do that. Do you want me to hold off on the interview until you get back?'

'No, sir, go right ahead. I doubt I'll be long here anyway.'

'All right. Well, at least things are moving. You'll let me know of any further developments?'

'Of course, sir,' Hillary promised. Then left to break the bad news to Claire.

She was going to have to trust Hillary with her car and hand over the keys.

CHAPTER FIFTEEN

Susan Leigh ushered their unexpected visitor into her patient's room with a cheery smile. 'Hello, Dot. I've got a surprise for you. There's someone here to see you. Isn't that nice?'

Dorothy Cornwallis, Susan had explained, had moments of lucidity, but mostly she was unaware of where she was, and often failed to recognise either her husband or son when they called.

Now Hillary glanced around the pleasant room, hoping that she would never end up in such a place, and drew a chair closer to the frail old lady half-dozing in her chair by the window. She'd asked the nurse to stay — both as a potential witness to whatever was said, but mostly because she wanted a professional present, if things became emotional or difficult.

'Hello, Mrs Cornwallis. My name is Hillary. Is it all right if I talk to you for a bit?'

The old lady looked at her vaguely. 'Hillary? Are you Mattie's girl?'

Hillary smiled but shook her head. 'No, sorry. I'd like to talk about the old days. Back when you lived in Lower Barton. Is that all right?'

She withdrew an enlarged photograph of Keith Coltrane from her bag. She'd had one made up at the start of the investigation, knowing a visual aid very often helped aid a witness's memory. So far, she'd had little cause to show it to anyone though.

Now she held it up in front of the old lady. She'd come in the hope that this woman might be able to shed some light on both her son and husband's relationship with the dead man, but she could already tell she was on a hiding to nothing.

'This is the vicar. Do you remember him, Dorothy?' she encouraged. 'He was a kind man, so everybody tells me.'

Dorothy stared at the photograph and frowned. Then she began to sing something — a song vaguely recognisable, maybe something from the eighties. Duran Duran perhaps?

'Dot likes to sing,' Susan put in, from where she was sitting on the edge of a single bed and watching the proceedings eagerly. 'She'll stop in a minute, don't worry. Believe it or not, it's a good sign when she does that. She often has a good spell after singing. I dare say songs from when she was younger trigger off memories.'

Hillary hoped she was right. 'Your son Trevor liked the Reverend, didn't he? He used to spend some time at the vicarage, playing tennis with his friends,' she tried again.

Dorothy suddenly stopped singing. 'He was a bad man,' she said flatly.

Hillary, surprised by the sudden clarity of her words, scrambled to make sense of them. She couldn't be speaking of her son, obviously. Again, she held out the photograph. 'Who was a bad man? Do you mean this man, Dorothy?'

'He was a bad man,' she insisted. And then nodded exaggeratedly, for extra emphasis.

And suddenly, Hillary felt a distinct chill settle around her which had nothing to do with the room's heating system. Instead, the chill came from within her. It was something she'd felt before, when realisation suddenly coalesced with a cold sense of foreboding.

With some effort, she mentally readjusted the way she'd been thinking, and looked at the old woman with new eyes. 'How was he a bad man, Dorothy?'

'He just was,' the old lady shrugged graphically.

Hillary nodded. And began to think. Was it possible a woman could be married to a man for all that time, and not come to understand his true nature?

When Keith Coltrane came to the village, Dorothy Cornwallis had a safe if unfulfilling marriage. She had a son, a husband, and a position in life that she must have valued. But that life could have been wiped out at a stroke if Peter's fantasy of running off with the handsome young vicar had played out.

'Dorothy,' she said quietly. 'Peter *liked* Keith very much, didn't he?'

'Disgusting. Letter. Filthy,' Dorothy said, then began to sing again. She sang for some time, but Hillary was happy to let her, because now her mind was racing.

Somehow, all those years ago, Dorothy must have seen the letter that her husband had written to Keith Coltrane. Perhaps Peter had agonised over it for several days, refining it, writing draft after draft until he had it right? Unaware that his wife, suspicious of all those darts nights, and quiz nights, and squash games, had been watching him and wondering. And checking up on him.

From what Peter had told her, Hillary was confident that his love for the vicar had been unreciprocated. But would this woman have known that? All her life, she must have at least suspected that her husband's love for her was lacking something vital. But whilst there was nobody else in Peter Cornwallis's life, she had probably been able to convince herself that everything would be all right. After all, so she would have reasoned, every married couple compromised to some extent, didn't they? And so what if their love life *was* somewhat lacklustre — there was more to life than hearts and roses and romance, right?

But having a less-than-passionate marriage was one thing. Having a rival — a handsome, *male* rival, living right on your doorstep, was another. How long had it taken for the new vicar to become a threat to her? One, moreover, that needed removing?

Dorothy suddenly stopped singing. She looked at Hillary and frowned. 'Are you Mattie's girl?'

Hillary shook her head again. 'No. I work for the police, Mrs Cornwallis,' she said, more for her own benefit than for this old woman who wouldn't remember her five minutes from now.

'Do you remember when Reverend Coltrane was killed in his church?' she tried again, but with no real hope of getting anything helpful from the process.

'The shovel,' Dorothy said, and nodded.

'Yes, he was hit over the head with a shovel,' Hillary agreed. It had been a spade, but she thought now was hardly the time for semantics. She might believe, in her gut, that she was now face to face with the killer of Keith Coltrane, but she also knew there was very little she could do about it.

Even if she could get a coherent statement from the old lady — and she knew that was a non-starter — there was no way the CPS would prosecute her. And what would . . .

'Hid it. I'm not silly,' Dorothy said, a crafty smile briefly lighting up her face.

Hillary regarded her thoughtfully. 'You hid it? Hid it where, Dorothy? You can tell me,' she encouraged.

'In the hiding place,' Dorothy said. 'Under the stairs. Is it teatime yet?'

At this, Susan, who had become very quiet indeed over on the bed, spoke up. 'Soon, Dot. Would you like some chocolate biscuits?'

But Dorothy Cornwallis was nodding off to sleep now.

For a few moments, Hillary watched her. She felt frustrated, uncertain, annoyed and tired. As the old woman started to snore, she admitted defeat and reluctantly got to her feet. 'Well, thank you for your help,' she said to Susan, as she gathered up her things about her and prepared to leave.

'You shouldn't take any notice of what she says,' Susan Leigh said anxiously, but there was uncertainty in her voice now as she looked at the sleeping old lady. 'They're often vague and confused. Don't know what they're saying half the time, they don't,' she insisted.

Hillary smiled a vague smile and left her to organise the promised tea and biscuits. And thought, a little sadly, that the motherly woman would probably never be able to think of the old woman in her care in quite the same way again.

* * *

When she returned to HQ, Claire's car didn't have a scratch on it, and Hillary had done some hard thinking.

She found the communal office empty, and supposed that, by now, Peter Cornwallis had been processed and was with Rollo Sale in the interview room, with Claire and Gareth watching from the observation room.

She walked to Gareth's desk and rummaged for his notes on the Cornwallis family and finally found their old address at Lower Barton. Leaving a note on Gareth's desk to say that she'd gone back to the village, she returned to the car park and climbed wearily into Puff, wondering if she was being stupid, just plain stubborn, or both.

When Peter had fallen on his sword and confessed to the murder of Keith Coltrane, she had assumed that he was covering for his son. It had made sense. Peter had probably believed — for all these years — that his son had killed Keith because he'd found out that his father was planning to leave his family and run off with the man that Trevor himself had so admired.

And how the guilt of that must have eaten away at Peter all this time.

So, she had gone to the care home to talk to the mother, in the hope of gaining some kind of confirmation of Trevor's guilt. Only to have the whole case abruptly turned on its head.

But really, Hillary mused forlornly, what did she have to go on to make a case for Dorothy Cornwallis as the killer of Keith Coltrane? A few muttered words from a confused old lady, and her own years of experience solving murder cases, plus her gut instinct. True, she had a motive, but then so did many others.

Unless Dorothy Cornwallis's 'hiding place' turned out to be real. And Hillary could find it. And the spade that had killed Keith Coltrane was still in existence and hidden there.

The odds on that happening had to be astronomical. And yet here she was, driving her ancient car towards a small village, intent on searching a house which, for all she knew, multiple strangers had lived in over the years before moving on somewhere else. Any one of whom could have found the spade and tossed it out years ago!

She was also starting to really feel the effects of yesterday's hospital stay, coupled with the long and trying day she was now having. And she wanted nothing more than to go home to her boat, have some soup and go to sleep.

But that would have to wait.

* * *

The Cornwallises had lived in Dashwood Cottage back in the day, and as she pulled up in front of it, Hillary could see that it probably wouldn't have changed much since they were there. There was no extension, no added garage, no major landscaping to the grounds. Which all boded well. The less the house had been mucked about, the less likely it was that the interior had undergone major changes either.

And when she rang the bell, and it was answered by a woman not quite as old as Dorothy Cornwallis, her hopes rose even higher.

Hillary showed her ID. 'Hello. Mrs . . . ?'

'Miss. Blackwater. Christina Blackwater. Is there something wrong?' She was a tall, heavyset woman with bright blue eyes and had a slight wheeze as she spoke.

'Oh no, nothing you need worry about, Miss Blackwater,' Hillary assured her. 'As you may have heard, we're taking another look at the murder of the vicar here thirty years ago?'

'Oh yes, I've heard all about that. The village is positively abuzz with it. Please, do come in,' she offered eagerly.

Hillary accepted, somewhat wearily, and stepped into the hall. 'I don't suppose you were living around here when it happened?'

'Oh no,' the old lady said with evident regret. 'I moved here in . . . let me see . . . 1995. Or was it 1994? My word, time does fly! I'm originally from Kent.'

Hillary again felt her hopes rise. 'You must have bought the place direct from the Cornwallis family then?' she said. She knew from Keith's notes that the family had left the village just a few years after the murder.

'Was that their name?'

Hillary nodded, but her eyes were already going around the hall and finding that there was indeed a small cupboard door fitted under the stairs. 'Miss Blackwater, this might sound odd, but do you mind if I look under your stairs?'

'My stairs?' the old lady repeated, looking distinctly startled. And as well she might. As she spoke, she too turned to look at the cupboard door. 'Oh my. I think I keep the spare heaters in there. In case the electric goes off, you know?'

Hillary hid a groan. That was all she needed — having to lug heaters about! A limp lettuce leaf had nothing on her right now. 'That's all right, Miss Blackwater,' she forced herself to say brightly. 'I'll be careful of them. It would help us out though, my having a quick look around. If you don't mind?'

'Oh, of course, of course.' She waved a hand vaguely at her to go ahead but was still looking bemused.

Hillary was conscious of her hovering about in the background as she opened the cupboard door, relieved to see that it was relatively uncluttered inside. There were indeed two spare gas heaters, but they only had a large cardboard box filled with who-knew-what to keep them company.

Once she'd wheeled the heaters out of the way, Hillary ducked into the space and used the torchlight on her mobile phone to look around.

Just as old mother Hubbard had discovered before her, the cupboard was bare.

Hillary couldn't help but laugh out loud. So much for that. That would teach her to tilt at windmills!

And that was when she saw it. The tallest wall — the one opposite the angled rise of the staircase above — had been lined with yellowish pine planks, reminiscent of a 1970s sauna. And in one of the planks was a knot hole. Just the right size, and in just the right position for someone to put a finger in and pull.

Hillary duly put in her finger and pulled, and a small section of the planks moved outwards, revealing a narrow shelving unit. At some point, a previous owner of the cottage must have wanted extra storage for something and had set it up. Jars of preserves maybe?

The shelves were all bare. But there, leaning against the wall, its metal surface glinting darkly in the poor light from her phone, was an old, wooden-handled spade.

Hillary backed out carefully, her heart thumping.

She closed the cupboard door after her and saw Miss Blackwater looking at her curiously. Hillary smiled wanly at her.

'I'm sorry, Miss Blackwater, but I'm afraid I'm going to have to inconvenience you a little longer,' she apologised, and lifting her phone to call HQ, she requested the presence of crime scene and forensic officers.

Miss Blackwater looked positively thrilled!

* * *

It was the following Monday morning before the case was all but tied up.

All three of them were in the superintendent's office, where he'd called them in to join him the moment the forensic report had come in.

Traces of blood and hair had been found on the blade of the spade, and a DNA sample, taken from Moira, confirmed a familial match. The trace elements of organic evidence did indeed belong to her sibling.

It wasn't often such an old specimen was able to produce results, and one of the boffins had make a joke about divine intervention, whilst the superintendent had been more inclined to think that the undisturbed storage space where it had resided for so long had had more to do with it.

'Of course, there'll be no prosecution,' Rollo concluded, nudging the initial CPS report that was lying on his desk. 'Someone's been to try and talk to Mrs Cornwallis, but . . .' he shrugged.

Hillary nodded. 'She probably sang to them for most of the time.'

Claire shook her head. 'You've let Peter Cornwallis go, I take it, sir?'

Rollo nodded. 'He's on his way home as we speak. He was stunned to learn of the find in his old home. He simply can't believe his wife did it. He looked dazed, poor man. I had him driven home in a patrol car. I called his son too. He sounded as shocked as his father, but he agreed to drive to Malmesbury so that he could make sure his father was all right. Reading between the lines, I got the distinct feeling that he'd suspected his father of the crime all along, but never his mother.'

'I expect after Keith was killed, Peter found it impossible to act normally,' Claire mused. 'He probably had a guilty conscience written all over him.'

Hillary stirred in her chair. 'I think father and son may have suspected each other. Both were keeping guilty secrets about the Reverend after all — the son about the drugs, and the father about his feelings for the dead man. And the Cornwallis men struck me as being intelligent and not totally insensitive.

'It would have been impossible for them, I think, not to sense there was something odd in each other's behaviour after the murder. Peter probably assumed Trevor had discovered his feelings for the Reverend and hadn't taken kindly to it.'

'Wouldn't they have talked about it?' Claire asked, then instantly shook her head, and answered her own question. 'No, course they wouldn't. They'd each be scared of what the other one might say. No dad wants to hear his son's a killer, or vice versa.'

Hillary nodded. 'Yes. I imagine they just tried to forget about it and put it behind them. Not sure how that would have worked,' she added with a sigh. 'I can't imagine they'd ever have been comfortable at family get-togethers.'

'So what happens now?' it was Gareth who asked the question.

'Nothing,' the superintendent said flatly.

'Except we can now label the file as solved and closed,' Hillary put in.

'For what *that's* worth,' Claire said, a little bitterly. 'It's been a strange one, this, hasn't it? I mean . . . what was it all about? Was the victim gay or not? Was he going to run off with Peter Cornwallis or was it all in their heads? We don't even know how the murder happened — not for sure.'

'Oh, I think it's fairly clear,' Rollo contradicted her. 'Mrs Cornwallis found out about her husband's infatuation and confronted the vicar about it. Some sort of argument or misunderstanding formed and in a moment of madness, she struck out. Then, in a panic, hid the weapon and never said a word about it. She was lucky she was never suspected, or DI Keating would have found the spade the moment he searched the house.'

There was a small silence at this. Then Claire said, 'So we're saying then that the vicar was probably just a good bloke, doing a good job, and was killed simply because Dorothy Cornwallis believed he was trying to take her husband away from her?'

She looked around the room, and let her eyes linger longest on Hillary, who smiled at her wryly. 'I don't have a crystal ball, Claire. But best guess, I think that's about right. Like you said, it's been a strange one. I don't know about the rest of you, but I don't feel my usual sense of accomplishment once a case is over.'

'Yeah, me neither,' Claire agreed. 'I mean, what was the point of it all? Keith's still dead and his family — what's left of it — don't give a tinker's cuss. We can't even lock up the killer. It all seems so sad and pointless somehow.'

Hillary shrugged and got to her feet, which broke up the meeting. But as they trooped out of the door, Rollo said, determinedly cheerfully, 'We're still going to meet up at the Black Bull after work for a celebratory drink though, yes?'

'Too right, guv,' said Claire. Gareth nodded, as did Hillary, after a moment's hesitation.

Once in her office though, Hillary twirled slightly to and fro in her swivel chair, her computer left off, her mind wandering a little.

Was Claire right? Was justice really not served unless the killer was in jail, and all the t's were crossed, and the i's dotted? Or did it not matter that they would never know — for sure — the whole story?

Perhaps. Perhaps not. But she was pretty sure that, right about now, Peter and Trevor Cornwallis would be meeting up at Peter's house in Malmesbury. And who knew? Now that the family secrets were all out in the open, maybe they could make something good come out of the whole complicated mess?

As the murdered man himself would probably have pointed out, God could work in mysterious ways.

"At that moment, her mobile phone rang.

She answered it absently. 'Hillary Greene.'

'Oh yes, Mrs Greene. This is Kurt Winstanley. From the clinic?'

Hillary abruptly stilled the movement of her chair. Suddenly, the background noise of her everyday life faded, and she came preternaturally aware of everything — from the weight of the bones in her body to the air that moved over the pores of her skin.

And then she heard her voice, as if it came from somewhere outside of herself, talking calmly. 'Oh yes. Mr Winstanley. Thank you for calling. I take it you have the results of the biopsy?'

'I have. And it's good news.'"

THE END

THE JOFFE BOOKS STORY

We began in 2014 when Jasper agreed to publish his mum's much-rejected romance novel and it became a bestseller.

Since then we've grown into the largest independent publisher in the UK. We're extremely proud to publish some of the very best writers in the world, including Joy Ellis, Faith Martin, Caro Ramsay, Helen Forrester, Simon Brett and Robert Goddard. Everyone at Joffe Books loves reading and we never forget that it all begins with the magic of an author telling a story.

We are proud to publish talented first-time authors, as well as established writers whose books we love introducing to a new generation of readers.

We have been shortlisted for Independent Publisher of the Year at the British Book Awards three times, in 2020, 2021 and 2022, and for the Diversity and Inclusivity Award at the Independent Publishing Awards in 2022.

We built this company with your help, and we love to hear from you, so please email us about absolutely anything bookish at feedback@joffebooks.com

If you want to receive free books every Friday and hear about all our new releases, join our mailing list: www.joffebooks.com/contact

And when you tell your friends about us, just remember: it's pronounced Joffe as in coffee or toffee!

ALSO BY FAITH MARTIN

DI HILLARY GREENE SERIES
Book 1: MURDER ON THE OXFORD CANAL
Book 2: MURDER AT THE UNIVERSITY
Book 3: MURDER OF THE BRIDE
Book 4: MURDER IN THE VILLAGE
Book 5: MURDER IN THE FAMILY
Book 6: MURDER AT HOME
Book 7: MURDER IN THE MEADOW
Book 8: MURDER IN THE MANSION
Book 9: MURDER IN THE GARDEN
Book 10: MURDER BY FIRE
Book 11: MURDER AT WORK
Book 12: MURDER NEVER RETIRES
Book 13: MURDER OF A LOVER
Book 14: MURDER NEVER MISSES
Book 15: MURDER AT MIDNIGHT
Book 16: MURDER IN MIND
Book 17: HILLARY'S FINAL CASE
Book 18: HILLARY'S BACK
Book 19: MURDER NOW AND THEN
Book 20: MURDER IN THE PARISH

MONICA NOBLE MYSTERIES
Book 1: THE VICARAGE MURDER
Book 2: THE FLOWER SHOW MURDER
Book 3: THE MANOR HOUSE MURDER

JENNY STARLING MYSTERIES
Book 1: THE BIRTHDAY MYSTERY
Book 2: THE WINTER MYSTERY
Book 3: THE RIVERBOAT MYSTERY
Book 4: THE CASTLE MYSTERY
Book 5: THE OXFORD MYSTERY
Book 6: THE TEATIME MYSTERY
Book 7: THE COUNTRY INN MYSTERY

Manufactured by Amazon.ca
Bolton, ON

39882971R00127

first ten, and when you can recite them easily, go to the next ten. Each time you finish a block, run through the previous words to make sure you still have them. You'll find the cues provided by the consonants very helpful. If one of the words gives you trouble, substitute an alternate. What you want at this stage is to be able to reel off the 110 words in order.

Next, practice the codes in random order so that you'll be able to rapidly come up with the right word for any pair of digits. Flashcards are one way to get the job done. There are also online sites and cell phone apps to drill you on your code words. Find them by searching the Internet for "major system memory training." Space out your practice sessions and continue until the code words come to you easily. That is all there is to it. You will be ready to look for opportunities to put this effort to good use. And here is an added benefit: On those nights when you have trouble drifting off to sleep, just review the 110 code words: "zoo . . . tie . . . hen . . . ma . . . zzzzz . . . "

life—addresses, phone numbers, ID numbers, credit card numbers, prices, measurements, product numbers, dates, and times—a basic mastery of the major system is all that is necessary. You will find suggestions for getting up to speed on it in the Memory Lab section.

Variations

Memory competitors have modified the major system for use in memory contests. These innovations have been described as an "arms race" among competitors, a search for ways to encode memory information ever more quickly and efficiently. Ben Pridmore, a top British mnemonist, remembers numbers and dates with an expanded major system that includes separate codes for digits up to 1,000. Its advantage is that a long number can be memorized as a sequence of three-digit chunks rather than two-digit chunks as with the major system. This gives Pridmore fewer images to juggle when he tries to retain a long number. Of course, the downside is that his system requires massive practice to use effectively. Pridmore has employed it to give impressive performances, such as at the 2008 World Memory Championship, where he memorized 1,800 digits in one hour.

Dominic O'Brien, an eight-time world champion, developed a variant of the major system based on representing numbers with people—he associates a different person with numbers from 00 to 99. Each person is also associated with a characteristic action, so 13 is represented by Al Capone carrying a bottle of liquor, and 15 is Albert Einstein writing on a blackboard. The clever feature of this system is that it can encode a four-digit number with only one image. Say O'Brien wants to remember 1315. He imagines Al Capone (13) writing on a blackboard (15). By combining the person from the first two digits with the action from the second two, he can retain a long number with half as many images as the major system requires. Variations like O'Brien's and Pridmore's make sense for determined memory competitors who can justify the Olympian effort required to master and use them proficiently. But for a recreational mnemonist, these are systems to admire from a distance.

Chao Lu's System

The approach Chao Lu took to memorize 61,890 digits was similar to the major system. He tackled *pi* by working on groups of ten digits at a time, dividing each group into two-digit chunks. He then encoded each chunk as a concrete word using a set of codes he had established for the digits 00–99. He wove the code words for each ten digits into a vivid story. Here's the one he used for the first ten decimal places of *pi*: "a piece of a **rose** (14) was bitten off by a **parrot** (15) and delivered to **Lei Fang** (a famous Chinese soldier—92) at a **cow house** (65), who was smoking a **cigarette** (35)." Each story connected in some way to stories before and after it, creating long chains of narratives. Although the system was simple in principle, managing the massive number of stories required an enormous amount of memory rehearsal.

Chao Lu's strategy provided him with two essential aids for remembering numbers. The first turned a number into the kind of object the memory system can easily retain—one that is concrete, visual, and meaningful. His 00–99 code words did that. The next requirement was to bind the codes together so he could retrieve them from memory in the proper order, and that was the function of the stories he created. This two-pronged approach—one focused on encoding individual memory items and the other focused on organizing them—is common to other powerful memory devices, most notably the memory palaces that we'll talk about in Chapter 14.

A Final Thought

The numbers we encounter in life vary in importance, and some of them certainly should be recorded securely rather than trusted to memory. However, there are many others where a mnemonic strategy can be viable. It's true your pride will suffer if you botch it and have to backtrack to retrieve the number, but it is also true that this very possibility will motivate you to really work at it, and in the process increase your mnemonic skill. And remember that along the way you will be exercising your high-level mental abilities, relying on your own mental resources rather than external devices. These are the very cognitive processes most closely associated with intelligence and applicable to all manner of mental challenge.

The best way to get started remembering numbers is to practice the technique of finding a pattern. When the number is not too long, and when you will use it in the near future, this strategy can be all you need to retain it. The acrostic and number-shape approaches are useful in special circumstances. To progress further, a serious practitioner of the memory

arts should consider taking on the major system. It is no walk in the park, to be sure, but it is quite doable at a level appropriate for a recreational mnemonist. You may find, as I have, that it is satisfying to master such a powerful system, and it puts you in the company of a long succession of mnemonists going back centuries.

In the Memory Lab:
How to Master the Major System

In this installment, we tackle learning the 110 code words that are essential for using the major system. The first step is to master the sounds associated with each digit as given earlier in the chapter. A memory cue for them is the sentence **Satan may relish coffee pie,** which decodes to 0123456789. A helper image is depicted below. Once the codes are secure in memory, you are ready to start on the 110 words. The table that appeared earlier (on page 149) gives the set of code words I use. If you don't like a word or find it hard to remember, think of a better one that decodes to the same number. Online resources are available to suggest code words for specific numbers— try searching for "major system word generator."

The best way to learn a list this long is in blocks. Start with the

"Satan may relish coffee pie" is a mnemonic for remembering major system codes for the digits 0123456789.

11

Remembering Skills

The barista behind the espresso machine looked at the code on the next cup in the queue—a medium-sized skinny vanilla latte—and moved into action. Put four pumps of sugar-free vanilla into the cup. Grind and tamp the coffee. Pull two shots of espresso and mix it with the vanilla. Measure the right amount of skim milk into a metal pitcher. And then the crucial step: Use the steam wand to aerate the milk and bring its temperature to 150 degrees. She completed the order by mixing the milk into the cup with just the right amount of foam on top. After she'd secured the lid, the latte was ready for the customer to pick up. The barista turned at once to the next cup. At this busy location, she sometimes pushes through 100 drinks an hour.

But this order was not finished. "Excuse me! Excuse me," the customer called out. "This latte is not hot enough." The barista may have been skeptical—her equipment is carefully maintained to get the temperature exactly right. In fact, the complaint could well be more about a coffee prima donna than the temperature of the drink. But if any of that passed through her consciousness, it didn't show, because her training kicked in. After establishing eye contact with the customer, she began to make things right. If she were a less experienced barista, she might have recalled the Starbucks acronym for dealing with unhappy customers—**LATTE**: **L**isten, **A**cknowledge, **T**ake action, **T**hank the customer, and **E**xplain what might have caused the problem. But she didn't need acronyms: She was a seasoned hand who knew how to respond to a customer problem, and she carried it out smoothly.

The barista's job is all about skill, not only the motor skills needed to operate the equipment, but also the cognitive and people skills she needs to interact with customers in a way that will keep them coming back for more. The barista, like all of us, possesses a broad range of skills that go far beyond her job, a skill collection that defines who she is as a person. Skills give us efficient, predictable ways to achieve our goals. They are at work when we prepare meals, drive cars, use computers, and play sports. They are at the core of the surgeon's technique, the stockbroker's advice, and the politician's deal making. As we saw in Chapter 1, skills rely on a specialized form of memory that is distinct from our memory for facts and personal experiences. You see evidence for this when you ask skilled people how they do what they do; they often cannot come up with a satisfactory explanation—their skill is something they can't put into words.

How Skills Are Acquired

The barista learned to make lattes by watching a trainer demonstrate the technique, an experience that left behind a memory of how to make one. This is how most skills start out: through the acquisition of basic knowledge that is retained as an explicit memory. The long-term memory systems described in Chapter 1, most of which are involved in learning a skill, are shown again below. The barista retained the trainer's demonstration as an episodic memory. She also knew a number of facts about lattes—the different varieties, the different sizes, her favorites—which she had picked up here and there before she took the barista job. She relied on this explicit knowledge at first. In fact, if we were to watch her closely as she prepared her first latte, we might have seen her lips moving ever so slightly as she mentally talked herself through the process by recalling what her trainer showed her. These were slow, inefficient productions, and they required

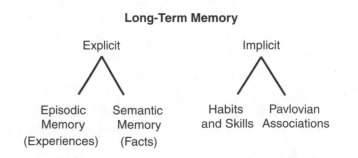

Long-Term Memory

Explicit   Implicit

Episodic   Semantic   Habits   Pavlovian
Memory   Memory   and Skills Associations
(Experiences) (Facts)

that she stay focused by devoting her cognitive resources exclusively to each step.

As our barista served up more lattes, we would see rapid improvement. Each time she successfully completed the required sequence, the behavior pattern was strengthened as a skill memory. This is a system specialized for carrying out efficient movements to achieve a specific goal. Unlike the explicit memory system, skill memory is established gradually, improving with each success, as illustrated in the graph below. We would see this as a series of small enhancements, like using the steam wand more deftly or pulling espresso shots more smoothly. She will also improve in a less obvious way by learning to pay attention to the things that matter—what to watch as she aerates the milk to get the right amount of foam and how to judge the quality of a shot as she pulls it. These perceptual skills are every bit as important as the motor skills involved in operating the machine. With each advance, the skill becomes better established in her implicit memory system and less dependent on her explicit, conscious knowledge. She moves from "knowing that" (explicit knowledge) to "knowing how" (skill).

More practice will lead to easier and smoother operations until they are so secure she can exchange pleasantries with a customer as she works or even allow her thoughts to drift to topics far removed from her espresso machine. These are distractions she wouldn't have been able to manage previously without spoiling a drink. Psychologists describe the behavior as automatic because it requires little conscious control.

The fact that automatic skills are almost effortless leads to huge benefits when the skill is embedded in a complex process. A pianist whose finger movements for a well-practiced piece have become largely automatic is able to apply her cognitive resources to the work's expressiveness, giving

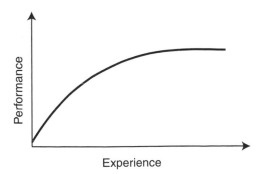

it gaiety, excitement, or surprise. A less practiced performer must reserve conscious attention to handle fingering details. The expert surgeon who has practiced specialized procedures to the point where they are automatic frees up his high-level mental abilities to handle unexpected problems and to plan the next steps.

Some skills are more about mental operations than physical movements—handling an unhappy customer, programming a computer, controlling air traffic, or memorizing the order of a deck of playing cards. Interestingly, their development is similar to more physical skills like playing a piano or using a scalpel. At first these skills are dependent on explicit knowledge consciously remembered and put to use, step by step. The new chess player needs to recall the way pawns and rooks, kings and queens move and then sort through the options available for each. But with practice, the basics of play become automatic and players become able to use their cognitive resources for more strategic and complex aspects of the game.

Mnemonic skills develop in the same way. Say you want to become better at remembering names by using the strategy from Chapter 7 cued by the acrostic "Friendly Llamas Seek People"—**F**ind a feature, **L**isten to the name, **S**ay it back, and **P**ractice. Initially, it will take effort to hold the four steps in mind, and you may even need the helper image repeated below. At this stage you are relying on explicit memory to carry out the strategy. But as with the barista at the espresso machine, each success strengthens

The Friendly Llama, a helper image used to recall an acrostic relevant for learning a name.

the process as a skill memory, and the routine becomes easier to follow. More practice also leads to refinements as you learn how to spot people's distinguishing features, what to do with difficult names, how to mentally practice new names, how to work names into conversations. You become less and less dependent on explicit memories for guidance, and you find it takes less attention and mental effort to carry out the steps. Eventually you won't need the Friendly Llama at all because your implicit memory system will be directing the action. The key steps now occur almost effortlessly, making the mnemonic superfluous.

Getting from "Good Enough" to "Good"

Most skills will get to a point where your performance no longer improves with practice. You may discover your tennis skill is stuck at an intermediate level no matter how often you play. Your cooking may not be soaring to culinary heights, even though you put dinner on the table every night. What's happened is that your practice is maintaining the status quo: Your skills aren't getting sharper, but they're not diminishing either.

What separates you from others who continue to improve? Motivation certainly plays a part. It could well be that you are at peace with your performance and have no serious interest in improving. Many skills are like that. Whether it's playing softball, making home repairs, or managing investments, many of us are satisfied with a skill level far short of real expertise.

But what about skills you would like to improve? Motivation alone isn't enough to bring this about. You've always wanted to be a better cook, but it just isn't happening. And then there's your tennis game. The development of expertise requires more than just wanting it. In fact, studies of high achievers reveal that they make focused efforts to hone their skills. Psychologist Anders Ericsson, a leader in this research, has studied top performers in areas as diverse as chess, music, medicine, bridge, computer programming, sports, and memory skill. These are individuals whose performance curves have risen way above the level of "good enough" as shown on the graph on the next page. Ericsson and his colleagues discovered common elements in the ways elite achievers practiced. For them practice is a serious endeavor. They work to get as much gain as possible from each session; they reflect on what was successful, and they figure out how to do

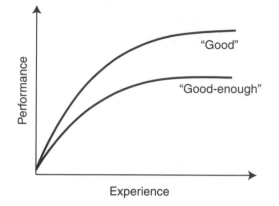

better. Ericsson called this "deliberate practice," and it applies to a Sunday golfer as much as to an Olympic hopeful. He found three features of deliberate practice that work together to keep skill development moving forward, putting it on a trajectory to become "good."

1. Target Specific Improvements

The best way to improve skills is to focus on specifics. The tennis player may work on her serve, the cook on his sautéing technique. The barista, having mastered the fundamentals, might decide to upgrade her technique for steaming milk so that she can consistently produce the finely aerated, creamy foam of top-quality lattes. By singling out foam for improvement, she leaves other parts of the skill as they are, largely automatic steps she performs easily. Focusing on the foam process changes it from being automatic to being consciously controlled. She can now apply her attention, working memory, and reasoning abilities to improve it. There can be no chatting with customers at this stage because she will need her cognitive resources to work out the fine points of making better foam. It is no surprise that Ericsson and his colleagues have found that improvement is demanding mental work.

An important part of deliberate practice is problem solving. The barista must figure out how to get the steam wand to produce small rather than large bubbles in the milk and then learn how to stir them into the creamy texture she wants. It will take repeated tries, but if she stays focused, it is within her grasp, and with even more practice the new routine will become largely automatic. At this point she can talk to customers and still produce high-quality foam.

2. Value Feedback

Unless the barista can determine the quality of the foam she is producing, she can't improve—feedback is essential for deliberate practice to work. In her case, a more experienced coworker could serve as a coach to provide feedback and suggest practice goals. In fact, this is the ideal situation for skill development. In the world of elite performers, coaches and trainers are highly prized for just these reasons. If the barista can find such a person, she will be able to improve her skills quickly.

When finding a coach isn't practical, you must look for another way to solve the feedback problem. Say you're a mnemonist who wants to improve your memory for names. What feedback will be most useful? And how can you get that feedback? Simply knowing how many names you remembered from an event isn't specific enough to help you improve your technique. You would do better to find a time soon after the event to reflect, a time when you can still recall how well you performed on each of the four Friendly Llama steps. You may make notes on your observations while your memory is fresh and then work out practice goals for your next opportunity. Each skill presents its own challenge. Finding a practical way to get feedback must be a priority for anyone interested in improving because without it, practice only reinforces errors and inefficiencies.

3. Get Lots of Practice

There is one more essential ingredient in deliberate practice: it has to be repeated over and over. How much practice? That depends on the complexity of the skill and the aspirations of the performer. In competitive fields like music, chess, surgery, or science, elite achievers typically invest ten years of serious work to become top performers.

That kind of commitment is out of reach for a recreational golfer, musician, or mnemonist. The amount of practice they can manage is not only compromised by other life interests, but it also can be undermined by the logistics of finding practice opportunities. How they juggle priorities, find opportunities, and marshal self-discipline will determine where they wind up on the continuum between "good enough" and "good."

Mental Rehearsal

Not all practice has to involve activities in the outside world. It can also take place in the mind. Top athletes use mental rehearsal as part of their practice for competitive events. Here is a successful Olympian springboard diver talking about his preparation:

> I did my dives in my head all the time. At night, before going to sleep, I always did my dives. Ten dives. I started with a front dive, the first one I had to do at the Olympics, and I did everything as if I was actually there. I saw myself on the board with the same bathing suit. Everything was the same. . . . If the dive was wrong, I went back and started over again. It takes a good hour to do perfect imagery of all my dives, but it was better than a workout.

Mental imagery has become a fixture in Olympic training circles. At the 2014 Sochi Winter Games, the United States brought nine sports psychologists to assist athletes in preparing for their events, and using imagery to improve skills was a major focus. Earlier studies of Olympic contenders have shown that the most successful competitors reported using more imagery than the less successful ones.

The idea that you can improve a skill by mentally practicing it is a well-researched principle in psychology. It is supported not only for sports but also for performing surgery, playing music, executing dance routines, landing airplanes, carrying out laboratory tasks, and recovering from strokes.

If you decide to give mental practice a try, it's best to wait until you've mastered the basics of the skill with hands-on practice and you're familiar with environments where it will be used. This is important because mental rehearsal works best when your imagined performance closely mimics the actual physical sensations of performing the skill—and you will need experience to be able to construct this imagery. The correspondence between real and imaginary should be as close as you can manage, starting with how the setting will look to you as you perform the skill, even what you will be wearing. The sensations of physical movements are an important part of mental rehearsal. The pianist should be able to feel her fingers working the keys; a softball pitcher should feel the windup before the mental throw; and a mnemonist should feel the pressure of a handshake during the imagined introduction. Even the emotions that accompany the skill—being nervous or feeling excited—will make the imagery more realistic and thus more effective.

Suppose you want to improve your ability to remember names of people you meet at a party or a business conference. You could picture yourself carrying out the Friendly Llama strategy successfully and retaining the names of imaginary people you will meet at a forthcoming event. Ideally, you will have been to the actual room where the introductions will take place so you can visualize it in your mind, but if not, you will need to picture a similar setting. You will see yourself there in the clothes you'll be wearing, and you will imagine behaving as you hope to behave at the real event. I recommend that you prepare a written script to guide the imagery, especially at first. Here is an example:

> *I am coming into the room for the meeting . . . I'm wearing my blue sports coat and gray trousers . . . no tie today . . . I am carrying my tablet. . . . I see the setup, the chairs, the table, the screen, the coffee urn. . . . I recall my retention intention for today . . . I seriously want to learn as many new names as I can. . . . I am looking forward to it and feeling pumped about my prospects. . . . I start noticing people I don't know . . . I check them out. . . . I wonder who they are and what they are like . . . I look for distinguishing features . . . I nod to a woman I know . . . she is standing with a man I want to meet . . . I have picked out a feature I can use to remember this guy—it's his abundant head of hair—and note it as I go over . . . I feel my legs moving as I go over to where she is . . . we say hello . . . as she begins to introduce me to the new person, I make eye contact . . . I give him my full attention . . . I feel my arm extend . . . I experience the handshake . . . I keep my full attention on him as he says his name . . . I hear him say "Jay" . . . I repeat it . . . "Glad to meet you, Jay" . . . I note his distinguishing feature again . . . we talk . . . I mentally repeat his name to myself . . . I excuse myself to say hello to someone else . . . I repeat "Nice meeting you, Jay" as I leave. . . .*

Scripts can be about more than just the skill; they can also create motivation, as this one does, and they can prepare you to cope with difficulties you might encounter. For example, you could get overwhelmed when you're being introduced to a lot of people, one after the other. You may know from experience that once that sinking feeling hits, you tend to give up trying to retain the names. Instead of giving up, prepare yourself for this situation by adding a section to the script in which you imagine that it happens and you deal with it. You might see yourself becoming overwhelmed, recognize what is happening, and respond by turning your attention inward, taking a breath, refocusing, and then going back to the Friendly Llama strategy. By rehearsing a coping response in advance, you increase the chances you can pull it off at the real event.

You can work from a written script or you can read it into a recording device and play it back to yourself. In either case, the goal is to create the images it describes. As you experiment with mental rehearsal, keep in mind that it is itself a skill and takes practice to master. Its two key requirements are making the imagery as vivid as you can and controlling it so that you can accurately portray the skill you are practicing.

You can use this rehearsal technique either to develop a skill or to prepare for a specific occasion. When you use it for development, it will be most effective in conjunction with actual practice. When you use it to tune up a skill for an upcoming event, the method will work best if you carry it out close to the time when you will need the skill.

The Leaky Bucket Problem

Just because you master a skill doesn't mean you will always perform it well. Suppose you successfully complete a training course in cardiopulmonary resuscitation (CPR). Will you be able to carry it out successfully if you encounter an emergency in six months? In a year? There will almost certainly be some drop in performance, but how much? That was the question British researcher Ian Glendon and his colleagues asked in a study of shop-floor and office workers who took a CPR course from professional instructors. Those who performed well were recruited to come back for a retest after different periods of time. When they arrived for the test, they were taken to a room where they found a "casualty," a manikin instrumented to record details of the CPR effort. This allowed experts to judge whether each participant would have maintained a real person's vital functions well enough to allow survival. The graph on the facing page shows how skill levels lapsed in a major way over the one-year period. After twelve and a half months, only fourteen percent of the CPR attempts would have been adequate to save the victim.

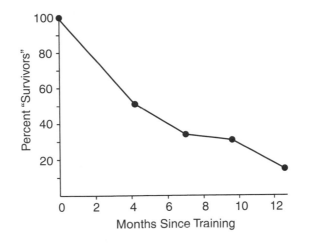

CPR competency in the months following CPR training.

This is the leaky bucket problem—a loss of competence over time when you don't practice a skill. Just how much loss depends on the skill. You are not likely to forget how to swim or ride a bike, even if you don't practice. The simple structure of repetitive movements guided by environmental cues makes these activities resistant to decay. But when a skill is replete with multiple steps and time pressures, it can degrade quickly. This is what happened in the CPR study, because CPR requires that a sequence of actions be performed precisely at a specified rate with little feedback available to signal its being done correctly. Over time there is slippage—steps can drop out, the compressions can become too shallow, the tempo can become too rushed. Regular practice is the only remedy. The Red Cross recommends a CPR refresher every three months, and the graph shows this is none too soon.

With more complex skills, practice must be even more frequent or performance will suffer. The great pianist Ignacy Paderewski famously observed, "If I miss one day's practice, I notice it. If I miss two days' practice, the critics notice it. If I miss three days' practice, the public notices it." Other demanding skills are similar in their practice requirements. A typical F-15 pilot must fly thirteen practice sorties a month to maintain adequate proficiency for real missions. And when it comes to the Olympics, hopefuls organize their lives around practice, both real and imaginary.

A Final Thought

Many people who take my memory classes hope to learn techniques that will instantly give them a better memory. Of course, it doesn't work that way, no more than learning how a latte is made will instantly make you a competent barista. In any complex skill, expert performance comes from an interplay between the explicit and implicit memory systems, an interplay that requires practice. This insight is especially important for anyone who aspires to be a practitioner of the memory arts. Because it's a skill based on techniques that can be described easily, it's seductive to believe that knowledge of the techniques is all you need. But explicit knowledge is only a starting point. An appropriate amount of deliberate practice must take place because practical utility won't come until the techniques become established as smoothly flowing procedures in the implicit memory system.

In the Memory Lab: The Link Method

This installment of the Memory Lab introduces a useful way to remember a series of memory items in a specific order. We look at an example of the method here, and then in Chapter 13 we'll examine it more thoroughly.

The Link Method is especially useful when you want to move easily from one item in a series to the next. For example, imagine you're working your way through a mental grocery list. You've just picked up the butter, and now you need the next item on the list. The Link Method will help bring it to mind.

Here we construct a memory aid for recalling the three components of deliberate practice in order. To add a practical context, suppose I'm preparing to deliver a lecture on this material, and I don't want to rely on notes. The Link Method allows me to move through the topics in order without external memory aids. Although the application here involves only three topics, the process could be extended to link as many topics as I wished.

The three components of deliberate practice are (1) target specific aspects of the skill, (2) get feedback on performance, and (3) practice. To apply the Link Method, I create associations between the pairs of components in the order I want to recall them.

To improve skills →
       Target specifics →
              Get feedback →
                     Practice

Every arrow will become a visual image linking the items on either side of it. The diagram shows I need three visual images to create the three links.

First Link: To Improve Skills → Target Specifics

I used a juggler to suggest skills and a bull's-eye to represent targeting specifics, as shown below. Combining them by showing bull's-eye targets being juggled gave the association I was looking for. During the lecture, when I get to improving skills, I mentally look for an association to that topic, and I recall the juggler image. The bull's-eyes will help me remember the first component of deliberate practice: targeting specifics of the skill.

The first of three images to link together the steps involved in deliberate practice. Here skill learning (the juggler) is associated with targeting a specific skill component (the targets).

Second Link: Target Specifics → Get Feedback

An interesting feature of the Link Method is that each association is independent of the others. So, to create the second link, I put the juggler aside and looked for something to connect "targeting specifics" and "feedback." Because "feedback" is abstract and not easily represented as a visual image, I looked for a substitute word that could suggest "feedback." I chose "food" and then imagined a target with "food" in the center, as depicted below. This will be enough to get me to recall "feedback." During the lecture, as I finish talking about targeting specifics, I mentally look for an association with "targeting," recall this image, and know the next topic is "feedback."

Third Link: Get Feedback → Practice

When I'm ready to make the third point, I will search for an association with feedback and recall the third link, shown on the facing page. It displays a hapless musician being pelted with hostile feedback as a disappointed audience hurls tomatoes. He obviously needs more practice, an implication that will cue the last topic. As you look at these images, keep in mind that effective memory cues are idiosyncratic.

The next visual image used in the link method. The second step of deliberate practice, getting feedback, is connected with the previous step, targeting a specific skill component.

The final link for remembering the three steps of deliberate practice. It associates feedback with more practice.

These images work for me, but if you were delivering the lecture and using the Link Method, your images would likely be different.

Once I have the links, I run through them in my mind several times before the lecture to make sure they will come easily to me as I move from topic to topic. If I choose the link images well, I'll be comfortable speaking without notes, and the lecture will follow the path I intend for it.

12

Remembering Life

James McGaugh is a leading authority on memory. As a top researcher, he has published scores of scientific papers and has been lauded for his major insights about the memory system. It was because of his prominence that Jill Price emailed him on June 8, 2000:

> I am thirty-four years old and since I was eleven I have had this unbelievable ability to recall my past, but not just recollections. My first memories are of being a toddler in a crib (circa 1967) however I can take a date between 1974 and today, and tell you what day it falls on, what I was doing that day, and if anything of great importance . . . occurred that day I can describe that to you as well. I do not look at calendars beforehand and I do not read twenty-four years of my journals either. Whenever I see a date flash on the television (or anywhere else for that matter) I automatically go back to that day and remember where I was, what I was doing, what day it fell on and on and on and on and on. It is non-stop, uncontrollable and totally exhausting.

Ms. Price hoped that McGaugh, Larry Cahill, and their colleagues at the University of California, Irvine, could help her gain some control of her memories so that they were not so draining of her energy. McGaugh agreed to a meeting, but he was deeply skeptical that her memory could be that remarkable. Researchers call this form of remembering "autobiographical memory," and everything that was known about it then suggested that what she claimed was impossible.

As McGaugh's team put Price through an extensive series of memory tests, it became clear that she indeed had phenomenal autobiographical memory. Her old journals allowed the researchers to test her recollections against what she had written years earlier. Her memories invariably checked out. In one surprise test, they asked her to write down the date that Easter fell on each year between 1980 and 2003. Not only did she give the dates, but she also volunteered what she had been doing on each day. For example, she reported that on Easter Sunday, March 30, 1986, her parents were in Palm Springs and three friends were staying with her at their house. In 1989, Easter was on March 26, and she remembered spending it with a friend. The journal entries matched her memories.

Interestingly, the tests showed that Price's memory for other types of information—numbers, words, pictures, and diagrams—was undistinguished. She reported that she had trouble remembering school material. But for life events that she found interesting or personally relevant, her memory was jaw-dropping.

McGaugh and Cahill studied Price's memory over several years and documented capabilities never previously suspected by researchers. Price patiently assisted their efforts, and over time she began to make peace with her extraordinary memory, eventually writing a book, *The Woman Who Can't Forget,* about the role it had played in her life.

Word about McGaugh's work spread, and other people with similar abilities were discovered. Unlike Price, they valued their uncommon proficiency. But like Price, they could recall daily experiences for calendar dates picked at random, and their memories checked out, just as hers did. McGaugh and his team carefully studied many of them with interviews, memory tests, and even brain scans. They named this rare ability "highly superior autobiographical memory" (HSAM). I will come back to what they learned about it, but first consider how the rest of us remember our past. It's totally different, and it will provide a context to appreciate these special people and see what they have to teach us if we want to remember our own lives better.

What We Remember

Those of us without Jill Price's abilities will forget most of what happens to us in life. It's true that each day adds new memories—the conversation at breakfast, the search for a parking space, the meeting with a colleague, the lunch at the deli. These events will usually be recallable for days, weeks, or even longer when a good memory cue is available—if you go back to that deli next month, you may still be able to recall details of what you and a friend talked about. Nonetheless, most of this information is doomed to be forgotten. But not all of it. What is it about the memories we retain?

Gillian Cohen and Dorothy Faulkner, two British researchers, attempted to find out by asking 154 people between twenty and eighty-seven years of age to identify their most vivid memories and to write a few words about each. The bar chart below shows the top nine themes in the memories people recalled. Taken together they account for over eighty percent of all memories reported. What is it about these events that allowed them to be remembered while so many others were lost to time? Cohen and Faulkner believe that each one was (1) personally important, or (2) unusual, or (3) emotionally significant, or some combination of these qualities.

The memory advantage of novel events deserves special note. The ease with which we retain the odd, the rare, the unusual, and the unexpected is shown by the fact that seventy-three percent of memories found in that study involved situations that are not routine—a first love, a trip abroad, an illness. The memorability of such distinctive experiences is dramatically illustrated in a study by David Pillemer and his colleagues at Wellesley College. They tracked down graduates who had been out of school for twenty-two years and asked them what they remembered from their first year of college. As the graph on the facing page shows, most of these memo-

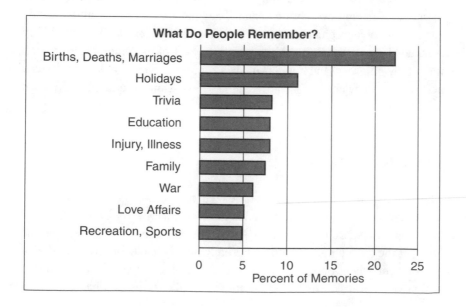

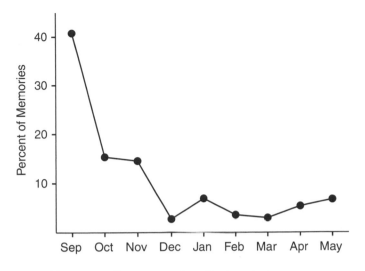

First-year college memories after twenty-two years.

ries came from one month—the month they arrived. This was when they encountered one fresh experience after another as they met roommates, talked with advisors, found their way around campus, and attended classes. These first-time experiences left lasting impressions. Later experiences, on the other hand, were "same old, same old," not distinctive enough to register well in memory.

Feelings are the other powerful memory enhancer. This was evident in the Wellesley study, where the great majority of remembrances were linked to emotion. You'll find the same is true of your own long-lasting memories. If you go back to your experience of college or high school and pay attention to the first memories that come to mind, they will most certainly have an emotional component that helped make them memorable—those first high school dances, accomplishments with the photo club, camaraderie at a football game.

Emotion has a special relationship to memory because of its ability to strengthen memories as they are created. The neurochemicals that accompany emotion affect the brain areas where memories are formed, and the result is a vivid, durable representation of the event. A notable example is a "flashbulb memory," an emotional experience preserved in compelling detail and capable of lasting a lifetime. Following is an elderly Danish man's memory of the invasion of Denmark on April 9, 1940, when he was thirteen years old.

> I was woken up by a thundering noise, never heard anything like it. Opened the skylight in the attic and looked towards the south. Over the woods nearby, squadrons of big grey planes are coming, three at a time, right above the tree-tops. One can see the pilots in their cockpits, and the sides of the planes are wavy sheet metal with big black and white crosses on them. I run downstairs to my family—consisting of my mother and grandmother. My mother is furious. The radio has announced that we are occupied by the Germans.

This memory had a lot going for it. Not only was the event important and unusual, but it also evoked strong emotions. In fact, it was probably the emotional content that's responsible for its crystal clarity and many details, the signature characteristics of flashbulb memories. Danish psychologists Dorthe Berntsen and Dorthe Thomsen used a variety of methods to check the accuracy of flashbulb memories recalled by elderly Danes who had lived through the invasion. Most checked out as substantially correct despite a retention period of more than sixty years.

A more recent event that produced flashbulb memories for many was the September 11, 2001, attack on the World Trade Center in New York. If you were old enough at the time, you probably have a clear memory of hearing about it. Is that memory coming back right now? Can you say where you were and what you were doing? How you learned about the attack? What you did next? If you can answer these questions, you have a flashbulb memory, and you are not alone. Not only do Americans who were at least adolescents at the time overwhelmingly remember it well, so also do residents of Britain, Belgium, Italy, Romania, Japan, and other countries. This was a flashbulb event worldwide.

In the Middle Ages, emotion was intentionally deployed for mnemonic purposes in powerful ways, creating flashbulb memories in the process. Here is historian Morris Bishop describing those times:

> Another curious aspect of medieval justice was the method of impressing dates and decisions on witnesses' memories, since written records were scanty or inaccessible. Boys who served as witnesses were solemnly cuffed or flogged to vivify their memory until old age. Coultron records that "Roger de Montgomery had thrown into the water his son Robert of Bellême, clad in a

fur coat, . . . in testimony and in memorial that the [property] of the abbot and his monks extended as far as that point."

By associating an emotional experience with a crucial fact, the medieval judge ensured that the location of the abbot's property line would be safe with young Robert for a long time as a flashbulb memory. Similarly, those who served as witnesses to marriages would sometimes follow the ceremony by hitting one another to make sure they remembered the union, a serious responsibility in a time with no formal record keeping.

Emotional memories are usually relatively accurate, but not always. In fact, sometimes they contain vivid and compelling errors. Consider flashbulb memories for September 11, 2001. Several days after the attack Lia Kvavilashvili and her colleagues at the University of Hertfordshire asked a large sample of people to describe how they had heard about it. They contacted the same people two years later and asked them to remember the event again. About ten percent of their participants showed major distortions in what they remembered. For example, a day after the event, one woman recalled that she had heard about the attack when she went to pick up her granddaughter at a playground. Two years later, she remembered hearing about it from a clerk in a dry cleaning establishment. She recalled both memories vividly. Instances like this show a risk associated with emotional memories. Because they seem so real, we accept them uncritically. But an impressive body of research shows that they regularly contain errors. The lesson for us as students of memory is to keep in mind that vivid memories are not guaranteed to be accurate. Any memory, even a flashbulb experience, can be in error.

The Bump

Suppose you write down the first fifty memories of your life you can think of. It will turn out that quite a few of them will be from the last year or so, but put those aside and look only at the older memories. What periods of your life did they come from? If you are over fifty, you'll find a disproportionate number of memories from the time when you were fifteen to thirty years old. This "bump" is illustrated in the graph on page 176, derived from studies of people in their seventies who were given a series of cue words

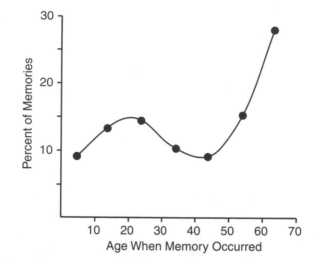

An autobiographical bump occurs between the ages of fifteen and thirty when people over fifty recall memories from their lives.

like *cat, flower,* and *ticket* and asked to recall a memory for each word. When scientists plotted the ages those events occurred, they discovered "the bump." This has turned out to be a surprisingly robust finding. It not only holds for memories spontaneously recalled and memories triggered by cue words, but also for memories cued by odors or recalled in life stories.

The bump is probably due to a combination of factors. It seems no coincidence that it occurs in the years when the cognitive system is at peak efficiency, when people score their highest on memory tests and when their reaction times are the quickest. It is also a crucial time for social development. During these years we navigate adolescence and find our adult identity. Major chapters in our life story are written as we take on college, careers, marriage, and children. These many experiences will often have all the features associated with strong memories—personal importance, novelty, and emotional content. It is indeed a special time of life, and the bump reflects it.

What about Earlier Memories?

Just as the bump represents our best remembered years, the period before it qualifies as the worst. When adults are asked to recall early memories, they seldom remember experiences before about the age of three. Freud called this dearth "childhood amnesia." It's not that children younger than three don't remember things; it's that their memories don't last. Even by the time a child is six, memory for the early years has largely faded. Part of the reason is brain development. Key memory structures are too immature in very young children for them to hold on to their experiences for very long. There are also social factors at work. Children have to learn how to put the bits and pieces of their remembered experiences together to form coherent stories of what happened. Interactions with their parents and other adults gradually teach this skill. As they get better at expressing their existing memories, the children's retention of new information also improves. By the time they are eight or nine, both nature and nurture have brought their memory systems to a point where their new memories are as robust as those formed by adults.

The Life Story

Another milestone in memory development occurs as people move into their teenage years and begin to organize their memories into a life story. This is a time when adolescents face a daunting agenda: establish gender identity, deal with tricky peer relationships, sort out educational options, and work through changing family dynamics. These challenges prompt interest in their own stories, an interest seen in the tendency of many teens to keep a diary—about a third of the college students I teach say they did so during these years. The life stories they are beginning to formulate will continue to evolve throughout their lives, and as this happens, memories will link together to capture different aspects of their experiences. An after-school job in high school will leave behind more than a bunch of isolated memories. Instead, the memories will form a story about this activity during those years, a narrative involving people, events, emotions, and responsibilities, all with special meaning for the person involved. Researchers call collections of memories like this a "chapter" in the life story. Memories from other aspects of a person's life will form other chapters—the years in the college dorm, a serious romantic relationship, a parent's illness. Each chapter pulls together memories of related events into a narrative structure that gives context and meaning. As the years pass, the life story will be expanded, updated, edited, revised, and reinterpreted. It serves as our personal perspective on the past, one that shapes how we see the present and how we look toward the future.

Because life stories organize autobiographical memories, they can play a role in retrieving them. Martin Conway, a prominent researcher, has theorized that such memories are organized as a hierarchy with three levels. At the highest level are collections of memories ordered chronologically according to a particular theme to form a chapter, such as "my years in the dorm." A second level consists of situations in the chapter where a group of memories took place. For example, "my freshman roommate, Jared," identifies a general situation with many dorm memories. At the lowest level in Conway's hierarchy are memories of specific episodes like "the time Jared screwed up my computer."

To see the system in action, suppose my wife asks if I remember the small garden she planted years ago when we lived in California. How will I locate that memory among the many thousands of experiences I've had? It may be that the cue she gave me, "small garden in California," will be enough to let me immediately retrieve the memory, but since this was long ago, directly retrieving it could well fail. If so, I might still be able to find the memory if I come at it from my life story as shown in the box below. I would begin by mentally going back to those California years, a chapter in my life story, and recalling a duplex we lived in at the time. This setting is associated with many memories, and it's where I would have experienced the garden. There I discover cues to bring the garden memory to mind—and to remember how much we enjoyed the taste of those tomatoes right off the vine. The life story, with its hierarchical organization, provides an alternate access to personal memories. It is slower and less efficient than a good cue

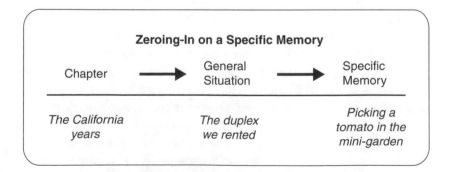

that takes us directly to the memory, but it can save the day when available cues are inadequate.

Highly Superior Autobiographical Memory (HSAM)

What about those people like Jill Price who have such amazing memories for autobiographical experiences? How do they do it? Can we learn anything from them that will help us better remember our own lives?

Although many questions remain, there have been enlightening discoveries about those with HSAM. Four scientific articles have now appeared about them as well as two books by HSAM individuals. In addition to Jill Price's story, Marilu Henner has written a self-help book titled *Total Memory Makeover.* Henner is an accomplished actress and author of other self-help books on health and diet. Her new book describes her HSAM and makes recommendations to readers about ways to improve their ability to remember their pasts. I'll come back to her suggestions later. One key finding about HSAM is enthrallment with the calendar. Those with HSAM can give the day of the week for any date as long as it's in the period of their lives where they have detailed memory, usually after about the age of eleven or twelve. They know when leap years occur, which months have identical calendar pages, and which years are identical for all months. Their memories are tied to specific dates, and this gives them a way to organize their memories so they can recall them easily and systematically. And with each rehearsal, the memories become stronger. Jill Price recalls that December 19, 1980, was the last day of school in tenth grade just before Christmas vacation. On December 19, 1981, she went shopping with Dean and Harry in Beverly Hills. She can continue remembering December 19ths right up to the present. It is striking how ordinary her memories for these dates are. These are not important events or especially noteworthy or charged with strong emotions; they are just daily happenings, the kind of things the rest of us easily forget. By tying the events to dates, she created specific cues that allow her to remember them, and she does this frequently. For example, as she blow-dries her hair each morning, she mentally flips back through the same day of the month in previous years to recall what happened. Marilu Henner and others with HSAM report similar practices.

Perhaps not surprisingly, a commonality among people with HSAM is a marked tendency toward obsessiveness—not enough to qualify as a psychological disorder but definitely more than the average person. They collect and carefully organize clothing, music CDs, mugs, hats, stuffed animals, and *TV Guide*s. The McGaugh team believes their need for order and their tendency toward obsessiveness may be linked to HSAM. It could explain their calendar fascination as a way to organize their memories, and it could motivate their habitual rehearsal of past years.

There is one other common element among these remarkable people: Those who have it value their special ability. None of the individuals studied, not even Jill Price, would give up their special memory if they could. One woman, Louise Owen, put it like this: "I think it makes me live my life with so much more intention and so much more joy. . . . I know that I am going to remember whatever happens today. What can I do to make today special? What can I do to make today stand out?"

Strengthening Autobiographical Memory

Is there anything we can learn from HSAM people to improve our autobiographical memory? Actually, any of us could adopt some of their practices: they are people who deeply value memories of the past; they enjoy the process of reminiscing, and they rehearse their memories on a regular basis. Although their calendar abilities seem out of reach, most of us can improve our ability to reminiscence, and we can choose to take more pleasure in reviewing our past.

Of course, not everybody needs to improve. Some people frequently recall events from their past and enjoy doing so. Deliberate autobiographical remembering is a part of who they are. Other people, though, are much less reflective and don't intentionally access their autobiographical memories unless there is a practical reason for it. In between these extremes are all manner of gradations. As a general rule, women engage in autobiographical remembering more than men. They typically recall past experiences more vividly and report them in more detail, giving special prominence to the thoughts and feelings involved in the event.

The suggestions here are for those not given to autobiographical reflection who would like to strengthen it. After all, memory of our lives is arguably our most important possession, the basis for our sense of self and the storehouse for life's lessons. It seems worthy of effort if it isn't getting the attention you think it deserves.

A word of caution: not all autobiographical remembering is healthy. When people ruminate about old hurts or lost opportunities, or when they reminisce to escape the present, or when they dwell on memories of people no longer present, they make themselves vulnerable to depression. Constructive reminiscing takes two forms. It's healthy to review your life and the path you've followed, to appreciate who you are and how you came to be that way. You may recall experiences that became turning points in your life and reminisce about them to discover what they meant for you, experiences like the one this student reported:

> In my sophomore year, I took an English literature course. I loved the course material, enjoyed writing papers, and felt pretty good about it until . . . I wrote an essay on my interpretation of a poem. I felt I had great insight into a special meaning within the verse. When the paper was returned, the teacher told me I didn't have any understanding of the material and she hoped I wasn't going to be an English major. I remember her pinched face and small, tight mouth as she said these things to me. I thought no way do I want to be like her. So I changed my major from English to Sociology.

Reminiscing also serves as a learning tool because it allows you to look at how you handled situations in the past. Consider the memory that basketball superstar Michael Jordan has about the time he failed to make the varsity basketball team when he was a sophomore:

> It was embarrassing, not making that team. They posted the roster and it was there for a long, long time without my name on it. I remember being really mad, too, because there was a guy who made it that really wasn't as good as me. . . . Whenever I was working out and got tired and figured I ought to stop, I'd close my eyes, and see that list in the locker room without my name on it, and that usually got me going again.

Most memories won't have as strong an impact as these. They will be a mix of experiences, some positive, some negative, some neutral. For most people, the overwhelming majority of autobiographical memories will be positive—studies typically find a ratio of positive to negative memories of more than two to one. It may be for this reason that constructive reminiscing promotes positive feelings and a sense of well-being. In fact, constructive reminiscing under the guidance of a psychotherapist is a recognized treatment for depression. With that background, here are suggestions for improving autobiographical memory.

Acquiring Strong Memories

A good first step is to put extra effort into acquiring rich autobiographical memories in the first place. When I was in Seattle not too long ago, I had an opportunity to have dinner with my sister, her partner, her two daughters, and one of their husbands. It is rare for all of us to be together. I wanted to remember the occasion well, so I adopted the three-step process Marilu Henner recommends for situations like this: Anticipate—Participate—Recollect. She learned it from her father who also valued memory. He engaged her entire family in carrying out the three steps for festive occasions like Christmas gatherings, beach parties, and birthdays. Henner has warm memories of these experiences, and to this day she follows her father's process.

In my case, I approached the anticipate phase by looking ahead to the event with positive expectations, making plans to remember what would take place. This gave me a sense of mission during the event that I think increased my enjoyment. The next step, participate, occurred at the dinner, where I made a conscious effort to fully experience what transpired so that I could form strong memories. As the evening passed, I found myself noting certain moments that seemed especially worth remembering. The final step took place back in Anchorage several days later when I chose a quiet place to travel back in time and relive the event. The result was a rich memory for that experience.

What to Reminisce About

You may find it useful to spend some time identifying aspects of your life story that would be interesting to reminisce about. These could be experiences that helped shape your personality and values, or added richness to your life, or taught important lessons, or simply are rewarding to revisit. Here are three suggestions for finding them.

Major Chapters in Your Life Story

Say you divided your life into its most important segments. What would they be? These are the chapters I am referring to here. A chapter can be whatever you want it to be, but for me, memories in a chapter have a common theme; they cover an extended time period like weeks, months, or years; and they have a distinct chronological order. Marilu Henner suggests identifying life-story chapters by imagining you are going to write an autobiography or produce a documentary about yourself. How would the story develop? The box below shows chapter possibilities based on her suggestions and other sources. In one study of middle-aged people, the average number of chapters they found in their life stories was eleven, although it varied among individuals. Henner recommends eight to fifteen chapters.

Finding Other Life-Story Themes

Some meaningful memories do not fit neatly into a chronological order but still have a common theme. If I recall hiking trips, for example, there is no particular connection between them other than they involved hiking, so they don't neatly arrange into a chapter. Nonetheless, it is satisfying to revisit them, and once I think of one trip, another is easily brought to mind. This is also true for the artist who thinks back to the creations she has worked on, or the woodworker and his projects, or the baseball fan's all-time favorite games. Topics that might be associated with memories like these are shown in the box on the next page. By identifying such areas, you open up opportunities for pleasant reminiscing.

Personal Mementos

Memory recall requires memory cues, and mementos can be especially effective—pictures from a vacation, a high school yearbook, a coffee mug made by a friend—all can be powerful reminders. The traditional way to collect and organize small mementos is the scrapbook. People keep them

---

Possibilities for Life Chapters

Places you've lived	Jobs	Children
High school	College	Grandchildren
Brothers / sisters	Childhood	Marriage
Parents	Hobbies	Divorce

Other Memorable Themes

Turning points in life	Friendships	Pets
Lessons from life	Outdoor adventures	Romances
Vacations	Family events	Mentors
Sporting activities	Spiritual experiences	Great meals
Work projects	Collections	Cars

---

for various reasons—to document events, to chronicle the past, to create pleasing displays—but every item carefully glued in place is a memory cue for an event meaningful to the scrapbooker, and this makes scrapbooks potent aids to autobiographical memory in the same way photo albums are. When you select a memento for inclusion, you identify it as something worth remembering. As you handle the object to secure it on the page, relevant memories come to mind, making them stronger.

Other sources of memorabilia also provide strong cues. Hearing a bar of music associated with a happy time, preparing stuffing for Thanksgiving dinner, smelling roses can all bring back memories that would be inaccessible otherwise. Studies have identified jewelry, stuffed animals, letters, and diaries as helpful cues for women. Men showed better reminiscence to sports equipment, cars, and trophies of past accomplishments. Memorabilia also play a role in the lives of people with HSAM—they are avid collectors and organizers of bits and pieces from the past.

The Act of Remembering

Suppose you have chosen a memory to explore. How might you recall it to get the richest experience? For example, say I want to remember a trip my wife and I took to San Francisco. Memory expert Dominic O'Brien recommends starting with a specific detail and working outward from there. The first detail that comes to my mind is the registration desk at the hotel. As I bring that into focus, other details start returning—the pleasant woman who checked us in, riding in the antique elevator, the four-poster bed. More memories easily follow—climbing steep sidewalks, friendly people we met, the smell of the waterfront. As one memory cues the next, I re-create the experience.

The way you picture memories as you recall them can affect how vivid they seem to you—the most powerful approach is to recall the experience from an "internal" perspective. This means I remember the cable car ride as it looked to me through my own eyes rather than picturing the ride as it would appear to an external camera recording the scene. Marilu Henner reports she always remembers this way, but most of us can't do this with all our memories. Instead, our memories are a mix of internal and external perspectives. Both viewpoints are seen in a memory recalled by a twenty-one-year-old undergraduate:

> I see myself dancing at a party at the university. I remember my clothes and my legs (the way they moved). Suddenly I am "inside my own body" looking out. A guy I know a little walks by and says as he passes, "You look good today."

She began with an external perspective but switched to an internal perspective as the memory unfolds. If she maintains that perspective, she will find that the emotions she remembers are more intense and the sensory details richer than they would be from an external viewpoint.

For recent memories, you will find an internal perspective relatively easy and natural to adopt. Older memories, which can be weaker and less detailed, may come to mind only from an external perspective, probably because they have faded to the point where they no longer have the sensory richness needed for an internal view. Forcing a memory like this into an internal perspective won't be a benefit. But when you can recall a memory readily from either an internal or external vantage point, the internal perspective will be a richer experience.

It's helpful to keep in mind that a specific memory doesn't always have to be recalled in the same way—a fresh perspective can sometimes provide a new take on an old memory. Henner identified four ways to re-create an experience. In the "horizontal" approach, the memory is recalled like a linear story—we arrive in San Francisco at the airport, take a taxi, check in, and so on. She uses the analogy of a DVD video for this kind of recall, cuing up one scene after the other as you move through the event. The "vertical" approach looks closely at one part of the experience—the lunch we had on the pier with the view, the table, the server, what we ordered, and the feelings of that moment. A "mushroom" approach starts with the San Francisco memory and uses it as a cue for wherever it leads, such as a time on the Atlantic City waterfront. A fourth type of retrieval is to capitalize on spontaneous recollections when they occur, such as when a random sight or sound brings to mind a part of the San Francisco trip. Usually we pay little attention to such involuntary memories, but when the situation permits, we can choose to hold them in consciousness, let them develop, and thus bring back the experience.

As you work on improving reminiscing, you will find the three structured retrieval strategies of Chapter 5 helpful. The mnemonic from that chapter, shown in the figure below, can help in remembering them. The "shotgun" strategy uses free association to find retrieval cues that activate other memories. The "return to the scene" strategy takes you back to the setting where the memory occurred to mentally re-create it and look for memory cues. The "wait-and-try-again" strategy allows time to pass between retrieval efforts. It can be surprising and rewarding to discover just what can come back when you stumble on the right cue after using one of these techniques. But don't overdo efforts to dredge up long-lost memories. If you struggle and struggle to remember, you can find yourself "recalling" a compelling false memory that never happened, an invention that you inadvertently created by overzealous efforts. So, give these techniques a chance, but if they don't produce the memory you were seeking, move on to other memories that can be more readily recalled. These are more likely to be valid reflections of the past.

A mnemonic for recall strategies: the shotgun approach, the return to the scene approach (the cop), and the wait and try again approach (the clock).

In the Memory Lab:
Creating a Habit of Reminiscing

If you want to spend more time reflecting on your life, you could follow the lead of people with HSAM and develop a habit of reminiscing. Marilu Henner speaks for all of them when she says, "I know that part of the reason I have such a strong memory is because I spent my entire life instinctively reviewing my past." In this installment of the Memory Lab, we look at the mechanics of establishing a habit of autobiographical reminiscing. Doing so gives me the opportunity to discuss habits and their creation, which is useful knowledge for any practitioner of the memory arts.

Habits are a special kind of memory similar to skills, the topic of the last chapter, but with their own characteristics. Reading is a skill; sitting down with the newspaper at breakfast is a habit. Both are behavioral sequences established by repetition, but skills are complex, flexible, and directed toward a specific goal like understanding the printed word. Habits are simpler, more situation specific, and less flexible. In fact, if I am eating breakfast in a restaurant, I don't feel a strong need to have the newspaper before me because my newspaper habit is connected to breakfast at my own kitchen table.

Because habits are automatic routines, we do them without conscious effort. This makes them particularly useful when we want to establish a desirable new behavior. If reminiscing can become a habit, it will be activated whenever you are in the triggering situation. Once that happens, you'll enter what Henner calls an "autobiographical state of mind," where you begin thinking about the past. This prompts you to take it from there and examine an aspect of your life.

As the diagram on the next page shows, a habit begins with a triggering cue. Next the behavior occurs—in this case, reminiscing. The last step is a positive outcome that acts like a reward to encourage the behavior in the future. Habits are established by repeating the sequence over and over.

Finding a Trigger

What you're looking for is a specific setting where you can pause to reflect on your life, one where you can have a few private minutes to

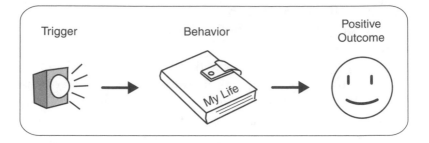

The three-step sequence that is repeated over and over to create a habit.

reminisce. People with HSAM report habitually reviewing their past in situations such as when shaving, when going to sleep, when awakening in the morning, when stuck in traffic, when waiting for an appointment, or when writing in a journal. The most powerful triggers are those that have the same sensory cues each time—the same sights, sounds, smells. An example is Jill Price blow-drying her hair in the morning, a trigger that initiates her habit of reviewing memories from previous days with the same date.

Carrying Out the Behavior

You will need topics to reminisce about, and it will help at this stage if you have them picked out ahead of time. Consider developing a list of possibilities such as specific life chapters or themes or events. Each day you can select one from the list. The amount of time you spend reminiscing is your call, but I recommend that you keep it short at first, just a few minutes.

Experiencing a Positive Outcome

For most people, the reward for reminiscing is built into the process. Reviewing the past to understand the path you've followed or to solve a problem is usually satisfying. Even when the memories are unpleasant, you may be able to adopt a perspective that gives them a different, more constructive meaning. Here is Marilu Henner's take on this:

. . . try to think of bad memories with the same appreciation you have when going through an archive box you haven't touched in ten years. Each item that comes out tells a story, and seeing it many years later gives new insight to how you understood it when it actually happened. A current perspective gives you a more objective understanding. You begin to clearly recognize why you made certain choices and how you would respond differently to similar circumstances in the future.

Overall, you should expect most of your reminiscing to be a good experience. This is what makes reminiscing constructive and why it seems to be associated with well-being. A positive outcome to reminiscing is also important at this stage because it serves as a reward that facilitates habit formation by encouraging repetition.

How Long Will It Take?

A habit is considered completely formed when it becomes automatic. You'll know when this happens: The trigger situation will put you into an autobiographical frame of mind in which you will want to reminisce. Unfortunately, you can't know in advance just how many repetitions it will take. In one study, students undertook to develop simple habits like eating a piece of fruit with lunch or running fifteen minutes before dinner. On average, it took sixty-six days to develop the behaviors into automatic habits. Individual students, though, were all over the map, ranging from eighteen days to 254 days! The moral is to be patient if you want a true habit to develop.

13

The PARIS Mnemonics

What if you could find versatile and practical ways to boost your memory in everyday situations like remembering shopping lists, errands, appointments, travel directions, and even speeches and presentations? It turns out you can do just that by tapping in to a small group of tried and proven mnemonic strategies that have wide applicability and are worthy additions to the repertoire of any mnemonist. These five techniques are named below and paired with an image associated with their acronym, PARIS. You have seen some of them in the Memory Lab sections of previous chapters, where I introduced them as techniques for remembering material from the chapter. Now let's take a closer look at these and related mnemonic templates.

Peg Words

Here is a mental notepad that will help you retain any information that can take the form of a list. I call on it often—it helps me remember what I want

Peg Words
Acrostics and Acronyms
Rhymes and Rhythm
Imagery
Stories

to get done before a trip, items to buy at the store, commitments I make at a staff meeting, or tasks and ideas that come to me in the middle of the night. Most often, it is information I will need for only a day or two. The peg words are a set of concrete objects you associate with the items you want to remember, words you can readily retrieve at a later time. The mnemonic is based on an easy-to-remember set of rhymes:

One is a Bun	Six is Sticks
Two is a Shoe	Seven is Heaven
Three is a Tree	Eight is a Gate
Four is a Door	Nine is Wine
Five is a Hive	Ten is a Hen

Once you've established the peg words in your memory—which won't take long—you can use them to remember any list up to ten items by associating the first item on the list with a bun, the second with a shoe, the third with a tree, and so on. The key to making this work is creating dramatic, distinctive imagery of the memory items interacting with the peg words. So, if you want to pick up onions, a tomato, and celery at the store, you first create an image of onions and a bun—perhaps an onion sandwich with a huge pile of sliced onions inside the bun. Next you move to the tomato and try to get something going with the shoe. You might visualize a shoe that has just stepped on a ripe tomato, making a yucky mess. You could associate the celery with a tree by imagining a magnificent giant celery tree.

Once you're at the store, reciting the rhyme—"one is a bun; two is a shoe; three is a tree"—will bring back the images and trigger memory for the items. Research studies show what will be clear to anyone who tries it: If your images create a good connection between the peg words and the list items, the mnemonic will serve you exceedingly well. And you needn't worry that you might confuse the new images with those left over from the last list you memorized. This just doesn't happen in practice. The newest association will be the one you recall—it's similar to parking your car when you go to work. Where you left your car yesterday doesn't confuse you about where you parked today.

Its Two Strengths

The peg word strategy excels in two areas where mnemonics can aid memory. First, it helps organize material to make it easier to retrieve when you need it. The peg words technique uses our well-learned ability to count as its organizing principle—as you mentally run through the digits, each item on your grocery list is cued in turn. Second, peg words can improve the memorability of individual memory items with better encoding. Here again, peg words get high marks. When you use imagery to connect "onions" on your grocery list with "bun" as a peg word, the odds of remembering the onions shoot up. As you will see, not all the PARIS mnemonics are equally strong in both organizing and encoding, and this makes the peg word strategy noteworthy. It is a simple, powerful, elegant way to remember a list.

Its Weakness

Like any of the imagery methods, this strategy is more difficult to use when the material is not easy to visualize. Consider a to-do list that includes "check out insurance." You decide to put "insurance" on your peg word list, but no concrete image comes to mind to represent it. A way around the problem is the substitute word approach. You look for a concrete word that *sounds* close enough to "insurance" to suggest it—perhaps "insect." Now you create an image associating the substitute word with a peg word. Later when you use the peg word to recall "insect," its sound helps you remember "insurance." We saw this technique used to remember names in Chapter 7. Substitute words work, but they add a complication that takes effort to overcome.

Peg Word Variations

Rhyming words are only one of several ways to set up a useful peg word system. In fact, we saw an alternate approach in Chapter 10, when we looked at the "major system" for remembering numbers. That system also associates concrete objects with specific digits, but the objects are selected based on the letters in their names. This gave pairings like 1—tie, 2—hen, and 3—ma. Their key features are the consonants t, n, and m, the established codes for the digits 1, 2, and 3. Vowels and other sounds were added to create concrete words. The major system can readily give a concrete word for each number from 0 to 99, as we saw in that chapter. Some mnemonists use this system to remember lists in the same way I use the rhyming peg words. It has the advantage that it can handle more than ten items. Another possibility is to construct peg words from the alphabet with pairings like

A—ape, B—boy, and C—cat. Any of these systems will work, and it comes down to personal preference. I reserve the major system for remembering numbers and use the rhyming peg word system for remembering lists. I find I can recall the rhyming words more rapidly with less effort than the words of the other systems.

Acronyms and Acrostics

You'll recall these two mnemonic forms from the Memory Lab segments of earlier chapters. Called "first-letter mnemonics," for obvious reasons, they provide useful ways to organize and remember items on a list. Unlike the peg word method, these mnemonics work as well with abstract words as they do with concrete ones. That is why I chose an acronym (PARIS) to encode this chapter's five mnemonic techniques. We saw another example in Chapter 8 to encode three ways to strengthen prospective memory (ICE)—which refers to Implementation intentions, Cue imagery, and Exaggerated importance.

Acronyms are usually short, typically no more than five or six letters. It helps if they are pronounceable, and the best ones, like PARIS and ICE, form recognizable words. Other well-known acronyms are HOMES to encode the Great Lakes (Huron, Ontario, Michigan, Erie, and Superior) and RAPPOS to recall the First Amendment protections of the U.S. Constitution (religion, assembly, petition, press, opinion, and speech).

The RAPPOS mnemonic is interesting in that it includes "opinion," a protection not listed in the First Amendment—it's covered as free speech. The inventor of the acronym probably added it to encourage pronunciation of both Ps, something that might not happen if the acronym were RAPPS.

Acrostics are conceptually similar to acronyms, but their strength is that they form a meaningful phrase, and this allows them to support longer lists such as the Romantic Dragon acrostic of Chapter 4—"Romantic Dragons Eat Vegetables And Prefer Onions"—which cues seven principles for strengthening memories: Retention intention, Deep processing, Elaboration, Visualization, Association, Practice, and Organization. An equivalent seven-letter acronym (REDAVOP, perhaps) is cumbersome and more difficult to remember. Even for shorter lists, an acrostic can be a good choice if the only available acronym is unpronounceable or awkward. That was the case in Chapter 7 with the mnemonic for remembering how to learn names and faces: Find a Feature, Listen, Say it, and Practice. The acrostic "Friendly Llamas Seek People" is better than the awkward acronym FLSP.

As acrostics get longer and longer, they lead to ever more clumsy sentences. Consider this fifteen-word acrostic for chemistry's Electromotive Series: "Poorly Canned Sausages Make A Zulu Ill. Therefore Let Highly Clever Men Slay Good Pigs" (Potassium, Calcium, Sodium, Magnesium, Aluminum, Zinc, Iron, Tin, Lead, Hydrogen, Copper, Mercury, Silver, Gold, Platinum). The complex acrostic is definitely easier to remember than the chemical list, but it will take some effort and rehearsal to master. The acrostic's creator was wise to develop it as two relatively short sentences, a kindness for those who must learn it. In general, as the length of the memory list increases, the acrostic becomes more and more contorted. At some point, it becomes prudent to move to what is known as a "memory palace," an approach I will describe in the next chapter.

A strength of acronyms and acrostics is that by encoding the first letters of the items in a word or phrase, they give the list an organization that helps you remember it. An added benefit is that they let you know how many items you must recall and when recall is complete. Their weakness is that they don't provide much help in making the items more memorable— they assume the first letter of each one will be enough to cue its memory. This may or may not be true. Go back to the acronym RAPPOS and see if it succeeds in cueing the protections of the First Amendment. If you missed some, you are not alone. It's not that the specific protections are difficult words or that the protections are unfamiliar; the problem is that they have not been associated together well enough to allow the single-letter cues to retrieve them. For many of us, this acronym can only work if we strengthen and associate memories for the protections so that we could recall them even with the acronym's relatively weak cue. This will require practicing the mnemonic until the protections easily come to mind.

Rhymes and Rhythms

Wonder which way to turn that screw? Say, "Righty tighty, lefty loosey." Come upon a person in shock? Have the person lie down and think, "If the face is red, raise the head. If the face is pale, raise the tail." Planning on serious partying? Keep in mind that "Beer on whiskey, very risky; whiskey on beer, never fear."

Rhymes and rhythms have long been used as mnemonic aids and for good reason—both are effective memory cues. To see why, take another look at the Henry limerick from Chapter 9.

Henry

There once was a boy named Henry
Who tried to improve his memory.
He practiced facts that he faced
With retrieval well spaced,
And found his recall exemplary.

Once you recall that easy first line you are well on your way, because the second line has to conform to it by (1) rhyming with "Henry," (2) adhering to the standard limerick rhythm, and (3) making sense. It is as if three pieces of a jigsaw puzzle are suddenly in place—rhyme, rhythm, and meaning—and the next piece must interlock with them. As memory researcher David Rubin pointed out, these three features drastically narrow the possibilities for what can come next, and this allows the memory system to more easily find the words that follow. Rhyme, rhythm, and meaning function as both memory cues and memory constraints. This is why we find mnemonic structures like rhyming maxims or limericks easy to remember.

Rhyming mnemonics always have a rhythm that emphasizes the rhyming words. In the Henry limerick, it's

There ONCE was a boy named HENRY
Who TRIED to improve his MEMORY.

It is this intonation pattern that allows rhyming to work well as a memory retrieval strategy. Normally we don't search our memory for rhymes. We can easily do it—bye, sky, high, die—but only if we intend to. The contribution of the sing-song rhythm is that it emphasizes words that must rhyme. This signals "rhyming mode," cueing the memory system to search for appropriate matches.

Rhythm can work as a memory cue even without rhymes, and it has played a role in extraordinary memory feats. During the age of the Roman Empire, it was not unknown for people to memorize the entire *Aeneid*, an epic poem of almost 10,000 lines written by Virgil in about 20 B.C. The distinctive rhythm of the poem's lines, a sound pattern known as dactylic hexameter, provided the structure that made such a massive undertaking possible. In the present day, there are millions of Muslims, called Hafiz, who have committed the entire *Quran* to memory. This work, written in Arabic, contains more than 6,000 verses and 80,000 words. As in the *Aeneid*, its lines do not rhyme. What is especially impressive is that many Hafiz do not speak Arabic, and therefore the words they memorize have no meaning to them. Their effort begins with learning to pronounce Arabic words to bring out the rhythm of the *Quran*'s passages. That rhythm becomes their principal memory aid as they laboriously master verse after verse during perhaps three years of study.

Rhyme and rhythm are unusual among the mnemonic forms in this chapter because they can be used for purposes other than remembering a list. They facilitate memory for all sorts of verbatim text. The text might contain a principle, like the Henry limerick, or a suggestion, like the mnemonic for turning a screw, or it can be a major work like the *Quran*. Rhyme and rhythm stand as a container for any verbal content a memoirist wants to embed in it.

*I*magery

Imagery is, of course, everywhere in the memory arts, and we have encountered it often in this book. Here we look at a fundamental, imagery-based technique that is the simplest and most basic of all mnemonic strategies. Called the "link method," it helps you remember a list by creating a series of visual associations between pairs of memory items, building a chain of associations that eventually includes the entire list. We saw an example in Chapter 11, where I used the link method to remember topics for a lecture.

Because of its simplicity, memory teachers often use it to demonstrate the power of mnemonics to new students. Harry Lorayne, the great memory performer and memory trainer, was a master at this. Students at his workshops were barely settled into their seats when he had them remembering a list. The following selection, taken from one of his many books, captures his approach. Here Lorayne talks his readers through using the link method to retain this list of objects: envelope, airplane, wristwatch, pill, insect, wallet, bathtub, and shoe.

Starting with **envelope/airplane**, begin by visualizing an envelope. Then mentally "attach" that to airplane: a gigantic envelope is flying like an airplane;

an airplane is licking and sealing a gigantic envelope; millions of envelopes are boarding or disembarking an airplane; you're trying to stuff an airplane into an envelope. You need only one picture, so select one I've just suggested, or one you've thought of yourself and *see* it. . . .

Airplane/Wristwatch. The new thing, wristwatch, must be brought to mind by airplane. Can you see yourself wearing a large airplane on your wrist instead of a watch? Or maybe there is a gigantic wristwatch around each wing of the airplane, or a gigantic wristwatch is flying like an airplane. . . . *See* one of those pictures in your mind.

On he goes, pair after pair, with nonstop patter to help his students create graphic visual images that link each pair on the list. After he finishes, he has them remember the items, which they find they can do with relative ease. Then, in a final flourish, he challenges students to recall the list backwards. Lo and behold, they discover that this too was easy. With his audience amazed and motivated, Lorayne is ready to move on to the next workshop topic.

The link method is well suited for Lorayne's purposes because it requires little preparation. There are no peg words to memorize, no acrostics to invent, just imaginative associations to connect pairs of objects. Once the associations are in place you can move up or down the list item by item.

A weakness of the link method is that it creates a chain of associations only as good as its weakest link. If you forget one of them, you can become stymied. And if you forget the first item on the list, you may find yourself with a catastrophic failure in which you can't recall any of the items. The lesson here is to rehearse the list well enough to establish the links securely in your memory. What I do if I have even the slightest worry about remembering the first item is create a starting link to make sure I can bring it to mind. I use an image of a boat anchor and associate it with the first list item.

On the mnemonic scorecard, the peg word system is superior to the link method because it doesn't have the "weakest link" problem. If you forget a word in the peg word system, nothing else is compromised; you just move on. But despite its shortcoming, the link method has advantages. It is easy to apply—there's no need to bother with mentally manipulating peg words. It also is particularly useful when all you want to remember is the next item on a list—say when you must remember the next topic in a speech or the next product on a shopping list. With the link method, your recall effort goes right to the one association relevant at that moment, the association that gets you to the next item on the list.

Stories

For centuries, the collective memory of entire cultures was maintained by stories told by one generation to the next. Stories are natural mnemonic devices. They work well because they play to the strengths of the memory system. They are based on meaning; they organize the material; they encourage deep processing; they contain elaborations, and they provide associations. These strengths no doubt explain why stories are so often trusted with important information—the wisdom of Aesop, the parables of the bible, the cultural lessons of folk tales.

The mnemonic benefits of the story can be harnessed simply by adding a narrative to forgettable information, and it can be used in conjunction with any other memory aid. Suppose you are using the peg word mnemonic to remember a shopping list, and you come to an association between "bun" and "onions." If your image of an onion sandwich on a bun seems uninspired, you could invent a story to pump it up: "This sandwich," you might say to yourself, "has been entered in a national food competition for a huge prize. It features extra sweet onions that are sure to please the judges." A quick, fanciful story like this can go a long way to ensure that the image will be available when you need it.

Stories can also be used as a primary memory aid. We saw an example of this in Chapter 10 in the way that Chao Lu memorized the first 61,890 digits of pi. He remembered each pair of digits as a concrete object, and then he wove a group of objects into a story that he connected to other stories. He repeated the process until he had the long chain of stories that allowed him to retain that massive number of digits.

We can use the story approach in the same way by creating a narrative around items we want to remember. To remember a shopping list—onions, tomato, celery, milk, and bread—you can create a plot to pull the items together. Here is one possibility.

An **onion** walks into a bar and sits next to an overripe **tomato**. The barkeep, a tall stalk of **celery**, comes over, and the **onion** orders **milk**. **Celery** slides the drink down the bar. The **tomato** sneers, "milk in a bar?" and continues to eat her **bread,** carefully dunking each bite in her martini.

It helps to visualize a story as well as verbalizing it, and a rehearsal or two is always a good idea. Research supports the story method as an effective mnemonic. In one study, college students remembered six times as many words after weaving them into a story as they did without a story. The technique has been especially successful when the material was tested after periods longer than a few days. It has also been shown to work with older adults and may be easier for them to use than other mnemonics.

A story achieves its memory benefit by using narrative to organize memory material and provide memory cues to recall it. A coherent story carries out these two functions well. But like the link method, the organization and cueing are provided by the memory material itself, so if you forget one thing, there can be a domino effect.

Stories work best when the list of memory items is not too long. Chao Lu held each story segment to about five memory items. That was also the size of my grocery list example. Imagine expanding that story to accommodate fifteen items—it would take a significant investment of time and effort, and the final product would likely be a convoluted tale, one with real possibilities for slippage. But when the lists are not too long, say, ten or fewer items, the story mnemonic is an entertaining and satisfying way to exercise the memory arts. When I ask students in my memory classes to try different mnemonics for lists and pick a favorite, the story mnemonic is always among their top choices.

A Final Thought

The PARIS mnemonics are general-purpose memory strategies for use with any memory material you can plug into them. They let you forgo written notes and electronic devices for routine memory needs and instead engage your wits and your knowledge of memory. For example, do you really need a written list when you go to the store? Wouldn't it be rewarding to go to the store without a written list and still come home with every item you intended to buy? And couldn't you just call up that to-do list with a PARIS strategy? What about the questions you want to ask the doctor? Or the topics you'll use to enliven that obligatory phone call to your mother-in-law?

The PARIS mnemonics can also be used to pump up natural memory. For a business presentation, you could retain the points you want to make in a list mnemonic—Introductory remark → The problem → Option 1 → Option 2 → Recommendation. By picking a concrete word to cue each point and linking them together, you can run over the presentation easily before the meeting. When you go to make the points, you will probably not need the mnemonic, because the rehearsals will have put the information at your fingertips and prepared your natural memory to perform well. This strategy is useful in any setting—presentations, job interviews, sales pitches— where you need to speak without notes or PowerPoint.

Of course, you don't have to use mnemonics to retain the kinds of information I've talked about—a pad of sticky notes and a pencil will get you through all those situations. But the PARIS strategies are rewarding exercises because they give you, as a recreational practitioner of the memory arts, a chance to accept a mental challenge and meet it. They allow you to step away from ubiquitous smart phones and iPads and exercise your mental resources. The reward is not only personal satisfaction but also the knowledge that you are putting to good use your most sophisticated mental processes—working memory, attention, top-down control, self-discipline, and self-reliance.

There is still one more technique to add to your mnemonic repertoire, one more option for holding on to slippery information. Like the PARIS mnemonics, it is applicable to memory material that can be put in the form of a list. This final strategy is rightfully considered the pinnacle of the ancient memory arts, one taught to students for centuries and extolled by luminaries from Cicero and Thomas Aquinas right up to Joshua Foer and Dominic O'Brien. This remarkable method of memory enhancement is the topic of the next chapter.

 ## In the Memory Lab:
Test Driving the Paris Mnemonics

The best way to get a feel for the PARIS mnemonics is to try them out. Except for the rhyme/rhythm format, they are well suited for remembering not only shopping lists and to-do lists, but also appointments, passwords, and directions. Your test drive can start with random, concrete words, and I've provided the five short lists on the facing page for that purpose. In each case, the goal should be to use one of the mnemonic formats to retain the list for a day or two. As you carry this out, enjoy your successes but also pay attention to slippages. Often you can learn a lot about the practicalities of specific mnemonics by trying to understand why you forgot something. Now the lists:

Peg words: meadow, stork, elbow, package, fox
Acronym: organ, steeple, knuckle, basin, eagle
Acrostic: prune, sword, lemon, spoke, statue
Imagery (link method): reed, nail, road, urn, wine
Story: edge, dairy, rattle, monarch, brim

14

The Memory Palace

Between 2001 and 2006, Andrew Card Jr. was the chief of staff for President George W. Bush. It was Card's responsibility to manage the president's daily schedule on a 24/7 basis, doing whatever was needed, from arranging key meetings to knowing the time of the president's next haircut appointment. It was a high-stakes job filled with endless, crucial, and not-so-crucial details. Card held the position longer than any of his predecessors in the last fifty years.

If you assume that Card designed and maintained an elaborate finely tuned filing system or a computerized spreadsheet to keep track of his responsibilities, you're mistaken. Reports say he seldom took notes at meetings and kept his desk clean, almost empty, with no paper in evidence. In fact, Andrew Card's notes and reminders and schedules were all in his head. He managed his pressure-cooker job almost solely by means of a remarkable mnemonic system called a "memory palace," the contents of which he juggled constantly as tasks, issues, and people came and went.

A memory palace is a group of fixed, well-known locations that one can easily imagine—say rooms in your home or different spots along a street in your neighborhood. It is often called the "Method of Loci" ("places" in Latin). To use a palace, you create visual associations between specific places and the information to be remembered—so, you could retain a grocery list by imagining each item at a different place in your palace—in the linen closet, on the dining room table, in the bathtub. Later, at the store, you mentally go to each place, discover the images you've created, and remember the items.

Card's memory palace was the kitchen of his boyhood home. Its features served as mental storage locations—the stove, the countertop, cabinets, and other kitchen furnishings. The information he stored there was more complex than a grocery list, but the principle was the same. Each fact or task was represented by a mental image associated with a specific place. A 2005 *Washington Post* story described the memory palace in operation.

> When tackling matters of top priority, Card [imagines standing] at the stove, working his "front and back burners." Intelligence reform is cooking this morning. He needs to call several people: 9/11 commission Chairmen Tom Kean and Lee Hamilton, Reps Duncan Hunter and James Sensenbrenner, and House Speaker Dennis Hastert. They are "on my right Front Burner," he says.
>
> "Then I shift gears to my left front burner, which is second most important," Card says. He will help the president hire a Cabinet secretary, then move to his right rear burner (hiring White House staff for the second term). "I do all that in my kitchen," Card says. "Now the things I want to put off for a long time, I put in the freezer. But then I can go to my freezer and generally remember things that I put there a long time ago." He will store matters that were resolved or tabled yesterday in a cupboard.

In an interview with me in 2009, he elaborated on his palace, describing other locations, each designed to serve a bustling office that needed to handle an ever-changing mix of ongoing work, new demands, crises, and important people. He used the oven for situations that needed to stay warm for a day or two before they could be resolved; the microwave held projects that needed to be done quickly, and the sink was for messes that needed cleaning up. When a memory item was no longer needed, Card took its memory image to the disposal and "let go" of it. He said he always paused before putting anything in the disposal, asking himself if he really wanted to get rid of it because he would almost certainly forget it once he let it go.

Card told me he seldom took notes at meetings, deciding instead what he wanted to remember and mentally putting that in the proper spot in the kitchen. Information he needed during the meeting he would retrieve from the kitchen. Periodically during the day he would "clean the kitchen" by mentally running through it, updating this, acting on that, and refreshing the information stored there. Card had used this system for decades.

Card's interest in memory palaces began in high school when he had a chance encounter with a memory performer who told him about the procedure. That conversation created a lifelong interest in mnemonic technique.

Soon he was applying the methods to his schoolwork and his afterschool job at a fast-food restaurant. The mental challenge of mnemonics appealed to him, and his skill increased, eventually carrying over to his duties at the White House. Did he think his natural memory was unusually good? I asked him. He said that he did not believe so. Instead, he attributed his remarkable ability to mental discipline in maintaining his kitchen. It was a process that was engaging and rewarding to him.

The Method of Loci in Antiquity

The Method of Loci that Card made such good use of has been a valued memory aid for more than two millennia. Legend has it that it was discovered in Greece about 500 B.C. by a renowned poet, Simonides, also known as "the honey tongued." Cicero, writing four centuries later in about 50 B.C., gave the best surviving account of the event. It seems that a nobleman planning a feast in his own honor contracted with Simonides to write an ode for the occasion extolling the nobleman's greatness. When it was read at the feast, the nobleman was taken aback by a section devoted to the exploits of two youthful gods, Castor and Pollux. Incensed, the nobleman told Simonides he would pay only half the agreed-upon price and that he should collect the other half from the two gods. Shortly thereafter, a servant told Simonides that there were two young men outside waiting to see him. But when he went out he found no one. At that very moment, the roof collapsed, killing all and mangling them so badly that identification was impossible. Simonides, however, was able to remember who was sitting where around the table by picturing the scene. That visual memory allowed relatives to claim the bodies. Later Simonides reflected on the experience and formulated the Method of Loci, based on the principle that an organized set of known places could help a person remember anything associated with them.

Simonides lived at the beginning of the classical Greek period when architecture flourished and democratic forms of government were emerging. Education became more valued, literacy more common, and written works more available. One might think that moving from an oral to a written culture would reduce memory demands, not increase them. But classical archaeologist Jocelyn Penny Small suggests that writing in fact had the opposite effect, creating a need for memory skill and a market for the memory arts. To understand why, consider the nature of written texts at the time.

When we think of "writing," we imagine what printed words look like on a page like this one, but what you are reading is writing that has been refined by innovations unknown to the Greeks and Romans. They experienced writing in a form that came to be called *scriptio continua,* used until about A.D. 1000, in which there were no spaces or punctuation between words, sentences, or paragraphs. The next paragraph appears in *scriptio continua* format and then is followed by the same words presented in the modern format. *Scriptio continua* was usually read aloud syllable by syllable, not word by word, and the reader listened to the sounds as he spoke them, using sound along with the letters on the page to decode the message. The manuscript itself was a long scroll. A major work like the *Iliad,* which spans more than 400 pages in a modern book, comprised twenty-four scrolls. There were no chapter titles, no headings, no table of contents, no index, and sometimes no manuscript title. Pity the poor reader who forgot a point and returned to the scroll to check it. Indeed, far from rendering memory skill obsolete, the written word made it essential. It would be many centuries before such niceties as spacing between words, upper and lower case, punctuation, paragraphing, headings, and consistent spelling came into wide use.

```
THUSITWASTHATSIMONIDESDISCOVERYPROVIDEDATECHNIQUETHAT
HADPRACTICALVALUEFORSTUDENTSANDSCHOLARSITWASPICKED
UPANDDISSEMINATEDBYTHESOPHISTSAGROUPOFITINERANT
INTELLECTUALSWHOTUTOREDSTUDENTSINPHILOSOPHYSPEAKING
ANDWRITINGARISTOTLEPROVIDEDANADDITIONALBOOSTFORTHE
METHODBYENDORSINGITANDITISLIKELYTHATHEWASSKILLEDIN
ITSUSE
```

(Thus it was that Simonides's discovery provided a technique that had practical value for students and scholars. It was picked up and disseminated by the Sophists, a group of itinerant intellectuals who tutored students in philosophy, speaking, and writing. Aristotle [350 b.c.] provided an additional boost for the method by endorsing it, and it is likely that he was skilled in its use.)

When Greece was added to the Roman Empire in 146 B.C., memory strategies spread to the West and became part of a standard curriculum taught to privileged sons of the wealthy on their way to high-status careers. The memory skills they learned benefited them in more ways than just as a study aid because memory ability itself was highly valued by the Romans. Its signature demonstration was in public oratory. Standout orators like Cicero were widely admired, and crowds were dazzled by their ability to deliver eloquent presentations without notes. The Method of Loci provided support for these deliveries and more. Memory scholar Mary Carruthers believes that the great orators used their memory palaces creatively to analyze complex situations, invent winning arguments, and handle objections from opponents.

Matteo Ricci

Although the concept of a memory palace is straightforward, many details about how memory palaces were actually used are elusive. What role did they play in education? How long was the information remembered? In what settings other than oratory were they useful? Most ancient descriptions of memory techniques are general and brief because it was assumed that their application was common knowledge. There is a notable exception, however: a sixteenth-century priest named Matteo Ricci. Although he was many centuries removed from the heyday of the Roman era, he had mastered the same memory arts and even studied from texts written in Cicero's day. His story provides insights into real-world applications of these memory aids. Before I tell it, though, let me fill in a few developments from the intervening years.

The classic memory arts—visualization, organization, and association, along with the Method of Loci—continued to be taught and practiced in the Roman Empire until it collapsed around the year 500. Massive upheaval followed as great cities fell into disarray, the educational infrastructure vanished, and literacy declined dramatically. Among the casualties were the memory arts, which disappeared from use. Surprisingly, though, in the thirteenth century, the arts were revived when scholarly monks discovered long-lost Roman texts that described them. One of these monks was the great Catholic theologian Thomas Aquinas, a Dominican friar born in 1225, who studied the ancient works, became expert in the memory arts, and used them to advantage in writing his influential works. Thomas came to the conclusion that memory skill was important to a Christian seeking salvation because "memory of many things" is a prerequisite to wise moral choices. With his endorsement, the Method of Loci became not just a practical skill but one considered morally virtuous. The Dominicans, and later the Jesuits, taught Thomist views widely and helped spread the use of the memory arts among the educated elite. Well before the sixteenth century, training in memory was common in the schools and colleges of these religious orders.

Matteo Ricci, born in Italy in 1552, received that training. Later the memory skills he learned contributed to his success as a Jesuit missionary to China. When historian Jonathan Spence wrote *The Memory Palace of Matteo Ricci*, his remarkable book about Ricci's life and times, he unearthed many details about Ricci's training and life that offer revealing glimpses of the mnemonic practices of his day.

Ricci joined the Jesuits in 1571 and attended the prestigious Jesuit College of Rome for much of his training. The Jesuits, founded in 1540, took pride in being at the forefront of the intellectual issues of the day and prepared students for this distinction with heavy workloads in the humanities, theology, science, and mathematics. Training in memory was an integral part of their education, and Ricci had access to expert memory instruction. Spence believes one of his memory teachers may have been Francesco Panigarola, who was said to be able "to roam across a hundred thousand memory images, each in its own fixed space." Ricci likely constructed many memory palaces as part of his education, something like a memory city with different structures to hold different subjects.

Ricci's memory palaces probably had varied forms. Some were certainly buildings such as the grand cathedrals he would have known, each with many locations within its walls for memory images. Other palaces were probably familiar routes he traveled around Rome or his home city of Macerata. The landmarks along these journeys would have been ideal memory locations. Some of his palaces may have been figurines in the form of statues or images of fictional characters. The drawing on the next page, which dates from 1533, is an example. It is a personification of "grammar," one of the seven liberal arts Ricci would have studied. Historian Frances Yates, whose book, *The Art of Memory,* was my source for this drawing, believes that figures like this were in use in Roman times and in the Middle Ages as variations on the Method of Loci. The mysterious-looking objects and lettering around Gramatica are thought to be memory cues for grammatical principles, each one occupying a specific location in the drawing,

A memory figurine in the form of a personification of grammar. The inscriptions located around the figurine are memory cues for grammatical principles. Such figures are variations on the Method of Loci.

thus creating a memory palace for that information. Every liberal art was represented by a figure with a distinct persona. Grammar was portrayed as a stern old woman as we see here. Rhetoric, on the other hand, was more glamorous, depicted as a tall warrior princess carrying cues for various figures of speech. Other personifications provided images for logic, arithmetic, geometry, astronomy, and music. Ricci could well have studied such images, possibly customizing and elaborating them, to create memory palaces for key ideas in each subject.

By the end of his studies, Ricci would have had a sizable collection of memory palaces to take with him on his missionary adventures. His ability to use information from his education in future years was largely dependent on how well these memory aids functioned because there would be few Western books available to refresh his knowledge. His first stop was India, in 1578. He traveled with few personal possessions on a grueling six-month voyage by sail. In 1582 he left India for China, where he spent the rest of his life.

Ricci's first task there was to learn the language, and he applied his memory skills to the task. He studied Chinese ideographs and began to memorize them, almost certainly in a memory palace. By 1585 he was able to speak Chinese without an interpreter and read the language, albeit in a halting way. By 1594 he was fluent to the point where he could converse easily and compose letters and essays in Chinese that were well received by native speakers. In the process, he discovered that the Chinese were extremely interested in memory techniques. Following is his description of a party he attended in 1595 with the educated elite of Nanjing. The subject of memory strategies came up, and he offered to provide a demonstration.

> I told them they should write down a large number of Chinese letters in any manner they chose on a sheet of paper without there being any order among them, because after reading them only once, I would be able to say them all by heart in the same way and order in which they had been written. They did so, writing many letters without any order, all of which I, after reading them once, was able to repeat by memory in the manner in which they were written; such that they were all astonished, it seeming to them a great matter. And I, in order to increase their wonder, began to recite them all by memory backward in the same manner, beginning with the very last until reaching the first. By which they all became utterly astounded and as if beside themselves. And at once they began to beg me to consent to teach them this divine rule by which such a memory was made.

Here we see a master mnemonist at work. Spence, Ricci's biographer, believes that hundreds of ideographs were involved in this demonstration. If you experiment with memory palaces, you will discover they are not hard to use if you have plenty of time to create the necessary imagery. You will even find you can recall a list just as easily backward as forward. But using a palace as Ricci did, on the fly at the spur of the moment under pressure, is a totally different undertaking. His success shows the massive amount of practice he must have had with this technique.

The Chinese interest in memory gave Ricci an opening to build relationships with prominent people to increase his status and develop social contacts. One of these people was the governor of the province in which Nanjing is located, who was eager for his sons to do well on Chinese civil service exams. These difficult, high-stakes tests covered a staggering amount of material, and the results could significantly advance or hold back opportunities available to the young men who took them. Ricci offered to teach the governor's sons Western memory arts to prepare for the test. For that purpose, he wrote a small book in Chinese on memory palaces and presented copies of the book to the governor and his three sons. Unfortunately, his plan did not succeed, and the reason for its failure provides a valuable insight into the use of the Method of Loci.

It wasn't that the sons failed the exam—actually, they did well. They just did not find Ricci's memory techniques helpful and chose to study for the test in their own ways. In hindsight, this is not surprising. Although memory palaces are simple in concept, their application to complex material requires skill and experience. The three sons had to draw on only a written description of the technique to memorize a massive amount of difficult information without first practicing the system. Difficulties and discouragement were to be expected. A useful rule for anyone interested in using memory palaces is to start with modest projects and expect a learning curve.

Ricci's memory technique wasn't the only thing that interested the Chinese. They were hungry for Western knowledge of mathematics and science, as well as some aspects of philosophy. Ricci saw another way to open doors, and he began to prepare Chinese translations of these topics, translations that could be widely circulated to an influential readership. Ricci reasoned that if they liked these materials, they might become open to more religiously themed works.

In some cases, such as Euclid's *Elements of Geometry*, he worked from source books in Latin. But in others, Spence believes he wrote from memory. Spence found material in Ricci's Chinese books from exotic Western works that he almost certainly did not have access to in China—including passages from Aesop's fables and minor Greek philosophers and ancient Roman poets, excerpts from books whose importance could not have justified inclusion on Ricci's arduous travels. Spence found Ricci's translations faithful to the original sources. These were subjects Ricci had studied at the Jesuit College decades earlier, material he likely registered carefully in memory palaces he constructed at the time.

Long-Lasting Memories

If Spence is correct that many of Ricci's translations were from memory palaces created decades earlier, his memories were very durable indeed. Contemporary studies show that about thirty percent of the information learned in academic content courses—history, civics, psychology, science—is forgotten in the first year and that this number increases to as much as seventy percent after four years.

What explains the longevity of Ricci's memories? Two features of memory palaces may have contributed. First, establishing a memory palace requires deep processing, organization, and visualization. The result would be strong initial learning, a contributor to long-lasting memories. Second, once they are established, memory palaces allow a person to rehearse their content easily without study materials like books or notes. Ricci could at any time mentally journey through his palaces, recalling each fact in turn. For him, the palaces were mental versions of flashcards. Ricci was a committed student, and if he rehearsed material now and then during his college years, those rehearsals could have led to the kind of strong long-lasting memories I referred to in Chapter 9 as the "permastore." These are memories for academic content that you learn so well through spaced retrieval practice that they last for decades, sometimes as long as fifty years. For example, if you take a sequence of courses in Spanish, each of your classes provides another opportunity for you to rehearse vocabulary and grammar, leading to long-lasting memory even if you never use the language after college. So too it might have been with Ricci's memory palaces.

Memory Arts in Decline

Although memory training was well established in Catholic universities of Ricci's era, forces were in play that led to its decline in the broader European culture. The invention of printing a century earlier meant that books were now plentiful, eliminating a motivation for memory training. Critics lambasted memory training as rote, irrelevant learning, criticisms brought on by pedantic teachers who used the methods to force students to memorize useless facts. Protestant reformers asserted that the use of imagery in memory techniques was an ungodly Catholic practice that would lead to idolatry. There were also new ideas in the air with the Age of Reason and the Scientific Revolution just beginning. All of this meant that for a growing number the Method of Loci, with its places and images, was either (1) no longer needed, (2) too pedantic and rigid, (3) too Catholic, (4) too old school, or (5) some combination. The end result was that the memory strategies Ricci practiced with such great skill were on a slide into obscurity, and they never recovered.

Memory Palaces in the Twenty-First Century

There is no question that memory palaces served a valuable purpose in earlier times, but do these ancient mnemonic devices have any relevance in today's world? It's a fact that there are few situations outside of memory competitions where the Method of Loci is regularly put to use these days. This is probably due to the effort and practice the technique requires as well as ambiguity about just where you might use it in modern times. I was initially motivated to try the Method of Loci out of curiosity to see how it worked, but I quickly learned that memory palaces are not only fascinating as a mnemonic strategy but of genuine practical utility. Here are several of my memory projects to illustrate possibilities and perhaps suggest an application in your life.

Lists

Any of the list-based memory applications of the last chapter—shopping lists, to-do lists, appointments—can be handled with a memory palace. A memory palace is my mnemonic of choice when the list is long, say more than ten items. The most valuable application for me is as an aid to learning student names.

A few days before a new class begins, I put the names of students enrolled in the course into a memory palace I reserve just for this purpose. Its locations follow a route down a busy street and into a shopping mall. I know the area well, and I can easily travel it in my imagination. A typical class requires about thirty locations, although the route has accommodated as many as seventy. They are organized in sets of ten to aid in rehearsing them. Using the class list, I create a memory cue for each name at a specific spot. For example, if the name is "Elliot Beck" and the next location is a table at the Panda restaurant, I use the name-learning techniques of Chapter 7 to create an image at that spot to suggest Elliot's name. I might picture the politician "Eliot Spitzer" sporting a birdlike *beak* sitting at the table. Next I move to "Gretchen Burns" and create a memory image for her name in a specific chair at the Tiger Paws Nail Salon, the next location on my route. I rehearse the memory palace until I know the class list well—literally forwards and backwards. On the first day of class, when I meet each student, I associate a face with a name I already know, and that reduces my workload significantly. Immediately after class I go back through the memory palace. As I get to each name, I work on recalling the face that went with it to practice the connection. By the second week, I usually have learned peoples' names, and I no longer need the memory palace. I will slowly forget which names are where in the palace over the next few months, and I won't use the palace again until the next class.

A Personal Organizer

Andrew Card's impressive application of a memory palace to manage the White House was especially interesting to me because the content he remembered was constantly changing as new items were added and old ones became passé. I decided to experiment with a similar system just to see how it worked. That was almost a decade ago, and I continue to find it useful. It has replaced appointment calendars, memo pads, and sticky notes for managing details of my daily life.

This memory palace is located in my garage. It consists of a series of sites, like Card's kitchen stove with its four burners, each site with several locations for memory images. The first site in my palace is a shelf on the far wall of my garage next to the door. I imagine four objects on the shelf—a steel wedge for splitting wood, a garden digging tool, a box of plant food, and a hose nozzle—each is a possible location for a memory image. The objects are spaced evenly on the shelf and well illuminated. It's important to note that this shelf is in my imagination. The real shelf is not as orderly, and objects come and go from it. But the shelf in my memory palace will always be as it is. I remember miscellaneous tasks and appointments by associating a memory cue with one of the locations. For example, I need to renew my membership in a professional association, so I have an image of the steel wedge deeply driven into the group's logo, splitting it in two. The garden tool is associated with the next meeting of an advisory committee I serve on, and the plant food box has a big bite out of it to remind me of my next dental check-up. If I needed, I could create a memory aid for the date and time of the appointment, but it won't be necessary. I review the memory palace often, and when I get to the box, I refresh my memory of the appointment—May 7 at 9:00 A.M.

The next site is another shelf farther down the wall of the garage. It holds other objects that define locations for memory images. Today there are cues for a home repair I've been putting off, a broken drill bit I should replace and backup printer ink I need. When I take care of one of these tasks, it will be quickly forgotten, and the location will become available for a new item.

Ten additional sites follow, located in cabinets, in a tool box, in drawers, and on a workbench. Each site contains objects that serve as locations I associate with reminders relevant to a specific area of my life—a site for a community group I'm active in, one for my memory class, sites for hobbies and interests, one for family, another for friends, a site for health, and a place for this book project. I visit the memory palace almost every weekday morning. It is a peaceful time for me as I mentally go to each site to find what is stored there. When I'm finished, I have a plan for the day.

Remembering Facts

A traditional use for a memory palace is to hold static information such as the facts Ricci retained from his college days. I am a private pilot, and I have a memory palace devoted to aviation facts. It is constructed in my imagination around the plane I fly. I picture a domed structure on the left wing, and within it I have set up memory locations in three separate clusters. Each location contains images to cue facts about airspace rules and practices. In front of the plane, parked next to the propeller, is another imaginary memory area in the form of a large black FAA Suburban. Locations on the vehicle are associated with cues for various regulations. Protocols for different flight situations are represented by memory cues in an imaginary hangar on the right wing. Weather facts are on the tail surfaces. I use this memory palace primarily in the spring, at the beginning of my flying season, to rehearse and refresh key facts so that they'll easily come to mind if I need them.

In constructing a memory palace for facts, the suggestions presented in Chapter 9 are useful. The first step is to organize the material and segment it into bite-sized facts. Next is finding a cue for each that can be visually linked to a location in the memory palace. Once all the cues have been associated with specific locations, the facts can be rehearsed by mentally traveling through the palace.

The steps for remembering factual material are summarized in the Henry mnemonic from Chapter 9, shown again on the facing page. Henry's stop sign cues the process: Segment—Cue/Rehearse—Review. The Henry limerick, cued by the "H," emphasizes the importance of spaced rehearsal, and the dumbbell provides a cue for the Rule of Five. The "DD" stands for "desirable difficulty," a reminder that rehearsal will be most beneficial

Henry, a mnemonic for ways to remember facts from Chapter 9. These same techniques can be applied to establishing facts in memory palaces.

when it requires some effort to recall the facts. A memory palace takes this approach for remembering facts to the next level.

Remembering a Deck of Cards

There is something about remembering the order of a deck of playing cards that appeals to people interested in the memory arts, and that includes me. It is one of the standard events at memory competitions, where the winners show astounding skill. The current world record for memorizing a single deck of fifty-two cards is twenty-one seconds. Former world champion Dominic O'Brien once memorized fifty-four decks of cards (2,808 total) in a single effort. These card-memory feats are done with memory palaces.

My ambitions are far more modest. For me, it's about a recreational challenge, not competition, and speed in memorizing is not a priority. I keep a deck of cards on my desk, and every now and then the deck catches my eye. I shuffle the cards and give it a go. When I remember them all, life is good.

The first requirement is to have a way to encode cards so that they can be placed in a memory palace. Card values, like "two of clubs" or "three of diamonds," are too bland to be remembered easily, so mnemonists associate them with concrete objects. My approach is similar to one described by Harry Lorayne and others. In it, a "two of clubs" becomes "coin" and a "three of diamonds" becomes "dame." Both are words that can be visualized in a memory palace. The complete list of code words is in the table below, and if you look closely, you'll see the pattern. Each code word begins with the letter of a suit, like "c" for "clubs." Cards of the same value have similar sounding code words—coin, dune, hen, and sun code the value "2" in the four suits. The origin of this pattern is the major system, described in Chapter 10, for remembering numbers. In it, a "2" is represented by "n," "3" by "m," "4" by "r," and so on. If you know the major system, this card code is particularly easy to learn, and that was its selling point for me. Memory competitors like Joshua Foer and Dominic O'Brien use more complex coding systems that allow them to put several cards at the same memory palace location. The effort these systems require makes sense when speed is the top priority. Even the less demanding system I use requires plenty

Concrete Words Used to Remember Specific Cards

	Suit			
	Clubs	Diamonds	Hearts	Spades
Ace	Cot	Date	Hat	Suit
2	Coin	Dune	Hen	Sun
3	Comb	Dame	Ham	Sum
4	Car	Door	Hare	Seer
5	Coal	Doll	Hail	Sail
6	Cage	Dash	Hash	Sash
7	Cake	Dock	Hog	Sock
8	Cave	Dove	Hoof	Safe
9	Cop	Dab	Hoop	Soap
10	Case	Dose	Hose	Suds
J	Club	Diamond	Heart	Spade
Q	Cream	Dream	Queen	Steam
K	King	Drink	Hinge	Sing

of practice with the code words to be facile with them, and this is essential before moving on to remembering cards. (If you decide to experiment with card memory, try starting out with one suit, say clubs, and get proficient in remembering the order of this group as a first step.)

The memory palace needs fifty-two locations. Mine begins in my home and continues around my neighborhood; it is organized in sets of 10. To remember the cards, I create an image linking the code word for each card to a location in the memory palace. So, if the current card is the four of hearts ("hare") and the current location is the mailbox on my neighbor's house, I imagine a rabbit with long ears and a woeful expression stuffed into the mailbox. The suggestions in Chapter 4 for memory images are helpful here. I make the images as distinctive and unique as I can manage and try to get them to interact with the locations in some way. Once I finish the cards, I come to my Moment of Truth when I recall them by going back through the palace.

A Final Thought

A memory palace makes use of two different features of our sophisticated visual system. One is the ability to remember locations so we can find our way in the environment. The other is the ability to remember the objects we encounter. These two features, memory for location and memory for objects, fulfill the two essential requirements of a list mnemonic: they organize material, and they provide encoding assistance to remember individual items. Together they make the Method of Loci the most powerful mnemonic system ever devised for retaining disconnected information that can be given a visual representation. Its most obvious use, of course, is to remember a list. But an application sometimes overlooked is using it to permit easy rehearsal of important information. Here the memory palace is used like flashcards to make memory strong enough that it can be recalled whenever it is needed without the palace.

 In the Memory Lab:
A Memory Palace for This Book

This is the last installment of the Memory Lab, and in it I invite you to create a memory palace to help you recall a key point from each of the preceding chapters. Think of this as an approximation of the kinds of memory palaces Matteo Ricci used to remember college subjects.

The first step is to establish the locations in the palace. Select them on a fixed route you can physically travel such as around your home or in your neighborhood. For example, the route might be kitchen table → stove top → kitchen sink → bathroom tub → computer station → book shelf. You need thirteen locations. Mentally run over the route until you have it down.

The thirteen images you will place at these sites are shown on pages 218–220; there is one from each chapter, and they cue major ideas and memory strategies of the book. Before you begin to locate them in the memory palace, I suggest you prepare a written summary of the facts you want each image to cue. You can use it later to check your memory.

Now place the thirteen cues at the thirteen sites by imagining them interacting with these places. Rehearse the palace by moving through it, recalling each image and associated facts. One advantage of a memory palace is that you can rehearse anywhere, even in bed when you are slow getting to sleep. In fact, medieval monks believed that being in bed at night was one of the best settings for memory work because there are few distractions. Wherever you carry them out, spaced retrievals are essential if, like Matteo Ricci, you want to retain the information over time.

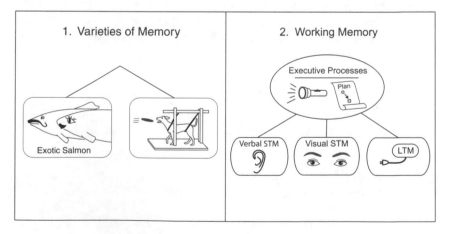

Memory images from Chapters 1–2.

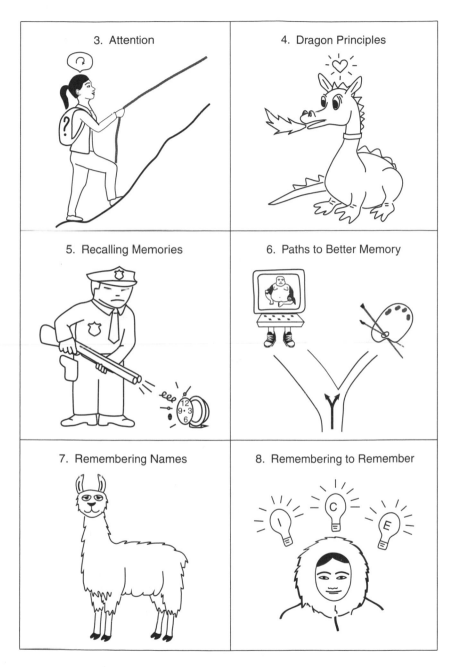

Memory images from Chapters 3–8.

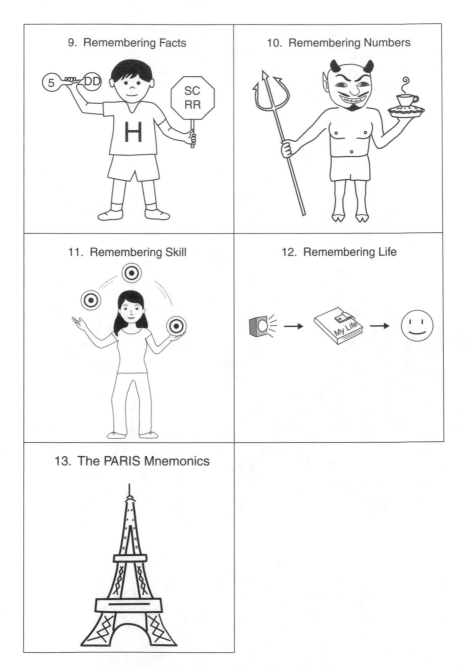

Memory images from Chapters 9–13.

15

Mindsets and Memory

Suppose you meet a nice couple at the dog park while you're watching your pet romp around. You chat, and later, as you are leaving, you bid them good-bye, calling each by name. This is a memory success, and you deserve to feel good about it as you and your dog head back to the car.

It's human nature to have an opinion about why you succeeded in remembering their names that day. Perhaps it was because your natural memory ability is especially good. Or maybe your success was due to the effort you put into remembering the names and the memory strategy you used. The difference between chalking up a success (or failure) to natural ability or to personal effort may seem like a trivial distinction. But it is not. The way you interpret memory outcomes can influence your attitude about your memory—how you think it functions and what it would take to improve it. That attitude can even affect what you try to remember.

Carol Dweck, a researcher at Stanford University, calls these two different attitudes "mindsets." With a fixed mindset you see your performance as the result of a relatively unchangeable ability like natural memory. A growth mindset is a belief that outcomes reflect your effort and technique, that improvement is possible if you work at it. To see these two mindsets at work, consider a study by Dweck and Claudia Mueller.

The two psychologists asked fifth-grade children to solve reasoning problems like the one on the next page. There were three separate work sessions. After the first session, each child was told he or she had done really well. Along with the good news, some children were praised for their natural ability: "You must be smart at these problems." Other children were praised for their effort: "You must have worked hard at these problems." Mueller and Dweck believed that these different forms of praise would encourage the children to adopt either a fixed or a growth mindset

Which answer completes the pattern?

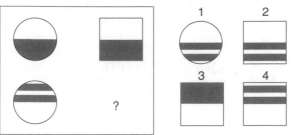

A reasoning problem similar to those given to fifth-grade children in the Mueller and Dweck study.

for evaluating their success, and the purpose of the study was to see if there were delayed consequences from the mindsets. The researchers suspected there could well be, especially if the children encountered a situation where they didn't succeed. After all, if doing well means you're smart, what does it mean when you fail? On the other hand, if doing well comes from working hard, failure has different implications.

To explore this issue, the researchers gave the children a dose of failure in the second work session, presenting them with a new set of problems much harder than the first. After the children finished, they were told that they had done a lot worse on the second set. Now the stage was set for the third session, when they were given problems similar to the easier ones they had first worked on. How would they rebound from failure? Would the kind of praise they received make a difference? The graph on page 223 compares the number of problems children solved in the first and third sessions. Those who had been praised for effort actually improved their performance, while those praised for ability showed a drop. What was going on?

Mueller and Dweck believe that the different mindsets gave failure different meanings for the two groups of children. When those who had been praised for being smart subsequently experienced failure, they were inclined to see it as a lack of ability, which made them less motivated to work on additional problems. The children who had been told they succeeded because they worked hard were likely to interpret the failure as a lack of effort, which led them to be more motivated in the third session.

The children also differed in the kinds of challenges they were willing to undertake in the future. Right after that first successful session, they

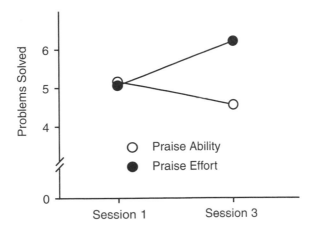

Performance on reasoning problems before and after a session where children experienced disappointing outcomes.

were asked what other kinds of reasoning problems they might like to work on. Most of those who had been praised for being smart (sixty-seven percent) chose options like "problems that aren't too hard so I won't get many wrong." They wanted to avoid failure, and they were drawn to safe choices involving easy problems. The children who had been praised for effort overwhelmingly (ninety-two percent) chose the option "problems I'd learn a lot from even if I won't look so smart." For these children, failure was much less negative, and they were attracted to challenging problems that offered a chance to learn better strategies.

There is now a large body of research on the importance of mindsets. A recent review summarized eighty-five studies and concluded that "mindsets matter." Whether people view ability as a skill that can be improved or a fixed entity influences many areas of human performance, including school achievement, success in sports, corporate leadership, dieting, and the dynamics of romantic relationships. Those with a growth mindset were more open to new learning; they were more resilient after failure, and they were more willing to take on challenges.

This insight is relevant to the practitioner of the memory arts. When you recall the movies nominated for this year's Academy Awards, and your friend says "You have a good memory," it's tempting to give credit to your natural memory. In fact, that's what your friend meant by the compliment. While this is flattering and empowering at the time, it is problematic in the long run because it doesn't prepare you to deal well with memory failures, which you are sure to experience at some point. This can limit your memory skill because failures can be more helpful than successes when it comes to improving memory—provided you are able to learn from them. Having the right mindset about memory outcomes, one that emphasizes growth through effort and strategy, sets the stage for improvement. It will also make you more willing to take on memory challenges where failure is a possibility—learning the names of new people in a group, retaining a phone number without writing it down, or making a presentation without notes. With a growth mindset, you'll be more likely to give situations like these a try and learn from them.

Mindsets and Stereotypes

A growth mindset is particularly beneficial to the elderly, who are bombarded with the widespread stereotype that advancing age leads to biologically driven cognitive decline and associated memory problems. Many older people embrace this notion, and we see evidence of it when someone forgets the name of a book he read last week or the dry cleaning she intended to pick up. Chagrined, they say "oops, a senior moment." The comment is understandable. Most elderly are aware that their memory is not as sharp as it once was, and the "senior moment" comment reflects this personal experience as well as societal stereotypes about aging. But in truth the actual reason for the memory slip will never be known—maybe it was age-related and maybe it wasn't. It is a fact that people of all ages forget. Calling this particular slip a "senior moment" will not be helpful if they're interested in improving their memory. To see why, think about what that expression means. It implies that the memory slip was a consequence of age and therefore is a permanent, fixed condition that will produce more memory errors in the future. Although it was a flip comment, it can undermine attempts to improve memory and even become a self-fulfilling prophecy—once this stereotype is taken to heart, expectations drop and the stage is set for lower memory performance regardless of any age-related factors that may or may not be operating.

Stereotype effects can be dramatic, as shown in a clever study of people between the ages of sixty and seventy conducted by Catherine Haslam and her colleagues at the University of Exeter. The participants were told that the purpose of the study was to investigate the way people of different ages performed on cognitive tests, and among the materials they were given was a magazine article about the association between aging and memory decline. Next came the ingenious twist in the experiment. Half the group was told that the study was made up of people between forty and seventy—this put them at the "old" end of the continuum. The other half was told that the study involved people between sixty and ninety, which put them at the "young" end. All the participants took a memory test—reading stories and then recalling them either immediately or after a thirty-minute delay. The results are shown in the bar graph below. Those who saw themselves as old conformed to the stereotype with poor memory performance. As you look at the figure, keep in mind that the only age difference between the two groups was in their minds.

Researchers have studied the impact of stereotypes on cognitive performance extensively, and the effects are well documented. The process begins when something in a situation triggers the stereotype, like the magazine article in the Haslam study. With the stereotype activated, those who thought of themselves as old tended to expect that they would do poorly on the coming memory test, and as a result they didn't try to the same extent as people who saw themselves as young.

Stereotype effects can have devastating consequences. Haslam and her colleagues found that activating an age stereotype can artificially lower

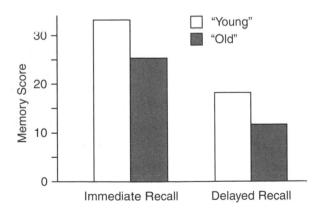

A comparison of memory test scores for senior citizens who thought they were either the youngest members of the group being tested ('young") or the oldest members of the group ("old").

some seniors' test scores on a screening exam to the point where they meet the diagnostic criteria for dementia, a diagnosis that is bad news indeed for the individual who receives it. For many elderly, dementia tops cancer as their most feared health affliction. And the diagnosis brings with it a new and even more pejorative stereotype.

The good news is that not everyone succumbs to stereotypes. Those most likely to accept them are people with fixed mindsets about abilities, and if they are in a vulnerable group like the elderly, they are more likely to apply the stereotype to themselves. When people are encouraged to adopt a growth mindset, they become less susceptible to stereotypes.

Researchers Jason Plaks and Allison Chasteen, working with a group of senior citizens in their seventies, investigated whether a change in mindset could have an immediate effect on memory. They gave some materials advocating a growth mindset and others materials supporting a fixed mindset. Next, all were given a memory test. Those who read material supporting a growth perspective outperformed the fixed mindset group by fifteen percent, a memory difference large enough that it could well be noticeable in daily life.

The elderly are not the only people who can derive special benefit from a growth mindset. Adopting this attitude can help anyone who has low expectations about their memory ability. This could be someone who has been diagnosed with a learning disability, or attention-deficit/hyperactivity disorder, or mild cognitive impairment, or a traumatic brain injury. Low expectations can also be a carryover from past performance problems, such as academic failures. Any one of these situations can create a nagging belief that you have a cognitive deficiency that includes a bad memory. When this belief is coupled with a fixed mindset that the cognitive abilities can't be improved, low expectations and weak motivation become locked in, creating an additional handicap that will further degrade performance. But a person's limitations can never be known with certainty. Adopting a growth mindset that says effort and strategy can improve performance will allow a person to move forward to the maximum extent possible.

Fostering a Growth Mindset

We pick up mindsets from the world around us—parents, peers, teachers, celebrities, and the media. They become our assumptions about how abilities come about and what can be done to improve them. We can have different mindsets for different abilities: for example, we might believe that athletic ability is fixed but that music ability comes about through practice, or vice versa. We can even hold both mindsets about the same ability, believing, for example, that although natural memory ability is fixed, memory skill can be improved with effort and strategy. These mindsets are not carved in stone. The studies reviewed in this chapter illustrate that mindsets can be changed by interventions such as the type of praise a teacher gives or the educational material people read.

A practitioner of the memory arts is in a good position to cultivate a growth mindset about memory because the techniques are based on learned skills and practice. But one more ingredient is necessary, and it has to do with the mnemonist's goals. Carol Dweck has identified two different forms achievement goals can take, and only one of them fully supports growth.

The one she recommends is called a "mastery goal," which focuses on developing and maintaining competence. Mastery goals are about taking on challenges and meeting them, and they accommodate failures as part of the process. Improvement is the name of the game. Dweck contrasts mastery goals with "performance goals," in which you seek praise for your successes and try to avoid the negative reactions that can result from failure. With performance goals the need to prevent failure becomes more important than the need to stretch and develop. When these goals dominate, progress in memory skill can be slowed or even derailed.

I believe that the best way to set the stage for continued progress is to deliberately interpret successes and disappointments as reflections of effort and strategy. Work on mastery goals, aim for small improvements, and find satisfaction in the process.

A Final Thought

A discussion of the growth mindset is an appropriate way to end this book. As we have seen in the previous chapters, there is abundant knowledge available about how to improve memory skill. Revolutionary advances in the scientific understanding of memory offer a better foundation than ever before for memory strategies that address the challenges of daily life—names and faces, numbers and facts, skills and intentions, even the events of your own life. To take advantage of real opportunities for memory development, all you need to add is a growth mindset and a commitment to improving your skill.

It's ironic that so many possibilities for improving memory have become available at the same time all manner of electronic devices have appeared to manage the information in our lives, relieving us of the need to be responsible for retaining it ourselves. When it comes to storing and accessing information, it could be argued that the need for traditional memory arts is on the wane. Given a smartphone and an Internet connection, you can meet many of the memory challenges I've addressed in this book. But people who are drawn to the memory arts—and I hope this book has helped make you one of them—are not motivated solely by managing information, just as a person who chooses to walk rather than drive is motivated by more than getting from point A to point B. Walking or biking offers opportunities for self-reliance, healthy exercise, and personal satisfaction. So it is with memory. Memory strategies and techniques are a complement, or even an antidote, to electronic devices, which have become so useful and seductive that they foster alarming levels of dependency.

I hope you'll take on the challenge of strengthening your memory in some area of your life, whether it be remembering names or studying more effectively or learning a new skill. And for readers who have a deeper commitment to mnemonic techniques, those who only grudgingly resort to sticky notes and the like, I offer this:

Every Day
Find a Way
To Put in Play
The Memory Arts

Notes

Introduction

Page 1

Here is Dan Rookwood: Rookwood, D. (2011, August 24). Technology overload. Retrieved May 12, 2014, from *www.gq.com.au/life/editors+pick/technology+overload,13897.*

Page 2

A survey of 3,000 Britons: Quinn, B. (2007, July 13). Mobile phones "dumbing down brain power." Retrieved May 12, 2014, from *www.telegraph.co.uk/news/uknews/1557293/Mobile-phones-dumbing-down-brain-power.html.*

Page 3

consider the story of Scott Hagwood: Hagwood, S. (2007). *Memory power: You can develop a great memory—America's Grand Master shows you how.* New York: Free Press.

Page 3

Hagwood bought a book: Buzan, T. (1991). *Use your perfect memory: Dramatic new techniques for improving your memory* (3rd ed.). New York: Plume.

Chapter 1

Page 9

H. M.'s epilepsy resulted from: Two books were my sources for details about H. M. Corkin, S. (2013). *Permanent present tense: The unforgettable life of the amnesic patient, H. M.* New York: Basic Books; and Hilts, P. J. (1996). *Memory's ghost: The nature of memory and the strange tale of Mr. M.* New York: Touchstone.

Page 10

Scoville was undeterred: In 1974, Scoville called the operation "a tragic mistake" (Corkin, 2013, p. 47).

Page 10

As Milner told a reporter: Hilts (1996, p. 110).

Page 10

"This patient's memory defect": Scoville, W. B., & Milner, B. (1957). Loss of recent memory after bilateral hippocampal lesions. *Journal of Neurology, Neurosurgery and Psychiatry, 20*, 14.

Page 11

Milner's ongoing work: This research was reported in 1962 in an obscure paper that is summarized in Milner, B., Squire, L., & Kandel, E. (1998). Cognitive neuroscience and the study of memory. *Neuron, 20*, 445–468. The figure on page 12 was derived from the data presented in their Figure 2.

Page 12

a different picture emerged: Squire, L. R. (2004). Memory systems of the brain: A brief history and current perspective. *Neurobiology of Learning and Memory, 82*(3), 171–177.

Page 13

Tulving proposed: Tulving, E. (2002). Episodic memory: From mind to brain. *Annual Review of Psychology, 53*(1), 1–25.

Page 14

Children develop the ability to time travel: Russell, J., Alexis, D., & Clayton, N. (2010). Episodic future thinking in 3- to 5-year-old children: The ability to think of what will be needed from a different point of view. *Cognition, 114*(1), 56–71.

Page 14

Older adults who have trouble remembering: Addis, D. R., Wong, A. T., & Schacter, D. L. (2008). Age-related changes in the episodic simulation of future events. *Psychological Science, 19*(1), 33–41.

Page 14

Tulving believes that this kind: Tulving, E. (2005). Episodic memory and autonoesis: Uniquely human? In H. S. Terrace & J. Metcalfe (Eds.), *The missing link in cognition: Origins of self-reflective consciousness* (pp. 3–56). New York: Oxford University Press.

Page 14

Semantic memory is thought to start: Diekelmann, S., & Born, J. (2010). The memory function of sleep. *Nature Reviews Neuroscience, 11*(2), 114–126.

Page 15

Such memories are called "implicit": The distinction between explicit and implicit memory is also referred to as a distinction between "declarative" and "nondeclarative" memory. The terminology is used interchangeably in research reports.

Page 16

Ronald Reagan's struggle: Altman, L. (1997, October 5). Reagan's twilight— A special report: A president fades into a world apart. *New York Times.* Retrieved from *www.nytimes.com/1997/10/05/us/reagan-s-twilight-a-special-report-a-president-fades-into-a-world-apart.html*

Page 17

expert radiologists: Myles-Worsley, M., Johnston, W. A., & Simons, M. A. (1988). The influence of expertise on X-ray image processing. *Journal of Experimental Psychology: Learning, Memory, and Cognition, 14*(3), 553–557.

Page 17

experienced computer programmers: Davies, S. P. (1991). The role of notation and knowledge representation in the determination of programming strategy: A framework for integrating models of programming behavior. *Cognitive Science, 15*(4), 547–572.

Page 17

the best-known psychology experiment: The drawing is from Yerkes, R. M., & Morgulis, S. (1909). The method of Pawlow in animal psychology. *Psychological Bulletin, 6*(8), 257–273.

Page 17

He described the curious case: Claparède, E. (1911/1995). Recognition and self-hood (Ann-Marie Bonnel, Trans.). *Consciousness and Cognition, 4,* 371–378.

Page 20

Cicero spoke for many ancients: Cicero, *De orotore,* II, lxxxvii, 357.

Page 21

the "substitute word technique": This terminology is from Lorayne, H., & Lucas, J. (1974). *The memory book.* Briarcliff Manor, NY: Stein and Day. Lorayne promoted the technique to remember abstract words, people's last names, and foreign vocabulary. When used to remember foreign vocabulary words, the technique has been called the "keyword mnemonic" by psychologists and has been studied extensively. This research is reviewed by Worthen, J. B., & Hunt, R. R. (2010). *Mnemonology: Mnemonics for the 21st century.* New York: Psychology Press. Also see Desrochers, A., & Begg, I. (1987). A theoretical account of encoding and retrieval processes in the use of imagery-based mnemonic techniques: The special case of the keyword method. In M. McDaniel & M. Pressley (Eds.), *Imagery and related mnemonic processes: Theories, individual differences, and applications* (pp. 56–77). New York: Springer-Verlag.

Page 23

about as much memory enhancement: McKelvie, S. J. (1995). The VVIQ as a psychometric test of individual differences in visual imagery vividness: A critical quantitative review and plea for direction. *Journal of Mental Imagery, 19*(3–4), 1–106.

Chapter 2

Page 24

Short-Order Cook: Daniels, J. (1985). *Places/Everyone.* Madison: University of Wisconsin Press. Copyright 1985 by the Board of Regents of the University of Wisconsin System. Reprinted by permission of The University of Wisconsin Press.

Page 27

the work of influential British researcher Alan Baddeley: Baddeley, A. (2007). *Working memory, thought, and action.* New York: Oxford University Press.

Page 28

the seat of consciousness: Baddeley (2007, pp. 314–316).

Page 28

was prepared from one such source: The averages for ages eighteen through eighty-seven are from Table B.6 in Wechsler, D. (1997). *WAIS-III administration and scoring manual* (3rd ed.). San Antonio, TX: Psychological Corp. The averages for ages six, eight, ten, twelve, and fourteen are from Table B.7 in Wechsler, D. (2003). *WISC-IV administration and scoring manual* (4th ed.). San Antonio, TX: Psychological Corp. The ninetieth and tenth percentiles are estimates calculated as plus and minus 1.28 times the standard deviation values given in the tables.

Page 29

only a moderate decline over the lifespan: Alloway, T. P., & Alloway, R. G. (2013). Working memory across the lifespan: A cross-sectional approach. *Journal of Cognitive Psychology, 25*(1), 84–93. Larger age effects are found for visuospatial working memory than verbal working memory. See Murre, J. M. J., Janssen, S. M. J., Rouw, R., & Meeter, M. (2013). The rise and fall of immediate and delayed memory for verbal and visuospatial information from late childhood to late adulthood. *Acta Psychologica, 142*(1), 96–107.

Page 30

what bedevils older people: Darowski, E. S., Helder, E., Zacks, R. T., Hasher, L., & Hambrick, D. Z. (2008). Age-related differences in cognition: The role of distraction control. *Neuropsychology, 22*(5), 638–644.

Page 30

reading comprehension can be predicted: Daneman, M., & Carpenter, P. A. (1980). Individual differences in working memory and reading. *Journal of Verbal Learning and Verbal Behavior, 19*(4), 450–466.

Page 30

In tests of reasoning ability: Oberauer, K., Süß, H.-M., Wilhelm, O., & Sander, N. (2008). Individual differences in working memory capacity and reasoning ability. In A. R. A. Conway, C. Jarrold, M. J. Kane, & J. N. Towse (Eds.), *Variation in working memory* (pp. 49–75). New York: Oxford University Press.

Page 30

Students mastering a computer language: Shute, V. J. (1991). Who is likely to acquire programming skills? *Journal of Educational Computing Research, 7*(1), 1–24.

Page 30

In a study of airplane pilots: Sohn, Y. W., & Doane, S. M. (2004). Memory processes of flight situation awareness: Interactive roles of working memory capacity, long-term working memory, and expertise. *Human Factors, 46*(3), 461–475.

Page 30

The connection to working memory: Conway, A. R. A., Cowan, N., Bunting, M. F., Therriault, D. J., & Minkoff, S. R. B. (2002). A latent variable analysis of working memory capacity, short-term memory capacity, processing speed, and general fluid intelligence. *Intelligence, 30*(2), 163–184.

Page 32

"We're back to the action": Hambrick, D. Z., & Engle, R. W. (2002). Effects of domain knowledge, working memory capacity, and age on cognitive performance: An investigation of the knowledge-is-power hypothesis. *Cognitive Psychology, 44*(4), 339–387.

Page 33

their findings are shown in the bar graph: From Table 9 in Hambrick & Engle (2002).

Page 34

In a definitive analysis: Cowan, N. (2000). The magical number 4 in short-term memory: A reconsideration of mental storage capacity. *Behavioral and Brain Sciences, 24,* 87–114. Also see Cowan, N. (2010). The magical mystery four: How is working memory capacity limited, and why? *Current Directions in Psychological Science, 19*(1), 51–57.

Page 34

to some extent may be inherited: Ando, J., Ono, Y., & Wright, M. J. (2001). Genetic structure of spatial and verbal working memory. *Behavior Genetics, 31*(6), 615–624.

Page 36

The Picture Superiority Effect: Classic studies are described by Paivio, A. (1971). *Imagery and verbal processes.* New York: Holt, Rinehart & Winston. A summary of theories to explain the picture superiority effect appears in McBride, D. M., & Dosher, B. A. (2002). A comparison of conscious and automatic memory processes for picture and word stimuli: A process dissociation analysis. *Consciousness and Cognition, 11*(3), 423–460.

Page 36

Researchers estimate: Van Essen, D. C., Anderson, C. H., & Felleman, D. J. (1992). Information processing in the primate visual system: An integrated systems perspective. *Science, 255*(5043), 419–423.

Chapter 3

Page 38

On an August evening in 1967: The most complete account of Margetts's story is Shapreau, C. (2006, February 12). Lost and found. And lost again? *Los Angeles Times.* Retrieved from *www.latimes.com/local/la-tm-violin7feb12-story.html#page=1.*

Page 40

"The secret of a good memory is attention": Edwards, T. (1891). *A dictionary of thoughts: Being a cyclopedia of laconic quotations from the best authors, both* *ancient and modern*, p. 342. New York: Cassell. Retrieved from *http://books. google.com/books*.

Page 41

One of their attention tests: A study that used the attention control test is Kane, M. J., Bleckley, M. K., Conway, A. R. A., & Engle, R. W. (2001). A controlled-attention view of working-memory capacity. *Journal of Experimental Psychology: General, 130*(2), 169–183.

Page 41

A large body of research supports: McCabe, D. P., Roediger, H. L., McDaniel, M. A., Balota, D. A., & Hambrick, D. Z. (2010). The relationship between working memory capacity and executive functioning: Evidence for a common executive attention construct. *Neuropsychology, 24*(2), 222–243.

Page 42

The two forms of attention evolved together: Allport, A. (1989). Visual attention. In M. I. Posner (Ed.), *Foundations of cognitive science* (pp. 631–663). Cambridge, MA: MIT Press.

Page 43

The third network is neurologically distinct: Buckner, R. L., Andrews-Hanna, J. R., & Schacter, D. L. (2008). The brain's default network: Anatomy, function, and relevance to disease. *Annals of the New York Academy of Sciences, 1124*, 1–38.

Page 44

Researcher Jonathan Smallwood calls this type: Smallwood, J., McSpadden, M., & Schooler, J. W. (2008). When attention matters: The curious incident of the wandering mind. *Memory and Cognition, 36*(6), 1144–1150.

Page 44

In one study, research participants were fitted: Reichle, E. D., Reineberg, A. E., & Schooler, J. W. (2010). Eye movements during mindless reading. *Psychological Science, 21*(9), 1300–1310.

Page 46

Researchers have found that restoring working memory: Clapp, W. C., Rubens, M. T., & Gazzaley, A. (2010). Mechanisms of working memory disruption by external interference. *Cerebral Cortex, 20*(4), 859–872.

Page 47

As the exam sits on his desk: A review of studies examining how worry, self-talk, and interfering thoughts affect test anxiety and performance is provided by Zeidner, M. (1998). *Test anxiety: The state of the art*, pp. 31–40. New York: Plenum Press.

Page 48

Athletes and coaches are well aware: Hatzigeorgiadis, A., Zourbanos, N., Galanis, E., & Theodorakis, Y. (2011). Self-talk and sports performance: A meta-analysis. *Perspectives on Psychological Science*, *6*(4), 348–356.

Page 48

"just do it": Cousins, S. O., & Gillis, M. M. (2005). "Just do it . . . before you talk yourself out of it": The self-talk of adults thinking about physical activity. *Psychology of Sport and Exercise*, *6*(3), 313–334.

Page 48

"Am I going to do this or not?": Senay, I., Albarracín, D., & Noguchi, K. (2010). Motivating goal-directed behavior through introspective self-talk: The role of the interrogative form of simple future tense. *Psychological Science*, *21*(4), 499–504.

Page 48

help test-anxious students stay focused on the test: Zeidner (1998, pp. 373–377).

Page 48

which enhances motivation by activating: Kang, M. J., Hsu, M., Krajbich, I. M., Loewenstein, G., McClure, S. M., Wang, J. T., & Camerer, C. F. (2009). The wick in the candle of learning: Epistemic curiosity activates reward circuitry and enhances memory. *Psychological Science*, *20*(8), 963–973.

Page 48

"When it is said that attention will not take a firm hold": Halleck, R. P. (1895). *Psychology and psychic culture*, p. 54. New York: American Book. Retrieved from *http://books.google.com/books*.

Page 49

"Flow is a subjective state": Csikszentmihalyi, M., Abuhamdeh, S., & Nakamura, J. (2005). Flow. In A. J. Elliot & C. S. Dweck (Eds.), *Handbook of competence and motivation* (pp. 598–608). New York: Guilford Press.

Chapter 4

Page 54

A retention intention sets the stage for good remembering: Specifying a plan in advance and committing to it is called an "implementation intention," a powerful cognitive strategy discussed in Chapter 8.

Page 55

In an important study: Craik, F. I. M., & Tulving, E. (1975). Depth of processing and the retention of words in episodic memory. *Journal of Experimental Psychology: General, 104*(3), 268–294. The figure on page 55 plots data from their Figure 3 for "yes" responses to "words presented twice."

Page 56

Deep processing even shows up in brain scans: Nyberg, L. (2002). Levels of processing: A view from functional brain imaging. *Memory, 10*(5–6), 345–348.

Page 57

One of the best ways to elaborate memory: Pressley, M., McDaniel, M. A., Turnure, J. E., Wood, E., & Ahmad, M. (1987). Generation and precision of elaboration: Effects on intentional and incidental learning. *Journal of Experimental Psychology: Learning, Memory, and Cognition, 13*(2), 291–300.

Page 58

Primal themes like survival: Nairne, J. S., & Pandeirada, J. N. S. (2008). Adaptive memory: Is survival processing special? *Journal of Memory and Language, 59*(3), 377–385.

Page 58

In one notable effort, Lionel Standing: Standing, L. (1973). Learning 10,000 pictures. *Quarterly Journal of Experimental Psychology, 25*(2), 207–222.

Page 58

Peter of Ravenna: Yates, F. A. (1966). *The art of memory*, p. 120. London: Pimlico.

Page 58

Francesco Panigarola: Spence, J. D. (1985). *The memory palace of Matteo Ricci*, p. 9. New York: Penguin Books.

Page 59

"Now nature herself teaches us": Appears in Yates (1966, p. 25).

Page 59

"Suppose someone must memorize": Appears in Carruthers, M., & Ziolkowski, J. M. (2003). *The medieval craft of memory: An anthology of texts and pictures*, pp. 209–210. Philadelphia: University of Pennsylvania Press.

Page 59

Modern research shows: The effectiveness of bizarre imagery is reported by McDaniel, M. A., & Einstein, G. O. (1986). Bizarre imagery as an effective memory aid: The importance of distinctiveness. *Journal of Experimental Psychology: Learning, Memory, and Cognition, 12*(1), 54–65. Benefits at longer retrieval intervals were found by O'Brien, E. J., & Wolford, C. R. (1982). Effect of delay in testing on retention of plausible versus bizarre mental images. *Journal of Experimental Psychology: Learning, Memory, and Cognition*, 8(2), 148–152.

Page 60

Colored images are five to ten percent: Wichmann, F. A., Sharpe, L. T., & Gegenfurtner, K. R. (2002). The contributions of color to recognition memory for natural scenes. *Journal of Experimental Psychology: Learning, Memory, and Cognition*, 28(3), 509–520.

Page 60

Movement has also been shown: Matthews, W. J., Benjamin, C., & Osborne, C. (2007). Memory for moving and static images. *Psychonomic Bulletin and Review*, 14(5), 989–993.

Page 61

Dominic O'Brien, a legendary memory competitor: O'Brien, D. (2000). *Learn to remember: Practical techniques and exercises to improve your memory*, p. 65. San Francisco: Chronicle Books.

Page 61

Harry Lorayne: Lorayne, H. (2007). *Ageless memory: Simple secrets for keeping your brain young*, p. 86. New York: Black Dog & Leventhal.

Page 61

Joshua Foer: Foer, J. (2011). *Moonwalking with Einstein: The art and science of remembering everything*, p. 3. New York: Penguin Press.

Page 62

Later, when he is trying to retrieve: Foer (2011, p. 183).

Page 63

one of the best established principles: Dempster, F. N. (1988). The spacing effect: A case study in the failure to apply the results of psychological research. *American Psychologist*, 43(8), 627–634.

Page 63

"Rule of Five": O'Brien (2000, p. 81).

Page 63

Other mnemonists offer similar spacing advice: Hagwood, S. (2007). *Memory power: You can develop a great memory—America's Grand Master shows you how*, p. 72. London: Free Press. Lorayne, H., & Lucas, J. (1974). *The memory book*, p. 32. Briarcliff Manor, NY: Stein & Day.

Page 64
In a now classic study: Bower, G. H., Clark, M. C., Lesgold, A. M., & Winzenz, D. (1969). Hierarchical retrieval schemes in recall of categorized word lists. *Journal of Verbal Learning and Verbal Behavior, 8*(3), 323–343.

Page 64
"What assists the memory most?": The memory teacher was Consultus Fortunatianus. His memory advice appears in Carruthers & Ziolkowski (2003, pp. 296–297).

Page 64
"a single glance of the mind's eye": Carruthers, M. (1998). *The craft of thought: Meditation, rhetoric, and the making of images, 400–1200*, p. 63. New York: Cambridge University Press.

Chapter 5

Page 69
"Having lived most of his life": Smith, S. M. (1988). Environmental context—dependent memory, p. 13. In G. M. Davies & D. M. Thomson (Eds.), *Memory in context: Context in memory*. Oxford, UK: John Wiley & Sons.

Page 70
Memory trainer Tony Buzan recommends: Buzan, T. (1991). *Use your perfect memory: Dramatic new techniques for improving your memory* (3rd ed.), pp. 161–162. New York: Plume.

Page 71
It has been shown to recover: Fisher, R. P., & Geiselman, R. E. (2010). The cognitive interview method of conducting police interviews: Eliciting extensive information and promoting therapeutic jurisprudence. *International Journal of Law and Psychiatry, 33*(5–6), 321–328.

Page 71
"Try to put yourself back": Fisher, R. P., & Geiselman, R. E. (1992). *Memory-enhancing techniques for investigative interviewing: The cognitive interview*, p. 100. Springfield, IL: Charles C Thomas.

Page 71
conducted an instructive experiment: Erdelyi, M. H., & Kleinbard, J. (1978). Has Ebbinghaus decayed with time? The growth of recall (hypermnesia) over days. *Journal of Experimental Psychology: Human Learning and Memory, 4*(4), 275–289. The figure on page 72 is based on their Figure 3.

Page 72

The strategy aids memory in two ways: Payne, D. G. (1987). Hypermnesia and reminiscence in recall: A historical and empirical review. *Psychological Bulletin, 101*(1), 5–27. Mulligan, N. W. (2006). Hypermnesia and total retrieval time. *Memory, 14*(4), 502–518.

Page 73

You will combine the gist and specifics: My presentation follows the fuzzy trace theory of Brainerd, C. J., & Reyna, V. F. (2005). *The science of false memory*, pp. 83–91. New York: Oxford University Press.

Page 74

"dumped in and tagged": Moscovitch, M. (2008). The hippocampus as a "stupid," domain-specific module: Implications for theories of recent and remote memory, and of imagination. *Canadian Journal of Experimental Psychology, 62*(1), 66.

Page 75

Researchers believe that memories briefly enter a malleable phase: Dudai, Y. (2012). The restless engram: Consolidations never end. *Annual Review of Neuroscience, 35,* 227–247.

Page 75

responses from a pair of identical twins: Sheen, M., Kemp, S., & Rubin, D. C. (2006). Disputes over memory ownership: What memories are disputed? *Genes, Brain and Behavior, 5*(Suppl. 1), 9–13.

Page 76

Most of the twin pairs: Sheen, M., Kemp, S., & Rubin, D. (2001). Twins dispute memory ownership: A new false memory phenomenon. *Memory and Cognition, 29*(6), 779–788.

Page 76

We can even mix up information: Loftus, E. F. (2005). Planting misinformation in the human mind: A 30-year investigation of the malleability of memory. *Learning and Memory, 12*(4), 361–366.

Page 76

Loftus began her study: Loftus, E. F., & Pickrell, J. E. (1995). The formation of false memories. *Psychiatric Annals, 25*(12), 720–725.

Page 77

Other researchers have replicated: Hyman, I. E., Husband, T. H., & Billings, F. J. (1995). False memories of childhood experiences. *Applied Cognitive Psy-*

chology, *9*(3), 181–197. Porter, S., Yuille, J. C., & Lehman, D. R. (1999). The nature of real, implanted, and fabricated memories for emotional childhood events: Implications for the recovered memory debate. *Law and Human Behavior*, *23*(5), 517–537.

Page 77

when they were debriefed: Loftus & Pickrell (1995, p. 723).

Page 77

memory confidence has been shown: Wells, G. L., Memon, A., & Penrod, S. D. (2006). Eyewitness evidence: Improving its probative value. *Psychological Science in the Public Interest*, *7*(2), 45–75.

Page 77

two hundred cases in which DNA evidence: DNA exonerations are tracked by The Innocence Project. Retrieved June 15, 2014, from *www.innocenceproject. org*.

Page 77

there is no completely reliable way: Bernstein, D. M., & Loftus, E. F. (2009). How to tell if a particular memory is true or false. *Perspectives on Psychological Science*, *4*(4), 370–374.

Chapter 6

Page 83

Memory, he wrote: Cicero, M. T. (1890). *Orations of Marcus Tullius Cicero*, p. 528. (C. D. Yonge, Trans.) (Vol. 4). London: Bell & Daldy. Retrieved from *http://books.google.com/books*.

Page 83

memory took two forms: Yates, F. A. (1966). *The art of memory*. London: Pimlico.

Page 84

"If I am asked what is the one great art of memory": Quintilian 11.2.40.

Page 84

William James . . . put the idea to the test: James, W. (1890). *The principles of psychology: Authorized edition, unabridged* (Vol. 1, pp. 667–668). New York: Dover Publications. Retrieved from *http://books.google.com/books*.

Page 84

Edward Thorndike, a leader in the early research: Thorndike, E. L. (1911).

The principles of teaching: Based on psychology, p. 241. New York: A. G. Seiler. Retrieved from *http://books.google.com/books*.

Page 85
published by Swedish researcher: Klingberg, T., Fernell, E., Olesen, P. J., Johnson, M., Gustafsson, P., Dahlström, K., et al. (2005). Computerized training of working memory in children with ADHD—A randomized, controlled trial. *Journal of the American Academy of Child and Adolescent Psychiatry, 44*(2), 177–186.

Page 85
all of whom show working memory problems: The connection between working memory and ADHD is reviewed by Alderson, R. M., Kasper, L. J., Hudec, K. L., & Patros, C. H. G. (2013). Attention-deficit/hyperactivity disorder (ADHD) and working memory in adults: A meta-analytic review. *Neuropsychology, 27*(3), 287–302. The role of working memory in beginning reading and mathematics education is examined by Gathercole, S., & Alloway, T. P. (2008). *Working memory and learning: A practical guide for teachers*. Los Angeles, CA: SAGE.

Page 86
The mood in the research community: Melby-Lervåg, M., & Hulme, C. (2013). Is working memory training effective? A meta-analytic review. *Developmental Psychology, 49*(2), 270–291. Rabipour, S., & Raz, A. (2012). Training the brain: Fact and fad in cognitive and behavioral remediation. *Brain and Cognition, 79*(2), 159–179. Shipstead, Z., Redick, T. S., & Engle, R. W. (2012). Is working memory training effective? *Psychological Bulletin, 138*(4), 628–654.

Page 87
The market for brain-fitness software: Jones, S. M. (2011, March 1). Retailer banks on brain fitness to expand stores. Retrieved June 16, 2014, from *http://articles.chicagotribune.com/2011-03-01/business/ct-biz-0302-marbles-20110301_1_brain-fitness-retailer-banks-sales-associates*.

Page 87
Jungle Memory spare no words: Retrieved June 15, 2014, from *http://jungle-memory.com/pages/how_it_works*.

Page 87
Mindsparke's pitch: Retrieved June 15, 2014, from *www.mindsparke.com/better_memory.php*.

Page 88
published in the prestigious British journal: Owen, A. M., Hampshire, A.,

Grahn, J. A., Stenton, R., Dajani, S., Burns, A. S., et al. (2010). Putting brain training to the test. *Nature, 465*(7299), 775–778.

Page 88

It has been described as: Kabat-Zinn, J. (1994). *Wherever you go, there you are,* pp. 3–9. New York: Hyperion.

Page 88

developed a widely adopted eight-week mindfulness training program: Kabat-Zinn, J. (1990). *Full catastrophe living?: Using the wisdom of your body and mind to face stress, pain, and illness.* New York: Bantam.

Page 89

Christian Jensen and his collaborators: Jensen, C. G., Vangkilde, S., Frokjaer, V., & Hasselbalch, S. G. (2012). Mindfulness training affects attention—Or is it attentional effort? *Journal of Experimental Psychology: General, 141*(1), 106–123.

Page 89

especially for attention: Chiesa, A., Calati, R., & Serretti, A. (2011). Does mindfulness training improve cognitive abilities? A systematic review of neuropsychological findings. *Clinical Psychology Review, 31*(3), 449–464.

Page 89

Memory also seems to profit: Chambers, R., Lo, B. C. Y., & Allen, N. B. (2008). The impact of intensive mindfulness training on attentional control, cognitive style, and affect. *Cognitive Therapy and Research, 32*(3), 303–322. Mrazek, M. D., Franklin, M. S., Phillips, D. T., Baird, B., & Schooler, J. W. (2013). Mindfulness training improves working memory capacity and GRE performance while reducing mind wandering. *Psychological Science, 24*(5), 776–781.

Page 89

ability to remember old personal memories: Heeren, A., Van Broeck, N., & Philippot, P. (2009). The effects of mindfulness on executive processes and autobiographical memory specificity. *Behaviour Research and Therapy, 47*(5), 403–409.

Page 90

In one large project: Laurin, D., Verreault, R., Lindsay, J., MacPherson, K., & Rockwood, K. (2001). Physical activity and risk of cognitive impairment and dementia in elderly persons. *Archives of Neurology, 58*(3), 498–504.

Page 90

Arthur Kramer and his associates: Kramer, A. F., Hahn, S., McAuley, E., Cohen, N. J., Banich, M. T., Harrison, C., et al. (2001). Exercise, aging, and cognition: Healthy body, healthy mind? In W. A. Rogers & A. D. Fisk (Eds.), *Human factors interventions for the health care of older adults* (pp. 91–120). Mahwah, NJ: Lawrence Erlbaum.

Page 90
These results have been confirmed: Guiney, H., & Machado, L. (2013). Benefits of regular aerobic exercise for executive functioning in healthy populations. *Psychonomic Bulletin and Review, 20*(1), 73–86. Smith, P. J., Blumenthal, J. A., Hoffman, B. M., Cooper, H., Strauman, T. A., Welsh-Bohmer, K., et al. (2010). Aerobic exercise and neurocognitive performance: A meta-analytic review of randomized controlled trials. *Psychosomatic Medicine, 72*(3), 239–252. Voss, M. W., Nagamatsu, L. S., Liu-Ambrose, T., & Kramer, A. F. (2011). Exercise, brain, and cognition across the life span. *Journal of Applied Physiology, 111*(5), 1505–1513.

Page 91
show better academic achievement: Grissom, J. B. (2005). Physical fitness and academic achievement. *Journal of Exercise Physiology, 8*(1), 11–25.

Page 91
fit children have more brain volume: Chaddock, L., Pontifex, M. B., Hillman, C. H., & Kramer, A. F. (2011). A review of the relation of aerobic fitness and physical activity to brain structure and function in children. *Journal of the International Neuropsychological Society, 17*(6), 975–985.

Page 91
results suggest small improvements: Kamijo, K., Pontifex, M. B., O'Leary, K. C., Scudder, M. R., Wu, C., Castelli, D. M., et al. (2011). The effects of an afterschool physical activity program on working memory in preadolescent children. *Developmental Science, 14*(5), 1046–1058. Tomporowski, P. D., Lambourne, K., & Okumura, M. S. (2011). Physical activity interventions and children's mental function: An introduction and overview. *Preventive Medicine, 52*(Suppl.), S3–S9.

Page 91
twelve weeks of aerobic exercise: Pereira, A. C., Huddleston, D. E., Brickman, A. M., Sosunov, A. A., Hen, R., McKhann, G. M., et al. (2007). An in vivo correlate of exercise-induced neurogenesis in the adult dentate gyrus. *PNAS Proceedings of the National Academy of Sciences of the United States of America, 104*(13), 5638–5643.

Page 91
follow government guidelines: Retrieved June 15, 2014, from *www.cdc.gov/physicalactivity/everyone/guidelines/adults.html*.

Page 92

based on average gains found in available research: Computer training improvements were taken from the meta-analysis of Melby-Lervåg & Hulme (2013). The working memory gain plotted at point *a* is the percentile equivalent of Cohen's *d* = 0.65, the mean of the verbal (*d* = 0.79) and visuospatial values (*d* = 0.52) given in the paper. The transfer effect size plotted as point *c* corresponds to Cohen's *d* = 0.16, the average of verbal (*d* = 0.13) and nonverbal (*d* = 0.19) for transfer effects given by these authors. Smith et al. (2010) is the source for the exercise effects on working memory; Hedge's *g* = 0.56 is plotted as point *b* in the figure. It is the seventy-first percentile. The meditation memory improvement shown is based on the average of the gains reported by Jensen et al. (2012), Chambers et al. (2008), and Mrazek et al. (2013). This average, Cohen's *d* = 0.59, is plotted in the figure as the seventy-second percentile.

Chapter 7

Page 98

surveys find that forgetting names: Devolder, P. A., & Pressley, M. (1991). Memory complaints in younger and older adults. *Applied Cognitive Psychology*, *5*(5), 443–454.

Page 98

Researcher Lori James studied memory: James, L. E. (2004). Meeting Mr. Farmer versus meeting a farmer: Specific effects of aging on learning proper names. *Psychology and Aging*, *19*(3), 515–522. The figure on page 99 shows results from her Experiment 1.

Page 101

some researchers believe specialized neural circuitry: Kanwisher, N., & Yovel, G. (2009). Face perception. In G. G. Berntson & J. T. Cacioppo (Eds.), *Handbook of neuroscience for the behavioral sciences* (Vol. 2., pp. 841–858). Hoboken, NJ: John Wiley & Sons.

Page 101

But if you interact with her: Johnston, R., & Edwards, A. (2009). Familiar and unfamiliar face recognition: A review. *Memory*, *17*(5), 577–596.

Page 101

"What you select could be anything": Lorayne, H., & Lucas, J. (1974). *The memory book*, p. 88. Briarcliff Manor, NY: Stein & Day.

Page 102

People differ significantly: Bindemann, M., Avetisyan, M., & Rakow, T. (2012). Who can recognize unfamiliar faces? Individual differences and observer consistency in person identification. *Journal of Experimental Psychology: Applied, 18*(3), 277–291.

Page 103

memory expert Kenneth Higbee observed: Higbee, K. (2001). *Your memory?: How it works and how to improve it* (2nd ed.), p. 197. New York: Da Capo Press.

Page 104

Seniors appear to be especially vulnerable: Stevens, W. D., Hasher, L., Chiew, K. S., & Grady, C. L. (2008). A neural mechanism underlying memory failure in older adults. *Journal of Neuroscience, 28*(48), 12820–12824.

Page 105

Mnemonist Scott Hagwood recommends: Hagwood, S. (2007). *Memory power: You can develop a great memory—America's Grand Master shows you how,* p. 107. London: Free Press.

Page 105

research is consistent with his advice: Mangels, J. A., Manzi, A., & Summerfield, C. (2010). The first does the work, but the third time's the charm: The effects of massed repetition on episodic encoding of multimodal face–name associations. *Journal of Cognitive Neuroscience, 22*(3), 457–473.

Page 105

Psychologist Peter Morris: Morris, P. E., Fritz, C. O., Jackson, L., Nichol, E., & Roberts, E. (2005). Strategies for learning proper names: Expanding retrieval practice, meaning, and imagery. *Applied Cognitive Psychology, 19*(6), 779–798.

Page 105

When Harry Lorayne amazed audiences: Lorayne was a regular guest on TV variety shows in the 1960s and 1970s, such as those hosted by Jack Parr, Ed Sullivan, and Johnny Carson. His signature feat was to learn the name of everyone in the audience, sometimes hundreds of people. First he was introduced to each individual, and then he would have them all stand. As he identified each by name, they sat down, one after the other, until no one was left standing.

Page 108

Laboratory studies show that both college students: Carney, R. N., & Levin, J. R. (2012). Facing facts: Can the face–name mnemonic strategy accommodate additional factual information? *Journal of Experimental Education, 80*(4),

386–404. Groninger, L. D., Groninger, D. H., & Stiens, J. (1995). Learning the names of people: The role of image mediators. *Memory*, *3*(2), 147–167. Yesavage, J. A., Rose, T. L., & Bower, G. H. (1983). Interactive imagery and affective judgments improve face–name learning in the elderly. *Journal of Gerontology*, *38*(2), 197–203.

Page 108
In two studies in which students had learned: Both are reported by Morris et al. (2005).

Page 109
Dan Gabor, a business coach: Gabor, D. (2011). *How to start a conversation and make friends* (Revised ed.). New York: Touchstone.

Page 109
Called the "name game": Morris, P. E., & Fritz, C. O. (2000). The name game: Using retrieval practice to improve the learning of names. *Journal of Experimental Psychology: Applied*, *6*(2), 124–129. Morris, P. E., & Fritz, C. O. (2002). The improved name game: Better use of expanding retrieval practice. *Memory*, *10*(4), 259–266.

Page 110
have used it with as many as twenty-five: Morris, P. E., Fritz, C. O., & Buck, S. (2004). The name game: Acceptability, bonus information and group size. *Applied Cognitive Psychology*, *18*(1), 89–104.

Page 110
As Dale Carnegie observed: Carnegie, D. (1936). *How to win friends and influence people*, p. 79. New York: Pocket Books.

Chapter 8

Page 112
By one estimate, over half of the daily memory problems: McDaniel, M. A., & Einstein, G. O. (2007). *Prospective memory: An overview and synthesis of an emerging field*, p. 193. Thousand Oaks, CA: Sage.

Page 112
Although precise numbers aren't known: Weingarten, G. (2009, March 8). Fatal distraction: Forgetting a child in the backseat of a car is a horrifying mistake. But is it a crime? *The Washington Post*. Retrieved from *www.washingtonpost. com/lifestyle/magazine/fatal-distraction-forgetting-a-child-in-thebackseat- of-a-car-is-a-horrifying-mistake-is-it-a-crime/2014/06/16/8ae0fe3a-f580-*

11e3-a3a5-42be35962a52_story.html. Some estimates of heatstroke deaths attributable to parental forgetting are higher than Weingarten's. See *www.kidsandcars.org/heatstroke.html* retrieved on December 27, 2014.

Page 113
"The wealthy do, it turns out": Weingarten (2009).

Page 113
but this is no ordinary memory: McDaniel & Einstein (2007).

Page 113
"slumbers on in the person": Freud, S. (1960). *The psychopathology of everyday life.* (A. Tyson, Trans.), p. 152. New York: W. W. Norton.

Page 114
detected through either top-down or bottom-up processes: This view is known as multiprocess theory in the professional literature (McDaniel & Einstein, 2007).

Page 114
something has to give: Marsh, R. L., Hicks, J. L., & Cook, G. I. (2005). On the relationship between effort toward an ongoing task and cue detection in event-based prospective memory. *Journal of Experimental Psychology: Learning, Memory, and Cognition, 31*(1), 68–75.

Page 114
McDaniel and Einstein believe is our preferred way: McDaniel & Einstein (2007, p. 54).

Page 115
Researchers call this a "focal cue": McDaniel & Einstein (2007, pp. 59–62).

Page 117
psychologist Peter Gollwitzer: Gollwitzer, P. M. (1999). Implementation intentions: Strong effects of simple plans. *American Psychologist, 54*(7), 493–503.

Page 117
how an implementation intention works its magic: McDaniel, M. A., & Scullin, M. K. (2010). Implementation intention encoding does not automatize prospective memory responding. *Memory and Cognition, 38*(2), 221–232. Rummel, J., Einstein, G. O., & Rampey, H. (2012). Implementation-intention encoding in a prospective memory task enhances spontaneous retrieval of intentions. *Memory, 20*(8), 803–817.

Page 117

especially helpful when the cue for the intended action: McDaniel, M. A., Howard, D. C., & Butler, K. M. (2008). Implementation intentions facilitate prospective memory under high attention demands. *Memory and Cognition*, *36*(4), 716–724.

Page 118

added benefit for older people: Chasteen, A. L., Park, D. C., & Schwarz, N. (2001). Implementation intentions and facilitation of prospective memory. *Psychological Science*, *12*(6), 457–461.

Page 118

The desired action must be a goal you really want: Sheeran, P., Webb, T. L., & Gollwitzer, P. M. (2005). The interplay between goal intentions and implementation intentions. *Personality and Social Psychology Bulletin*, *31*(1), 87–98.

Page 118

Some fine points about implementation intentions: Ellis, J. A., & Freeman, J. E. (2008). Ten years on: Realizing delayed intentions. In M. Kliegel, M. A. McDaniel, & G. O. Einstein (Eds.), *Prospective memory: Cognitive, neuroscience, developmental, and applied perspectives* (pp. 1–27). New York: Taylor & Francis Group.

Page 118

helps in many self-control situations: Gollwitzer, P. M., & Sheeran, P. (2006). Implementation intentions and goal achievement: A meta-analysis of effects and processes. In M. P. Zanna (Ed.), *Advances in experimental social psychology* (Vol. 38, pp. 69–119). San Diego, CA: Elsevier Academic Press.

Page 119

it can do this in one of two ways: Kliegel, M., Guynn, M. J., & Zimmer, H. (2007). The role of noticing in prospective memory forgetting. *International Journal of Psychophysiology*, *64*(3), 226–232.

Page 119

the cuing stimulus should be in focal attention: McDaniel & Einstein (2007, pp. 59–62).

Page 120

Einstein and McDaniel report that participants: Einstein, G. O., & McDaniel, P. M. A. (2004). *Memory fitness: A guide for successful aging*, p. 135. New Haven, CT.: Yale University Press.

Page 120

create them at the spot: Nowinski, J. L., & Dismukes, R. K. (2005). Effects of ongoing task context and target typicality on prospective memory performance: The importance of associative cueing. *Memory, 13*(6), 649–657.

Page 120

And the more important the task: Kliegel, M., Martin, M., McDaniel, M. A., & Einstein, G. O. (2004). Importance effects on performance in event-based prospective memory tasks. *Memory, 12*(5), 553–561.

Chapter 9

Page 124

Herbert Spitzer carried out a classic study: Spitzer, H. F. (1939). Studies in retention. *Journal of Educational Psychology, 30*(9), 641–656. The figure on page 125 is from his Table 2, time period B1.

Page 125

Their shapes are usually similar: Rubin, D. C., & Wenzel, A. E. (1996). One hundred years of forgetting: A quantitative description of retention. *Psychological Review, 103*(4), 734–760.

Page 125

a powerful, reliable way to enhance memory: Roediger, H. L., Agarwal, P. K., McDaniel, M. A., & McDermott, K. B. (2011). Test-enhanced learning in the classroom: Long-term improvements from quizzing. *Journal of Experimental Psychology: Applied, 17*(4), 382–395.

Page 126

Washington University researchers: Roediger, H. L., & Karpicke, J. D. (2006). Test-enhanced learning: Taking memory tests improves long-term retention. *Psychological Science, 17*(3), 249–255.

Page 127

The results are shown in the bar graph: My graph is based on Figure 1 in Roediger & Karpicke (2006).

Page 127

Multiple-choice tests are a useful way: McDermott, K. B., Agarwal, P. K., D'Antonio, L., Roediger, H. L., & McDaniel, M. A. (2014). Both multiple-choice and short-answer quizzes enhance later exam performance in middle and high school classes. *Journal of Experimental Psychology: Applied, 20*(1),

3–21. But also see McDaniel, M. A., Anderson, J. L., Derbish, M. H., & Morrisette, N. (2007). Testing the testing effect in the classroom. *European Journal of Cognitive Psychology, 19*(4–5), 494–513. Little, J. L., Bjork, E. L., Bjork, R. A., & Angello, G. (2012). Multiple-choice tests exonerated, at least of some charges: Fostering test-induced learning and avoiding test-induced forgetting. *Psychological Science, 23*(11), 1337–1344.

Page 128

the primary studying method: McIntyre, S. H., & Munson, J. M. (2008). Exploring cramming: Student behaviors, beliefs, and learning retention in the Principles of Marketing course. *Journal of Marketing Education, 30*(3), 226–243.

Page 128

the memory boost it provides is short lived: Roediger, H. L., & Karpicke, J. D. (2006). The power of testing memory: Basic research and implications for educational practice. *Perspectives on Psychological Science, 1*(3), 181–210.

Page 129

He calls it "desirable difficulty": Bjork, R. A. (1999). Assessing our own competence: Heuristics and illusions. In D. Gopher & A. Koriat (Eds.), *Attention and performance XVII: Cognitive regulation of performance: Interaction of theory and application* (pp. 435–459). Cambridge, MA: MIT Press.

Page 129

you may not be able to recall it at all: Bahrick, H. P., Hall, L. K., & Baker, M. K. (2013). *Life-span maintenance of knowledge*, p. 226. New York: Psychology Press.

Page 130

Bjork and his colleague: Landauer, T. K., & Bjork, R. A. (1978). Optimum rehearsal patterns and name learning. In M. M. Gruneberg, P. E. Morris, & R. N. Sykes (Eds.), *Practical aspects of memory* (pp. 625–632). New York: Academic Press. Whether expanding retrieval practice leads to more efficient learning than constant spacing is debated by researchers.

Page 130

Professional mnemonists endorse this approach: Buzan, T. (1991). *Use your perfect memory: Dramatic new techniques for improving your memory* (3rd ed.), p. 82. New York: Plume. Hagwood, S. (2007). *Memory power: You can develop a great memory—America's Grand Master shows you how*, p. 72. New York: Free Press. Lorayne, H., & Lucas, J. (1974). *The memory book*, p. 32. Briarcliff Manor, NY: Stein & Day. O'Brien, D. (2000). *Learn to remember?: Practical techniques and exercises to improve your memory*, p. 81. San Francisco: Chronicle Books.

Page 131

students report they rarely use it: Karpicke, J. D., Butler, A. C., & Roediger, H. L. (2009). Metacognitive strategies in student learning: Do students practise retrieval when they study on their own? *Memory, 17*(4), 471–479.

Page 131

memory researcher Jennifer McCabe: McCabe, J. (2011). Metacognitive awareness of learning strategies in undergraduates. *Memory and Cognition, 39*(3), 462–476.

Page 132

an "illusion of competence" after restudying: Bjork (1999).

Page 132

Researcher Mark McDaniel and his collaborators: McDaniel, M. A., Howard, D. C., & Einstein, G. O. (2009). The read-recite-review study strategy: Effective and portable. *Psychological Science, 20*(4), 516–522.

Page 133

the most popular student self-testing strategy: Wissman, K. T., Rawson, K. A., & Pyc, M. A. (2012). How and when do students use flashcards? *Memory, 20*(6), 568–579.

Page 133

the evidence doesn't support this concern: Carpenter, S. K. (2012). Testing enhances the transfer of learning. *Current Directions in Psychological Science, 21*(5), 279–283.

Page 133

taught a group of students how to classify birds: Jacoby, L. L., Wahlheim, C. N., & Coane, J. H. (2010). Test-enhanced learning of natural concepts: Effects on recognition memory, classification, and metacognition. *Journal of Experimental Psychology: Learning, Memory, and Cognition, 36*(6), 1441–1451.

Page 134

The SCRR Method: Similar to the cue word method in Bellezza, F. (1982). *Improve your memory skills*. Englewood Cliffs, NJ: Prentice-Hall.

Page 134

there is a memory benefit to delaying: Butler, A. C., Karpicke, J. D., & Roediger, H. L. (2007). The effect of type and timing of feedback on learning from multiple-choice tests. *Journal of Experimental Psychology: Applied, 13*(4), 273–281.

Page 135

three perfect passes may be better: Karpicke, J. D., & Roediger, H. L. (2007). Repeated retrieval during learning is the key to long-term retention. *Journal of Memory and Language*, *57*(2), 151–162.

Page 135

five additional rehearsals spaced a week apart: Rawson, K. A., & Dunlosky, J. (2011). Optimizing schedules of retrieval practice for durable and efficient learning: How much is enough? *Journal of Experimental Psychology: General*, *140*(3), 283–302.

Page 136

a visual approach called "mind mapping": Buzan, T., & Buzan, B. (1996). *The mind map book: How to use radiant thinking to maximize your brain's untapped potential*. New York: Plume.

Page 137

this repository of long-lasting information: Bahrick, H. P. (1984). Semantic memory content in permastore: Fifty years of memory for Spanish learned in school. *Journal of Experimental Psychology: General*, *113*(1), 1–29. The figure on page 137 is the average of Spanish–English and English–Spanish tests given in his Table 6 and expressed relative to the scores of his Group 0 who took the test immediately after completing their last Spanish course.

Page 138

permastore memories vary in strength. Memories with intermediate strength will sometimes be able to be recalled and other times not, as discussed by Bahrick, Hall, & Baker (2013).

Page 138

long-lasting memories have been found: Bahrick, H. P., Bahrick, P. O., & Wittlinger, R. P. (1975). Fifty years of memory for names and faces: A cross-sectional approach. *Journal of Experimental Psychology: General*, *104*(1), 54–75. Bahrick, H. P., & Hall, L. K. (1991). Lifetime maintenance of high school mathematics content. *Journal of Experimental Psychology: General*, *120*(1), 20–33. Schmidt, H. G., Peeck, V. H., Paas, F., & van Breukelen, G. J. P. (2000). Remembering the street names of one's childhood neighbourhood: A study of very long-term retention. *Memory*, *8*(1), 37–49.

Page 138

memory for high school classmates: Bahrick, Bahrick, & Wittlinger (1975).

Chapter 10

Page 141

a place in the *Guinness Book of World Records:* Retrieved June 25, 2014, from *www.guinnessworldrecords.com/world-records/1/most-pi-places-memorised*. Other mnemonists have claimed to have broken Chao Lu's record, but the claims have not been accepted by the Guinness organization at this time.

Page 141

Chao Lu was inspired: Estimates of the value of pi were proposed many times, even as far back as 1650 B.C. Zu Chongzhi earned special note because he computed a particularly accurate version to seven decimal digits in A.D. 480. It remained the best estimate of pi for 800 years. The quotation from Chao Lu was retrieved on June 25, 2014, from *www.newsgd.com/culture/peopleandlife/200611280032.htm*.

Page 141

Chao Lu planned to recite 90,000 digits: Retrieved June 25, 2014, from *www. pi-world-ranking-list.com/lists/details/luchaointerview.html*. His preparation is described by Hu, Y., Ericsson, K. A., Yang, D., & Lu, C. (2009). Superior self-paced memorization of digits in spite of a normal digit span: The structure of a memorist's skill. *Journal of Experimental Psychology: Learning, Memory, and Cognition, 35*(6), 1426–1442.

Page 141

he cooperated with Chinese and American psychologists: Hu, Ericsson, Yang, & Lu (2009), and Hu, Y., & Ericsson, K. A. (2012). Memorization and recall of very long lists accounted for within the Long-Term Working Memory framework. *Cognitive Psychology, 64*(4), 235–266.

Page 144

The Number-Shape System: Most of my number–shape examples come from Buzan, T. (1991). *Use your perfect memory: Dramatic new techniques for improving your memory* (3rd ed.), p. 52. New York: Plume; and O'Brien, D. (2005). *How to develop a brilliant memory week by week*, p. 42. London: Duncan Baird.

Page 147

Allan Paivio traced its early form: Paivio, A. (1971). *Imagery and verbal processes*, p. 168. New York: Holt, Rinehart & Winston.

Page 147

To get a feel for the code: The answers: 95, 72, 68, 55.

Page 147

Now try your hand at finding words: Some possibilities: 41, rod, or rat or radio; 19, tub or dope or teepee; 47, rock or rug or rag; 35, mule or mail or mole.

Page 147
"a beautiful naked blonde": Lorayne, H., & Lucas, J. (1974). *The memory book*, p. 105. Briarcliff Manor, NY: Stein & Day.

Page 150
Researchers have found that the major system: Patton, G. W., D'Agaro, W. R., & Gaudette, M. D. (1991). The effect of subject-generated and experimenter-supplied code words on the phonetic mnemonic system. *Applied Cognitive Psychology, 5*(2), 135–148.

Page 150
Mnemonist and memory researcher Kenneth Higbee: Higbee, K. L. (1997). Novices, apprentices, and mnemonists: Acquiring expertise with the phonetic mnemonic. *Applied Cognitive Psychology, 11*(2), 147–161.

Page 150
Francis Bellezza, a researcher at Ohio University: Bellezza, F. S., Six, L. S., & Phillips, D. S. (1992). A mnemonic for remembering long strings of digits. *Bulletin of the Psychonomic Society, 30*(4), 271–274.

Page 151
Ben Pridmore, a top British mnemonist, remembers numbers: Pridmore's system is described at *http://mnemotechnics.org/wiki/Ben_System,* retrieved on June 25, 2014. He was the overall winner at the 2008 World Memory Championship based on ten events. Memorizing 1,800 numbers in an hour is currently his best performance in that event.

Page 151
Say O'Brien wants to remember: O'Brien calls his person–action approach the "Dominic System" and describes it in O'Brien (2005).

Page 153
The approach Chao Lu took: Hu & Ericsson (2012); also see Hu et al. (2009).

Page 153
Satan may relish coffee pie: Memory trainer Francis Fauvel-Gouraud seems to be the originator of this mnemonic. Fauvel-Gouraud, F. (1845). *Phreno-mnemotechny: Or, The art of memory*, p. 120. New York: Wiley and Putnam. Retrieved from *books.google.com/books*.

Page 153
the set of code words I use: My code words were largely derived from those presented by Higbee, K. (2001). *Your memory: How it works and how to improve it* (2nd ed.), pp. 219–222. New York: Da Capo Press; and Bellezza, F. (1982).

Improve your memory skills, pp. 119–123. Englewood Cliffs, NJ: Prentice-Hall. The newer online word generators for the Major System are even better sources.

Chapter 11

Page 155

the Starbucks acronym: Duhigg, C. (2012). *The power of habit: Why we do what we do in life and business*, p. 145. New York: Random House.

Page 157

These perceptual skill are every bit as important: Causer, J., Janelle, C. M., Vickers, J. N., & Williams, A. M. (2004). Perceptual expertise: What can be retained? (pp. 306–324). In N. J. Hodges & A. M. Williams (Eds.), *Skill acquisition in sport*. New York: Routledge.

Page 157

Psychologists describe the behavior as automatic: Moors, A., & De Houwer, J. (2006). Automaticity: A theoretical and conceptual analysis. *Psychological Bulletin, 132*(2), 297–326.

Page 158

Some skills are more about mental operations: Rosenbaum, D. A., Carlson, R. A., & Gilmore, R. O. (2001). Acquisition of intellectual and perceptual-motor skills. *Annual Review of Psychology, 52*, 453–470.

Page 159

has studied top performers: Ericsson, K. A., & Lehmann, A. C. (1996). Expert and exceptional performance: Evidence of maximal adaptation to task constraints. *Annual Review of Psychology, 47*, 273–305.

Page 160

Ericsson called this "deliberate practice": Ericsson, K. A. (2006). The influence of experience and deliberate practice on the development of superior expert performance. In K. A. Ericsson, N. Charness, P. J. Feltovich, & R. R. Hoffman (Eds.), *The Cambridge handbook of expertise and expert performance* (pp. 683–703). New York: Cambridge University Press.

Page 160

An important part of deliberate practice is problem solving: Ericsson, K. A. (2003). The acquisition of expert performance as problem solving: Construction and modification of mediating mechanisms through deliberate practice.

In J. E. Davidson & R. J. Sternberg (Eds.), *The psychology of problem solving* (pp. 31–83). New York: Cambridge University Press.

Page 161

elite achievers typically invest ten years: Ericsson, K. A., Krampe, R. T., & Tesch-Römer, C. (1993). The role of deliberate practice in the acquisition of expert performance. *Psychological Review, 100*(3), 363–406.

Page 162

Here is a successful Olympian: Orlick, T., & Partington, J. (1988). Mental links to excellence. *The Sport Psychologist, 2*(2), 112.

Page 162

At the 2014 Sochi Winter Games: Clarey, C. (2014, February 22). Olympians use imagery as mental training. *The New York Times.* Retrieved from *www. nytimes.com/2014/02/23/sports/olympics/olympians-use-imagery-as-mental-training.html.*

Page 162

Earlier studies of Olympic contenders: Murphy, S. M. (1994). Imagery interventions in sport. *Medicine and Science in Sports and Exercise, 26*(4), 486–494. Ungerleider, S., & Golding, J. M. (1991). Mental practice among Olympic athletes. *Perceptual and Motor Skills, 72*(3, Pt. 1), 1007–1017.

Page 162

a well-researched principle in psychology: Driskell, J. E., Copper, C., & Moran, A. (1994). Does mental practice enhance performance? *Journal of Applied Psychology, 79*(4), 481–492. Suinn, R. M. (1997). Mental practice in sport psychology: Where have we been, where do we go? *Clinical Psychology: Science and Practice, 4*(3), 189–207. Schuster, C., Hilfiker, R., Amft, O., Scheidhauer, A., Andrews, B., Butler, J., et al. (2011). Best practice for motor imagery: A systematic literature review on motor imagery training elements in five different disciplines. *BMC Medicine, 9*(75), 1–35.

Page 162

works best when your imagined performance: Smith, D., Wright, C., Allsopp, A., & Westhead, H. (2007). It's all in the mind: PETTLEP-based imagery and sports performance. *Journal of Applied Sport Psychology, 19*(1), 80–92.

Page 163

I recommend that you prepare a written script: For suggestions on preparing scripts, see Williams, S. E., Cooley, S. J., Newell, E., Weibull, F., & Cumming,

J. (2013). Seeing the difference: Developing effective imagery scripts for athletes. *Journal of Sport Psychology in Action*, 4(2), 109–121.

Page 164

keep in mind that it is itself a skill: Gould, D., Voelker, D. K., Damarjian, N., & Greenleaf, C. (2014). Imagery training for peak performance. In J. L. Van Raalte & B. W. Brewer (Eds.), *Exploring sport and exercise psychology* (3rd ed.), pp. 55–82. Washington, DC: American Psychological Association.

Page 164

British researcher Ian Glendon: Glendon, A. I., McKenna, S. P., Hunt, K., & Blaylock, S. S. (1988). Variables affecting cardiopulmonary resuscitation skill decay. *Journal of Occupational Psychology*, 61(3), 243–255.

Page 165

a loss of competence over time: Sabol, A., & Wisher, R. A. (2001). Retention and reaquisition of military skills. *Military Operations Research*, 6(N1), 59–80. Arthur, W. J., Bennett, W. J., Stanush, P. L., & McNelly, T. L. (1998). Factors that influence skill decay and retention: A quantitative review and analysis. *Human Performance*, 11(1), 57–101.

Page 165

The Red Cross recommends: Retrieved June 25, 2014 from *www.redcrossrefresher.com/q/first-aid-cpr-and-aed/choices*.

Page 165

The great pianist Ignacy Paderewski: The quote is from Francis, C. (2009). *Wisdom well said*, p. 331. El Prado, NM: Levine Mesa Press.

Page 165

A typical F-15 pilot: Levy, C. P. (2006). *A comparison study of F-15C fighter squadron ready aircrew program flying hour scheduling vs. the Rand Corporation's flying hour scheduling linear program (AFIT/IOA/ENS/06-04)*. Wright-Patterson Air Force Base, OH: Air Force Institute of Technology.

Chapter 12

Page 170

"I am thirty-four years old": Parker, E. S., Cahill, L., & McGaugh, J. L. (2006). A case of unusual autobiographical remembering. *Neurocase*, 12(1), 35.

Page 171

write down the date that Easter fell on: She made one mistake listing the twenty-four Easters by giving a date that was two days off. Two years later, she was asked without warning to repeat the task. This time she was correct on all the dates and gave very similar memories for each of the days. When she was shown her earlier responses, she immediately pointed out the incorrect date (Parker et al., 2006).

Page 171

McGaugh and his team carefully studied many: LePort, A. K. R., Mattfeld, A. T., Dickinson-Anson, H., Fallon, J. H., Stark, C. E. L., Kruggel, F., Cahill, L., & McGaugh, J. L. (2012). Behavioral and neuroanatomical investigation of Highly Superior Autobiographical Memory (HSAM). *Neurobiology of Learning and Memory, 98*(1), 78–92.

Page 172

Gillian Cohen and Dorothy Faulkner: Cohen, G., & Faulkner, D. (1988). Life span changes in autobiographical memory. In M. M. Gruneberg, P. E. Morris, & R. N. Sykes (Eds.), *Practical aspects of memory: Current research and issues, Vol. 1: Memory in everyday life.* (pp. 277–282). Oxford, U.K.: John Wiley & Sons. Additional details are provided by Williams, H. L., Conway, M. A., & Cohen, G. (2008). Autobiographical memory. In G. Cohen & M. A. Conway (Eds.), *Memory in the real world* (3rd ed.), pp. 21–90. New York: Psychology Press.

Page 172

David Pillemer and his colleagues: Pillemer, D. B., Goldsmith, L. R., Panter, A. T., & White, S. H. (1988). Very long-term memories of the first year in college. *Journal of Experimental Psychology: Learning, Memory, and Cognition, 14*(4), 709–715. The figure on page 173 is based on their Figure 1.

Page 174

"I was woken up by a thundering noise": Berntsen, D., & Thomsen, D. K. (2005). Personal memories for remote historical events: Accuracy and clarity of flashbulb memories related to World War II. *Journal of Experimental Psychology: General, 134*(2), 257.

Page 174

This was a flashbulb event worldwide: Curci, A., & Luminet, O. (2006). Follow-up of a cross-national comparison on flashbulb and event memory for the September 11th attacks. *Memory, 14*(3), 329–344.

Page 174

"Another curious aspect of medieval justice": Bishop, M. (2001). *The Middle Ages*, p. 217. Boston: Mariner Books.

Page 175

by hitting one another: Bishop (2001, p. 116).

Page 175

Emotional memories are usually relatively accurate: Reisberg, D., & Heuer, F. (2004). Memory for emotional events. In D. Reisberg & P. Hertel (Eds.), *Memory and emotion* (pp. 3–41). New York: Oxford University Press.

Page 175

Lia Kvavilashvili and her colleagues: Kvavilashvili, L., Mirani, J., Schlagman, S., Foley, K., & Kornbrot, D. E. (2009). Consistency of flashbulb memories of September 11 over long delays: Implications for consolidation and wrong time slice hypotheses. *Journal of Memory and Language, 61*(4), 556–572.

Page 175

an impressive body of research shows: Talarico, J. M., & Rubin, D. C. (2009). Flashbulb memories result from ordinary memory processes and extraordinary event characteristics. In O. Luminet & A. Curci (Eds.), *Flashbulb memories: New issues and new perspectives* (pp. 79–97). New York: Psychology Press.

Page 175

This "bump" is illustrated in the graph: Redrawn from Figure 2 in Rubin, D. C. (2002). Autobiographical memory across the lifespan. In P. Graf & N. Onta (Eds.), *Lifespan development of human memory* (pp. 159–184). Cambridge, MA: MIT Press.

Page 176

The bump is probably due to: Rubin (2002, pp. 173–174).

Page 177

it's that their memories don't last: Bauer, P. (2012). The life I once remembered: The waxing and waning of early memories. In D. Berntsen & D. C. Rubin (Eds.), *Understanding autobiographical memory* (pp. 205–225). New York: Cambridge University Press.

Page 177

Part of the reason is brain development: Bauer, P. J. (2007). *Remembering the times of our lives: Memory in infancy and beyond*. Mahwah, NJ: Lawrence Erlbaum.

Page 177

Children have to learn how: Nelson, K., & Fivush, R. (2004). The emergence of autobiographical memory: A social cultural developmental theory. *Psychological Review, 111*(2), 486–511.

Page 177

By the time they are eight or nine: Bauer (2012, p. 208).

Page 177

The life stories they are beginning to formulate: Habermas, T., & Bluck, S. (2000). Getting a life: The emergence of the life story in adolescence. *Psychological Bulletin, 126*(5), 748–769.

Page 177

Researchers call collections of memories: Thomsen, D. K. (2009). There is more to life stories than memories. *Memory, 17*(4), 445–457.

Page 178

Martin Conway, a prominent researcher: Conway, M. A., & Pleydell-Pearce, C. W. (2000). The construction of autobiographical memories in the self-memory system. *Psychological Review, 107*(2), 261–288.

Page 179

Four scientific articles have now appeared: Parker et al. (2006). LePort et al. (2012). Ally, B. A., Hussey, E. P., & Donahue, M. J. (2013). A case of hyperthymesia: Rethinking the role of the amygdala in autobiographical memory. *Neurocase, 19*(2), 166–181. Patihis, L., Frenda, S. J., LePort, A. K. R., Petersen, N., Nichols, R. M., Stark, C. E. L., McGaugh, J. L., & Loftus, E. F. (2013). False memories in highly superior autobiographical memory individuals. *Proceedings of the National Academy of Sciences, 110*(52), 20947–20952. Also see comments on a case in Baddeley, A. D. (2012). Reflections on autobiographical memory. In D. Berntsen & D. C. Rubin (Eds.), *Understanding autobiographical memory* (pp. 81–82). New York: Cambridge University Press.

Page 179

Jill Price recalls that December 19, 1980: Price, J. (2008). *The woman who can't forget: The extraordinary story of living with the most remarkable memory known to science—A memoir*, pp. 27–28. New York: Free Press.

Page 179

a marked tendency toward obsessiveness: LePort et al. (2012).

Page 180

One woman, Louise Owen: Finkelstein, S. (Producer). (2010, December 19). Endless memory. Parts 1 and 2. *60 Minutes.* New York: CBS.

Page 180

In between these extremes: Cornoldi, C., De Beni, R., & Helstrup, T. (2007). Memory sensitivity in autobiographical memory. In S. Magnussen & T. Helstrup (Eds.), *Everyday memory.* (pp. 183–199). New York: Routledge. Merriam, S. B. (1993). Butler's life review: How universal is it? *International Journal of Aging and Human Development, 37*(3), 163–175.

Page 180

women engage in autobiographical remembering: Grysman, A., & Hudson, J. A. (2013). Gender differences in autobiographical memory: Developmental and methodological considerations. *Developmental Review, 33*(3), 239–272.

Page 181

not all autobiographical remembering is healthy: O'Rourke, N., Cappeliez, P., & Claxton, A. (2011). Functions of reminiscence and the psychological well-being of young-old and older adults over time. *Aging and Mental Health, 15*(2), 272–281.

Page 181

Constructive reminiscing: Westerhof, G. J., & Bohlmeijer, E. T. (2014). Celebrating fifty years of research and applications in reminiscence and life review: State of the art and new directions. *Journal of Aging Studies, 29*, 107–114.

Page 181

"In my sophomore year": Pillemer, D. B. (2001). Momentous events and the life story. *Review of General Psychology, 5*(2), 130.

Page 181

"It was embarrassing, not making that team": Pillemer (2001, p. 127).

Page 181

majority of autobiographical memories will be positive: Walker, W. R., Skowronski, J. J., & Thompson, C. P. (2003). Life is pleasant—and memory helps to keep it that way! *Review of General Psychology, 7*(2), 203–210.

Page 181

under the guidance of a psychotherapist: Hallford, D., & Mellor, D. (2013). Reminiscence-based therapies for depression: Should they be used only with older adults? *Clinical Psychology: Science and Practice, 20*(4), 452–468.

Page 182

the three-step process: Henner, M. (2012). *Total memory makeover: Uncover your past, take charge of your future*, pp. 3–5. New York: Gallery Books.

Page 183

Marilu Henner suggests identifying life-story chapters: Henner (2012, pp. 140–143).

Page 183

In one study of middle-aged people: Thomsen, D. K., Olesen, M. H., Schnieber,

A., & Tønnesvang, J. (2014). The emotional content of life stories: Positivity bias and relation to personality. *Cognition and Emotion*, *28*(2), 260–277.

Page 184
Studies have identified jewelry: Habermas, T., & Paha, C. (2002). Souvenirs and other personal objects: Reminding of past events and significant others in the transition to university. In J. D. Webster & B. K. Haight (Eds.), *Critical advances in reminiscence work: From theory to application* (pp. 123–139). New York: Springer.

Page 184
they are avid collectors: LePort et al. (2012).

Page 184
Memory expert Dominic O'Brien: O'Brien, D. (2000). *Learn to remember: Practical techniques and exercises to improve your memory*, p. 144. San Francisco: Chronicle Books.

Page 184
The way you picture memories: Rice, H. J. (2010). Seeing where we're at: A review of visual perspective and memory retrieval. In J. H. Mace (Ed.), *The act of remembering: Toward an understanding of how we recall the past* (pp. 228–258). West Sussex, UK: Wiley-Blackwell.

Page 185
"I see myself dancing at a party": Berntsen, D., & Rubin, D. C. (2006). Emotion and vantage point in autobiographical memory. *Cognition and Emotion*, *20*(8), 1193.

Page 185
Forcing a memory: Vella, N. C., & Moulds, M. L. (2014). The impact of shifting vantage perspective when recalling and imagining positive events. *Memory*, *22*(3), 256–264.

Page 185
Henner identified four ways: Henner (2012, pp. 87–90).

Page 187
"I know that part of the reason": Henner (2012, p. 24).

Page 187
Habits are a special kind of memory: Graybiel, A. M. (2008). Habits, rituals, and the evaluative brain. *Annual Review of Neuroscience*, *31*, 359–387. Wood,

W., & Neal, D. T. (2007). A new look at habits and the habit-goal interface. *Psychological Review, 114*(4), 843–863.

Page 187

"autobiographical state of mind": Henner (2012, p. 177).

Page 187

Habits are established by repeating: The key operation is pairing the cue and the behavior over and over. The positive outcome motivates the sequence so that it occurs often enough to form the habit. Once the habit is firmly in place, the positive outcome is believed to be unnecessary (Wood & Neal, 2007).

Page 189

"try to think of bad memories": Henner (2012, pp. 38–39).

Page 189

In one study, students undertook to develop: Lally, P., van Jaarsveld, C. H. M., Potts, H. W. W., & Wardle, J. (2010). How are habits formed: Modelling habit formation in the real world. *European Journal of Social Psychology, 40*(6), 998–1009.

Chapter 13

Page 191

you needn't worry that you might confuse: Massen, C., & Vaterrodt-Plünnecke, B. (2006). The role of proactive interference in mnemonic techniques. *Memory, 14*(2), 189–196.

Page 191

The peg word strategy excels in two areas: These two key functions of mnemonics are discussed by Bellezza, F. S. (1996). Mnemonic methods to enhance storage and retrieval. In E. L. Bjork & R. A. Bjork (Eds.), *Memory* (pp. 345–380). San Diego, CA: Academic Press.

Page 192

peg words get high marks: Worthen, J. B., & Hunt, R. R. (2011). *Mnemonology: Mnemonics for the 21st century.* New York: Psychology Press.

Page 193

Other well-known acronyms: Evans, R. L. (2007). *Every good boy deserves fudge: The book of mnemonic devices.* New York: Perigee.

Page 194

"Poorly Canned Sausages": Anonymous. (1972). *A dictionary of mnemonics,* p. 27. London: Eyre Methuen.

Page 194
Planning on serious partying?: Anonymous. (1972, p. 26). Follow this advice at your own risk!

Page 195
memory researcher David Rubin pointed out: Rubin, D. C. (1995). *Memory in oral traditions: The cognitive psychology of epic, ballads, and counting-out rhymes.* New York: Oxford University Press.

Page 195
memorize the entire *Aeneid*: Carruthers, M. (2008). *The book of memory: A study of memory in medieval culture* (2nd ed.), p. 21. New York: Cambridge University Press.

Page 196
committed the entire *Quran* to memory: Luo, M. (2006, August 16). Memorizing the way to heaven, verse by verse. *The New York Times.* Retrieved from *www.nytimes.com/2006/08/16/nyregion/16koran.html.*

Page 196
"Starting with envelope/airplane": Lorayne, H. (2007). *Ageless memory: Simple secrets for keeping your brain young,* p. 41. New York: Black Dog & Leventhal.

Page 197
On the mnemonic scorecard: Bellezza (1996).

Page 199
In one study, college students: Bower, G. H., & Clark, M. C. (1969). Narrative stories as mediators for serial learning. *Psychonomic Science, 14*(4), 181–182. Also see Worthen & Hunt (2011, pp. 72–73).

Page 199
tested after periods longer than a few days: Boltwood, C. E., & Blick, K. A. (1970). The delineation and application of three mnemonic techniques. *Psychonomic Science, 20*(6), 339–341.

Page 199
shown to work with older adults: Drevenstedt, J., & Bellezza, F. S. (1993). Memory for self-generated narration in the elderly. *Psychology and Aging, 8*(2), 187–196.

Chapter 14

Page 202
Reports say he seldom took notes: Leibovich, M. (2005, January 5). Pressure

cooker. *The Washington Post*. Retrieved from *www.washingtonpost.com/wp-dyn/content/article/2006/03/28/AR2006032800445.html*.

Page 203
A 2005 *Washington Post* story: Leibovich (2005).

Page 204
Simonides, also known as "the honey tongued": Yates, F. A. (1996). *The art of memory*, p. 42. London: Pimlico.

Page 205
There were no chapter titles: Small, J. P. (1997). *Wax tablets of the mind: Cognitive studies of memory and literacy in classical antiquity*, pp. 11–25. London: Routledge.

Page 206
Memory scholar Mary Carruthers believes: Carruthers, M. (1998). *The craft of thought: Meditation, rhetoric, and the making of images, 400–1200*, p. 9. New York: Cambridge University Press.

Page 206
The great Catholic theologian Thomas Aquinas: Yates (1966, pp. 81–90) describes how Thomas restated the principles of the Method of Loci for the medieval period. Memory skill as a step on the path to moral perfection is discussed by Carruthers, M. (2008). *The book of memory: A study of memory in medieval culture* (2nd ed.), p. 88. New York: Cambridge University Press. Thomas's own memory skill is described by Carruthers (2008, pp. 3–9).

Page 207
"to roam across a hundred thousand memory images": Spence, J. D. (1985). *The memory palace of Matteo Ricci*, p. 9. New York: Penguin Books.

Page 207
It is a personification of "grammar": This is Plate 7a in Yates (1966). Other depictions of grammar for mnemonic purposes were also in play at this time as variations on the Method of Loci. Interesting examples of "towers of grammar" are examined by Mittelberg, I. (2002). The visual memory of grammar: Iconographical and metaphorical insights. Retrieved July 2, 2014, from *www.metaphorik.de/en/journal/02/visual-memory-grammar-iconographical-and-metaphorical-insights.html*.

Page 208
Rhetoric, on the other hand: Spence (1985, p. 8).

Page 209
"I told them they should write down": Spence (1985, p. 139).

Page 210
They just did not find Ricci's memory techniques helpful: Ricci's instructions also suffered from some cultural disconnects with Chinese readers as discussed by Hsia, R. P. (2010). *A Jesuit in the forbidden city: Matteo Ricci 1552–1610*. Oxford, UK: Oxford University Press.

Page 210
Contemporary studies show: Custers, E. J. F. M. (2010). Long-term retention of basic science knowledge: A review study. *Advances in Health Sciences Education, 15*(1), 109–128.

Page 211
forces were in play that led to its decline: Yates (1966). Rossi, P. (2000). *Logic and the art of memory: The quest for a universal language* (S. Clucas, Trans.). Chicago: University of Chicago Press.

Page 213
When I take care of one of these tasks: Once I have no more use for a memory cue at a specific location, it just goes away. Andrew Card experienced the same when he took a memory cue to his disposal. It is an interesting phenomenon researchers have studied as "directed forgetting." Baddeley, A., Eysenck, M. W., & Anderson, M. C. (2009). *Memory,* pp. 221–224. New York: Psychology Press.

Page 215
My approach is similar to one: My list generally follows Lorayne, H., & Lucas, J. (1974). *The memory book*, p. 137. Briarcliff Manor, NY: Stein & Day. These mnemonists use a peg word system to remember the deck of cards, not a memory palace. I find the memory palace is easier to manage.

Page 216
use more complex coding systems: Foer, J. (2011). *Moonwalking with Einstein: The art and science of remembering everything*, pp. 165–167. New York: Penguin Press. O'Brien, D. (2005). *How to develop a brilliant memory week by week*, pp. 149–151. London: Duncan Baird. O'Brien also explains how he set up a memory palace to hold 2,808 cards.

Page 218
medieval monks believed: Carruthers (1998, pp. 173–174).

Chapter 15

Page 221
Carol Dweck, a researcher at Stanford: Dweck, C. (2006). *Mindset: The new psychology of success*. New York: Random House.

Page 221
a study by Dweck and Claudia Mueller: Mueller, C. M., & Dweck, C. S. (1998). Praise for intelligence can undermine children's motivation and performance. *Journal of Personality and Social Psychology, 75*(1), 33–52.

Page 222
compares the number of problems children solved: My figure shows data averaged across Studies 1, 3, and 5 from Mueller & Dweck (1998) as presented in her Figure 2.

Page 223
A recent review summarized: Burnette, J. L., O'Boyle, E. H., VanEpps, E. M., Pollack, J. M., & Finkel, E. J. (2013). Mind-sets matter: A meta-analytic review of implicit theories and self-regulation. *Psychological Bulletin, 139*(3), 655–701.

Page 224
the widespread stereotype that advancing age: Chasteen, A. L., Kang, S. A., Remedios, J. D. (2012). Aging and stereotype threat: Development, process and interventions. In M. Inzlicht & T. Schmader (Eds.), *Stereotype threat: Theory, process and applications* (pp. 202–216). New York: Oxford University Press. Hess, T. M., & Emery, L. (2012). Memory in context: The impact of age-related goals on performance. In M. Naveh-Benjamin & N. Ohta (Eds.), *Memory and aging: Current issues and future directions* (pp. 183–214). New York: Psychology Press.

Page 224
conducted by Catherine Haslam: Haslam, C., Morton, T. A., Haslam, S. A., Varnes, L., Graham, R., & Gamaz, L. (2012). "When the age is in, the wit is out": Age-related self-categorization and deficit expectations reduce performance on clinical tests used in dementia assessment. *Psychology and Aging, 27*(3), 778–784.

Page 225
the impact of stereotypes on cognitive performance: Inzlicht, M., & Schmader, T. (2012). *Stereotype threat: Theory, process, and application*. New York: Oxford University Press.

Page 225

Those who thought of themselves as old: Stereotype effects arise in several ways. Sometimes they can be similar to "choking" under pressure, but with the elderly it appears more often to be a loss of motivation. Hess, T. M., Hinson, J. T., & Hodges, E. A. (2009). Moderators of and mechanisms underlying stereotype threat effects on older adults' memory performance. *Experimental Aging Research, 35*(2), 153–177.

Page 226

encouraged to adopt a growth mindset: Hong, Y., Coleman, J., Chan, G., Wong, R. Y. M., Chiu, C., et al. (2004). Predicting intergroup bias: The interactive effects of implicit theory and social identity. *Personality and Social Psychology Bulletin, 30*(8), 1035–1047.

Page 226

Researchers Jason Plaks and Allison Chasteen: Plaks, J. E., & Chasteen, A. L. (2013). Entity versus incremental theories predict older adults' memory performance. *Psychology and Aging, 28*(4), 948–957.

Page 226

can help anyone who has low expectations: A paper discussing this point from the perspective of neurologically impaired individuals is Kit, K. A., Tuokko, H. A., & Mateer, C. A. (2008). A review of the stereotype threat literature and its application in a neurological population. *Neuropsychology Review, 18*(2), 132–148.

Page 227

Carol Dweck has identified two different forms: Dweck, C. S. (1986). Motivational processes affecting learning. *American Psychologist, 41*(10), 1040–1048. Also see Hastings, E. C., & West, R. L. (2011). Goal orientation and self-efficacy in relation to memory in adulthood. *Aging, Neuropsychology, and Cognition, 18*(4), 471–493. Stout, J. G., & Dasgupta, N. (2013). Mastering one's destiny: Mastery goals promote challenge and success despite social identity threat. *Personality and Social Psychology Bulletin, 39*(6), 748–762.

Index

Accuracy of a memory, 74–78
Acronyms. *See also* PARIS acronym
 ICE acronym (Implementation
  Intentions, Cue Imagery, Exaggerated
  Importance), 116–121, 193
 Memory Lab regarding, 200–201
Acrostics. *See also* Friendly Llamas Seek
  People acrostic; Romantic Dragons Eat
  Vegetables and Prefer Onions acrostic
 how skills are acquired, 158–159, 158*f*
 Memory Lab regarding, 66–67, 67*f*
 mental rehearsal and, 163
 name-person connection and, 103–105,
  104*f*
 overview, 53
 PARIS acronym and, 193–194, 201
 remembering numbers and, 144, 152–153
Active monitoring, 114
Aeneid, 195
Age
 physical exercise and natural memory
  and, 90–91
 stereotype effects and, 224–226, 225*f*,
  268*n*–269*n*
 working memory and, 29–30, 29*f*, 233*n*
Alzheimer's disease, 16
Anticipate-Participate-Recollect technique,
 182
Anxiety-based distraction, 46–47,
 235*n*–236*n*. *See also* Distraction
Appearance, 55
Aquinas, Thomas, 206–207
The Art of Memory (Yates), 207–208
Artificial memory
 improving, 93–95
 Memory Lab regarding, 95–96, 95*f*, 97*f*
 overview, 83

Association. *See also* Dragon Principles
 direction of, 96
 organization and, 65
 overview, 3, 61–62, 193
 remembering names and, 101–103
 substitute word technique, 21–23, 22*f*
Attention
 automatic actions and 39–40, 45
 distracting situations, 45–47
 explicit memory and, 40
 forms of, 42–45, 44*f*
 Memory Lab regarding, 50–52, 50*f*, 51*f*,
  52*f*
 mindfulness meditation and, 88–90
 overview, 38–42, 41*f*
 retention intention and, 53–54
 staying focused, 47–50
 working memory and, 26–28, 35
Attention Control Task, 41–42, 41*f*
Autobiographical memory. *See also* Life,
  remembering
 autobiographical bump and, 175–177, 176*f*
 childhood memories, 176–177
 emotion and, 173–175
 hierarchy, 178–179
 highly superior autobiographical memory
  (HSAM) and, 171, 179–180
 life story and, 177–179, 178*f*
 Memory Lab regarding, 187–189, 188*f*
 novel events and, 172–173
 overview, 170–171
 strengthening, 180–186, 186*f*
 what we remember, 171–175, 172*f*, 173*f*
 automatic actions, 157–161, 187, 189

Backward digit test, 28–29, 31*f*
Bahrick, Harry, 137–138

Bang Goes the Theory, 87
Bellezza, Francis, 150
Baseball, 32–34
Berntsen, Dorthe, 174
Binding images, 51–52, 51*f*, 52*f*, 79
Bjork, Robert, 129, 130, 131–132
Bottom–up attention, 42–43, 44*f*, 114–115.
   See also Attention
Bower, Gordon, 64
Bradwardine, Thomas, 59–60
Buddhist meditative practice, 88–90
Buzan, Tony, 3, 70

Cahill, Larry, 170–171
Calendar, 145–146
Card, Andrew Jr., 202–204, 213, 267*n*
Carnegie, Dale, 110
Carruthers, Mary, 206
Challenges, creating
   remembering numbers and, 142–143
   staying focused and, 49–50
Chasteen, Allison, 226
Childhood amnesia, 177
Childhood memories, 176–177
Chongzhi, Zu, 254*n*
Chunking
   expert and novice, 34
   the major system for remembering
      numbers and, 151–152
   working memory and, 31–34, 33*f*
Cicero, 83, 204, 206
Claparède, Eduarde, 17–18
Cognitive interview, 71
Cohen, Gillian, 172
Color, 60–61
Cowan, Nelson, 34
Competence, illusion of, 131–132
Competence loss, 164–165, 165*f*
Composition, 64–65
Computer training, 85–88, 245*n*. *See also*
   Technology
Connections, 61–62
Consciousness, 28,34
Conway, Martin, 178
Craik, Fergus, 55
Cramming, 128, 132
Csikszentmihalyi, Mihaly, 49
Cue imagery, 116, 119–120, 193. *See
   also* ICE acronym (Implementation
   Intentions, Cue Imagery, Exaggerated
   Importance)
Cues
   focal, 115–116, 121

improving natural and artificial memory
   and, 95–96, 95*f*, 97*f*
mind maps and, 136, 136*f*
prospective memory and, 113–116
recalling memories and, 78–79
retrieval of information and, 69
SCRR method (Segment, Cue, Retrieve,
   Review) and, 134, 135*f*
self-testing and, 133
Curiosity, 48–49

Daniels, Jim, 24
Deck of cards, memorizing, 215–217, 216*f*
Declarative memory. *See* Explicit memory
Deep processing. *See also* Dragon
   Principles
   face memory and, 102
   memory palace and, 211
   organization and, 65
   overview, 55–56, 55*f*, 193
Default-mode network, 43–45, 44*f*. *See also*
   Attention
Deliberate practice, 160–161, 160*f*. *See also*
   Practice
Depression, 181
Direct visual associations, 20–23, 20*f*, 22*f*,
   35, 35*f*. *See also* Visual mnemonics
Distraction. *See also* Attention
   bottom-up attention and, 42–43
   distracting situations, 45–47
   staying focused, 47–50
Division, 64–65
Dragon Principles. *See also* Romantic
   Dragons Eat Vegetables and Prefer
   Onions acrostic
   association, 61–62
   deep processing, 55–56, 55*f*
   elaboration, 57–58
   improving artificial memory and, 94, 95
   Memory Lab regarding, 66–67, 67*f*
   organization, 64–66, 65*f*
   overview, 53, 193
   practice, 62–64
   prospective memory improvement and,
      118
   recalling memories and, 79
   remembering facts and, 125
   retention intention, 53–54
   visualization, 58–61
Dweck, Carol, 221–223, 227

Edwards, Tryon, 40
Einstein, Gilles, 113–114, 120

Elaboration, 57–58, 65, 193. *See also*
    Dragon Principles
Elite achievers, 159
Emotion, 62, 173–175
Engle, Randall, 32–33
Episodic memory. *See also* Explicit
    memory
  connecting facts, 14–15
  hippocampus and, 12
  how skills are acquired, 156*f*
  mental time travel and, 13–14, 230*n*
  overview, 13
  reconstructing memories and, 73–74
  substitute word technique, 21–23, 22*f*
Erdelyi, Matthew, 71–72
Ericsson, Anders, 159–160
Exaggerated importance, 116, 120–
    121, 193. *See also* ICE acronym
    (Implementation Intentions, Cue
    Imagery, Exaggerated Importance)
Executive processes, 27, 27*f*
Exercise, physical, 90–91, 92–93, 92*f*, 93*f*
Exercising memory, 83–84. *See also*
    Practice
Expanding the meaning, 65. *See also*
    Meaning
Experiences, 12–15, 156–158, 156*f*
Explicit memory. *See also* Episodic memory;
    Semantic memory
  creating, 40
  how skills are acquired, 156*f*, 157–158
  overview, 15, 231*n*
  substitute word technique, 21–23, 22*f*
External cues, 115–116, 121–122. *See also*
    Cues

Face memory, 101–108, 104*f*, 107*f*
Facts, remembering
  Memory Lab regarding, 139–140, 141*f*
  memory palace and, 214–215
  overview, 12–15, 124–125, 139
  permastore and, 137–139, 137*f*
  practice and, 125–136, 125*f*, 126*f*, 127*f*,
    129*f*, 135*f*, 136*f*
  repeated memory practice and, 127–132
  retrieval practice, 132–136, 135*f*, 136*f*
Faulkner, Dorothy, 172
Features, finding
  Friendly Llamas Seek People acrostic
    and, 103–104
  how skills are acquired, 158–159, 158*f*
  name-person connection and, 103–104
Feedback, 161, 168–169
Feelings, 173–175
Flashcards, 133, 134, 135*f*

Flexibility, 26
Flow, 49–50
Fluid intelligence, 30–31, 31*f*
Focus, 47–50
Foer, Joshua, 61, 62, 94
Forgetting, 40, 76, 110, 124–125, 129,
    137–138, 267*n*
Freud, Sigmund, 113
Friendly Llamas Seek People acrostic. *See*
    also Acrostics
  how skills are acquired, 158–161, 158*f*
  mental rehearsal and, 163
  name-person connection and, 103–106,
    104*f*, 108–109
  overview, 194
Fritz, Catherine, 110
Future events, remembering, 112–113. *See*
    also Prospective memory

Gabor, Don, 109
Gates, Bill, 132–133
Glendon, Ian, 164
Goals, 49–50
Gollwitzer, Peter, 117–118
Growth mindset. *See* Mindsets

H. M., 9–12, 15, 229*n*
Habits. *See also* Implicit memory
  attention and, 40
  autobiographical memory and, 187–188,
    188*f*
  distracting situations and, 45–47
  how skills are acquired, 156*f*
  overview, 15–17, 263*n*
Hagwood, Scott, 3–4, 105
Halleck, Reuben, 48
Hambrick, David, 32–33
Haslam, Catherine, 224–225
Heeren, Alexandre, 89
Helper image, 66–67, 67*f*. *See also* Imagery
Henner, Marilu, 179, 182, 183, 185–186,
    188–189
Higbee, Kenneth, 150
Highly practiced activities, 45–46. *See also*
    Distraction
Highly superior autobiographical memory
    (HSAM), 171, 179–180, 188
Hippocampus, 9–10, 11
Hypermnesia, 72

ICE acronym (Implementation Intentions,
    Cue Imagery, Exaggerated
    Importance). *See also* Acronyms
  Memory Lab regarding, 122–123, 123*f*
  overview, 122, 193

prospective memory improvement and, 116–121
Illusion of competence, 131–132
Image interconnections, 60
Imagery. *See also* Visual mnemonics
    acrostics and, 66–67, 67f
    attention and, 50–52, 50f, 51f, 52f
    color and movement, 60
    creating, 22, 58–61, 80, 119
    individual differences,23, 67
    interconnections, 60, 79
    link method, 196–197
    mental rehearsal, 162–164
    PARIS acronym and, 196–197, 201
    peg words and, 190–193
    remembering numbers and, 144–146, 145f
Implementation intention, 116, 193, 236n, 248n. *See also* ICE acronym (Implementation Intentions, Cue Imagery, Exaggerated Importance)
Implicit memory. *See also* Habits; Pavlovian associations; Procedural skills
    direct visual associations, 20–23, 22f
    how skills are acquired, 156f
    overview, 15–17, 231n
Information retrieval. *See* Retrieval of information
Intelligence, 30–31, 31f

James, Lori, 98–99
James, William, 84
Jensen, Christian, 89
Jordan, Michael, 181
Jungle Memory, 87

Kabat-Zinn, Jon, 88–89
Karpicke, Jeffrey, 126–127
Keyword mnemonic. *See* Substitute word technique
Kleinbard, Jeff, 71–72
Klingberg, Torkel, 85–86
Korsakoff's syndrome, 17–18
Kramer, Arthur, 90
Kvavilashivili, Lia, 175

Landauer, Thomas, 130
Language, 25–26
Last names, 106–108, 107f. *See also* Names, remembering
Letter chain approach, 109
Life, remembering. *See also* Autobiographical memory
    autobiographical bump and, 175–177, 176f
    childhood memories, 176–177

highly superior autobiographical memory (HSAM) and, 171, 179–180
    life story and, 177–179, 178f
    Memory Lab regarding, 187–189, 188f
    overview, 170–171
    strengthening, 180–186, 186f
    what we remember, 171–175, 172f, 173f
Life story, 177–179, 178f, 182–183
Link Method
    overview, 166–169, 167f, 168f, 169f
    PARIS acronym and, 196–197, 201
Listening
    Friendly Llamas Seek People acrostic, 104
    how skills are acquired, 158–159, 158f
    name-person connection and, 104
Lists, 190–193, 212–213
Lobotomy, 9
Loftus, Elizabeth, 76–77
Long-term memory
    attention and, 40–42, 41f
    how skills are acquired, 156f, 157–158
    massed practice and, 128
    memory palace and, 210–211
    overview, 19
    spaced memory recall and, 129–132
    working memory and, 27, 27f
Lorayne, Harry, 61, 94, 101–102, 105–106, 147–148, 196–197, 215–216, 246n
Lu, Chao, 141–142, 151–152, 198–199, 254n
Lucas Jerry, 101–102, 147–148

Major system
    Memory Lab regarding, 153–154, 153f
    remembering numbers and, 146–152, 148f, 149f
Margetts, David, 38–39, 40
Massed memory rehearsal, 128
Mastery goals, 227
McCabe, Jennifer, 131–132
McDaniel, Mark, 113–114, 120, 132
McGaugh, James, 170–171
Meaning
    deep processing and, 55–56, 55f
    organization and, 65
Meditation, mindfulness, 88–90, 92–93, 92f, 93f
Mementos, 183–184
Memories
    alterations of, 74–78
    reconstructing, 73–74
Memorization, 84–85
Memorization, rote, 84–85
Memory, science of, 4–5

Memory arts
  history of, 206–211, 208*f*
  improving artificial memory and, 93–95
  overview, 2–5, 227–228
Memory cues, 52
Memory failure, 111
Memory Lab. *See also* Mnemonic approaches
  attention, 50–52, 50*f*, 51*f*, 52*f*
  autobiographical memory, 187–189, 188*f*
  direct visual associations, 20–23, 22*f*
  Dragon Principles, 66–67, 67*f*
  improving natural and artificial memory,
    95–96, 95*f*, 97*f*
  memory palace, 217–218
  overview, 19–20, 218*f*, 219*f*, 220*f*
  PARIS acronym, 200–201
  picture superiority effect, 36–37, 36*f*, 37*f*
  prospective memory improvement and,
    122–123, 123*f*
  recalling memories, 78–80, 79*f*, 80*f*
  remembering facts, 139–140, 141*f*
  remembering names, 110–111
  remembering numbers, 153–154, 153*f*
  remembering skills, 166–169, 167*f*, 168*f*,
    169*f*
  rhyming, 139–140, 141*f*
  substitute words, 21–23, 22*f*
Memory map, 136, 136*f*
The Memory Palace of Matteo Ricci
  (Spence), 207
Memory palace system
  history of, 204–206, 206–211, 266*n*
  Memory Lab regarding, 217–218
  overview, 202–204, 217
  in the twenty-first century, 212–217,
    215*f*, 216*f*
Memory systems, 12, 15, 19, 156
Mental imagery, 23. *See also* Imagery
Mental skills, 16–17
Mental time travel, 13–14, 230*n*
Method of Loci system
  history of, 204–211, 208*f*
  Memory Lab regarding, 217–218
  overview, 202–204, 217
  in the twenty-first century, 212–217,
    215*f*, 216*f*
Milner, Brenda, 10–12
Mind maps, 136, 136*f*
Mindsparke, 87
Mindfulness meditation, 88–90, 92–93, 92*f*,
  93*f*, 243*n*
Mindsets
  fostering a growth mindset, 226–227
  overview, 221–224, 222*f*, 223*f*, 227–228
  stereotypes and, 224–226, 225*f*

Mnemonic approaches. *See also* Memory
    Lab; Visual mnemonics
  acronyms and acrostics, 193–194
  direct visual associations, 20–23, 22*f*
  how skills are acquired, 158–159, 158*f*
  improving artificial memory and, 93–95
  the major system for remembering
    numbers, 146–152, 148*f*, 149*f*
  overview, 3, 5
  peg words and, 190–193
  rhyming and, 139–140, 141*f*
  substitute words, 21–23, 22*f*
Molaison, Henry, 9–12, 12*f*. See also H. M.
Morris, Peter, 105, 110
Motivation, 47, 54, 118, 159
Movement, 60–61
Mueller, Claudia, 221–223
Multitasking, 46. *See also* Distraction

Name game approach, 109–110
Name-person connections, 103–108, 104*f*,
  107*f*
Names, remembering. *See also* Substitute
    word technique
  last names, 106–108, 107*f*
  many names in a group introduction,
    108–110
  Memory Lab regarding, 110–111
  name-person connection and, 103–108,
    104*f*, 107*f*
  overview, 98–100, 99*f*, 100*f*, 110
  remembering the person, 101–103
Natural memory
  improving, 83–93, 92*f*, 93*f*
  Memory Lab regarding, 95–96, 95*f*, 97*f*
  overview, 83, 91–93, 92*f*, 93*f*
Nondeclarative memory. *See* Implicit
    memory
Numbers, remembering
  an acrostic for, 144
  find a pattern, 143–144
  the major system for, 146–152, 148*f*,
    149*f*
  Memory Lab regarding, 153–154, 153*f*
  overview, 141–143, 152–153
Number-shape system, 144–146, 145*f*,
  152–153

O'Brien, Dominic, 61, 63–64, 128, 151,
  184, 215
Organization
  memory palace and, 211
  overview, 64–66, 65*f*, 193
  remembering facts and, 136, 136*f*
  working memory and, 31–34, 33*f*

Overconfidence, 115, 131–132
Owen, Louise, 180

Paderewski, Ignacy, 165
Paivio, Allan, 147
Panigarola, Francesco, 58, 207
PARIS acronym. *See also* Acronyms;
    Acrostics; Link method
  acronyms and acrostics, 193–194
  imagery, 196–197
  Memory Lab regarding, 200–201
  overview, 190, 190*f*, 199–200
  peg words, 190–193
  rhymes and rhythms, 194–196
  stories, 198–199
Patterns in numbers, 143–144
Patton, Gary, 150
Pavlov, Ivan, 17
Pavlovian associations. *See also* Implicit
    memory
  direct visual associations and, 20–23,
    20*f*, 22*f*
  how skills are acquired, 156*f*
  overview, 17–18, 18*f*
Peg words, 190–193, 201
Penfield, Wilder, 10
Perception, 89
Performance
  fostering a growth mindset and, 227
  how skills are acquired, 156–158, 156*f*
  improving skills and, 159–161, 160*f*
Permastore, 137–139, 137*f*, 211, 253*n*
Personal organizers, 213–214
Physical exercise, 90–91, 92–93, 92*f*, 93*f*
Picture superiority effect, 36–37, 36*f*, 37*f*,
    234*n*
Pillemer, David, 172–173
Plaks, Jason, 226
Practice. *See also* Deliberate practice;
    Dragon Principles; Memory Lab;
    Repeated memory practice
  expanding retrieval practice, 130, 251*n*
  Friendly Llamas Seek People acrostic,
    105
  how skills are acquired, 158–159, 158*f*
  improving skills and, 159–161, 160*f*,
    168–169
  leaky bucket problem, 164–165, 165*f*
  memory palace and, 211
  mental rehearsal, 162–164
  name-person connection and, 105
  overview, 62–64, 193
  remembering facts and, 125 136, 125*f*,
    126*f*, 127*f*, 129*f*, 135*f*, 136*f*
  remembering names and, 109

repeated memory practice, 127–132
retrieval practice, 132–136, 135*f*, 136*f*
Practices. *See* Memory Lab
Price, Jill, 170–171, 179, 180, 188, 258*n*
Pridmore, Ben, 151, 255*n*
Problem solving, 160–161
Procedural skills. *See also* Implicit memory;
    Skills, remembering
  how skills are acquired, 156–159, 156*f*,
    157*f*, 158*f*
  improving, 159–161, 160*f*
  leaky bucket problem, 164–165, 165*f*
  overview, 15–17, 155–156
Prospective memory. *See also* Future
    events, remembering
  how prospective memory fails, 113–115
  ICE acronym (Implementation
    Intentions, Cue Imagery,
    Exaggerated Importance) and,
    116–121
  improving by mental preparation,
    116–121
  improving with external cues, 115–116
  Memory Lab regarding, 122–123, 123*f*
  overview, 112–113, 122
  performing an action at a specified time,
    121–122

Quintilian, 84, 88, 94
Quran, 196

Ravenna, Peter of, 58
Reading comprehension, 30
Read-rehearse-review, 132
Reagan, Ronald, 16
Reasoning ability, 30
Recall. *See also* Remembering information;
    Retrieval of information
  gist, 73–74, 76–77, 240*n*
  memory alterations and, 74–78
  Memory Lab regarding, 78–80, 79*f*, 80*f*
  mind maps and, 136, 136*f*
  overview, 68–69
  permastore and, 137–139, 137*f*
  reconstructing memories and, 73–74, 76
  remembering facts and, 126, 126*f*, 132
  spaced memory recall, 129–132, 129*f*
  strategies to help with, 70–73, 72*f*
Recognition, 126, 126*f*
Reconstructing memories, 73–74
Rehearsal. *See also* Practice
  memory palace and, 211, 214–215
  mental, 162–164
  remembering names and, 109
Relaxation training, 89

Remembering information. *See also* Recall;
  Retrieval of information
  memory alterations and, 74–78
  Memory Lab regarding, 78–80, 79*f*, 80*f*
  overview, 68–69
  reconstructing memories and, 73–74
  strategies to help with, 70–73
Reminiscing
  Memory Lab regarding, 187–189, 188*f*
  strengthening autobiographical memory
    with, 180–186, 186*f*
Repeated memory practice. *See also*
    Practice
  improving skills and, 161–162
  remembering facts and, 127–132
Restudying, 126, 126*f*, 128, 131–132
Retention, 35
Retention intention, 53–54, 118, 193, 236*n*.
  See also Dragon Principles
Retention of information, 137–139, 137*f*
Retrieval of information. *See also*
    Recall; Remembering information;
    Spontaneous retrieval
  autobiographical memory and, 186
  Memory Lab regarding, 78–80, 79*f*, 80*f*
  overview, 68–69
  prospective memory failure and,
    113–115
  reconstructing memories and, 73–74
  SCRR method (Segment, Cue, Retrieve,
    Review) and, 134, 135*f*
  strategies to help with, 70–73, 72*f*
Return to the scene strategy, 70–71, 78–80,
  79*f*, 80*f*, 186, 186*f*
Review, 134, 135*f*
Rhetorica ad Herennium, 58–60
Rhymes
  PARIS acronym and, 194–196
  peg words and, 192–193
  remembering facts and, 139–140, 141*f*
Rhythms, 194–196
Ricci, Matteo, 206–211, 208*f*, 218,
  266*n*–267*n*
Roediger, Henry, 126–127
Romantic Dragons Eat Vegetables and
    Prefer Onions acrostic. *See also* Dragon
    Principles
  association, 57, 61–62
  deep processing, 55–56, 55*f*
  elaboration, 57–58
  Memory Lab regarding, 66–67, 67*f*
  organization, 64–66, 65*f*
  overview, 53, 193
  practice, 62–64

  retention intention, 53–54
  visualization, 58–61
Rookwood, Dan, 1–2
Rote memorization, 84–85
Routines, 187–188, 188*f*. *See also* Habits
Rubin, David, 195
Rule of Five
  memory palace and, 214–215
  recalling memories and, 80
  repeated memory practice and, 128
  self-testing and, 135
  spaced memory recall and, 130–131
Rumination, 181

S*ay*
  Friendly Llamas Seek People acrostic,
    104–105
  how skills are acquired, 158–159, 158*f*
  name-person connection and, 104–105
Scoville, William, 9–10
Scrapbooking, 183–184
Scriptio continua writing form, 205
SCRR method (Segment, Cue, Retrieve,
    Review), 134, 135*f*
Segmenting, 134, 135*f*
Self-talk strategy, 48
Self-testing, 128–129, 131–132, 133–135,
  135*f*
Semantic memory. *See also* Explicit
    memory
  hippocampus and, 12
  how skills are acquired, 156*f*
  mental time travel and, 13–14
  substitute word technique, 21–23, 22*f*
Senior moment, 224
Shadow technique, 106
Shallow processing, 56
Sharing with others, 132–133
Sheen, Mercedes, 75–76
Short-term memory, 11, 24–25, 26–28, 27*f*.
  See also Working memory
Shotgun strategy, 70, 78–80, 79*f*, 80*f*, 186,
  186*f*
Simonides, 204–205
Skills, procedural. *See* Procedural skills
Skills, remembering
  H. M. and, 11
  how skills are acquired, 156–159, 156*f*,
    157*f*, 158*f*
  improving skills and, 159–161, 160*f*
  leaky bucket problem, 164–165, 165*f*
  Memory Lab regarding, 166–169, 167*f*,
    168*f*, 169*f*
  mental skills, 158

mental rehearsal, 162–164
overview, 155–156, 166
perceptual skills, 157
Small, Jocelyn Penny, 204–205
Smells, 61–62
Smith, Steven, 68–69
Sound, 55, 61–62
Spaced memory recall
remembering facts and, 129–132, 129*f*
self-testing and, 133–135, 135*f*
Spence, Jonathan, 207, 209, 210
Spitzer, Herbert, 124–125
Spontaneous retrieval, 114–115. *See also*
Retrieval of information
Standing, Lionel, 58
Stereotype effects, 224–226, 225*f*,
268*n*–269*n*
Stories, 198–199, 201
Stradivarius, 38
Substitute word technique, 21–23, 22*f*, 107,
231*n*–232*n*

Talking to yourself strategy, 48
Tastes, 61–62
Technology, 2–3, 85–88, 245*n*
Thomsen, Dorthe, 174
Thordike, Edward, 84
Top-down attention. *See also* Attention
curiosity and, 48–49
distracting situations and, 45–47
overview, 40–43, 41*f*, 44*f*
prospective memory failure and, 114
zoning out and, 45
Triggers
autobiographical memory and, 187–188,
188*f*
performing an action at a specified time
and, 121–122
prospective memory failure and,
113–115
Tulving, Endel, 12–13, 14, 55

Verbal short-term memory, 27, 27*f*
Video games, 85–88. *See also* Technology
Visual imagery, 23
Visual mnemonics. *See also* Imagery;
Mnemonic approaches; Substitute word
technique; Visualization
acrostics and, 66–67, 67*f*
attention and, 50–52, 50*f*, 51*f*, 52*f*
designing, 50–52
direct visual associations, 20–23, 22*f*
improving natural and artificial memory
and, 95–96, 95*f*, 97*f*
overview, 20
perceptual grouping, 51
recalling memories and, 78–80, 79*f*, 80*f*
working memory and, 35, 35*f*
Visual short-term memory, 27, 27*f*
Visualization. *See also* Visual mnemonics
memory palace and, 211
organization and, 65–66
overview, 3, 58–61, 193

Wait and try again strategy, 71–73, 72*f*,
78–80, 79*f*, 80*f*,186, 186*f*
Weak motivation for the goal, 47. *See also*
Distraction
Weingarten, Gene, 112–113
Working memory
age and, 29–30, 29*f*, 233*n*
attention and, 40–42, 41*f*
capacity, 28–33, 29*f*, 41, 65
chunking and organization in, 31–34, 33*f*
improving via technology, 85–88, 245*n*
limits of, 28–31, 29*f*, 31*f*
mindfulness meditation and, 89, 243*n*
nature and nurture of, 34–35, 35*f*
overview, 24–28, 27*f*
picture superiority effect, 36–37, 36*f*, 37*f*

Yates, Frances, 207–208

Zoning out, 44–45. *See also* Attention;
Default-mode network

About the Author

Robert Madigan, PhD, is Professor Emeritus of Psychology at the University of Alaska Anchorage, where he was an award-winning instructor. Dr. Madigan has taught memory classes in college and community settings for more than thirty years. He lives in Anchorage with his wife.